THE RAVENS OF SOLEMANO

OR

THE ORDER OF THE
MYSTERIOUS MEN IN BLACK

— Book Two —

Eden Unger Bowditch

bancroft
press

Also by Eden Unger Bowditch: *The Atomic Weight of Secrets*

ISBN 978-1-61088-104-3 (cloth) / $22.95
ISBN 978-1-61088-121-0 (school edition) $19.95
Published by Bancroft Press ("Books that enlighten")
P.O. Box 65360, Baltimore, MD 21209
410-358-0658
410-764-1967 (fax)
www.bancroftpress.com

Cover design and author photo: Steve Parke
Interior design: Tracy Copes
Chapter illustrations and diagrams: Mary Grace Corpus

Printed in the United States of America

TO NATEJULIUSLYRICYRUS AND OLIVE, THE DOG

THIS BOOK IS DEDICATED TO MY FATHER, DANIEL PHILIP UNGER.

DAD—YOUR SPIRIT ROAMS THROUGH THESE PAGES AND HAUNTS

THE HEART OF THE STORY. I MISS YOU SO.

TABLE OF CONTENTS

THE YOUNG INVENTORS GUILD

— Book Two —

PROLOGUE

The following article appeared in *The New York Times*, fall 1903 (actual date withheld).

FOUND DEAD IN TUNNEL

Body of Italian, Full of Stiletto Wounds, Near Jerome Park Reservoir

The body of a murdered Italian was found yesterday by John Martins, a foreman of the Jerome Park Reservoir, in the new tunnel which, when opened, will connect the reservoir with the High Bridge Aqueduct, within about 100 feet of the opening.

The body of a young man in his early 20s was in an advanced state of decomposition, although a scar was evident across the eyelid of the victim's left eye.

Martins notified Policeman Bailey of the King's Bridge Station and telephoned Coroner O'Gorman. When they examined the body, it was found that there were nine stiletto wounds in it—six in the back, two in the breast, and one in the stomach . . .

Near where the body had been there was found a long and murderous stiletto, with strange signs carved on the handle . . .

The New York City police came to the conclusion that the young man was Italian. This was because Italian coins were found in his jacket pocket, and because his rather worn clothes had tailoring marks in Italian. The trousers, it was noted, were made in *Italia.*

But in truth, these were not revelations of vast importance. These were not such terribly mysterious or, in the end, even important clues. The fact that he was Italian would matter little to the police of New York City. He could have been Greek or Armenian, or even from the United States. The police would never know what had happened in that tunnel or why. In the end, they would close the case. They would call it "murder by person or persons unknown," and only a handful of people far, far away would be faced with the darkest of facts.

The article did, however, fail to mention three terribly mysterious and infinitely more important clues. First, in the right hand of the victim was a corner of a map. It was a very tiny piece of a map that, when completely unfolded, would show, to someone who knew the region very well, a sliver of the *Appennini,* or Apennine, mountain range. Second, in the left hand, the victim held a fistful of black feathers. Third—and the utter and total absence of this clue from the written newspaper article was in no way the fault of the journalist, his editors, the coroner, or the police investigators at the scene, because this terribly mysterious and most important clue was gone by the time any of them even knew there was a body in that tunnel—hidden by a rock, much farther down the tunnel, in the shadows, there was an envelope, crumpled beyond recognition, with a broken wax seal and a torn note inside that, when it was intact, and the ink had not run from the wetness, and the note was legible, read simply, "They will be on the train."

CHAPTER ONE

BEFORE THE BIG BANG

OR

THE EMPTY SPACE

B efore the enormous explosion, there was calm. For the passengers on the train, this was a lovely calm.

This was not the kind of train one takes from town to country and back. It was not the kind of train one rides to work or to the fair. It was not the kind of train one takes across the continents or for holiday abroad. This train, unlike others, was, well, very much unlike others.

This train had a grand salon with a fine fireplace that warmed the whole car. On this train there was a spectacular laboratory filled with tools of invention. There was a grand observatory with a high glass-domed ceiling and telescopes with gears that allowed levers a great range of movement. There were beautiful sleeping compartments for each of the traveling families. And for several days, since the travelers first climbed on board, the train had made no stops. In fact, besides the few who were traveling together, there were no other passengers aboard at all.

But there was a dining car. Without a doubt, that car was a delicious experience of taste and smell. Before the explosion, five children and most of their parents sat around the long dining table.

"Well, this looks familiar," said thirteen-year-old Faye Vigyan-veta with a groan, looking out the window. The rain had stopped and the land was wet—brown and wet for miles and miles. A smallish man, dressed in black with a frilly apron and a chef's hat, stood beside her. He picked up a cinnamon stick with a pair of pincers and placed it beside her cup. Faye did not thank him or look up to acknowledge this presentation. She simply picked up the cinnamon stick and began to stir her tea. She looked at the boy across the table and rolled her eyes.

Ten-year-old Wallace Banneker, descendent of the great Benjamin Banneker and Louis Latimer, adjusted his glasses but said nothing. He looked down at the eggs on his plate. He knew what his father was going to say about a boy and his appetite, but Wallace was already full from the toast and jam.

This was not the case for the boy next to him. "I'll have another crumpet," said twelve-year-old Noah Canto-Sagas before swallowing the three he had in his mouth. "And the apricot jam, too . . . please?" He reached across Wallace's plate, barely skimming the jiggling eggs as he tried to grab the jam pot, which was just beyond his fingers. Wallace moved the pot closer so Noah could take it.

"Honestly, Noah." Faye shook her head as Noah poured the jam onto his crumpets. Noah smiled a food-filled smile at Faye. Faye again shook her head, long, dark chestnut hair falling freely down her back and over her shoulders.

"Can you pass the other pot of jam, Lady Faye?" Noah asked. Faye showed a look of disgust, but did, indeed, pass the jam.

Before they'd all gathered for breakfast, Faye had been working on her wing design, and Noah had been working with twelve-year-old Jasper Modest on a mechanical chess set. Jasper had been caught between fits of laughter with Noah and quick glances at Faye.

As he worked, Jasper tried not to stare, but Faye always looked so beautiful when she was concentrating. Her green eyes seemed to get even greener. He liked to watch her when her passion was pleasure. When she was, instead, angry, those green eyes could burn a hole right through you. Ever since the children had recovered their missing parents, Jasper had noticed that Faye had her mother's eyes—or rather, she shared the color. But Faye's eyes were like no others. No one had eyes so intense, so beautiful. While her mother was American, blond and tall, Faye's father was from India and gave Faye her beautiful bronze skin. Jasper noticed that, too.

As they sat around the table now, Jasper stole a glance over at Faye. She looked back, and her wrinkled nose at Noah turned into a disarming smile at Jasper. Blushing from his belly to his ears, Jasper quickly stabbed himself in the cheek with his fork, then knocked over his glass and dropped his napkin into his cocoa.

"It's because of the little bunny hole he makes in the softness of the sand. See?" came the voice of Lucy Modest. Lucy had followed Faye's gaze as she looked out the window. "Yesterday it wasn't as big, but we certainly did pass by his house."

"Quelle mémoire!" said her mother, Dr. Isobel Modest. "My girl *does* remember everything." And this was true. Lucy could remember everything. It's just that sometimes, things could be lost in the translation from Lucy's brain to a language anyone else in the world could understand.

"What house, Lucy?" asked Wallace, who saw no house.

"Is it an imaginary house?" asked Noah. "Or is it just invisible? Maybe you need to go back to sleep."

Earlier, Lucy had been like a sleeping kitten in her mother's lap. But Lucy had not been asleep. Not really. She had decided to pretend to sleep. This way, she could feel what it was like simply to sleep within her mother's grasp. Getting her mother all to herself was a rare and special thing for Lucy, and because this was so rare and special, she didn't want to miss it by sleeping. So there she had lain, experiencing the joy of her mother's slender legs against her almost seven-year-old cheek—at least until the train had lurched as it came to a curve around some rising hills on the plains.

"I hope nothing's tumbled over," Faye's mother Gwendolyn had noted as she straightened her skirt and adjusted strands of her blond hair that had come undone from the large bun at the nape of her neck.

Suddenly, Lucy had jumped up from her mother's lap. She looked around, her special bracelet in her mouth, and ran out of the room.

Lucy had then run through the doors and into her family's sleeping quarters. She opened the door to the room she shared with her parents and Jasper and quickly climbed onto her bed. She reached under her pillow and sighed with relief. The journal, she found, was safely tucked away. She leaned over and kissed it and straightened the ribbon that kept it closed.

This journal was precious to Lucy. In fact, it was precious to them all. But Lucy felt responsible, for it was her role to hold it and keep it safe. The lurching of the train might have sent her pillow flying, and then the journal could have flipped out of the bed and been torn—or even slipped out the window! She was glad it was safe and, checking once again that it was still beneath the pillow and hadn't disappeared (since things and people often did in Lucy's life), she then hurried back to the others.

———><•<———

Now, Lucy looked out the window at a stand of trees she knew they had passed before.

"There's the house, near the trees," she insisted, pointing in the direction Faye had been looking.

"There's no house, Lucy," Noah said.

"Silly, of course there is!" Lucy pointed more emphatically, her finger wagging.

"It's not there," Noah said, buttering another scone.

"Yes, it is quite," said Lucy. "He's dug it out himself. Oh, I hope his ears didn't get wet in the rain."

Noah threw a look at Jasper. "Rabbit?" Noah mouthed silently. Jasper nodded.

"We've passed this way exactly seven times," said Lucy. "There's the sand cherry turning red." Lucy identified a tight clump of bushy plants that had, in fact, turned a deep but mottled red. The last time, just days before, the leaves hadn't yet turned—or, at least, Faye didn't remember seeing anything so colorful from the window.

"It feels as if we've passed this way a hundred times," groaned Faye, pouring milk into her tea, "no matter what color the leaves are."

"As we must," said Dr. Rajesh Vigyanveta to his daughter. "It is for our own good."

"And what is that supposed to mean exactly, Father?" Faye asked. "How is any of this for our own good?"

"Faye, dear," said her mother soothingly, "there are things that just must be because ..." Looking at her husband, then the other adults, she simply said, "Because they must be. It is for the best." Gwendolyn Vigyanveta smiled at her daughter. Faye looked at her mother, who sounded more like a small-minded country girl than the world-class scientist she was.

Faye opened her mouth to argue, but caught Jasper's eye. She knew what he was saying with that look. He was right. There was no point complaining. Had Faye gotten anywhere complaining? At best, she simply failed. At worst, her complaining got them all into trouble.

Faye threw an angry glance at the mysterious man in black bringing a pot of tea to the table. At this point, she had no choice but to agree that the mysterious men in black (in their bunny ears, or frocks and pinafores, or bloomers and frilly bonnets) were likely there to guard them and meant no harm. Still, Faye saw them as her jailers. They made her furious, these horrid men with their lunatic dress and bizarre speech. To Faye, they had been kidnappers, stealing her from her life on the estate in India, taking her from her own home and her own creatures and her servants and her laboratory.

The other children and their parents, too, had all been dragged from their homes—Jasper and Lucy from London, England; Noah from Toronto, Canada; and Wallace from Long Island, New York, here in America.

Faye had to admit that life before—before the farmhouse outside Dayton, Ohio, before the train, before Miss Brett—had been lonely. Captive as she was, she was now among friends. Friends are the one thing she had never had before. But she could not believe that this was all "for their own good," as her parents seemed to believe. At least they tried to convince her of it, whether or not they really believed it themselves.

Noah, with his mop of red hair, pulled a small white chess pawn from his pocket. He attempted to balance it on his nose. Either by intention or misadventure, he flipped it into his not-yet-empty cup. With a shrug, he picked up the cup and slurped, finishing every last drop, except for the pawn. Faye made a grimace, placed her own cup daintily into its saucer, and tapped the cinnamon stick gently on the rim of her cup before putting it, too, on the saucer. Noah, who still had a full plate, reached for yet another crumpet from the basket of hot fresh treats being placed on the table by the man in black bunny ears. His mother, Ariana Canto-Sagas, her beautiful platinum necklace sparkling on her neck, picked up the basket and moved it out of reach of her son's hunting fingers.

The door to the salon opened, and Dr. Banneker appeared, filling the doorway with his brawny form. Stepping aside, he gestured and Miss Brett entered. All the children were delighted to see her. As always, their teacher looked lovely. She was so pretty and kind, and her smile brightened the room. Like everyone else, she seemed to have relaxed tremendously now that all the families were finally back together again.

Miss Brett had been with the children in confinement and isolation at Sole Manner Farm. She had been there when they first arrived, unsure of why they had come. She had been there, with them, as they feared and fretted, not knowing where their parents were.

And she had been there when he had come—the mysterious and terrifying man who had threatened all their lives.

Miss Brett had grown to love these children dearly. To her, they were more than pupils, and more than charges. She cared deeply for each and every one of them. She was so very glad to see them basking in pleasure with their parents again.

"Now that looks like a mighty fine spread," said Dr. Banneker, looking at the table. He pulled a chair out for Miss Brett, then went over to Wallace and put a large hand on his son's small shoulder. "You need more meat on them bones, son," he said, patting Wallace's shoulder. The boy winced. When his father wasn't trying to make him grow, he was reminding Wallace that, given all their brown-skinned ancestors of scientific fame and glory, he had mighty big shoes to fill. Sitting down beside Wallace, Dr. Banneker piled more eggs and cakes onto his son's plate, then did the same for himself.

"He's, well… That is certainly a full plate," Miss Brett said. She knew Wallace was not much of an eater, and that he would never finish that plate. That said, Miss Brett did notice how much Wallace had grown already. He was still small for his age, but the slightly pudgy little boy was leaner and taller than when they had met all those months ago.

<hr />

Before breakfast, Wallace, like the others, had been working on an invention—actually, an experiment with magnets. At the age of ten, he was quite a chemist.

Miss Brett had been sitting by the fire. "What are you doing there, Wallace?" Miss Brett had asked as she counted stiches. She was knitting scarves for each of the children.

"I've weighed this rare earth element and introduced a small layer of bismuth on one side, since, after consideration, I felt it would be the strongest elemental choice. See…" Wallace showed how the magnet in his hand caused the thimble on the armrest to roll away from him instead of toward him. "The bismuth has created a diamagnetic reaction," he said, "pushing away instead of pulling toward itself, repelling instead of attracting, as one would expect." Wallace adjusted his glasses and looked at Miss Brett, smiling.

Her hands had stopped knitting, and she simply stared. She had become quite used to being told things that were well beyond her ken. She often gazed blankly at the inventions and experiments of the brilliant children in her care. Though she was used to it, there were times when she was still shocked by what they could do.

She realized she was staring with her mouth open. She shook her head to break the spell and smiled broadly at him. "Well, now that *is* something," she finally said.

Wallace adjusted his glasses again. "I've considered that this would create the strongest magnetic force. We had decided that neodymium might be better than the cobalt." By "we," he'd meant he and his colleague, but before breakfast, his colleague had been busy feigning sleep in her mother's lap.

"How did you do all this?" Miss Brett leaned over to see his magnets.

"We used the small sintering furnace from the laboratory to heat the powder. I combined it with steel." Wallace held the plaster mold in his hand. It had cooled and was ready.

"Mmmm," said Miss Brett.

Opening the mold, he had smiled, dropping the magnet into his palm.

"You've made a perfect sphere." Miss Brett was amazed.

Wallace smiled and showed her another he had made earlier. The old one was perfect, too. He polished it against his shirt and nodded to himself. Yes, the alloy would make the strongest magnet.

He could already feel it tugging toward the coin in his pocket—the lucky coin his father had finally returned to him.

Wallace had managed to balance the magnet between the iron coils. Then he pulled the coin from his pocket. Carefully, Wallace got it to float between his magnets.

Miss Brett gasped. "Wallace, how clever! It…it's like magic!"

"It's science," he said.

"To me, science is magic," she said. "And these magnets are amazing."

"I've always loved magnets," Wallace said, "ever since my father read me Gilbert's *De Magnete* when I was four."

Miss Brett did not know who Gilbert was or what *De Magnete* was, either, though she could hazard a guess that it was a book about magnets.

"Lovely, Wallace! You've done it!" said Lucy, who had stopped by the window on her way back from checking on the journal. "What if we could get droplets of water to float?" Lucy watched the rain fall across the plains. "If there was enough iron in the water, we could use the property of diamagnetism and float water—or even a little froggy!"

"A froggy?" Noah asked from the pile of his chess pieces. "A floating froggy?"

Frogs aside, Wallace *did* start thinking of creating a diamagnetic field and floating droplets of water. As interesting as magnets were when pulling things to them, the idea of pushing things away—or both at the same time—was more fascinating.

"We could make a dynamo, a generator, using the magnetic reaction to generate power," Wallace said to Lucy.

"We could make a magnetic torch that lights itself, and we could carry it with us!" cried Lucy.

"An electro-magnetic torch," Wallace considered. He could clearly imagine the mechanism. It would never run out of power.

Miss Brett again shook her own head in amazement. Those heads carried more power than any magnet could create.

For months now, all of the children had been on a long, strange adventure. Though they seemed to have adjusted to the strange-ness, their lives had truly been turned upside-down. At the mo-ment, they all felt much safer than they had for weeks upon weeks. During those weeks, they had been left with nothing to cling to for support—nothing from their parents to reassure them. Wallace had not even had the lucky coin his father had given him; nor Noah his dog; nor Jasper and Lucy their special bracelets, given to them as babies; nor Faye her amulet, a gift from her mother. Miss Brett had seen the impact from the absence of these tokens of comfort.

Aside from Miss Brett, they only had each other. They had worked some fabulous inventions and made some fascinating dis-coveries, but Miss Brett soon learned that the children were miss-ing something important. No one had ever read stories to them. No one had read them lullabies or poems.

Well, there was one poem, if, indeed, it could be considered a poem. Miss Brett had never heard it before. But somehow, the chil-dren all knew it:

> Strange round bird with three flat wings,
> Never ever stops when it shivers and sings,

Never to be touched even if you are bold,
Turns the world to dust and lead into gold.

Three are the wings, one is the key,
One is the element that clings to the three.
Turns like a planet but it holds such power,
Clings to itself like the petals of a flower.

On weekends, the children had been taken from Miss Brett to houses in the city of Dayton, Ohio. There, nannies waited with arms opened wide. While the nannies had been wonderful to the children, promises of their parents' return had been nothing but a pack of lies. Every day, Jasper and Lucy had been told the same story about late-night returns and early-morning departures. But the truth was that, in all those months, their parents never came.

While Jasper and Lucy discovered that their parents were missing, they also discovered a secret journal. Seemingly ancient, this journal had contained no pages, only torn and tattered shreds of what once must have been. But within the bound covers, they had found written several mysterious dates—dates like "Naples in 1872," "Amsterdam in the mid-summer of 1740," and "Edinburgh in the late autumn of 1738." There was no explanation as to why these dates were there. The only clue was written on the cover. There were only three words: "Young Inventors Guild."

The children did not know what the Young Inventors Guild was. But they considered themselves to be the newest members. They had added their own date: "Dayton, Ohio, USA, 1903." They had written their own notes and drawings and ideas. They had added their own inventions and kept them in the Young Inventors Guild book. This was the journal Lucy now protected.

But how could wee Lucy truly protect it? And against untold dangers? The children and their teacher had all been in danger, as was their greatest invention—their flying machine. Someone came for it, and for them. Someone terrible. A monster disguised as a birdwatcher, who had placed Miss Brett in mortal danger.

Komar Romak.

———

"Oh, I'd love a biscuit," said Lucy, clapping her hands together. She reached over and took one, placing it on her napkin. She then reached for the crusts of toast from Jasper's plate. As Jasper reached up to stop Lucy, Wallace reached over Jasper's plate for the milk and Faye tried to take a spoon from the tea tray.

"Ouch!" Jasper and Lucy cried, pulling their arms back and rubbing their wrists. Wallace pulled his hand back, too. Across the table from Jasper, Faye also jumped back. The twinge in her neck had felt like a bee sting.

Noah's mother, sitting next to Faye, jumped as well. She had been reaching to take a lump of sugar next to Faye.

"What happened?" asked Faye, rubbing her neck.

"It was an electric shock," Jasper said, moving his bracelet up his arm to better rub the part of his wrist where it hurt.

"From all the way over here?" said Faye, rubbing her necklace. It felt hot. "I'm across the table from you. I was only reaching for—"

"You must have turned your head too quickly and pinched your nerve," her mother said quickly, looking at her husband. She reached over to rub Faye's neck, looking at her daughter with concern. Faye looked at Jasper. Silently, they agreed.

"There's something you're not telling us," insisted Faye.

Dr. Clarence Canto-Sagas seemed to plaster a smile on his face that did not extend beyond his lips. His eyes seemed to hold a different emotion, more like concern.

But suddenly, Lucy leapt up, nearly knocking over her plate. She jumped up and down, pointing toward the window.

"Look!" she cried. "There's someone coming toward us!"

Someone was an odd thing to call the large mechanical contraption lumbering toward them. It was not yet very close, but they could still hear the sound of clanging.

"Goodness, is that another train?" asked Miss Brett. Her vision could not clearly capture the thing.

"Not a train," said Jasper. "Father, do you—" But his father was running from the room.

Within seconds, his father returned, and then he, too, ran to the window.

Then, suddenly, they all felt a jolt—not as if they had hit something, but as if something had slapped the train with an electric hand.

"What is that?" Lucy asked, still pointing and jumping. "It's so shiny!" She hurried to the window, her nosed pressed against it. "It's so shiny, shiny, shiny!"

Miss Brett stood up, holding a plate of scones, and went over to Lucy.

There was, indeed, something shiny. Now—off in the distance, but not as far as the horizon—there was a very shiny sparkle, like a mirror or something silver. The strangest thing was that it seemed to be floating in the air. And even stranger, it seemed to be going away from the train, as if the train had been its origin.

"Goodness," Miss Brett said, without a clue as to what the shiny object was. She watched with the others as it looped past the lumbering contraption.

Dr. Ben Banneker stood up, throwing a look of concern to the other parents. The tension among them was thick.

"I don't know what that could be," said Jasper. All five children were pressed against the window, looking at the shiny thing that now seemed to be getting closer while still hovering well above the ground. "I thought it was getting smaller, but it looks to be the size—"

"The size of Faye's head," said Noah, pretending to measure Faye's head. "And, like Faye's head, it's getting bigger every second."

Though Noah was being funny, what he said was actually true—not about the size of Faye's head, but about this floating orb of energy, silver and glowing, looping back around and closer.

"Maybe it's getting bigger because we're moving toward it," said Noah, feeling he was wrong before he said it. No, it was moving with intent.

"Could it be a reflection from the silica in the sand?" asked Wallace, wiping and replacing his glasses, looking toward his father, then peering more intently through the window. He already knew that his suggestion was impossible. Reflections did not hover. Nor did they move through the air of their own volition.

"It's definitely not a reflection. It's hovering," said Noah, saying aloud what Wallace had realized silently, "and reflections don't hover like that. And they don't fly through the air." For now it was clear that, more than hovering, the floating orb was flying toward them—or perhaps circling around back toward them after it had gone around the metallic contraption. Either way, it felt as if something was wrong.

The man in the frilly apron came for the empty platters and teacups and pot. He was followed by the very short man with the very tall black top hat and the long black leather jerkin, and behind him, the man with the black chef's hat was carrying a fresh tea tray.

"Come look!" called Lucy. She took the frilly apron man's hand and pulled him to the window. "I've found a shiny thing!"

Dr. Tobias Modest caught the chef's-hat man's arm and whispered something in his ear. The man gasped. Then the parents all huddled together, exchanging inaudible words with the top hat man.

Faye's face went hot again, but it was Jasper who spoke: "What's going on, Father? Tell us, please!"

The frilly apron man hurried from the room, the top hat man and chef's-hat man following suit. Within seconds, the train seemed to pick up great speed.

"Take them to our room," Dr. Canto-Sagas said to Miss Brett. "I … we … Just take them, please."

"You know what's happening, too, don't you?" Noah said, rounding on his father. Clarence Canto-Sagas turned from his son.

Wallace looked up at the looming form of his own father. He opened his mouth to ask, but his father shuffled him along toward the door of the train car. As he was shuffled, he caught a glimpse of the hovering thing going back toward the lumbering contraption.

"You all know what it is, don't you?" Faye would not be moved so easily. She could see how the parents were avoiding the eyes of their children. "Are we in danger? Are we in danger from the machine, or from the shiny thing circling around it? I want to know and I want to know now!" Faye could feel the bile rising with her fury. Her cheeks felt hot and flushed. "I hate when you do this! I hate when you don't tell me what's going on! I hate it!"

"We...we don't..." But Faye's mother turned toward the window, fear clearly visible on her face.

With one arm, Miss Brett pulled the children to her, spreading that arm protectively around them as best she could. Unconsciously, she still clung to the plate of scones in her other hand.

"Go to room," the man in the chef's hat insisted in his odd mysterious-man-in-black accent as he tried to hurry the children and Miss Brett along to the sleeping car.

"What is the shiny thing?" asked Lucy, pulling away and pointing out the window. "It is lovely. Is it naughty or nice?"

But there was no answer, from either the parents or the mysterious men in black. Instead, the bonnet man returned to Dr. Banneker and left the children where they were.

From her apron, Lucy removed the spyglass she had made when they lived at Sole Manner Farm. She stood at the window. The other children moved to join her.

Miss Brett, suddenly aware of the plate of scones in her hand, started to place it on the table, then stopped abruptly.

"Get down!" shouted Dr. Banneker.

Noah turned toward him. "What's—"

And that's when something loud and strange happened. What it was might be called an explosion—but it was not *the* explosion.

It was nothing like what was to come.

CHAPTER TWO

ALL UP IN SMOKE

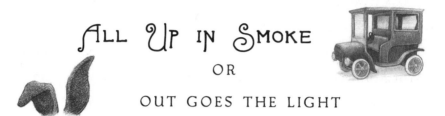

OR

OUT GOES THE LIGHT

Suddenly, as if the ground was on fire, lightning crackled across the plain. The electric lights on the train grew bright, then blew out. Only the dim glow of the few gas lamps still burned.

But no one really noticed that. It was the contraption they noticed.

Another bolt of lightning, coming across the ground instead of from the clouds, hit the contraption and blew it sky high. Lucy yelped and dropped her spyglass.

For a moment, there was silence.

"What was that?!" Jasper asked, breathless.

Then, with a jolt, everything in the room shook. The plate of scones flew from Miss Brett's hand, landing with a crash on the table. The jug of milk cracked open, knocking over the pitcher of juice, which rolled around, tipping over the glasses. The quake shook the very ground on which they rode. It shook the train, and even seemed to shake the hills around them. Rocks tumbled down and cracked as they fell, grinding along the train tracks. It felt like thunder rising from beneath them. It knocked almost everyone to the floor. Next to Wallace's elbow, a lamp tipped over and lit a bread basket on fire. He jumped up as Miss Brett grabbed the pitcher with the last bit of juice and managed to put out the small but growing flame.

The train started inching along instead of running smoothly. But then, with a big jolt, it seemed somehow to right itself back into its chugging groove and began to pick up speed.

"Look at you!" Noah said, laughing as he pointed at Jasper.

In his reflection in the glass window, Jasper saw his hair standing on end. Running his hand through it, he grinned. He looked at Noah. "You, too!" he said. Then, looking around the room, he saw that everyone's hair was standing on end from the static electricity.

Normally, the sight of them as they climbed to their feet, with hair like so many dandelions, would be enough to make everyone laugh, but their utter confusion and fear prevented it. Ariana felt the tips of her lovely locks, now floating out in every direction. Somehow, she alone could still look elegant and graceful.

"The light is still chasing itself across the ground," Lucy said, pointing at the crackles of electricity continuing to shoot across the fields around them.

Every light in the train suddenly seemed to light itself. Sizzling sounds of electricity came from everywhere. Without warning, the train turned sharply, knocking everyone right back to the floor.

Miss Brett was up in a flash, checking to see if the children were all right. Helping Dr. Isobel Modest to her feet, she asked if anyone else needed help.

"Get them to the rooms now!" shouted Dr. Tobias Modest.

Without a second request, Miss Brett herded the children from the dining car into the corridor of the sleeping car. Once again, the train lurched suddenly, and everyone found themselves in a pile on the floor—except Miss Brett, who had been thrown backwards through the corridor, back into the dining room.

Shaking themselves off, the children scrambled to get up.

Lucy climbed over the pile of children. Jasper could see panic in her face and tried to reach her.

"I have to get her!" cried Lucy, pushing Jasper's hand away as he tried to stop her. "She's fallen and she might be stuck." Lucy looked like a mad feral child, her hair still standing on end, a wild look in her eyes.

Pulling herself up, Lucy was not going to be separated from Miss Brett. She knew, somehow, that whatever was happening might mean that her parents would have to go away again, but not Miss Brett. Jasper would always be there, and Miss Brett must as well. If her parents were going to go, they mustn't take Miss Brett with them.

But the way was blocked by a chair that had overturned and tumbled into the corridor. With another lurch, Lucy lost her footing and fell back into the others. This time, Jasper grabbed her in his arms and pulled her to him. Helping Faye to her feet, Jasper took Lucy and followed the others into Noah's comfortable and elegant room. It seemed to be designed especially for Noah and his parents, as each bedroom seemed to have been decorated just for each of them.

In Noah's room, there was a large bed made of elegantly carved mahogany. A netted canopy draped over the posters. A writing table and a music stand were both near the window, though now leaning precariously against the wall. There were even portraits of Ariana on the wall that were now askew. Next to the big bed was a smaller bed, carved exactly like the other, but without the canopy. This was for Noah, who threw himself onto it.

"Well, here we are," he said, "locked up in a cabin while our parents go off without us."

"Going off like rotten fruit," grumbled Faye.

Jasper said gently, "Faye, you can't blame—"

"Can't I?" Faye said, more resigned than accusingly rude. "They're always going off, and I don't like the smell of it."

"Faye." Jasper wanted to calm her. Glancing over, he saw Lucy's telltale sign of fear and worry.

Lucy's hand went to her mouth, where she found her bracelet and began to chew. Over the last few days, she had fallen out of the habit of biting her nails or her bracelet, but the habit seemed to have returned.

"We don't know they will, or where, I mean, if . . . What about Miss Brett?" asked Wallace, not sure if he felt confident defending the decisions of their parents.

"She fell back into the dining car," said Faye. She considered. "She'll be fine and surely come back to us." But Faye was thinking of something else. "They know," she said quietly.

"You could see it in their eyes," Noah said, staring at the ceiling. "Those rascals are up to something."

"You mean our parents?" asked Faye. Noah caught her eye and her irony, but could not deny what she had said. He had meant the mysterious men in black, but the same thing held true for their parents.

Wallace stared out the window, trying to take deep breaths. His father had just shoved him aside. That, he could take. But without a word of explanation?

Suddenly, Wallace focused on what he was seeing. "Look!" he called.

In a moment, all five were staring back out of the window again. There was a definite cloud of smoke and dust and sand and dirt, and when it settled, it was clear that the contraption and the shiny thing were nowhere to be seen.

But they didn't have long to look, because then another violent shift came and knocked them all down, Noah's nose smashing and sticking against the glass window. Wallace's forehead was pressed against the glass by Jasper's elbow, which left a giant smudge. Some crumpet crumbs and jam from Noah's cheek hit the window as he slid his face across the glass.

The train had accelerated, and was now taking sharp turns at amazing speed.

Climbing up again, the children were dazed. The door opened, and Miss Brett came in, winded and disheveled, but more anxious about the children than about herself. The door shut quickly behind her. Someone had shut them in.

"Are you hurt, any of you?" she said, panting and leaning against the wall.

"Just a nose tweak," said Noah, rubbing his nose for emphasis.

"What's going on out there?" asked Jasper.

"I don't know," said Miss Brett. "Your parents...I think...well—"

"Come on!" said Faye. "Let's get our parents!"

"Wait!" cried Miss Brett.

"We can't!" said Faye. "If they're hurt, I want to help. If they're not, I want to shout at them!"

"Faye!" begged Miss Brett, though she could not reject Faye's honesty. "Children, please." But she went unheeded as the other children scrambled past Faye to the door and rushed to pull it open, ready to run from the room to see what was happening.

The man wearing big black bunny ears stood in the doorway, glowering. Despite the funny dark glasses and the black balaclava pulled over his chin, his face was stern.

"Stay in room!" he said gruffly.

"Mr. Bunny Ears!" said Lucy to the mysterious man in black. "What happened? What was shiny and why, why, *why?*"

Lucy certainly spoke for the rest of them, though this may not have been how they would have put it. They all stood firm. Someone knew what was happening, and the children wanted for once to know as well.

Miss Brett made her way to the front of the group, putting a hand on Lucy's shoulder.

"I want to know immediately if we have been put in danger," said Miss Brett, trying to remain calm. "Or more danger, I should say. This is unacceptable. I demand to speak with..." She thought of who seemed to be the most powerful voice among the parents. "Dr. Banneker. If he is unavailable, I'll speak with any of the other scientists."

"The watcher," Mr. Bunny Ears said.

"What?" said the children in collective confusion.

"Who," said the man.

"Who?" asked Noah, speaking for the rest of them. As usual, the odd accent and strange way of talking made everything the man in black said so very confusing. There *were* times Noah almost felt as if he were getting the hang of the mysterious men in black's odd language, but this was not one of those times.

"The watcher," said the man.

"And what on earth is that supposed to mean?" asked Faye, hands on hips, angry glint in her eye. Jasper knew that glint and

23

was glad it was not aimed at any of them.

"Who was the watcher? Or what?" asked Wallace, his voice cracking. He slid his hand into Miss Brett's and moved, ever so slightly, behind her.

"Was the watcher the shiny thing or the thing that blew up the shiny thing?" Noah said.

"Yes," said the man. He turned to leave, but Miss Brett caught his arm.

Then Jasper said, "I want to know, was it…" But the name caught in his throat.

"Was it Komar Romak?" Noah blurted out, swallowing hard, nodding to Jasper.

Komar Romak.

The mysterious men in black were no angels. Guardians or captors, they were a rather unlovable bunch, by all except Lucy. But Komar Romak was the monster they feared. He haunted their nightmares. Like the mysterious men in black, Komar Romak had been unthinkably odd—tall, strange, and skinny. If things had been different, if everything had been different, he might have been funny. In fact, at first, they had thought he *was* funny—before they knew better.

And still, they knew next to nothing about him. The mysterious men in black had explained nothing. They hadn't explained why this monster was haunting them. But as much as they did not know, they *did* know this: Komar Romak had only half a moustache, and Komar Romak could shed ropes that bound him and disappear out of a small locked room.

They wanted to know more and wanted to know it right now. Was this Komar Romak? Was he after them again?

Noah waited for an answer, but an answer did not come.

"Well, was it?" Faye said, more harshly than Noah had. "Was it him? Only he's been blown to smithereens. We're free of him, are we not? We must be free of him."

"Never," the man said. And with that, he walked hurriedly down the corridor and into the dining car, the door closing shut behind him.

Faye's cheeks grew scarlet. "Stay here," she said through gritted teeth as she went to follow the man. Miss Brett reached out to stop her, but Faye slid past.

It didn't matter, though. The door to the dining car would not open. Faye pulled and pulled, but the door would not budge. She grabbed at the handle and banged upon it with her fists, but no one came. Defeated, she looked at the other children, who had followed her out.

"Maybe we should go back into Noah's room and wait," Wallace said meekly.

Without a word, they walked into Noah's room.

The terrain was slightly different as they watched the light change from morning to afternoon. Their previous view had been nothing but empty space, plains, hills, and tumbleweeds, but now there were great piles of rocks, and they could see the mountains in the not-too-faraway distance. As they gazed out in silent thought, something happened that had not happened since boarding the train three days before.

The train slowed to a stop.

"Over here!" called Jasper, pointing out the window in the direction they had been headed.

Now that the train was no longer moving, they could see they had been wrong about the rocks. That is, what had appeared to be natural rocks were in fact blocks of stone—a vast pile of rubble that seemed once to have been a building. Or a few buildings. They could see that in the middle, partially fallen, stood what might have been a tower. But the tower, unlike the rest of it, looked to have been dismantled, not destroyed. Neat piles of rebar and bolts lay next to the base. Whatever it had been, it was no longer.

"Is this all from the machine thing that the shiny thing exploded?" asked Lucy, looking up at Faye. Faye shook her head and raised her shoulders. She hadn't a clue.

"Let me find out what—" Jasper began, but before he could leave the room to get some answers, answers came their way. The door to the cabin opened. It was one of the mysterious men in black—the one in the frilly apron.

"Why are we stopping?" Jasper asked.

"You must descend," the frilly apron man said.

Miss Brett stepped in front of Jasper. "We are not going anywhere until I know it is safe for the—"

"The children down," he insisted.

"Down where?" Faye moved to put her arms around Lucy.

"It will be with safety," the man said.

"Where's Mummy?" asked Lucy, chewing her bracelet mercilessly.

"Go," the man insisted.

Jasper and Lucy stepped forward. Miss Brett took a step to follow Jasper and Lucy, but the man blocked her way.

"The children," he said.

"Absolutely not," Miss Brett said, trying to get past the man. But he barred her way.

"Miss Brett!" cried Lucy, standing on the steps, but the man simply picked her up and placed her on the ground, off the train.

"I want Miss Brett!" cried Lucy. "I want Mummy!"

"I'm here, Lucy," Jasper said, trying to calm her.

"No!" yelled the little girl as she tried to reboard the train.

"Lucy!" Jasper tried to reach for her, but she pulled away. He swallowed hurt that felt like a lump in his throat.

The man refused to let the children back onto the train, or Miss Brett off it. Trying to collect herself, Miss Brett took a deep breath. "It...it will be... We must do as he says, children. I'm sure it will be..." She wanted to say it would be all right, but she did not know if that was true. But they had no choice—at least not any that she knew.

With mounting fear and growing sorrow, the children left Miss Brett behind and stood on firm ground for the first time in three days. They stepped into the ruins of at least two structures.

"What is this place?" Noah said. "Or rather, what was it? Because it certainly isn't what it was."

"What?" asked Faye, looking at Noah.

"I'm turning into Lucy, aren't I?" Noah grinned.

But he was right. As the children stood in the midst of rubble, Wallace bent down and picked up a broken beaker, and then the remains of a small Bunsen burner.

"This was a laboratory," he said with confidence.

"This was a magnifying transformer," Jasper said, finding what looked to be a piece of the secondary coil. There were other bits of twisted metal and something that Jasper guessed had been a part of the electromechanical oscillator. "Whose laboratory?"

"Mine," came a voice both whiny and cracked.

Jasper and Faye turned around. Noah stumbled slightly and froze when he saw from where the voice had come. Wallace instinctively reached for a hand and was glad when Noah didn't make fun of him for grabbing his. Wallace did let go of it immediately, though, not wanting to appear scared. Noah patted Wallace on the back, then stumbled again.

Lucy stood up from investigating rocks and pieces of wire. They all looked over to find a tall, skinny man with a tidy moustache, a somewhat beaky nose, and ears that stood out on either side of his very neat, parted black hair. He was clearly not one of the mysterious men in black, because he wore a crisp white shirt, and his face was plain and clear. He pulled from his pocket a white handkerchief and bent over to pick something up from the rubble.

"Who is that?" asked Faye.

"It is belonging to him," said one of the men in black, wearing a black derby hat and short black britches, long black stockings, and black shoes that curled at the toes. He seemed to appear out of nowhere. *Was he on the train?* thought Jasper. Where else could he have been? Wherever he came from, the mysterious man in the black derby hat was pointing at the man in the white shirt and moustache.

"What?" Noah shook his head as if that might clear things up.

"All of the light."

Without warning, Lucy ran over to the odd skinny man in the white shirt. She pulled down on his sleeve so the man tilted toward her. Then Lucy let go and, with a hand grasping one side each, pulled hard on his moustache.

"OUCH!" he cried. The man jumped, letting out a scream. He swatted at his face even after Lucy had released him, scrubbing away at his moustache with his white handkerchief as if something filthy had touched it.

"It's not the birdwatcher," said Lucy.

"You mean Komar Romak," Noah said. Odd as it had been, he understood why Lucy had tugged.

"By what insane and horrifically disgusting measure do you take such liberties with my moustache?!" cried the man, still wiping his moustache clean. It was no longer neatly combed, but rather quite bushy from being rubbed. "Komar Romak, indeed." He pulled from his pocket a tiny comb and proceeded to tidy his moustache.

"I wanted to be sure it was yours, on both sides," said Lucy sweetly. "You are tall and skinny and you might be him, but for the moustache. We are all very pleased that you are not the bad person we hoped you wouldn't be. Thank you."

"You honestly thought—"

"Yes," said Lucy, sincerely.

The man searched her face, then those of the other children. He stood at full height, dusted himself off, and attempted to straighten his moustache once again before replacing the comb in his pocket. He then extended his hand, holding the handkerchief. When no one reacted, he cleared his throat.

"You may shake my handkerchief," he said curtly. The others looked at one another, but Lucy reached out and took the corner of the handkerchief, shaking it as if it were a limp hand. The man pulled it back and returned it to his pocket.

"I am none other than—"

"Sir," said the man in the black derby hat.

The man in the white shirt turned without finishing his intro-
duction. He went to speak with the derby-wearing man. They spoke
in mutters, so none of the children could hear what they said. The
man pointed to various areas in the rubble, then up at the partially
disassembled tower. Seeming to remember the children again, the
odd skinny man in the white shirt looked at them, and then off behind them.

"Ah, yes, they've come for you," he said, gesturing toward the
rubble. The children looked to find that there, on the far side of the
ruins, away from the train, were three large black motorcars.

"Where did those come from?" said Noah to no one in particular. He certainly did not expect an answer.

"They have come for you, as I said." The odd skinny man rolled
his eyes.

"But who are you?" Faye asked, exasperated.

"Ah, more on that later."

"Later?" said Jasper. "You mean we're coming back here?"

"Heavens no," the man said, dismissively.

The derby-wearing man in black shuffled the children toward
the cars.

Lucy bent to pick up something. "Look at what someone left,"
she said, handing the paper to Jasper.

Jasper looked at the torn paper. On it was an equation, or part
of one, and, at the bottom, where the page was torn, it said, "ors Gui."

"And that is mine," said the man, plucking the paper from Jasper's hand with a thumb and forefinger as if he were touching
something contaminated. Deftly, and still with two fingers, he folded the piece of paper and put it into his jacket pocket. Then looking
around, he gestured grandly, "It's all mine."

"All the rocks, dust, and rubble?" asked Noah, not seeing much else.

"Hmmph," said the man, wiping his fingers. "Hmmph," he huffed again.

As the children were herded towards one car, Jasper looked to see the man take the scrap of paper out of his pocket and hand it to the derby-wearing man in black. The two spoke together softly as they walked toward the train.

If it's his, Jasper wondered, *why did he give it to the man in black?*

The odd skinny man stepped up onto the train, his white handkerchief protecting his hand from the railing. He turned toward the children, standing in the doorway. "Do not look, hear me?" he said, shaking a finger.

"What?" said Jasper, who was not sure he had heard the man correctly. "Don't look at what?" But the man had disappeared into the train. Jasper looked—that is, he instinctively looked around. What did the man mean?

"What about Mummy and Daddy and everyone else?" Lucy asked, standing firm in place.

"In go car," said the derby-wearing, mysterious man in black, who herded the rest of them into the automobile.

"I don't want to leave Mummy," Lucy said, her arms folded determinedly across her chest. "Or Miss Brett." The man merely picked her up and put her in the motor car.

"Miss Brett!" Faye shouted. She, too, suddenly realized they were without their teacher. From the looks on the boys' faces, they had realized it as well. Even so, the boys climbed into the automobile.

Faye reluctantly climbed in after Lucy, and the door was closed behind her. Looking out the back of the car, she saw the odd skinny man with the kerchief looking out the window of the train. He then moved away from it, leaving it dark and empty. The other two motorcars took off in opposite directions. The motorcar they were in began to drive directly away from the train.

From the window of the car, the children could see inside the salon. All of the parents were gathered there, standing together. Miss Brett was shaking her head. She was upset. Dr. Isobel Modest turned toward the window. Jasper thought his mother looked sad. Or perhaps she was worried. She looked right at him, though they were moving away from the train so swiftly that he could hardly see her face anymore. But he thought she said something—something to him. Then it was too far to see, and the late afternoon sun reflected in his eyes, but still he could make out Miss Brett as she left the salon through the door to the dining car.

Lucy began to wave, then began waving frantically from the back window, as if this would somehow stop something about to happen.

But it did happen. And it happened right there. With it came a terror the children had never felt before. What they saw would haunt them, and keep haunting them, long after they would come to understand what had happened.

The train, with everything and everyone in it, exploded before their eyes.

CHAPTER THREE

A Burning Confusion

OR

THE YOUNG INVENTORS

MISS THE TRAIN

"The train!!!" screamed Jasper, his hand pressed against the glass of the motorcar. Wallace seemed to be mouthing words that no one could hear. Noah just stared. Faye's face went white.

"Mummy!!!" screamed Lucy through the back window, her waving now a frantic blur. "Miss Brett!"

A huge plume of smoke grew like a thunder cloud, darkening the skies above them. At first, the impossible horror was beyond their enormous ken—beyond what even they could understand.

But what their eyes saw took a moment to hit their brains. Tears began to flow down Wallace's stricken face. He could not move and could not speak. Noah's mouth hung open as if it hoped something would arrive in it that might explain what had happened. Faye went from being frozen in her seat to shouting, banging her hands against the windows.

Jasper shook his head. He knew that all the shouting in the world could not undo what had just happened.

With each beat of their hearts, flashes hit them like more explosions. Faces of their parents, faces of each other—fire, heat, loss.

They were in a panic beyond panic. They were in a terror beyond terror. And they watched, helplessly, as the car continued to drive away from the explosion. The train was completely devoured by the smoke as they came to a hill and turned around the bend. The billows of smoke rose high above the top of the hill and cast a dark shadow over the otherwise white clouds floating gently against the blue sky.

"Stop the car!" shouted Noah suddenly, tears streaming down his face. The man driving did not appear to hear him. He drove on as if nothing had happened. Faye tried to smash the glass between them and the driver. But the glass seemed to be made of steel, and the window would not break. And the driver seemed to be made of the same hard, impenetrable material as the glass.

Lucy shouted and cried and waved furiously out of the back window, as if this would somehow bring back the train. Faye could not breathe. Suddenly, with a shove, she pushed the door open and jumped out of the moving car, skinning her knees and slicing the palms of her hands.

Gasping, on all fours, she could not feel the gashes on her hands and knees—only the air filling her lungs and, with it, a more vivid vision of the horror she had just witnessed. With the wind came the stinging smoke, now also filling her lungs. It did not stop her from sucking in what air she could.

The man in black turned the car around and slowed down. Noah then threw himself out after Faye, rolling as he hit the ground. As Faye dragged her bruised and scraped body up from the dirt and began to run, Noah just lay there, rocking from side to side.

The car jerked to a stop. Jasper grabbed for Lucy, but she jumped from the car, too, and ran after Faye. She was losing everyone. She had to catch Faye and bring her back. Jasper followed his sister.

Faye's lungs were not the only thing that burned, straining as she ran. Her brain felt as if it were on fire. Something about this was familiar to Faye—the need to run, the cold sweat that came from being trapped in a tiny space. She had felt it when her parents had first left her back in Ohio. She had felt the need just to get out of that carriage—that first big, black carriage. She had felt it at other times in her life—the fear of being trapped. Sometimes it didn't bother her, but other times it made her sick.

Her knees now stung and her elbows ached, but she ran until her legs felt as if they were on fire, too. The clouds and the mountains were in the way, so she couldn't even see if the smoke from the explosion was in front of her or if she was running in the other direction. It didn't matter.

And then she could run no further, and she fell to her bruised knees. Lucy came upon her, and Faye gathered the little girl in her arms and sobbed. Jasper fell to the ground next to them and held them tight.

They didn't know how long it was, but it was a long time— maybe minutes, maybe more. Finally, legs shaking, the three stood, clinging, as if letting go of each other would take away what strength they had as one. They walked to Noah, who had ceased his rocking and simply lay on his side. Reaching for him, Faye helped Noah to his feet. Silently, they walked back to the car.

Wallace—Wallace was alone in the car, curled into a very small ball on the backseat. He looked up, but it was as if he didn't see them through his swollen eyes and foggy glasses. He had not been able to save his mother years ago, and he had not been able to save his father now. Maybe the burners he used for smelting the metal alloys had somehow triggered the explosion. Maybe if he had made those electro-magnetic torches, the train wouldn't have needed so much fire. Maybe this was somehow his fault.

Once the others were back in the car, they could not speak. Their strength and their voices had given way to grief. It became very quiet, as each child began to search a broken heart for some answer—trying to reason, trying to deny what their eyes had seen. Leaning back in his seat, Noah put his arm around Wallace, who, curled tight, was so still it was frightening, and Faye put her arm around Noah. Brother and sister leaned close to the others, Jasper feeling Faye's hand slip into his. He squeezed the warmth of that living hand as if it brought life back into him by being there. There was nothing left in the world—nothing but each other.

Jasper didn't realize he had been biting his lip so hard until he tasted the salty blood. He didn't realize he had been clenching the fist of the arm that was around Lucy. He had been digging his hand so hard into the corner of the door that, when he opened his hand, he found his knuckles raw and his palms bruised.

He found that waves of anger peppered the sorrow that wrenched his soul. How could they leave him to take care of Lucy? But he knew this feeling was not reasonable—or was it?

Jasper stole a look at Faye, who clung now to her amulet. He could see the blazing in her eyes and knew she, too, had begun to feel anger. How could he feel anger when his parents had been killed? Guilt washed over him, only to be replaced by fear, and then anger again—and then sorrow.

In time, Lucy cried herself to sleep, now occasionally waving and sniffling from Jasper's lap where she lay. "Mummy," she would sob, or "Miss Brett," or "Daddy." Then she would whimper, "Mr. Silly

Black Bonnet." They were all gone.

Soon, amidst sniffs and sobs, they all fell into a fitful sleep.

⇒⊷⊶⇐

It was the sound that woke Jasper first. As his eyes reluctantly opened, he saw that the light had definitely waned in the sky. *It must be late in the afternoon,* he thought. He had been dreaming that he and Lucy were sailing little boats in the milk jug on the picnic blanket Miss Brett had laid. He and his sister each had a stick that they used to push the boats. "Mind the milk," he kept saying to Lucy.

As he woke, he couldn't quite remember where he was, and found that his empty hands were gripping a stick that was not there. Then, as his twilight sleep receded, he tried desperately to return to his dream. He did not want to wake. He did not want to know. He was fighting what he would find when his eyes were truly open.

But he could not fight it. In a flood, visions came pouring in like an unfriendly tide—visions that revealed the last moments before the car drove away. And he remembered.

Lucy had curled into a ball in Faye's lap. Faye, sleeping, held Lucy's hand, gently, occasionally pulling it to her cheek, whining softly in her unsteady sleep. It made Faye seem so fragile.

As Faye stirred, Jasper was careful not to look at her or show he was aware of her fragility. He knew that she would not want that.

Wallace and Noah had fallen asleep together. Wallace had burrowed into Noah's chest. Noah was snoring.

And then Jasper heard the sound again.

He looked out the window of the moving motorcar. He could see the last sliver of sun disappearing behind the high ridge of hills. As he watched the sky turn orange in the first fading light, he heard it. He blinked. It must have been his imagination. But then he heard it again. It made no sense.

Noah jumped up. Faye sat up, too. And then they all heard it.

"It's the train," Wallace said. "It's the sound of the train whistle."

"It can't be." Faye rubbed her swollen red eyes. "It's a different train."

But the whistle came again, and it was getting louder.

And then they saw it. As they came around the bend, there it was.

But it was impossible. It simply could not be. It had to be a different train. But, no, it was theirs. It was the one they had seen explode. The one containing everyone they loved. The one that was gone.

"It's our train!" shouted Lucy. "It's come back for us!"

"Lucy," Jasper said gently. This simply could not be. It could not.

"Look!" Lucy pointed. "It is!" And now tears were coming down her cheeks as a smile spread across her face. The waving of her arm wiped the tears away.

Jasper looked. He rubbed his eyes and looked again. It really did look like their train. In fact, it looked exactly like their train.

"But it can't be," Noah said, unbelieving. "We all saw it go up in smoke. It was . . . It couldn't . . ."

"I'm sure there must be some explanation," said Jasper, who did not sound sure of this at all. "Perhaps we only thought . . ." But he could not say.

"Maybe we're all asleep," said Noah. "Or dead."

"I'm not dead!" Lucy yelled, sticking her tongue out and trying to catch it between her fingers. "I'm not dead, and I've heard it. That means you're not dead and they're not dead and everybody else isn't dead, either."

As the motorcar approached and the sky darkened in earnest, the children were all pressed against the door that faced south. From there, they could see inside the train. The car slowed as they drove alongside it. The children could see the fireplace still lit in the salon. They could see the dining car, food on the table. They could even see inside Faye's bedroom, where everything seemed to be in place: her beautiful bed, and the soft silks that hung from the walls. Even the beads on the mirror were visible from the window.

And they saw through Noah's window, too, where the impression on the glass from Noah's nose and Wallace's forehead could be seen clearly, as the dying light from the outside made it visible from the light on the inside. There was the smudge, and the crumbs, and the jam.

And then the motorcar stopped. The driver got out and opened the door. In slow motion, the five passengers emerged. They just stood there, staring at the train they had seen destroyed. It was like looking at a ghost.

"But that's impossible," said Jasper in disbelief, speaking in little more than a whisper. He stepped gingerly toward the train and, with hesitation, touched it.

"It's really real, Jasper," insisted Lucy, her eyes as wide as saucers. "It really truly is really truly real."

"Yes," Jasper said, "it certainly feels like it's real."

"Haven't you learned?" said Noah, wiping his eyes. "Nothing is impossible anymore."

"Please," Lucy said to herself, her hands clasped under her chin and her eyes shut tight, "please belong to us, you lovely, lovely train. Please belong to us." She opened her eyes.

At the top of the stairs of the dining car was the man in the black bonnet. He stood for a moment, gathering his skirt as he descended the stairs.

"Hooray!" shouted Lucy, looking up at the sky. "Thank you, lucky star!"

"Dinner upon the table," said the black bonnet man in a gruff voice, gesturing for the children to climb aboard.

"Mr. Silly Black Bonnet!" cried Lucy. She ran up to him and clung to his leg. "It's you, isn't it? It *is* you!" she said, tears in her eyes as she looked up at the man attached to the leg she held. "Is it really the same you? It is, oh, it is!"

"I ... It is me," he said in a very awkward voice, unable to extricate himself from Lucy's grasp. He seemed to be enduring her affection with great strain.

"Oh, I'm so glad," said Lucy, clinging all the tighter. "I was so very worried you'd been blown to smoke. You and Miss Brett and Mummy and everyone. I am ever so pleased you are all un-blown up. Truly."

Standing there with Lucy attached to his leg, the man with the bonnet seemed to be at a loss as to what to do. He took one step back into the train with Lucy still attached. He was not able to get Lucy off his leg—that is, until Lucy jumped back on her own and screamed with pleasure.

The diminutive man with the black chef's hat stepped out from behind the man in the bonnet.

"Mr. Cheffy Hat!" said Lucy, throwing her arms around the waist of the other man, who was significantly shorter than the first. "Oh, you've not been exploded either! You're all in one bit!"

Suddenly, running down the stairs, pushing past Mr. Cheffy Hat and Mr. Silly Black Bonnet, came a very anxious teacher.

"Miss Brett!" all the children shouted as they ran to her, surrounding her in rather painfully hard embraces.

But Miss Brett returned them. She was as white as a sheet and looked deeply at each child as if to be sure that they, too, were really there. Faye's normally severe expression was gentle and soft, and Noah just laughed through falling tears.

"I wished and wished and wished," Lucy kept saying as she twisted around in Miss Brett's skirts. Wallace simply held tightly to Miss Brett's arm as if letting go might send her floating off into the universe, beyond his reach forever.

Jasper, however, looked deeply into Miss Brett's eyes. She hoped her eyes gave him some relief—that she was here, and here for them. It was Jasper who worried her the most, because Jasper did not only have himself to take care of—he had Lucy, too. Being responsible for another life was quite a lot for a young boy.

With effort, Miss Brett tore her eyes away from his to look upon the others—that, and by averting her eyes, Jasper wouldn't see how terrified she had been only moments before.

"What happened?" she asked them, tears pouring down her already reddened face faster than she could wipe them away. "I thought...I truly thought..." But she couldn't bring herself to say it.

"You tell us," said Noah. "We all thought you were gone."

"You thought... but I ... we ... you mean, *you* thought *we* were gone?" she asked.

"We saw ... we thought we saw ..." Wallace could not get it out. Somehow, even though they were all together now, the thought of saying what he saw felt too real, as if it would suddenly make *that* the horrid truth and make everything else disappear.

"There was a terrible explosion," said Miss Brett, "and I ... I ..." But she could not say, either. Her hand flew to her mouth, and she just shook her head as if to loosen the horrible thoughts trapped in there.

"Exploded," said Lucy, who had managed to squeeze through everyone else to get to the center, arms around her teacher's waist.

"Exploded?" Miss Brett said, confused. "Me?" She suddenly felt the need to get everyone safely back onto the train. Standing out there in the middle of nowhere, she felt more vulnerable, and she felt the children more vulnerable here than if they were inside. She felt this now that she knew they were safe. As she swallowed her words, she decided not to tell them how terrified she had been. She decided not to tell them what she had seen, right before her eyes—how it was *she* who had thought the worst had happened to *them*.

She decided not to tell them how the enormous explosion appeared to have utterly destroyed the car that carried them away from her.

CHAPTER FOUR

THE REDISCOVERED AND THE GONE AGAIN

OR

WHAT LUCY FOUND MISSING

"Mummy! Daddy!" Lucy shouted as she ran through the dining car, past the delicious roast beef and caramelized fennel with buttery artichokes and lemon sauce on the table.

The others moved far more slowly through the dining car. Wallace wanted to touch everything he saw—just a quick touch, to be sure each thing was real. Noah and Jasper seemed to wander somewhat in a daze. Faye stood for a long time, looking out the window and thinking. Only minutes ago, they believed themselves orphans, and now all seemed to be as it had been before. The emotional strain weighed heavy on them all, as if they had all experienced a nightmare together—but a nightmare that was incredibly real. Could it be that their parents were unharmed? That thought was a relief to Noah, and still unreal to Jasper and Wallace. For Lucy, this was all the result of her wishes.

Though Faye was relieved, too, the pangs in her gut that turned into lumps in her throat were symptoms of an unexplainable sense of betrayal.

How could any of this have happened? Or, even more disturbing, how could any of their parents have let this happen? Or, yet again, could it even have happened? They all knew what they had seen. It had been real.

But this was their train, no question. It contained everything it had before. They walked through the dining car to look at their rooms. Miss Brett followed quietly behind them.

"Mummy!" called Lucy, throwing the door open, but the room she and Jasper had shared with their parents was now empty.

"They're not under the beds," Jasper coaxed, touching his sister gently on the shoulder as she crawled out from under her parents' bed.

Lucy jumped up and ran back to Miss Brett, who was walking down the corridor with the others. "Where's Mummy?" the little girl asked, excitedly.

"I don't know, sweet angel." Miss Brett was wiping her eyes on her sleeve.

"Well, did you see them?" asked Faye. She, Noah, and Wallace were leaning against the window in the hall. They, too, had been to their rooms and found no sign of their parents.

"Of course I saw them. We were all together, and then …" Miss Brett was trying to think. She and the other adults had all been on the train.

"Maybe they can't hear us," said Lucy, hopefully.

Noah put his fingers between his lips and blew an ear-splitting whistle. Faye covered her ears and kicked him in the shin.

"They'd hear that," he said. But no one came.

"I don't understand," Miss Brett muttered to herself. She tried not to look concerned, but she was. How could they all disappear?

"Well, where did they go?" demanded Faye.

"I'm sorry, I don't know," said Miss Brett. "I ... I was alone in the dining car when I saw you ... when you drove away. Then I was distracted. I don't know where your parents went."

"Then everything is all right," Jasper said with an emphasis he did not really feel. "Miss Brett didn't see anything happen—anything bad—so surely they're fine."

Miss Brett hoped she hid well the horror she knew must still be reflected in her eyes. She nodded, but without firm conviction. Faye, Noah, and Wallace looked around their rooms once more. It was not as if there were places to hide. And why would their parents be hiding? More important, why would their parents be hiding from them?

All their rooms were as they had been. Noah fell back onto his bed, but not before checking, once again, that his smudge was still on the window. Lucy was busy chatting to herself and jumping on her bed. Jasper gingerly sat down on his bed, and Wallace simply stood, looking in his room.

"This is impossible," said Faye. She stood, looking around. She clutched her beaded necklace hanging from the tall mirror. It was exactly where she had put it the night before. She touched it carefully, as if it might dissolve in her hand. But it was real. She reached beneath her pillow. Her nightdress was folded, just as she had left it.

"Come," Miss Brett said, standing in the passageway between the rooms. "Some food will do us all good."

Wallace, still dazed, looked up at her. "Is this real?"

Miss Brett kissed the top of his head. "I believe it is real, Wallace. I believe we are all here and everyone is all right."

Reaching under her pillow, Lucy pulled out the ancient green journal tied with a pink ribbon. The others would have preferred a leather strap or twine—something more dignified—but Lucy had wanted to use her favorite bright-pink lace ribbon, and no one felt it right to argue.

Lucy gazed down upon the journal. Humming to herself, she untied the ribbon and opened the cover—and she gasped.

"They're gone!" she cried.

"Our parents?" said Wallace, looking into the room.

"They were under the pillow!"

"What?" asked Noah, following Wallace. "Who was under the pillow? Our parents?"

"Our pages. All of our lovely pages."

"What?! What are you talking about, Lucy?" Rushing into the room, Faye pushed past her colleagues and stared down at the empty journal. "They *are* gone!"

The five faces stared down at the empty space that once held all of their designs and inventions.

"Someone has stolen them," said Faye.

"And what's new about that, Faye?" asked Noah sardonically. "Everything of ours is always stolen. Our parents, for example."

"Bad form," Faye growled. "That simply is not funny."

Soon, they burst through the doors of the laboratory, and they could see that all the things there remained as they had left them. Even the rare earth sphere remained, hovering in its magnetic cell between the coils. There were, however, some overturned beakers and burettes. Two of the rare earth magnets had flung themselves up and attached themselves to the rim of the ceiling lamp, and one was lodged up the nose of a metal cupid hanging above a wall sconce. Wallace rightly assumed this had all happened when the train was racing at high speeds—more proof that this really was their train.

But their parents had simply disappeared.

Lucy, however, was not ready to believe it. "Mummy!" she called from up above. She was in the observation room with Wallace, the glass ceiling creating a strange echo when she called. She ran from the observation room and into the laboratory, where Noah, Jasper, and Faye waited. Wallace walked silently down to the laboratory.

"Lucy," Jasper said in a soft voice. With every empty room, he felt more certain that there was, indeed, something missing. "They may be busy with something, somewhere…"

"In a secret room," suggested Faye, the same worry hidden poorly on her face.

"They may not want to be disturbed." Jasper looked thankfully at Faye.

"Of course!" Lucy cried. "They must be in the salon. It's the only place we haven't checked." She ran toward the salon. It was in this salon that she last lay in her mother's lap, where they sat around the fire, and where the parents would go in the evenings to chat. "Mummy!" she called, turning the handle on the door to the salon. "Mummy, please open up. I won't be a bother. I promise I'll be as quiet as a mouse."

But it was locked.

They had to be in there, Jasper hoped.

"Mummy!" Lucy pounded on the door. Her voice cracked as only silence came from the other room. "Mummy!" Lucy's tears ran into her mouth. Her hand was hurting as she continued to pound.

Miss Brett, who had followed, beckoned to Lucy. "Come over here, sweet angel," she said. "Perhaps they—"

"Mummy!" whined Lucy, crying as she called out desperately. She dropped any pretense of play and panic filled her throat.

Miss Brett took a step toward her, but Jasper quickly blocked her way and eased himself toward the door.

"I'll go to her and see if they … or she …" He didn't want to think about what might not be behind the door. But he knew what he had to do.

Lucy was no longer pounding. She just stood by the door in tears, her head leaning against the handle. Jasper took a wire from his pocket. As he slipped it in the lock, Lucy looked up, offering thankful blinks to her brother. In a few moments, Jasper had unlocked the door. Lucy slipped in, but Jasper could not bring himself to follow. He knew what they would find. He didn't want to know, but he knew. He waited for what seemed like minutes, but was more likely seconds. Then, with a deep breath, he looked back at the others and entered the salon.

The room was empty. Except for Lucy. She sat, knees to chest, by the dying fire. The flames flickered across her face as she rocked herself. Jasper reached out for the hand that carried the fingers heading for her mouth.

"Lucy?" he said gently.

"Where's Mummy, Jasper?" Lucy said, wiping her nose on her sleeve.

"I don't know, but we'll find out." He took his sister's hand and she stood up. She hugged him suddenly and deeply, and he held her tightly in his arms as tears came down onto his cheeks.

It was Faye who still seethed as they entered the dining car. The chef's-hat man was placing baskets of steaming-hot bread near the places set for them at the table.

A warm onion tart was placed next to a bowl of buttery peas and a plate of roast beef.

"We're not hungry," said Faye.

"I'm hungry," said Noah. "I'm tired and scared and exhausted and miserable, and I am hungry."

"Where's Wallace?" asked Miss Brett.

No one had noticed that Wallace was not with them.

"He was in the observatory," said Lucy.

"He followed you down the stairs," said Faye, remembering. "I think he followed you into the laboratory."

Miss Brett walked into the laboratory and found Wallace at his table. He was working feverishly. There were metal cylinders and wires and light bulbs and magnets all over the table. She put her hand on his shoulder as she had done so many times before. She knew that distracting the children from their work was a delicate matter.

"Darling," she said gently. "Sweet angel, come in and have something to eat."

"I must finish this," said Wallace, wiping the fog from his glasses. "I need to secure this electro-magnetic mechanism. I need to create an electric torch so nothing will burn again."

"Oh, sweet angel." Miss Brett gathered him in her arms. "I think that is a noble plan. Come, though. You need some energy." She walked him slowly toward the dining car.

When Wallace and Miss Brett entered, the children were still standing, Faye scolding Noah for thinking of his stomach at a time like this. They seated themselves and reached for dishes, so it took a moment before the children noticed that Wallace was still standing.

"Why are there only six chairs at the table?" asked Wallace.

Faye stood up from her seat. "Where are they?" she asked loudly.

"I don't know, Faye," Jasper said.

"I'm not asking you, Jasper," she said. "I'm asking him."

The man in the chef's hat, holding a tray full of biscuits, looked surprised. "All is away," he said.

"Everything is always away," growled Faye. "I want to know what you've done with our notes, since you seem too dull-witted to tell us where you've taken our parents."

The man shook his head and left the room.

Miss Brett reached for Faye. "Faye, dear, why don't you—"

But Faye rounded on Miss Brett. "You must know!" she cried. "You were here!"

"But I—" Miss Brett was taken by surprise. "Faye, I—"

"You're not telling us what happened on the train," she said. "We all saw you blown to bits, and now you're here and they're not!"

"Dear, I . . . I wish I could tell you." Miss Brett was keeping her voice steady. "Your parents went to their compartments and locked the doors. I first went to tidy up in the dining car, and . . ." But she wasn't sure she could finish.

"And what?!" demanded Faye, who was now shouting.

"Don't talk to Miss Brett like that!" cried Lucy. "She loves us."

"And . . . and I saw the motorcar that you were in . . . I saw it drive away, and . . ." Miss Brett pulled a corner of her skirt to wipe her cheek, because the tears were falling into her mouth.

"And?" Faye's voice wavered. She was no longer shouting.

"And I saw it explode, with all of you in it." Miss Brett fell back into her chair, sobbing into her skirt.

Faye's stony defenses gave way slightly. She, too, fell back into her seat.

The beautiful meal sat uneaten and the room remained silent. Faye's anger turned into defeat as she realized she still did not know if her parents had been killed in an explosion that seemed, otherwise, never to have happened.

CHAPTER FIVE

WHAT LUCY UNDERSTANDS
OR
WHEN ONE WILL HAVE FLERN

Miss Brett had finally cried herself out. Once she had regained her poise, and after Lucy had come over and put her arms around her, Miss Brett knew, simply, that food would help, although eating seemed like an overwhelming task given everything else. She mustered her strength, trying to ignore the questions that plagued the children—the very same questions that roared in her own brain.

One question rose above the others and lay at the bottom of everything. Could this be connected to the elusive Komar Romak? Miss Brett had been trapped by that man. She knew firsthand how horrid he could be. And they had captured him, caught him, and cornered him. But he had escaped, somehow, from an inescapable hold. Could he still be following them, or was someone else behind this new threat? Whatever the answer, Miss Brett could not find room in her stomach with such a large weight filling it up.

"What I don't understand," Faye said, and Miss Brett could feel Faye coming with the question that had been burning in her own head, "is why that maniac Komar Romak would still be after us. He must have known we didn't bring the you-know-what."

"I know, I know!" cried Lucy raising her hand. "You mean our flying machine!"

"He must know it didn't come with us," said Faye. "Why is he still being such a bother?"

"How would he know we didn't have it?" asked Noah. "You think he was posing as a baggage steward?"

"Well." Faye thought about it. But a different question seemed to loom larger in her mind. Somewhere inside, she pondered the same question Jasper asked aloud:

"Are we sure that he was after the aeroplane?"

"What else could it have been?" said Noah. "He asked about it, didn't he?"

Faye considered the question. Had he asked for the flying machine? Had he said "aeroplane" or specifically noted what it was he wanted? They knew he wanted something and, at the time, it was only logical to assume he wanted their invention.

"Pardon me . . . um, please, Miss Brett, may I have some peas?" Wallace had been holding out his plate to her as she stared off without looking.

"Sorry, dear. Yes, of course," said Miss Brett. Still lost in thought, she spooned in much too much as Noah slipped his plate under her spoon to catch the next spoonful she was dishing out.

Had Komar Romak asked for the young inventors' flying machine? Miss Brett let her mind wander back to the time Komar Romak held her captive. "I wonder," she said to herself.

The possibility that he could still be pursuing them, and even still, the aeroplane, was beyond them all. Faye stared into her tea. Jasper put his arm out to pull Lucy's hand from her mouth. Noah had stopped moving, a fork poised to feed a mouth frozen in midair.

Blinking, he seemed finally to notice and stuffed the food between his lips.

Miss Brett looked at Wallace with deep concern. She picked up the serving spoon and scooped out the last of the peas onto Lucy's plate.

Komar Romak was still out there. He was still just over the horizon.

"How much longer?" asked Lucy.

"Longer for what?" Jasper said.

"Not you, silly. Mr. Poofy Trousers." Lucy pointed to the man serving tea. He wore what could only be considered a bathing cap, a pair of dark goggles, and poofy trousers that seemed to tie at the ankles.

"What is long?" the man asked.

"We are," said Lucy. "But how long?"

"Not for you," he said.

"For anyone?" Lucy asked.

"Not so," he said.

"Well, that's a good thing, yes?"

"So."

"So," said Lucy. Smiling to the others, she said, "Isn't that good to know?"

Noah once again held his fork halfway to his mouth. Faye sat holding her cup to her lips. Miss Brett still clutched the empty bowl, and Jasper just sat, his mouth agape. Wallace looked at the others, then at Lucy.

"Did you really understand him, Lucy?" asked Wallace.

Lucy looked at the others. "Well, of course I did, silly."

"Did you understand each other?" Noah asked, swallowing the

mouthful that had not yet made its way down. "He could understand you, too?"

"Of course," said Lucy. "What isn't to understand?"

"Well, what did he say? And what, pray tell, did you ask?" Faye took a sip from her cup.

"It won't be long, and then we won't be on the train anymore," Lucy said, as if this were a matter of fact that all would appreciate as such.

Noah coughed, his bite stuck in his throat. "Won't be long?"

"Well, where is it that we're supposed to be, then?" Faye's cup clattered in its saucer.

"I don't know, but we'll be there, won't we?" said Lucy, nibbling all of the crispy edges of her potato. "Maybe our mummies and daddies, too."

The table was quiet after that. Thoughts turned to parents. Would their parents be there? Would they want to be there if they could? Noah put his fork down. Suddenly, he was less hungry. All of this not knowing was filling his gut.

Like waves of confusion, each mystery crashed on the shores of his thoughts. Noah hoped that his deepest, darkest fears were not well-founded, and that, instead, his parents simply lacked a choice, and were forced to go away. But somehow, he felt that he was, once again, being left behind by people with more interesting, more important things to do. With a sharp pang, he thought of his mother. She could not be blamed for any of this.

Noah's mother, Ariana Canto-Sagas, was unlike the other parents. She was the only parent not constantly distracted by equations and laboratories. She was never found smelling of sulfur or needing to wipe dried bicarbonate from her spectacles. Ariana

Canto-Sagas was not a scientist. Ariana Canto-Sagas was an artist. She was a star. It was said, far and wide, that she had the voice of an angel and was even more beautiful. As a soprano, she reigned supreme. Kings and queens bowed to her artistic majesty. Her presence changed the molecular structure of the room as surely as an extra oxygen molecule changes water to hydrogen peroxide.

So Noah was angry at himself for feeling the way he was feeling. Wasn't it selfish of him always to want his world-famous mother to stay home, though he had indeed been thrilled the time his mother had been ill and couldn't go on tour with the opera? His father had tried to raise his spirits then, but his father was gone now, too.

Noah looked down at his plate. No, he was definitely not hungry anymore.

<hr />

After the sun began to go down, first on the right side, then on the left, they no longer knew whether they were headed east or west across the plains of America. And, in truth, it didn't matter.

As they walked into the salon to have hot chocolate, Miss Brett found that Lucy was yawning and rubbing her eyes. They were all tired and ready for the end of a rather harrowing day.

"Come on, sweet angel," Miss Brett said softly. "I'll help you into bed."

Jasper stepped toward them to help, but Miss Brett shook her head and smiled. The boy had enough to worry about. He didn't have to be the only one to carry his sister, too. "You go have that hot chocolate," she said. "I bet she'll be asleep before her head hits the pillow."

Jasper nodded and went with the others to sit by the fire. He was just staring at the flickering light when Noah's raised voice came into focus.

"Why do you ask me?" Noah was saying. "Me? What I have learned? I don't know any more than anyone else. I'd like to think I do, but I've got nothing."

"Well, you always have something witty to say," Faye said. "I just assumed you decided you knew everything."

"Well, we *will* know, won't we?" said Noah. "Once we have learned." Noah was tired, and not ready to take on Faye.

"'Have learned'? 'Have learned'?" Faye's voice rose, and then was shushed by Miss Brett, who had just come back from Lucy. "When, pray tell, will we have learned, Noah? We get nothing from these men—and nothing from our parents."

Jasper had been trying to get his head around why his parents did not simply tell them why they had to go. Wallace was afraid to ask his father, but felt his father must have a reason. Noah was grappling with his own guilt for being angry at them, but Faye—she was just angry. How dare they, she thought. How dare they leave her.

"I have learned ..." Noah started, but realized this was not true. He had not learned anything. He simply let the idea fade on its own without adding to it.

"Well, aren't you the lucky one?" said Faye. "I would love to have learned ... something. Instead, I know less than I did before."

"Well, perhaps real knowledge is knowing we know nothing," said Noah, a sheepish smile on his face.

"Sweet angels," said Miss Brett, "we will look back upon this time, once we all have learned, and the mystery will seem ..." But what would it seem? Miss Brett thought. Would it ever feel like they could make sense of it? Would it ever be all right? "It will seem like a long-ago dream."

"Or nightmare," said Faye in a pout.

A squeak came from the doorway.

"Is there any left?" asked the sleepy girl.

"Any of what?" asked Noah. "Potatoes?"

"Flern," said Lucy with a yawn.

"Excuse me, what?" Faye rubbed her ears.

"I'd like some flern, too," said Lucy.

"What?" everyone said at once.

"Flern," Lucy repeated. "I want some, too." She looked around, blinking in the firelight. "Don't I? What is flern?"

"What are you talking about?" Faye tried to get the grumpy look off her face, but Lucy was being so, well, Lucy. She could be as bad as those horrid mystery men. No wonder they could all understand each other.

"Flern," insisted the sleepy little girl. "What is it?"

"I have no idea," said Noah, yawning and rubbing his eyes.

"Yes, you do," demanded Lucy, rubbing her eyes as well. "Don't hide it from me. I'm a big girl."

"Flern?" Noah shrugged. "Never heard of it, Lucy, like most of what you say. That said, I'll sleep on it and see if I become enlightened." Noah leaned over and closed his eyes, flopping his head onto Wallace's. Wallace tried to push him off. Noah flopped the other way, pretending to sleep, leaning against the arm of the sofa.

"But you said you had some. You said you have flern, or that we all will, and once we have flern, everything bad will be far away." Lucy yawned again. "I'd like to know what it is. Maybe I don't want any. But if it helps us look back at the dream…"

"Oh, my." Miss Brett's hand went to her mouth as she stifled a giggle. "Sweet angel, you misheard us ... we said, 'have learned,' and you thought..."

But Lucy was already falling asleep against the doorjamb. Miss Brett stood up and again gathered Lucy in her arms. She looked back and saw that Wallace was fast asleep on the sofa. Noah, no longer pretending, had begun to snore, half hanging on the arm-rest. His snore seemed to dislodge him, and he more or less slid from the sofa to the floor, rolled over to the rug by the fire, and curled into a ball. Only Jasper and Faye were awake, though they both looked exhausted.

"Jasper, Faye," Miss Brett said softly, "do you mind putting a couple of the quilts on the sleeping boys? I think I'll leave them in here. No point waking them."

Jasper rose to get a quilt for Wallace. Faye reached behind her and grabbed the one from the chair. While Jasper tucked the edges of his quilt carefully around Wallace's sleeping form, Faye threw hers so that it covered Noah's head. Then Faye swallowed hard, got up, and straightened the quilt, tucking it under Noah's chin. His red hair was now mussed and in his sleeping eyes. Faye gently, and kindly, moved the hair aside.

"Mama," Noah muttered between snores, grinning in his sleep.

Faye quickly withdrew her hand, then looked over at Jasper, who had been gently removing Wallace's glasses. He looked over at Faye. Suddenly smiling, Faye and Jasper had to flee from the room at the risk of waking the boys with their laughter.

As they headed toward their respective bedrooms, Jasper looked at Faye and smiled a different smile. "You were so kind to make him comfortable," he said. "You must have reminded him of his mother."

Faye then did something so incredibly rare for her that Jasper thought it was just a trick of the light. She blushed. "I could do with learning kindness," she said. "I've been horrid to him—to all of you."

Jasper reached out to put a hand on her arm, wanting to assure her this wasn't the case. But at that moment, two things happened. One, he realized he couldn't lie. She *had* been horrid. And, two, Faye reached up her hand at the exact same moment. Their hands touched, their fingers wrapped around, and their eyes met. Very quickly, Faye and Jasper lowered and separated their hands and looked down, warm faces full of even more blushes.

"Um…" Jasper had no idea what he was going to say. It felt like the first day he saw Faye, when her beauty had shocked him before her vicious tongue lashed him out of his stupor. "We'd best head for bed."

Faye nodded and smiled. She opened the door to her room, then looked back and smiled again. "Yes," she said, "it's time for bed. See you in the morning."

It was time for bed, but sleep would be another thing. The feel of one another's fingers around their own lingered as Faye and Jasper each lay in bed that night. But thoughts about what would come, and where they were headed—and according to Lucy, very soon— would keep them awake long into the night.

CHAPTER SIX

DISAPPEARING PROMISES

OR

MISS BRETT MISSES HER PAGES

As the night waned, the train headed into the morning sun. Miss Brett watched the breaking light reveal what the night had held in shadow. Her sleep had been disturbed all night long. She could not settle herself, having gone all those hours believing the children were lost to her. Worried, she woke in a jerk several times during the night. So she was up every hour or so, and every time, she went to check on the children.

They, too, were tossing and turning—all except Noah, who lay so still she had wanted to check for breath. Luckily, he tended to snore, so she knew he was breathing. On every round she made, in the other beds, and on Wallace's couch in the salon, she found blankets kicked off onto the floors and heads where feet should be. Once, as she tucked in Faye, she found the girl awake.

"Miss Brett," Faye's sleepy voice said, "would you sit on the edge of my bed until I fall back asleep?"

Miss Brett smiled. This was the fiercely independent girl, the girl who had been so desperate for her own room back on the farm. Faye had been mortified that she would have to share a room with Lucy. And now, she wanted company to fall back asleep.

Miss Brett brushed the hair from Faye's eyes, "Do you miss sharing your bed with Lucy?"

"Mmm-hmmm," said Faye drowsily, curling on her side and clinging to Miss Brett's arm.

And with that, Faye slept. *Lucy was so warm and cuddly, and now you're on your own,* Miss Brett thought.

Miss Brett eased her arm from Faye's grasp and tucked her in. She caressed her cheek and kissed her forehead before leaving the room. *But we are with you,* she thought. *We are with you, Faye.*

Miss Brett learned something in those nighttime hours. She knew now that the train was headed in a straight line for the first time since boarding back in Ohio. Until that night, the train had twisted and turned, wending a serpentine path through fields and plains, hills and hollows. Not an hour went by that the train had not made some turn or reversed direction. But through the whole of the night, there had been no turns, no reversed directions, no sudden alterations. Miss Brett was certain that something had changed. They were heading somewhere now.

Exhausted herself, Miss Brett would let the children sleep late into the morning. Sleep, she believed, was the great healer. Even more than lessons, the children needed to rest their weary hearts and minds. She did, too, but that would have to come later. She would try to sit quietly and knit or mend, though she had found neither a helpful distraction in the night. She hoped the children, once awake, would find distraction in their laboratory. She would read to them, if they so desired. But she could not relax with a book of her own. She was finding it hard to focus, as her mind kept wandering back to the events of the previous day—and her unhappy discovery earlier that night.

It had happened when she was looking for something to occupy her mind. She'd taken out her knitting, but it felt wrong in her hands. She then took out some sewing, but put that back as well. The light would soon be peeking over the horizon. With no more hope of sleep, she thought it would be a good time to write in her diary. So much had happened, after all, and she wanted to keep track of her own thoughts.

However, when she went to her room and reached under her pillow, she had made a discovery that only added to her anxiety. She had not considered that anyone would enter her room. Nothing ever seemed out of place until that moment. But now her personal diary, her private journal, was gone. This was impossible, she thought, searching and searching again through her things. Could she have put it in a clothes drawer or in her writing desk? She looked, but she knew it would not be there. She knew exactly where she always put it, and it simply was not there. She bit her lip. Miss Brett had been keeping journals and diaries since she was small. This one she had been keeping since she first agreed to take this job. She had kept it throughout the strangest and most important chapters in her life. Suddenly, it was gone.

And there was nothing she could do. It was maddening. It was a reminder that, however well-fed she was, and however comfortable her bed might be, she was at the mercy of these mysterious men in black. It had to be them. They had taken it.

She had gone to the kitchen, where the man in the frilly apron was kneading dough for bread.

"Why have you taken my diary?" she demanded.

"It is kept," he said.

"I want it back," she said, her voice quavering.

"It is kept," he said, without looking up at her.

"Why did you take it?" she asked. "How did you know where I kept it? Are you spying on me?"

The frilly apron man did not answer.

She opened her mouth to protest, but realized, instantly, that it was a futile exercise—a useless waste of time. Instead, she turned on her heels and left the kitchen. But why her diary? She had been noting her thoughts and her concerns. Had she revealed too much? Angry and frustrated, she went back to her room and sat, watching the sun rise ahead of the train. They were heading east.

Dressing now, Miss Brett decided that, with the coming of the light, she would go sit in the salon. She lit the fire herself and, once again, brought some knitting. This time, it felt comfortable in her hands and, as she counted stiches, she began to relax. She sat by the fire and tried to let her pearling and knitting ease her mind. She had begun a new project—a long scarf for Faye, who was not used to cold weather. She had knitted mittens for all the children, and hats, too. And she had knitted a pair of booties for Lucy's bunny doll. She knew it was early, but she thought they might be nice Christmas gifts. There was always a chance they might be somewhere cold for Christmas.

———◦————

After a quiet breakfast late that morning, the children sat in silence in the salon. Again, it was a few moments before Miss Brett realized Wallace was not there. Miss Brett knew where he was. He was working on his electric torch. Miss Brett suggested the others might want to work on their experiments.

"I don't want to," said Lucy, who returned her bracelet to her mouth.

"We just aren't in the mood, Miss Brett," Jasper said, staring into the fireplace.

"I just can't concentrate," said Noah.

Miss Brett looked from one to the other. They needed something to distract them.

"Well, you need to organize that laboratory of yours," she said with a hint of sternness. "I have seen what a mess it can be—"

"That's Noah," said Faye, without looking up.

"Well, the whole place could use a tidying up." Miss Brett took Faye by the hand and helped her up. Then she did the same for Noah and Wallace. Jasper stood, helping his sister up as well. "Off you go." The lot of them started to leave, albeit reluctantly. She watched them go, noting that the shuffling didn't really seem to be getting them out of the room. "Wallace has been working on a most fascinating invention," she said.

Suddenly, they were off. Surely they would want to know what this invention was.

Miss Brett knew there was not, in fact, much to organize. She knew she was making up reasons to get them into the lab. But she also knew the children were happiest, or at least most content, when they were working on their inventions.

She waited a few minutes, then went back to see how things were going. They were as she had hoped they would be. Once the children were there, their minds filled with visions she could never understand. Miss Brett smiled and sighed. Seeing them consumed by their work meant they were not spending time fretting about all those things they could not control.

Miss Brett, on the other hand, could not help but worry. She did not have a brain full of magical distractions. How could she protect the children against things she could not see? Things she could not hear? Things she did not understand? What kind of guardian was she when she could not keep the children safe? When it came down to it, the children had been forced to rescue her at the farm, at great risk to their own safety.

After fluffing the pillows and folding the throw blankets, she headed back to her room. Out of habit, she reached for her diary and, once again, fretted about its absence. She'd just have to start another one and hide it better, she thought. She busied herself arranging her pillows and refolding the clothes in her drawers.

She looked out the window. Yes, the train was absolutely headed east. But to where?

———

It was late in the afternoon before Jasper realized Lucy was no longer in the laboratory. He looked up through the tall windows and saw the sun was on the other side of morning.

"She said she was tired," Wallace said, pointing toward the bedrooms. "She left about twenty minutes ago."

Leaving Wallace among the growing piles of magnetic spheres and cylinders and dynamos, Jasper walked through the laboratory unnoticed by Noah or Faye, each deeply engaged in their work. He quietly opened the door to the Modest family's sleeping cabin. Lucy was sprawled out on their parents' big bed. Her fingers were curled next to her mouth, a charm from her bracelet between her lips.

"Lucy." Jasper knew that Lucy would be famished if she didn't have lunch or her afternoon tea.

Lucy stirred and groaned.

Jasper wiped away the wisp of hair from his sister's eyes and gently rubbed her shoulder. As Lucy stretched across that big bed, Jasper found it hard to swallow for a moment. Moments like this, when he saw little Lucy in that big, empty room, on that great big bed, it hurt the most.

This was their parents' bed. Their parents had slept in that very bed, their heads on that very pillow. But their parents were not there now.

The first night on the train seemed ages ago. That night, Jasper and Lucy and the others had come aboard and found the laboratories and the beautiful dining car, and the special rooms made up for each family. And there, on the train, in the salon, the five children had arrived and found Jasper and Lucy's parents, Faye's parents, Wallace's father, and Noah's parents, alive and well. And now they were gone again.

Lucy opened one eye. With what seemed like a great deal of effort, she opened the other, until she had both of her very large brown eyes opened fully. Jasper was not fooled for a moment, however. Lucy was still asleep. Even Lucy's vast and seemingly endless memory would not have included this moment. If Jasper, believing her awake, would have stood and walked out, expecting her to follow, she would have simply closed those big eyes and flopped back onto her pillow.

"Lucy?" he said. "It's Jasper. Wake up." And this time there was a blink and a wink and a twinkle in her eyes, followed by a yawn. "There you are," he said, seeing the sleepy girl emerge from behind the rubbing and yawning and stretching.

He looked out of the window. He smiled. "Look, Lucy."

Lucy perked up and climbed across the bed to the window.

"That's the biggest, fluffiest cow I've ever seen!" Lucy said, pointing to a very large bison. She squealed with delight. "That one, next to the smaller one with the patchy thing on its hind leg. See? That one's dancing! I love it when they dance, prancing around like that!"

Yes, Lucy was awake, Jasper thought. Lucy couldn't keep her eyes off the dancing bison, rushing from window to window along the corridor as she and Jasper walked to the dining car, in which Jasper could hear the other three gathered for teatime.

As they entered the dining car, Jasper noticed immediately that Miss Brett was not present. Leaving Lucy with the others, he went to look for her in the last car—the salon. Its large fireplace was still lit with a warming fire, and that's where Miss Brett waited, sewing a ribbon onto Lucy's bunny rabbit doll.

Jasper walked up to her and placed a hand on her shoulder.

"It's time for tea, Miss Brett," Jasper said, his voice cracking.

"Yes, sweet angel, I know," Miss Brett said after she bit off the end of the thread and put it back in her sewing box. "But I wanted to have Lucy's bunny doll join us." Miss Brett stood up and put her arms gently around Jasper's shoulders, and he wrapped himself tightly around her waist.

"Well, that is certainly a strong hold you have on me, Jasper," Miss Brett said. "Were you afraid I would—" And she was going to say *disappear*, but she suddenly realized this was not the right thing to say at all. She knew, from the way he held onto her, that that's exactly what he thought. And who could blame him?

"Listen to me," she said, pulling away just enough to look deeply into his eyes. "As much as I can say it, I am not going anywhere. Do you hear?"

"I ... I know. It was only ... I was thinking of the night on the train, before Dayton, when our parents, before the morning, when they were suddenly gone, and ... I'm sorry." Jasper felt he was sounding like Lucy. "I'm being stupid."

"No you are not." Miss Brett almost sounded cross. "As far as I can help it, I will not disappear. I will not leave you children."

Taking Jasper by the hand, she let herself be led into the dining car for tea.

CHAPTER SEVEN

A DANGER CANNOT BE UNINVENTED

OR

WALLACE MEETS HIS TOWERING NEIGHBOR

Miss Brett opened her window as the delicate light of early morning began to build its strength. She expected to see the rocky terrain, but instead, she was met with a cityscape coming fast over the horizon. She sat back down and watched. Had they gone from the plains to the city in that short a time?

Where were they? This was a big city, to be sure. It was coming up fast, too. Within a few minutes, she recognized the Park Row Building against the skyline. Miss Brett knew what city she saw. The Park Row Building was, after all, the tallest office building in the world.

Miss Brett was looking at New York City.

She quickly dressed. It was best to be prepared. But she continued to watch as the train rolled past the city center, not slowing in the slightest. *What on earth?* Miss Brett thought. She could not think of anything that was out past New York City.

She jumped at the knock on her door. *Goodness*, she thought, catching her breath. She was rather on edge. She stood up, straightened her skirt, and opened the door. There were five faces looking at her. The children, like her, were all dressed.

"That is a very big building out there," said Lucy. "We're certainly not in the fluffy cow land anymore."

"No, dear, we're not," said Miss Brett with a smile. Looking out, she added, "And I cannot imagine where we're going."

"We're headed onto Long Island," said Wallace.

Of course, Miss Brett thought. *Wallace is from Long Island.* She wondered if Wallace's house was going to be on the way. She knew he lived there with his father. Wallace's mother had died several years before.

"Wallace, do you know where we are? Does this look familiar?" Miss Brett asked.

"Not yet," he said, distracted as he watched intently through the window. Adjusting his glasses as he watched the city rolling by, he added, "I mean, not so as I recognize the neighborhood, ma'am."

"Well, I'm sure we'll all know very soon," said Miss Brett in a positive tone. "Let's be sure we feed Noah before we head off on some adventure, shall we?"

"That's right," said Noah, rubbing his belly. "I need feeding every few hours. Otherwise, I might catch flern."

"You *are* flern," said Faye. "I thought you were a human being, but, clearly, I was wrong. You belong in a cage in a zoological park."

"Not so," said Noah. "As long as you feed me, I can be quite human." And his stomach growled on cue.

"Are you like a hummingbird?" asked Lucy, with concern. "A hummingbird needs to eat every few minutes or he can starve to death."

"Uh-oh, Luce," said Noah, pretending to take out a pocket watch. "You had better feed me before I expire."

With their sandwiches and biscuits and cakes barely finished, Faye was the first to notice. She stood up abruptly and pointed out the window. "Goodness, what is that?"

They all stood to see what Faye saw.

It was a tall tower. It appeared to be close to two hundred feet high. It rose from a brick building hardly visible from behind the trees. The structure was not far at all from the train tracks.

"We must be in Wardenclyffe-On-Sound," said Wallace, now standing by the window, marveling at the sight.

"What on what?" asked Noah, standing behind him.

"It's a community on Long Island. Really, it's a resort," said Wallace. "But there have been rumors about a scientific project."

Everyone was standing by the window now, looking out at the strange sight.

"Rumors, huh?" Noah smiled as the train slowed. They all stumbled slightly, bumping into one another as the train stuttered to a stop. "Looks like we can confirm those rumors right here and now."

The bunny ear-wearing man came into the dining car.

"We stop," he said, and departed.

Scrambling to get to the door, the children were stopped by the arm of Miss Brett.

"Please, children," she said, not scolding, but firm. "Let me lead, if you please. We don't know what's out there."

Miss Brett led her charges to the door of the dining car. *Will it be locked?* she wondered. *Will we be prisoners on the train?* But when she pressed against the door, it opened. She led the way out.

Descending the steps, each of them felt the ground beneath their feet, or at least they tried.

"I can still feel the train in me," said Lucy. "I'm still on the train from my ankles down, and a bit of my tummy."

Because they were not under duress and running for safety, they had the time to step upon the rocks and actually look around.

"Wardenclyffe-On-Sound is a lovely place," Miss Brett noted. Although there did not seem to be visitors, the place was tidy, and the flowerbeds filled with colorful blooms.

But it wasn't the blooms that Faye noticed. The huge tower rising above them was a very un-resort-like sight. And it really was massive. They all stood, staring upwards. *How ugly*, thought Faye.

"Amazing," said Wallace. "To think, it is real and it is here."

"It's your neighbor," said Lucy.

"That's right," Noah said. "Do introduce us, Wallace."

"Well," Wallace said, adjusting his glasses, "the train line was extended here around 1895. Then Mr. Warden, who is a very rich man, bought the land to build a resort. But he also seemed to be interested in inventions. This tower is going to be one of many."

"What does it do?" Miss Brett asked.

"Amazing things you cannot possibly fathom," came a voice that did not belong to any of them. But it was a voice they had heard before.

"It's you!" Lucy said enthusiastically. "It's really you, and you're not exploded!"

"I most certainly am not exploded, young lady," said the skinny man with the white handkerchief who they had last seen leaving the rubble of his laboratory to enter the train, just before it exploded.

"Well, it's really nice that you are not exploded," said Lucy politely. "We're ever so glad." She smiled. The man, however, merely twitched his lips, and only Lucy knew that behind that twitch was a less-than-a second smile.

"Good to see you're not dead," said Noah, reaching his hand toward the man. The man offered his handkerchief. Noah took it and shook it vigorously, as if it were the hand of an old friend.

"Well, I suppose it is a good thing not to be dead," said the man, now offering his handkerchief to Wallace, who did not understand what to do with the gesture and, therefore, looked the other way.

"Nice place you have here," Noah said, looking around.

The man harrumphed at Wallace, then looked at Noah and the others. He seemed resigned to something.

"Very well," he said. "As you are here, I shall show you my tower." The man shook out his handkerchief and placed it in his pocket.

"Sorry to be rude," Miss Brett said, "but who exactly are you?"

"Exactly?" The man's eyebrows rose high on his forehead.

"Well, I mean…that is…well, I'm Astraea Brett. And you are…?"

"I am Nikola Tesla," the man said. "I would have thought you all would know that, if nothing else. Nikola Tesla. But you can call me Mr. Tesla."

"It is, um, a pleasure to meet you, Mr. Tesla," Miss Brett said, pulling back her hand when she remembered the man obviously did not like to shake.

"Nikola Tesla?" Noah's own eyebrows shot up his forehead.

"The one and the only, yes." Mr. Tesla, without humor, presented himself with a gesture.

"Then—this is *your* tower!" Noah was clearly excited.

"Mr. Tesla is a brilliant inventor," Wallace said, looking up at the man and adjusting his glasses.

"Yes, my father and I were reading about you back in Toronto," said Noah.

"What did you read?" asked Jasper.

"Well, that he's been building a tower," Noah said. "Something of a radio tower, to create electricity, and—"

"Now, now," said Tesla, "don't attempt a feeble explanation of something about which you know only tiny portions. This tower will change the world, as will most of my inventions."

"Oh, lovely!" Lucy said, clapping her hands together. "A story!"

"Well, if you think I shall tell you all ..." But Tesla seemed to reconsider. "I suppose as you are members ..."

"Members?" Miss Brett looked confused.

It was then that the man in black bunny ears came over. He bowed, slightly, toward Mr. Tesla.

"Is it loaded?" Tesla asked.

"Near but more need," the man in bunny ears said.

"Well, I am needed," Tesla said dismissively, pulling a pair of gloves from his pocket and putting them on as he spoke. "I will have to tell you about my death ray another time."

He turned to follow the man in black toward the building.

"Death ray?" said Noah, Jasper, and Wallace all at once.

"Did you have something to do with the explosion?" Miss Brett called to him.

"All of the sparkly bits and stuff?" said Lucy.

"Yes, it was mine, the lightning ball," he said, not bothering to turn around. "It was mine, my creation. My terrestrial stationary waves."

Then Jasper shouted, "Do you know Komar Romak?!"

Tesla seemed nearly to trip over his feet as he stopped dead in his tracks. He gasped, catching his breath. "Do I know ... why on earth would you ask ... I ... well, I ..." But then he turned to the man in black next to him. The bunny-ears man shook his head, his ears flapping on either side of his face.

"No, and I will not speak of them." Tesla turned on his heels and continued walking toward the building that sat below the formidable tower.

"You blew up the shiny thing and the contraption," Lucy said.

"I did nothing of the sort," Tesla said, stopping, arms folded in protest. "I *was* the shiny thing."

"You were ..." And then Jasper got it. The "shiny thing" was a ball of lightning, hovering across the field. The contraption was the target, and it succeeded. "How did you create a lightning ball?" he said. "It is said to be impossible."

"Hmmph," said Tesla with a wave of his arm as he walked away.

"Then you blew up Komar Romak," Jasper said.

"But if you did that, then why is everyone still so worried?" said Noah.

"Komar Romak?" Tesla laughed, stopping and turning back around. "One does not simply blow up Komar Romak."

"So he's not dead?" asked Wallace.

"Not he," the bunny-ears man said.

"And not dead," Tesla mumbled, almost to himself.

"But it was you who blew up our train," Noah said. Then, upon rethinking: "Or didn't blow up the train, or ..."

"Yes, you told us not to look," Lucy said. Tesla had indeed warned the children not to look at the train.

"I have no time for this." Tesla stomped his foot and turned away from them. "Load up!" he shouted to the men in black. They followed him into the building.

"But..." began Faye. Without warning, she ran after them. The rest of the children followed. And far from stopping them, Miss Brett joined in the chase.

They entered what was clearly an unfinished laboratory. It housed gadgets and machines the likes of which the children had never seen. There were gears of enormous size and strange rods and wires everywhere.

"What is this place?" asked Faye, distracted from the object of her pursuit.

"This will be the brain, the epicenter, the very heart of the operation. It is here that the conduit and energy—the power—will be conducted to its ends." Tesla stood, full of pride, his arms spread as if introducing the greatest thing on the planet.

"What does it all do?" asked Lucy.

"Do?" Tesla's moustache quivered. "*Do*, child? It does everything. It is the power source and the power itself."

"Oh," Lucy said timidly, for she still had no idea what all this did.

"Well, is it safe to be in here?" Miss Brett asked.

"Safe?" Tesla seemed to recoil. "Are you one of that thieving fool's spies? That blue-collar genius of an idiot, Edison, tried to prove that my current was unsafe, but he was filled with lies, as you all know."

"Um, no," Miss Brett said. Her question had seemed logical if this was, indeed, the center of immense power. "No, I am not, and no, I don't know what you're talking about."

"Well, he shall never have my death ray! I will find the thieves!" declared Tesla. Miss Brett and the children were now certain that

Mr. Tesla was more than a little mad.

"You really have invented a death ray?" said Noah, trying to keep a straight face.

"Must you speak so loud?!" Tesla covered his ears. "I am working on perfecting the defense mechanism."

"Defense mechanism?" asked Jasper.

"Yes. It is a mechanism to prevent the weapon from being used for anything but defense."

Tesla leaned against a wide, low vat. It was no more than three feet high, but probably twice that in diameter. Lucy walked over to the vat. In it was what looked like a massive silver soup. "Mercury!" said Lucy in excitement. She touched the strange substance. It jiggled slightly. She giggled and touched it again. "It's my favorite metal, since it wiggles. Other metals are not anywhere as funny."

"Get away from that!" shouted Tesla. "That is the ammunition!"

"The mercury?" asked Jasper, pulling his sister to him and grabbing her hand as it moved toward her mouth. He'd have to warn her about touching things and then putting her hand in her mouth. Whatever the death ray was, mercury was poison and she had touched it.

"Yes, indeed, the mercury. It is genius," Tesla said. "The electrostatic generators require such turbines as I have yet to create, although, yes, we know how the idea came to be ... yes, and I'm sorry for it." The man seemed to retreat into his thoughts, turning to the bunny-ears man, who put a hand on Tesla's shoulder.

"It is true. A weapon from my hand should never be used to attack, only to defend. But as we know ..." Tesla looked at the bunny-ears man. "As we know, the most brilliant inventions borne of the best intentions can sometimes be the end of the world." Tesla suddenly broke into tears.

"We all protect," said the bunny-ears man.

"Yes, but we cannot unknow things, eh, brother? Once we bring something into the world . . . and, yes, I have learned from the long, long past, but still, as we know, we cannot uncreate something once it burns a hole for itself in this world." And he burst, again, into tears.

"Sir . . ." Lucy began, stepping toward him.

"No!" he said, startling the little girl back into her brother's embrace. "No, it is true. I am to blame for this, but it will not matter, yes? No. It is for the best, for now, to be taken to safety. Yes, secrecy and safety—a powerful pair."

The others looked at one another for guidance. Had Tesla invented something very dangerous? Or was he talking about something else? Jasper cleared his throat. "I'm . . . we're not exactly sure what you—"

"Then I leave you," Tesla said, turning on his heels once again and heading to the door. The children and Miss Brett walked toward him, hoping to follow him out and get some sort of explanation as to why they were here, but Telsa ignored them. He placed his hand on the doorknob and turned. Without warning and without a sound, all his hair, short as it was, was standing on end, and so was theirs—just as on the train during Komar Romak's attack.

Tesla turned. "I bid you adieu . . . ach, goodness!" He hurried over to one of the big machines and turned some knobs. "Not that it makes a difference, since it was only gathering, not expending." And with that, he left the room.

Miss Brett and the children all smoothed back their hair. All except Noah.

"I like it," he said. "It will be the new style!"

⟫●⟪

"It is done," said the bunny-ears man as Miss Brett and the children left the building. "The train waits."

"What is done?" asked Miss Brett.

"The loading," said the bunny-ears man.

"The loading what?" asked Noah.

But the bunny-ears man simply gestured for them all to get onto the waiting train, then boarded himself.

"Very well," said Miss Brett, as she led the children back onto the train.

CHAPTER EIGHT

From Land to Sea

OR

MYSTERIOUS MEN IN BLACK ON THE DECKS

Back on the train, things were as they had always been. A delicious supper was followed by warm milk by the fire. But there was so much to think about—more than ever, in fact. They were going somewhere, but the mysterious men in black kept all explanations to themselves.

Consequently, getting to sleep again was a feat. Troubled thoughts had led to troubled sleep these last couple nights, and at least a couple of the passengers on the train would meet in the hallways in the middle of the night.

Now, as the train went slowly toward some unknown destination, Faye wandered the hallways, thinking. Deep in her own thoughts, she came upon Noah, deep in his. At first, she slipped back into a doorway when she saw him there, standing and looking out the window. Then she realized he was singing quietly to himself.

Noah could be such an idiot, she thought, that witnessing his musical talent was always something of a shock. She had heard him play violin only twice and was very impressed both times. She had never heard him sing, though—not seriously. Nothing Noah ever did was serious. It was as if he didn't know how to be serious. But there he was, singing something operatic. And his voice was beautiful.

Faye quietly stepped back into the corridor. She stood and listened, not wanting to interrupt.

"That was beautiful," she said when he finished, stepping into the light.

"Gadzooks!" exclaimed Noah, his hand to his heart. "Are you trying to give a fellow heart failure?"

"Noah," Faye said, "you really have talent. Why are you always so ridiculous?"

"Thanks," he said with a sniff. "I think."

"I'm sorry, that didn't come out right," said Faye. "What I meant to say was that everyone thinks you're a bit ridiculous and then don't realize you're talented."

"When you say 'everyone,' you mean you, right?" Noah winked as he headed back to his room. "Don't worry. I won't tell anyone you were being nice. You don't want anyone to know you aren't the snow queen, correct, Lady Faye?" He waved and closed the door behind him.

Noah, for all his silliness, *was* absolutely right. This only served to make Faye really, really angry. Instead of walking the halls, she stomped back to her room and flung herself onto her bed. How dare he call her a "snow queen." How dare he! She *had* been awfully unkind. But hadn't he deserved it? Or had he?

Faye's anger began to change into an uncomfortable bemusement. Huffing and puffing was the behavior of a spoilt child. Noah had hit a sore spot. Taking a deep breath, she sat up. She would have to be better about it. She stood, took another deep breath, and went back into the corridor to look out the window. The train was not moving very fast. She had a feeling they were almost where they were going. She smiled to herself, glad to be leaving this train.

Meanwhile, Jasper was tossing in his bed. Lucy had been talking in her sleep, something about a unicorn and someone named Lulaberry and her buttercup hat pin. Finally, as Lulaberry seemed unable to descend her elephant, Jasper left Lucy to her babbling dream world, put on his slippers, and stepped into the corridor. The light of the moon was bright, and he could see that Faye was still standing, smiling to herself, looking out the window into the night. Jasper was not happy with the fact that whenever Faye smiled, he seemed to break out in a great red blush from ear to ear.

"Cheers, Jasper," Faye said, hearing him close his door. "I see you're having a good night's sleep."

"Yes, quite," he said. "Lucy is taking up the room with her night-talking."

Faye laughed. "I remember one dream she had. I woke up because she was pulling my arm, saying, 'If we don't fetch the grindle-cakes, the hydrogen molecules will leave without us!'"

Jasper had to laugh.

Then Faye looked at Jasper. Why, she thought to herself, did she feel the need to be so forthright with the boys? She must be tired. It weakened her. Faye felt the awkward silence that followed the laughter. She suddenly wanted to be alone. So Faye started toward her room, but after a few steps, she realized that Jasper might be hurt if she just walked away from him. She faced back around.

"Goodnight, Jasper," she said, turning away before he could see the blush in her cheeks.

Jasper stood there for a moment. Then, without thinking, he

walked back into his room and climbed into bed, forgetting to take off his slippers and totally unable to fall back asleep.

———————

The sound of a blaring horn filled the air. It was not yet dawn, but with the first hints of light, the six passengers could feel that the stuttering slow-moving train had, once again, stopped. The fog outside, though, made it impossible to see where they were.

Again, there was the sound of the horn. It could have been a foghorn, loud and deep. They could have still been on Long Island, but no one could be sure. Beyond the fog, though, there was daylight, and the children could see tall silhouettes against the grayness, swaying upon the water. These were certainly ships.

Miss Brett called to the children, not sure what was coming. She wanted everyone up and dressed before someone came to demand they leave the train or whatever else might be demanded.

As they rose from their beds, the fog began to clear. Looking out the windows of the cabin, Miss Brett saw grand ships lining docks. They were at a seaport.

The children hurried from their cabins to Miss Brett's room. She, in turn, was just opening her door when she met them outside of it.

"Miss Brett, where are we?" asked Wallace.

"Well, I don't know exactly," Miss Brett said. Turning, Miss Brett spotted the Park Row Building against the skyline. "We are still in New York. It must be New York Harbor."

"Are we taking a ship?" asked Lucy.

Miss Brett opened her mouth to answer, then, knowing full well that she could not, said simply, "We shall see, Lucy. We shall see."

They did not have to wait very long. Within moments, the man with the frilly apron came for them. He had a sack slung over his shoulder.

"To sea," he said, pointing to the water.

"What?" Miss Brett thought she had heard wrongly.

"Sea," he said. "Go."

"But I'm in my sleepy things. We all are," Lucy said.

This did not seem to matter to the man. "It goes," he said, gesturing for them to move along. But from his sack, he pulled a blanket and handed it to Lucy.

"What goes?" asked Noah, who then shook his head. "Never mind. Either you won't answer or you'll say something I don't understand." Resigned, he and the others allowed themselves to be pushed along, each handed a blanket as they went.

Coming to the door of the train car, the children and Miss Brett descended. Before them was a large, elegant steamship. Its gangplank was extended, and things were being loaded onto the ship by familiar men in black.

"Come," said a voice from beside the doorway.

It was a man dressed in a black captain's jacket and slacks, a black captain's hat, and dark, rectangular glasses. They followed him from the train.

"But my things!" Faye cried.

"Come," said the man again.

"I will not leave all of my things behind," said Faye. She ran back toward the train to fetch her belongings and, she hoped, put on some proper clothes.

"What about our things?" asked Noah. He thought of the postcards he kept from his mother, telling him about all of her adventures around Europe.

"Come all," insisted the man in the captain's uniform, his hand catching Noah by the shoulder as the boy tried to return to the train like Faye.

Faye, meanwhile, climbed aboard the train and ran down the corridor to her room. Pulling open the door, she stopped dead on the threshold.

Nothing was there—literally, nothing. Her beads, her shoes, her clothes, and even her bed and lamp were all gone. They couldn't have been off the train more than five minutes, but everything had vanished.

This made her very angry. She took several breaths before turning around and slowly heading back to the others.

The man in the captain's suit was still holding Noah by the scruff, though Noah seemed to have given up all hope of escape. Noah was the first to see Faye and was surprised to see her empty-handed.

"Where are your things, Faye?" Noah called as Faye walked towards them. Faye just shook her head. She didn't feel like shouting across to the others.

"What happened?" asked Jasper, his hand holding Lucy's tight.

"Everything was gone," Faye said once she was with them.

"Of course it is," Lucy said. "He told us they'd be bringing everything for us, silly."

"And when did he do that?" asked Faye in frustration.

"As we were walking," said Lucy. "But you ran back anyway."

Jasper looked at his sister. Clearly, she understood something the rest of them did not.

They marched together, following the man in the captain's uniform. Miss Brett hoped Lucy was right.

The man in the captain's suit pointed to the entrance. He turned and walked along the edge of the deck, then climbed a ladder, disappearing over the handrail above.

Not knowing what else to do, the children and Miss Brett boarded the ship, finding themselves in a most elegant entrance. The carpet was a deep red and looked as if it was made of silk. Lucy bent down and rubbed her hand on it.

"The floor's so soft," she said. "I could sleep on it." Lucy yawned, and the idea of just curling up right there did not seem like a bad idea at all.

But instead, the children and Miss Brett continued down a wide corridor with lovely paintings adorning the walls and Greek or Roman statues lining the hall, which opened to a big room with high ceilings, a giant chandelier, and a fountain in the center. The huge windows were as tall as the ceiling, and outside, where sea met sky, the horizon stretched as far as they could see. There was a large archway on each side of the room.

"One way must be the sleeping quarters," said Miss Brett. "The other must lead somewhere else."

A man in black wearing a very tall, fuzzy hat bent at the very top, a fuzzy black vest, and a large bow tie appeared in the archway on the left and gestured for them to follow. Yawning and exhausted, with the boat's gentle rocking making them wish for nothing more than a bed upon which to return to sleep, Miss Brett and her brood were led down the hallway.

The man stopped at the first door. He gestured for Miss Brett to go inside. She did not, instead staying with the children. He went and opened four other doors and gestured toward the children. Each cabin seemed to have been prepared exclusively for each of them. They knew this because of what each contained.

"Oh, my bunny doll!" Lucy hurried to one of the beds in the room next to Miss Brett's. Jasper looked around and quickly discovered that their cabin looked remarkably like the cabin on the train, except, notably, their parents' bed was missing.

"Look, they've brought our beds!" Lucy exclaimed.

"Don't be silly, Lucy. They couldn't possibly have," said Jasper. But whether or not they were the ones from the train, these beds were tidily made, pillows fluffed, and looked exactly like those they had just left. And there, on Lucy's bed, was her bunny doll, with its new ribbon sewn to its hat.

Faye, in her room, considered how all of her things had been missing from her cabin on the train. From the look of things, all of her possessions, including her bed, her bedclothes, and her dressing robe, were there. With these fellows, it seemed anything was possible.

"All right now," Miss Brett said from back out in the hallway. She looked outside. The sun was rising in the late October sky. "I want everyone to get back into bed and get some sleep—even if it's just for a morning nap." *Who knows what today will bring?* she thought.

"Oh, Miss Brett," said Lucy, "but I'm not the least bit sleepy." But she yawned an enormous yawn.

"We'll see about that," Miss Brett said, wrapping around Lucy's shoulders the blanket she had been given and pointing to Lucy's room. Lucy trudged through the cabin door into the room she would share with her brother.

She flopped onto her bed, then reached for Miss Brett, who had followed her in. Placing a kiss on Lucy's forehead, Miss Brett felt the little girl pull her face close and whisper something in her ear.

"How did you know, sweet angel?" Miss Brett whispered back. But not waiting for an answer, she said, "Now go to sleep."

"I'm not . . . not the least"—she yawned—"bit . . ." But she was curled up under her covers and asleep before she could conclude her denial.

Finding this move to the boat yet one more fantastical thing to consider among the fantastical things always happening to them, Jasper lay awake on his bed for some time before sleep accepted its welcome. Noah, like Lucy, let the ponderings give way to exhaustion, and to the sleep that followed immediately upon head hitting pillow. And Faye, finally, allowed sleep to come, knowing full well there was nothing she could do about her predicament.

It was Wallace, however, who did not sleep until he quietly snuck into Miss Brett's room. His teacher was asleep in her rocking chair. Wallace climbed into her lap, finding it a bit smaller than it had once been. And Miss Brett, upon finding the sleeping boy in her lap, woke groggily, carried him back to his room, tucked him in, and went back to sleep herself.

CHAPTER NINE

CLOTHES FOR THE OCCASION

OR

WHAT LUCY FOUND IN THE CLOSET

It was the gentle rocking of the ship that made for such a deep and comforting sleep. When Jasper woke, he found the sea all around them. They had sailed through the early morning.

Jasper watched the undulating ocean through his porthole, stretched, and then noticed Lucy was not there. Her bed had been carefully made, and she was not in it.

"Lucy?" he called, but there was no answer.

Quickly, he dressed, realizing he was not sure what time it was. It was daytime—perhaps close to noon. He wondered what the others were doing and if Lucy had gone to join them.

Opening his door, Jasper peeked out. He checked the lock on his door to be sure he wouldn't lock himself out if he closed the door behind him. Cautiously, he stepped out. Walking down the hall, Jasper decided to knock on the doors next to his. But neither Faye, Noah, Wallace, nor Miss Brett answered. Jasper walked a bit faster, but he did not know where he was headed.

Coming to the end of the hallway, he opened a door that led up to the deck. Breathing in the chilly sea air, Jasper felt refreshed. But the fresh air did not change the fact that he was alone. Where was everyone? They had to be here...didn't they?

But the disappearance of people he loved was part of life for him. He took another deep breath and walked along the deck. There was no land in sight—only sea to the horizon in every direction. At a door, he entered and found a staircase. He descended the wide spiral stairs and walked along another corridor. This led to another stairway. He walked down instead of up, and his nose soon met the smells of breads and cakes. This had to be the kitchen or the dining room. His stomach grumbled. Yes, he was hungry. He let his hunger lead him.

He opened the wide doors at the end of the walkway and entered a beautiful, sunlit room. There was a large table in the center of the room. And there they were. Jasper breathed deeply, relieved, feeling a bit silly that he'd worried about not finding them. They were, after all, on a ship in the middle of the ocean. Capturing his calm, he walked over to the table. The others sat around the table—except Lucy.

"About time," said Noah, still in his pajamas. He was, as usual, filling his face with food.

"I take it you slept well, Jasper," said Miss Brett. She was pouring tea into her cup.

"Yes, Miss Brett," he said. "Have you seen—" But he did not need to finish. Lucy came through another set of doors, skipping into the room, singing to herself. She, too, was in pajamas, but wore a warm, fuzzy dressing robe and a wooly cap.

"You're awake, Jasper!" she said happily, throwing off the cap and robe. "You were ever so not when I came up here. Everyone's been terribly slow to wake up. Noah came just before you."

Noah winked at Jasper and reached for another sandwich.

"I had better see if I can find one of our minders," Miss Brett said, putting her cup down. She suspected that, at the rate Noah was going, they would be needing some more sandwiches for Jasper. She went to find the kitchen.

"I've been playing on the decks. It is lovely here." Lucy twirled around and landed in a seat at the table. She took a piece of toast from the basket and piled jam upon it. "I've been investigating."

"Mind you don't fall down a rabbit hole," Noah said with a smile.

"Oh, there are no rabbits on the ship," said Lucy. "At least not where I've been looking. I'd love to find a bunny rabbit. Then Vercingetorix can have a wedding."

"What?" Noah goggled at Lucy.

"Who on earth is Vercingetorix?" Faye shook her head.

"And why should he marry a rabbit?" Noah's eyebrows were nearly hidden by his hair, they were so high up on his forehead.

Lucy picked up her bunny rabbit doll from her lap. "This is Vercingetorix," she said. "And you're all just making silliness at me because I wished for bunnies in a bunny hole." Lucy humphed.

"Moi? To shame!" declared Noah in mock offense. "I merely noted that it is very dangerous wandering into places that do not wish you to enter them."

"He means, be careful about exploring in places you shouldn't," Faye said sternly. "Strange as it may seem, I'd have to agree with Noah."

Noah put his hand to his heart and mock-fainted into Faye's lap.

"Oh, get off!" Faye said, wiping Noah from her lap as if he were a pile of crumbs. Noah slid to the floor in true crumb style.

"I would never go where I shouldn't go," said Lucy. "I only

went to peek in places I hadn't been."

Noah came up from the floor and looked into everyone else's confused faces. Then he shrugged and sat back down in his seat. He grabbed three pieces of toast, spread jelly and cream on each one, piled all three together, and then, in three bites, devoured it all.

"Find anything interesting?" Noah asked Lucy, reaching for the last piece of toast on the table. He received a slap from Faye, who took it herself.

"Oh, yes," said Lucy, her mouth full of toast. "I found the kitchen and the salon. And I found a grand closet filled with books—more books than I could count—and another filled with dress-up things."

"Dress-up things?" Faye hadn't a clue what Lucy meant.

"Well, there were hats and cloaks and funny wigs," said Lucy. "Since Halloween is in ten days, we can use those things for dress-up."

"We'll celebrate a holiday on the ship, you fancy?" Jasper thought about it and considered that they might be on the boat for more than one holiday. They might well be traversing the entire ocean, and that could take…Jasper could only imagine.

"Oh, it isn't the *first* holiday." Lucy giggled. Then, she spoke as if she was telling secrets: "Miss Brett's birthday is today, and I gave her a special birthday kiss filled with wishes and happy thoughts of cream custards and puddings and chocolate cakes."

"We forgot Miss Brett's birthday?" Wallace gulped, thinking of how kind she had been on his own birthday.

"How do you know?" Faye asked Lucy.

"Miss Brett told us," Lucy said. "It's the same day as Alfred

Nobel, who invented dynamite, and started the Nobel Prize. That's today."

Faye was amazed. She didn't remember ever having been told.

Miss Brett came back, carrying a large plate of hot crumpets and some raspberry tarts. All eyes turned to her.

"Yes?" she said.

"Happy birthday, Miss Brett," Wallace said, sheepishly. "We should have brought presents."

All the children wished her a happy birthday. A few moments followed where only the slurping of Lucy's tea could be heard.

"Children, no long faces," she said. "In truth, I forgot myself, until Lucy reminded me. I'd say we've had a great deal to think about these days." Miss Brett picked up the empty jam pot and went back to the kitchen to refill it.

Jasper quickly leaned toward his sister and whispered. "You could have reminded us, Lucy. It would have been the sporting thing to do."

"What do you mean?" she asked, honest confusion on her face.

"You remembered it was Miss Brett's birthday." Jasper was surprised at Lucy's thickheadedness. "And we didn't."

"But what about it?" Lucy asked, picking a currant from her scone and nibbling it like a bunny rabbit.

Jasper felt his face go red. How could Lucy be so thoughtless?

"Forget it," Jasper hissed as Miss Brett returned. Lucy looked hurt and shocked by his response. She looked down at her teacup, then put it back in its saucer, tears welling in her eyes. Jasper almost moved his hand to comfort her, but he didn't. Anger and guilt battled it out in his head and his heart.

"I didn't mean to do anything," Lucy mumbled.

"I ... I said forget it." Jasper patted Lucy on the shoulder. Lucy grinned and blinked and the tears, though no longer needed, fell.

"Where do you think we're headed?" Faye asked quickly.

"Well, I haven't a clue," said Miss Brett, looking out at the sea. "I only know we're going east, so we could be headed toward a number of places. Anyone care to guess?"

"Europe," said Jasper.

"India," said Faye, hopefully.

"Africa or England, or, perhaps, Atlantis," said Noah.

"Oh!" Lucy's eyes grew very big. "You think we might be going to Atlantis? It's the lost city. That would mean we'd be the ones to find it! They'll all be so pleased not to be lost anymore."

"I suppose we'll know soon enough," Miss Brett said, kissing Lucy on the head. She looked out at the sky hitting the sea, her fears unspoken about their journey.

"And when might that be?" asked Wallace.

Again, Miss Brett had no idea.

<hr>

After breakfast, the children settled in quickly, a talent they had acquired—and explored the ship. They learned that, however grand the ship was, they were certainly its only passengers. This did not surprise them, though, since the only members of the crew were the mysterious men in black.

Lucy showed the children the kitchen and the closet of books. They lit a lamp and found five shelves filled with books of all sizes. This was a deep closet that went back into darkness. What was remarkable wasn't that there were so very many books, but that they were all so different. Some had pictures, and some had only computations. Some were in Latin and some, handwritten, looked very old indeed. There was a book on navigation by a famous American navigator and a book on the history of Persia.

"And look!" Noah pulled a book from the shelf. "It's Jules Verne! *Voyages Extraordinaires.* And there's another," he said, pulling from the shelf another book by the same author. These, he could tell, were collections of stories.

After perusing the books and, with the help of Lucy's memory, putting them back on the shelves exactly where they belonged, Lucy took the children to other spots she'd discovered. While the broom closet was not very exciting, the costume closet was to everyone's interest. It was a strange collection of things that no one expected to find.

"You'd think the costumes would be all in black," said Noah.

"That would make the most sense." Faye held a very small shoe in her hand. It had no mate, and was very old. "I'd like to see the lady who could fit into this."

Lucy took the shoe and placed it easily, like Cinderella, upon her tiny foot. "It's for me," she said.

"But there's only one," said Faye. "And it's old. Probably from the century before last."

There were many things that looked at least that old. Folded on the shelves and hanging on hooks were old-fashioned coats and cloaks that seemed to be from the middle ages. There were beautiful dresses and hats, too. And strangely, almost all of them seemed to be small enough to fit the children.

"Do you think they were brought here for us?" asked Lucy. Having selected a lovely hat with silk flowers which she was now wearing, she held up a tiny dress that was just her size. The dress was made of velvet and lace. "I could be a princess."

"I doubt it," said Faye, who noticed that there were a few more single shoes in a corner. "It looks as if these are things people left on the ship."

"You mean passengers left them?" asked Wallace, wiping his glasses so he could better examine the costumes.

"Who knows?" Faye had no idea to whom these things belonged, only that they were not being worn by any of the men in black.

Noah pulled at a long piece of cloth folded neatly in a corner. It was huge, and seemed to be red and white. Under it was another giant cloth, this one black and white.

"What *is* this?" he asked, staring at the first cloth. Jasper grabbed one corner and Wallace another. Faye took the third, and Noah held his. They all began stepping back, until they came to the walls. Though the space was not large enough to spread out the cloth fully, they could see that it was some sort of a drapery, or perhaps a large tablecloth. It was rectangular, and the children had, unfortunately, opened it so that the long sides were against the walls. So they shuffled around to extend it the length of the corridor. It was indeed red and white, and checkered. Dropping it, they picked up the other cloth and began to unfold it as well. It was not checkered, but there was a black, angular design. It looked like "V" shapes facing toward the center, but they could not make out the complete image.

And then they heard footsteps.

"We'd better fold it back the way it was," said Jasper, figuring that these cloths were not part of the costume collection. Since he was fairly sure the mysterious men in black would not be too pleased with an invasion of the costume room in the first place, pulling out these special cloths would certainly get them all into trouble.

The children tried to refold the cloths neatly, but it was nearly impossible. They kept getting the corners crossed and finding that the ends did not meet. In addition, Lucy seemed to think it was fun to run through the billowing fabric and twirl through the center, pulling the corners out of the hands of her friends and giggling as she rolled herself up in a cocoon.

"Lucy!" groaned Jasper. "Get out of there! We're trying to fold these dratted things."

"You must not flop," came a voice full of menace. It turned out to be a man wearing a pair of black, octagonal welding goggles and a black three-pointed jester's hat. He was in a black leotard and poofy black bloomers. But judging by his voice, gravelly and deep, he was not amused.

"Oh—sorry," said Jasper, pulling Lucy from the mess of cloth.

"There is no sorry," growled the man, and even Lucy, who seemed to be fond of the men in black, stepped behind Jasper.

"The costumes are lovely," Lucy offered.

"Not so but left," he muttered.

"Um, may, um, may we . . ." But Lucy trailed off as the jester turned his back on her.

Grumbling to himself in words even Lucy could not understand, the man grabbed the black and white cloth and pulled it all into a ball. Then, he kissed it. And then, with a sudden flick of his wrists, he sent the huge cloth out clean and flat and, with amazing speed and remarkable skill, flipped and flopped his arms until the cloth was perfectly folded, as if it had been ironed. He did this all on his own. The children were amazed.

Then he did the same with the other cloth. He placed both of them on the shelf, closed the door to the closet, and left the children standing there. As he walked down the hall, he did a little skip and clicked his heels together.

"For a jester, he wasn't very funny," said Noah. "But he could most certainly fold."

CHAPTER TEN

Miss Brett's Birthday Surprise

OR

WALLACE'S MAGNETS GO ASTRAY

The children wandered down to the engine room, where they were shooed out by the engineer, who wore short black pants, long black stockings, and thick black boots. The engine room was noisy, and the children did not in the least mind leaving.

They went to the upper deck. Heading across it and into the first set of doors, they found themselves in a wide corridor with a set of double doors at the end. They opened the doors and were thrilled to find their laboratory just as they had left it. And, to their pleasure, they found an observation room connected to the lab. It was very much like the observation room in the train, with a rounded dome of glass as its ceiling. In the center was a huge telescope with enormous gears and many levers, so it could be positioned however they chose.

"We must tell Miss Brett!" said Lucy, jumping up and down. "She was just saying that we should learn about astral navigation." She tapped on the glass and was surprised at how thick it seemed to be. Her tapping made a very different sound than it did on a regular window, as if she were tapping on a stone wall.

So, following a late afternoon tea, they took Miss Brett to the upper deck.

"How fabulous!" she exclaimed when she saw the telescope.

Once they were able to position the telescope properly, they took turns looking out toward the horizon. They positioned the telescope to focus on the sliver of moon, which was visible though it was still light.

"You must be very careful when you look into the sky," Miss Brett said. "Looking at the sun can hurt your eyes."

"It's the magnification of the light," said Wallace.

"Well, what do you know? Look who's the astronomer," Noah said, patting Wallace on the back.

Miss Brett decided that schoolwork would focus on the ocean, the stars, and sailing. What an opportunity to study hands-on.

In the early evening, the children took Miss Brett to the room of books. She was thrilled to see so many volumes and longed to walk all the way to the back. She immediately considered this the perfect lending library for their on-board classes.

Wallace perused a large book called *The American Practical Navigator*, an encyclopedia of sea and navigation, full of equations and scientific information.

"This will be an excellent book to study while at sea," Miss Brett declared. "Be sure to care for it well and, when we are done, return it to where we found it." She figured it would help in different lessons—navigation as well as meteorology and oceanography. It was a wonderful encyclopedia of all things maritime.

They referred to the book when they discussed various navigational methods. She explained a sextant, having borrowed one from the mysterious captain in black.

"You see, this is how they navigate using the stars," said Miss Brett.

"And the planets," said Jasper.

"And the birds," added Lucy. Then, to a sea of questioning faces, she said, "They're celestial."

"Well, birds do a lot of flying about," said Wallace, "but I think the celestial object needs to be more fixed in the sky than a bird." Wallace was taken with *The American Practical Navigator*. The calculations were amazing.

Later, as the autumn sun descended, and the moon a thin bright streak in the sky, Miss Brett had them go outside on the deck. Because most sailing ships were not equipped with fabulous domed glass enclosures and enormous telescopes, she would teach them using ordinary equipment. Tonight, they would use one of the small telescopes positioned around the ship. Miss Brett also borrowed a map from the captain so they could use the sextant properly. The children were able to take some measurements and do some navigational investigations of their own. She brought blankets and asked one of the men in black to bring a tray of hot tea to arm them against the chill.

Holding the sextant, Wallace looked through the lens, but when Faye moved into position to look through the scope, Wallace stumbled while getting out of her way and dropped the sextant. It tumbled over toward the edge of the deck, but when he reached for it, frantic, it slid slowly across, stopping at the edge. When he tried to pick it up, the sextant would not move. Jasper leaned over and tried to help him pull it from the edge.

"What's going on?" Noah said. He tried to pull it up as well. "It's stuck," he said, "but it isn't stuck to anything."

But Jasper could see that the sextant was attached to a long, narrow, metal edge that ran around the outer perimeter of the top deck. *How odd*, he thought, using the back of a teaspoon from the tray to wedge the sextant from its position. He handed it back to Wallace, looking back down at what was clearly a magnetic strip. Why it should be there, he could not imagine.

"It is strange, isn't it?" Wallace said, taking one of his magnetic spheres from his pocket. He tried to place it on the magnetic strip, but the sphere jumped off and landed back on the deck. "They must have the same polarity."

"It must be used for something," said Jasper, standing up. It was growing darker. The sun was setting behind them.

Noah looked down at the strip. "Maybe to seal something?" He shrugged. "It's getting dark fast—and cold, too."

"We still seem to be heading more or less due east," Wallace said, standing next to Jasper.

"And away from South America," said Wallace.

Noah examined the map. "If we keep this course, we'll be heading for—"

"The Strait of Gibraltar," said Wallace, who was looking at the map as well.

The Strait of Gibraltar, thought Miss Brett. She looked down at the map. That would take them into the Mediterranean Sea. There were so many possible destinations in that part of the world, and Miss Brett had read about a variety of countries in that region. This would be the first time she would be traveling there—the first time she'd be traveling anywhere, in fact, besides the United States and England, where she'd visited her mother's family as a child. She wondered just where they would be pulling into port.

Noah was shivering, and had neither jacket nor muffler for warmth.

Walking over to Noah, Miss Brett placed a blanket on his shoulders. He smiled and thanked her. He looked at Jasper, who now had the same expression on his face as Noah. Miss Brett was so kind, he thought, and they hadn't even remembered her birthday.

"I'll get you some tea, shall I?" Miss Brett went over to the tray.

"I feel like a cad," said Noah to the others.

"She would never have forgotten our birthdays," said Wallace with a groan.

"I wish Lucy had said something," Jasper said, feeling gnawing resentment.

But they had a plan to make it up to Miss Brett. They had a plan to give something to the kindest woman they knew.

"Shhh." Lucy's finger was on her lips as she turned to the others. Her very groggy companions bumped into one another. Bleary-eyed, they agreed—well, those who could think despite the fuzzy sleep that filled their heads. Wallace nodded. Faye's eyes were fluttering, but she was awake enough to swat Noah in the head when he started to snore on her shoulder. Jasper kept rubbing his eyes and nodding in case anyone might be talking to him.

"But why are we all up so early?" Noah asked, yawning and rubbing the spot on his head that Faye had whacked in response. He and the others were all in their pajamas. They were sleepy not only because it was early, but because they had stayed up well past their normal bedtimes working in the laboratory.

The five young inventors had worked late into the night to finish. Wallace and Lucy had managed to make more magnets—not spheres, but round, flattened discs using the tiny furnace. Out of gears and thin metallic plates, they had created a device that also had sides of both positive and negative charges. By allowing the gears to stabilize the force, they could control the magnetic discs more easily.

Jasper's idea had helped to improve the strength of the magnets by using a process of nickel-plating with the neodymium he'd invented. Noah had concluded that the sign was too plain and quickly produced a copper wire that he bent in the shape of a heart. The wire heart balanced on top of a small battery. The balancing wire began to spin, becoming a three-dimensional whirring, twirling heart.

"We're lucky we had the miniature sintering furnace and the neodymium already crushed," Wallace had said as he'd cooled another compressed metal alloy.

"It's lucky you're such a big fan of Hans Oersted to think of these magnets in the first place," said Noah, rubbing his finger gently against the spinning copper heart.

"Well, Oersted did more than magnets and electromagnetic experiments," said Wallace, handing another magnet to Faye, who was organizing them for their project. "He was the first one to iso-late aluminium—"

"Everyone knows that, Wallace," Faye said, rolling her eyes.

Wallace adjusted his glasses and tried to let his face cool down before saying anything. When he could speak, he said, "My guess is that we'll need three more to make it work."

So now, with everything ready, they tiptoed down the hall, a set of magnets hovering next to them. As if by magic, the magnets floated above, and below, a very thin plate made mostly of iron. The plate carried a lovely birthday sign for Miss Brett.

Only the faintest clicking came from the gears in the mecha-nism, which Wallace held, and a gentle whir came from Noah's heart, spinning like a butterfly in his hand. And like a pleasant ghost that had only the intention of bringing belated birthday cheer, the sign floated in a very well-behaved manner.

"We had to be up before Miss Brett," said Lucy to Noah, "so we can wish her a happy new pretend birthday."

"Don't call it a new pretend birthday," groaned Faye. "It's a be-lated birthday—a delayed or otherwise slightly tardy birthday."

"Very well," said Noah, "though I think we outnumber Miss Brett and could just decide this is her new birthday."

The five children walked in one quiet mass to their teacher's door. There was no sound from within.

"You think she's still asleep?" asked Wallace. It was only 7 a.m., but Miss Brett was an early riser.

"I think so," said Lucy.

At that moment, the door to the room slid open. Startled, Lucy jumped and knocked into Wallace, who, in turn, bumped into Noah. The twirling heart shot out of his hands. The battery attached itself to the hovering disc as the gently floating phantom birthday sign flew like a demon into the hair of a not-yet-entirely-awakened Miss Brett.

Miss Brett cried out as she batted away the sign, thinking it was some mad bird or bat. The heart now poked her repeatedly in the forehead.

Wallace quickly recovered control and managed to get the thing out of Miss Brett's hair and back to its benign state.

"What was that devil…?!" Miss Brett was breathing hard, her heart pounding.

"Oh, Miss Brett!" Lucy was mortified. She burst into tears, feeling horrid that she had somehow managed to ruin their big surprise.

As if begging forgiveness, the sign fluttered down in front of Miss Brett, who read it and smiled. Noah quickly righted the heart and balanced it in its place atop the sign. Lucy smiled through her tears and gave a shuddering sigh of relief.

Laughing now, Miss Brett said, "Well, now, happy belated birthday to me."

The laughter followed them into the dining car. Miss Brett placed the whirring heart next to her plate and allowed the sign to float safely at a distance. On her seat, Miss Brett found a package.

"Goodness, what have you sweet angels been up to?" She opened the packages and found a beautiful cylinder. It had copper beading along the edges and a round glass on one side. Suddenly, she realized what it must be. Feeling along the side, she found a round button made of copper. She pressed it. Nothing happened.

Wallace adjusted his glasses. "You need to shake it," he said, shyly.

Miss Brett shook the cylinder, and a beam of light shot out of the glass end.

"Amazing!" she said.

"W-we all made it together," Wallace stammered.

"But Wallace invented it," Jasper said quickly.

"The electric torch." Miss Brett turned it on and off, remembering Wallace at work on it back on the train. She looked down at Lucy and smiled, placing the torch on the table. "I absolutely love it," Miss Brett said to Lucy. She held up her birthday sign all on her own.

Wallace placed his magnets in his pockets. It felt good to have something in his pocket, something that was his and he could hold. He was glad he had the magnets and felt that, somehow, they would come to some good use someday.

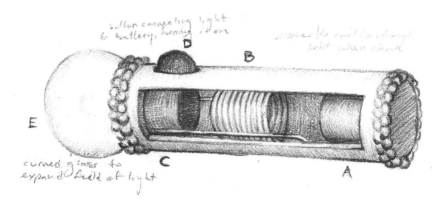

CHAPTER ELEVEN

HALLOWEEN SCARES
OR
WHAT LUCY SEES IN THE COOKING POT

C hilly and cold from the rain and the spray, Jasper pondered the power of magnets. After the gift to Miss Brett, myriad images went through his brain of the ways they could experiment. Did hot or cold temperatures affect magnetic fields? Might they create a truly zero electrical resistance? Could they magnetize metals that did not, themselves, have great magnetic strength? Magnets might be able to power cities and electric carriages and … the possibilities were endless. Perhaps, even, there was a way to make magnets work with opposing forces in unending motion.

"Do you think we could create a magnetic sphere that could move from one repelling magnet to another, Wallace?" Jasper said. "So it moves forever, perhaps in a circle?"

"It would certainly be possible," Wallace said. "In theory."

"Would it get faster and faster if the repelling magnets were stronger and stronger?" Jasper had been wondering about this. "Or would it always lose momentum?"

"I think it depends on the distance between the magnets, in relation to the force projecting the magnets from one point to another and back."

"Aha, force," said Noah, wandering over. "You two talking Newton's second law?"

"Not directly," said Wallace, now wiping the sea spray from his eyeglasses.

"Well, it's a good thing this saltwater isn't separated into elements, eh, Wallace?" Noah winked at Wallace. Wallace just blinked back.

"What do you mean?" asked Jasper, who was not as chemistry-oriented as Wallace. He could certainly apply some principles of chemistry to his inventions, but it was Wallace who was the real chemist among them.

Noah grinned and wandered off. Wallace replaced his glasses and looked at Noah as if he had just made a very lame joke.

"Because, as you know," said Wallace, "salt is sodium combined with chloride. Sodium alone, if thrown into water, would simply explode."

"Oh, yes, well, very funny," Jasper said.

"Yes, precisely," said Wallace. The boys continued to stare out at the sea.

The days after Miss Brett's birthday were proving to be colder, with a choppy ocean. The children spent much of their time inside, doing lessons with Miss Brett and working in the lab. Experiments in astral navigation were impossible, as they could not see any stars or planets through the thick layer of clouds. But this gave the children time to work on other important projects.

"Poor sailors," Lucy said, shivering as she and her brother came in from the cold. "They'll be terribly lost without the stars to guide them."

"Too right," said Jasper, placing his muffler around his sister's neck to warm her. "That's why there's so much treasure beneath the sea. The poor sailors and pirates couldn't navigate, and crashed upon rocks and uncharted islands."

He wanted to ask Faye about the sunken treasure of Shah Aurangzeb Alamgir, but Faye refused to do anything outside, or even talk about anything in the cold, cold sea. She insisted her Indian sensibilities were not suited for cold, wet, dank, miserable weather.

———◆———

"The question is," said Noah, entering the laboratory one day, "what are we going to be tonight?"

"What on earth are you talking about?" asked Faye, fed up with his silliness. She had been helping Wallace and Jasper with their moving magnets, using a magnifying glass to remove any particles from the spheres. Lucy, meanwhile, was at the microscope, trying to see if she could use a hair to paint faces on grains of sand. She had stiffened the hairs with a paste of flour and water, leaving just the ends soft. Then she had made a pigment, using saffron from the kitchen for yellow and, for black, simply ink.

Noah took Lucy's "hair" brush and painted a tiny face on the head of a nail. He tossed the nail, which flew to the magnetic sphere, appearing much larger in Faye's magnifying glass.

Faye jumped back. "What was that, you fiend?!" she yelled. She found the nail, then threw it back at him and went back to her work.

"I hope I'm your best fiend. It is October 31, after all," Noah said. "That means something to those of us from the real world."

"The real world?" Faye looked up from her magnifying glass and raised her eyebrows.

"For those of us from North America or Europe or Great Britain, it means that this is Halloween."

"Of course," said Wallace, without Noah's enthusiasm.

"And this means something?" asked Faye. "This is something important?"

"It's Halloween!" cried Noah. Jasper and Lucy nodded in agreement.

"What the devil is Halloween?" said Faye.

Faye's choice of words tickled the others, and even Wallace had to laugh.

"Exactly," said Noah.

"Exactly what?" Now Faye put down her magnifying glass.

"The devil, naughtiness, mischief," said Noah. "That's all part of Halloween."

"And dressing up in lovely costumes and eating sweets and playing games," added Lucy, imagining all these delights.

"Who does all this?" Faye asked, rather intrigued.

"Well, mostly adults, but children more and more," Wallace said. "I've seen children participate in our neighborhood, though I myself have never partaken in their antics."

"But you'd like to." Noah winked at Wallace.

"Well." Wallace looked down and adjusted his glasses. "Perhaps."

"It's a special night where spirits and ghouls arise," said Noah. "Where creatures of doom descend upon us and screams of phantoms and witches can be heard on the night winds. It's jolly good fun."

"Sounds like a nightmare," said Faye.

"Only in the most splendid way," said Noah. "I'm not sure if you English folk have as much fun as we do in North America, though."

"Oh, yes!" cried Lucy. "But we don't have any banshees or horrid witches and things. Only nice ghosts haunt us."

"Really," said Noah. "What a disappointment. I'd like to imagine the most terrifying hauntings."

Lucy's eyes bulged. "Like Komar Romak?"

"Absolutely not!" said Jasper.

Lucy's lip began to quiver. "But... but... he's a scary monster, and... and..."

"Never, Lucy," insisted Faye. "Out here? On the sea?"

"But he found us on the train." The little girl looked from face to face. "Can't he sneak in on us here?" Lucy's hand flew to her mouth.

"No, indeed, Lucy," Wallace said.

"He certainly would never come to any Halloween party," Noah said. "Never ever. It would not be allowed."

Lucy blinked and Jasper tried to look reassuring. Noah winked.

Quickly changing the subject, Faye said, "So you also have Halloween?"

"We do celebrate All Hallows Eve, but we also have Mischief Night," said Jasper, smiling when he saw Noah's eyebrows rise.

"That sounds like my kind of holiday," said Noah.

"Good god," moaned Faye. "Don't give him more menace to plan."

"Halloween is when most of the adults dress up," said Jasper, "but children get to do their bit on Mischief Night."

Noah moved closer, hands cupped around his ears.

"That's the night before Guy Fawkes," said Jasper. "You know, Bonfire Night. Lucy and I haven't really done much for Mischief Night, but we've read all about it. And we've seen the bonfires on Guy Fawkes Night. Mischief Night, though, is more than remembering Guy Fawkes."

"Such as…?" Noah had a mischievous gleam in his eye.

"I'll leave it to your imagination," said Jasper. "But Faye is likely right to worry. Anyway, Mischief Night isn't the only night of naughtiness."

"Oh, Jasper is right," said Lucy. "So many scary, naughty nights. All over the world. They had creepy scary dead days even back in Egypt. They were called all sorts of things, but they were celebrating dead things, which I suppose is not so bad if you miss your pet doggie or bunny rabbit. You know, there's Samhain in Ireland, and that means 'summer's end' in Gaelic, which is sort of like summer dying." Lucy looked at Noah. "And they have real ghosts."

"There's no such thing, Lucy," Jasper said.

"No, it's true, honestly," said Lucy.

"What?" Noah raised his eyebrows.

"It's only people dressing as ghosts. Mostly adults, but sometimes children."

"My mother has gone to Halloween galas dressed as Marie Antoinette and Cleopatra," said Noah.

"Were you ever allowed to go?" asked Lucy, her eyes wide with excitement.

Noah's smile wavered. "I … no, I never was allowed to go, but I did get to peek down from the banister when they had a party at our house in Edinburgh. Mother had all the great heads of state and stars of the stage over in costume."

"Heads?" asked Lucy. "All by themselves?"

"Oh, no they … they were attached to very silly bodies," Noah explained. "Very silly indeed."

"We never had anything like that," Wallace said, thinking about his parents.

"Neither did we," said Jasper, thinking about his own.

"I suppose Mummy and Daddy aren't celebrating tonight," Lucy said, her face suddenly sad.

"No," said Jasper softly. "I think they are not."

"I should hope they wouldn't celebrate without us," said Faye, indignant. "Wherever they are, they should be heartbroken and missing us dreadfully."

"I doubt my mother is mourning," said Noah. "She surely has great festivities to fill her time."

Jasper and Faye exchanged looks.

"You know she misses you, Noah," Jasper said, gently.

"Do I?" Noah did not return Jasper's look. His tone was more of wonder than anger.

"Maybe she feels better at a party?" asked Lucy, her hand on Noah's arm. "So she isn't missing you."

"Oh, she loves a good party," said Noah, recovering his composure. "She loves costume balls and all sorts of fetes."

"Maybe she's going to a Halloween party so she won't be sad," said Lucy, smiling.

"You know, I bet you're right, Lucy." Noah smiled at her, letting the little girl feel she succeeded in making him feel better. "When we lived in Edinburgh, she brought me a pumpkin tart from their costume party. I wonder if it was a Halloween party after all."

"Could have been." Lucy nodded, looking at her brother. "Right, Jasper? There are great parties all over Britain."

"In Scotland, they have Hallowtide," said Jasper, quickly joining in. He could see that cheering up Noah was an excellent way to distract his sister.

"That's when children get to collect cakes and sweets from all their grown-up neighbors!" said Lucy. "Wouldn't it be lovely if we could beg for sweets and everyone gave us delicious marzipans and chocolates and dried apricots glacés?"

"Dried apricots glacés?" Noah laughed. "I'd like a chocolate cake and orange sponge and vanilla sandwich cakes and trifle and meringues." He licked his lips with great delight.

"These English sweets and cakes are quite nice, but we have the loveliest of treats in India," said Faye. "Oh, how I miss honey cakes and gulab jamun."

"Gulab jamun?" Noah laughed again. "Who are you people?"

"Oh, how lovely, gulab jamun!" cried Lucy, rubbing her tummy.

"You know what that is, Lucy?" said Jasper.

"No," said Lucy, still rubbing her tummy. "What is gulab jamun?"

Now Faye laughed. "Milk balls."

"Milk balls?" Noah asked. Now everyone laughed, even Faye, who realized that did not sound so delicious.

"Well, they're dumplings, really," she explained, "soaked in honey and rose water."

Now Noah rubbed his tummy. "Mmmm, gulab jamun."

"Getting treats is the law on Hallowtide," said Lucy.

"I like that law," said Noah.

Wallace wiped his glasses and returned them to his nose. "I don't think it's a law as much as a tradition," he said, "since—"

"Honestly, you're all acting quite the fool. Law, indeed," Faye said. But though she looked and often felt superior to the others, was taller than all but Noah, and was older than all of them by nearly a year, the idea of cakes and sweets did have a strong appeal.

"I say it's a law," said Noah with a flare.

Jasper smiled conspiratorially. "Well, we *are* at sea..."

"And we can invoke Scottish law," said Noah.

"Oh, yes!" Lucy jumped up and down again. "Let's do!"

Faye humphed. Jasper smiled at her, then glanced over at Lucy. Faye understood immediately that this was a good distraction for the little girl, and for them all—to think about something other than their absent parents and uncertain future.

"Well then, I think this requires some planning," said Faye.

The children set about writing out a list of demands. They did it in the style of a declaration:

> We, the members of the Young Inventors Guild, have declared that Scottish law be set in place for All Hallow's Eve, or Hallowe'en, or Hallowtide, or the night of 31 October, or whatever other name by which it may be known. As such, to our knowledge, law requires that children be given treats upon demand.

Each member of the Young Inventors Guild signed the document—even Faye, as a result of Lucy's pleading. Now it looked truly official.

"And who do we give this to?" asked Lucy.

The five children headed off to find Miss Brett. Faye grumbled, but she kept behind the others so they couldn't see her grin.

—⟶◆⟵—

"You'll have to hold up your part of the deal," said Miss Brett when they found her in her room. "You'll have to dress up in costume this evening."

Soon, the children were at the closet of costumes.

Jasper and Noah each found a pair of short britches, but neither fit very well. Noah found what appeared to be an artifact from Viking times to wear on his head. It had horns coming out on each side. Jasper found a hat that seemed to be from Napoleon's army and a bright yellow silk scarf that he wrapped around his neck.

Wallace found a galabaya, a traditional robe of Arabia. This one was from Egypt, according to the inscription ("made in Cairo by a hand"). He found a scarf that, with the help of Faye, he wrapped around his head.

Faye herself looked beautiful. The dress she found looked as if it had been sewn just for her. It was pale yellow with a deep red-and-gold trim. There was a single pale yellow glove that matched the dress, and Faye wore this as well. There were no fancy shoes that fit her, but there was a single silk slipper. In the spirit of things, Faye wore the single slipper. Behind his own scarf, Jasper blushed.

Lucy wore a beautiful Elizabethan dress made of the finest red velvet and gold lace. It was trimmed in black silk thread, and the most delicate of flowers had been sewn into the trim. Upon her head, Lucy wore a flowered hat, which must have come from a much more modern era than the dress. Why, a modern lady in 1903 might very well have worn it—a very small lady, that is. The single shoe—well, that lovely little shoe must have come from a generation before the hat.

Lucy also found a lady's handbag with green and blue beads. In it was a small gear and a handkerchief—nothing else. The handkerchief had a lovely embroidered letter, but it was so ornate, the children could not decide whether it was an "H," an "A," or a "K," not that it mattered.

"We'll put our sweets in this handbag," Lucy said. "It will keep them safe."

"Our sweets safe in *your* handbag?" said Noah.

"I won't eat them all!" Lucy cried, indignant. "And it's not my handbag." But Lucy considered that perhaps it was. "H," "A," or "K" probably had little interest in returning from their century to retrieve it. And the kerchief was so lovely. She wished it were hers.

⟶➤●◄⟵

After a dinner concluded with a delicious pie of apples and caramel, which was hardly touched by the excited children, there was a mad dash to get into costumes. They knocked on several doors that night before anyone answered. They found one door that was partially opened, but when they peeked in, it was dark, and Lucy was desperate to leave it alone.

But by the time the others began to walk away from the dark room, Noah's eyes had begun to adjust, and he could see something hanging on the wall. *Yes*, he thought, *this is perfect*. Lucy had planted an idea, and a night of tricks and treats would be perfect. He slipped into the room.

As the others continued along the corridor, Lucy insisted that they knock on every door.

"But that's a maintenance closet, Lucy," groaned Faye.

"You never know," Lucy said, knocking for a third time on the closet door before she moved to the next.

"You must not knock!" came a sudden shout from down the hall. Lucy jumped. The others were startled, too. A hooded figure all in black, face obscured by the shadow of his hood, came billowing down the corridor after them, shaking a scolding finger. Wallace looked as if he'd seen a ghost.

"What do you mean?" Lucy whined. "Why not?"

"Very dangerous," he insisted. "Could bring death."

"Death?!" cried Lucy, shrinking into Jasper, looking around as if death might be lurking.

"Death," the hooded figure said. "And very bad teeth."

Lucy's hand shot to her mouth to check that her teeth were still there. Wallace, too, put his hand to his mouth, but as he did, he cocked his head to one side and considered the figure. Jasper's eyebrows went up, Wallace squinted through his glasses, and Faye folded her arms and looked dangerous.

"Oh, goodness!" cried Lucy. "Noah's gone missing!" And she burst into tears. "It's all my fault for knocking!" She buried her face in Jasper's side, mumbling, "Oh why did I want the party? Why, oh, why? ... Now he's gone! Like Mummy and Daddy!"

"Lovely." Faye tapped her foot in fury. "Just lovely. Well, if death hasn't carried Noah away, then I plan to throw him to the sharks! How utterly ghastly you are! Honestly."

Lucy sniffled and looked at Faye, confused. As Jasper patted his sister's back, he shook his head at the hooded figure. "Please try to have a bit of sense some of the time, *Death*," Jasper said.

Lucy's eyes darted between her brother and the hooded figure, who now seemed less terrifying and somehow diminished—even shrinking.

"What were you thinking, you idiot?" Faye demanded.

"Think I not," said the figure. "I trick, no treat."

"Oh, shut up!" Faye turned and knocked on the next door.

Lucy's eyes suddenly grew enormous. "Noah?"

Noah pulled the hood from his head. "Sorry, Luce," he said. "I thought it'd be funny."

"Well." Lucy wiped her nose on her lovely costume sleeve. "Maybe it is, a bit."

Noah hugged Lucy, but he felt wretched. "I'm going to put this back before someone misses it." He ran back down the corridor.

"Don't hurry back!" called Faye.

"He didn't mean to be horrid," Jasper said. Noah had looked mortified that Lucy was actually crying.

Noah ran back down the corridor. He knew the door was one of the middle ones by the stairwell. He grabbed the handle of the first door, but it was the wrong one, so he tried another. That handle turned, and he opened the door.

Luckily, he caught himself before he made a squeak.

He had entered a room full of hooded, robed mysterious men in black. Slowly, Noah slipped into the room to observe.

The men were not very interesting, however. They all seemed to be in silent contemplation. After a few minutes, or more likely one minute that seemed like more, Noah stifled a yawn. Was this some kind of ritual? Well, thought Noah, maybe he'd catch them again on a more interesting day. Odd, though, to know that under those robes must be the mysterious, oddly dressed men in black they were used to. Here, they were all dressed alike.

Noah slipped back out and found the next door to be the closet for the robes. He put his away. Then he caught up with the other children, who were not finding anyone at home behind any of the doors.

Finally, they knocked at a door in a lower deck corridor. They could hear someone coming.

The door opened.

"Treats, please," Lucy said, opening her empty beaded bag. She had taken the handkerchief and the gear out to make more room for sweets.

"What." It was a man in a tall black top hat and goggles. He had a watch chain and vest over a poofy black shirt.

"Treats. Please," said Lucy. "It's Halloween."

The man did not respond, as if he had not heard what Lucy said.

"Halloween. All Hallow's Eve. Hallowtide," said Noah. "Don't tell us you haven't heard of the most important holiday to be acknowledged by all of the good Earth's inhabitants, especially those of us at sea."

The man just stared at the children.

"Treats," Lucy said again, giving the sweetest little girl look she could muster.

"Treats," repeated the man.

"Yes, please," said Lucy, excitedly.

"What it?" the man asked.

"Treats," said Lucy.

"Oh, forget it," groaned Faye. "He hasn't a clue what—"

"Keep your hair on," Noah said.

Lucy rubbed her tummy. "We'd love something delicious."

"Go to kitchen," the man said.

"No, it must come from you," Lucy said. "Really, it must. Otherwise, it isn't the holiday treat adventure at all, and we'd just be children off getting something yummy from the kitchen and not getting to show our costumes to the people who supposedly have the delicious treats to give us, since we're asking for them on Halloween."

Faye swallowed hard and nodded with the rest of the children. Something was seriously wrong, as she'd actually understood what Lucy said.

The man looked Lucy up and down, then closed the door.

"Honestly." Faye turned, but Lucy knocked and the man opened the door again. He had a tray of dry crackers. Lucy took five and placed them in her bag. "I suppose those might be treats," she said, nodding at the man. "Thank you, sir. Thank you for the Halloween treats."

"Right. Treats." Noah coughed through crumb-filled lips as he fished a cracker from Lucy's bag. "Only if you're starving all alone on an island, or a monk after a hunger strike."

***

Somewhat discouraged, the children made a beeline to Miss Brett's room. Faye knocked. They could hear a strange noise from behind the door. Lucy looked up at Jasper, but he smiled down at her.

"What can this intrusion be?" came a cackling voice from within. The door opened, and a bent figure covered by a large red blanket answered. At first, Jasper felt Lucy's hand slink into his and tighten its grip on his fingers. "Who be knockin' at me door?"

"It's only children," said Lucy, squeezing behind Jasper.

"I love children," said the bent figure.

"Not to eat!" cried Lucy, squeezing harder to Jasper's ill-fitting britches.

The bent figure again cackled, and it reached out a hand that touched Lucy's arm. Lucy screamed, then suddenly laughed. She looked at the lovely, delicate hand that touched her.

Lucy's grip loosened on her brother. "May we have a delicious treat, you lovely, grumpy old witch?" she said with glee.

It was the lovely hand of Miss Brett that had reached out from under the blanket. Now, in the other hand, she held a bowl of meringues. Squealing with pleasure, Lucy took the meringues, one by one, and stuffed them into her handbag.

"Best be taking these, too," said Miss Brett, handing Noah a basket she had filled with wrapped honeyed biscuits. "You'll all be needin' your strength. Now off with you!" said Miss Brett as she closed the door.

"She's the loveliest old hag I have ever met," insisted Lucy, as she reached into Noah's basket and unwrapped a biscuit that simply oozed with honey. Her mouth now full of biscuit, she added, "I wonder what other treats will be given to us by darling ugly monsters."

Unfortunately for the children, this was the highlight of their culinary adventure through the corridors of the ship. No doors hid biscuits, and no other ghouls promised buns. They nibbled as they walked, but this served only to make them aware of how few treats they had managed to get. While Lucy seemed ever able to engage in the hunt, the others were getting tired and losing interest after running up and down the corridors from deck to deck.

It was this, and the memory of apple pie with caramel, that finally drew the children back to the kitchen.

⋙●⋘

"Where do they keep it?" said Lucy, peering over the counter at the row of jars and bottles, watching the sweet sugar syrup loll gently back and forth against its glass shores.

"Probably in the pantry," said Wallace with confidence, though he hadn't a clue which latched door led to the pantry.

"Look, I've found their store of chocolate," Faye boasted, pulling a handful of lovely chocolate chunks from a large tin next to a bread box. "We'd best not eat them all, since we're at sea, and we don't want the kitchen to run out," she muttered despite a chocolate-filled mouth. The others joined her until they had devoured all that Faye doled out to them—all except Noah, who quietly grabbed another hefty handful.

Lucy ran her fingers along the side of the massive wooden table that made up the center of the kitchen. She opened several pots and looked in at their emptiness. The last pot, however, simply could not be opened.

"What do you mean it can't be opened?" said Faye. She tried herself to pull off the lid. When it did not budge, she declared, "It must be rusted shut."

"I don't see any rust," Noah said, tugging at the lid.

"Look," said Lucy, pointing at the rim of the pot. "There's a little folding thing, and it's grabbing the edge."

"Who ever heard of a locking pot?" said Jasper in disbelief.

Faye had already gone to the knife drawer and grabbed a small knife with a wicked edge. She tried to pry off the lid, but did not have any success. Noah tried, again, to pull it off.

"Get me a hammer," said Faye. Jasper noted a slightly mad twinkle in her eye.

"What? Are you crazy?" Noah looked at Faye. "And create a gong out of the pot lid? That's not very clever if we're up to no good and don't want to be discovered."

"Something important must be in the pot," Faye said, trying

again with the knife. "Maybe it's a clue to everything—or, at least, something valuable and secret. Something that had to be hidden away."

"In a pot?" said Noah.

Faye looked around in vain. There was nothing else to use for prying.

"I say we throw it down and break it," said Faye.

"And break the wooden floor boards?" The iron pot was stronger than any wooden floor.

Then Wallace stepped closer. He ran his small fingers over the edge of the rim and around the handle on top. He took hold of the handle and turned. With a click, the seal was broken, and he was able to pull off the lid.

Everyone at once peered into the pot. This created some commotion, and several bumps on the head. The pot, as it turned out, held something completely unexpected—a small leather pouch, wrapped in a torn and crumpled page from a newspaper.

Lucy reached in and uncrinkled the paper in hopes of discovering a treasure, edible or otherwise. The pouch, unfortunately, contained neither treasure nor delights. It held a tiny piece of paper—the corner of a map. Perhaps it had been torn when removed from the pouch. But where the map had come from or what it meant, the children had no idea.

"Well, that's disappointing," said Noah.

While the others lamented the situation, Lucy attempted to straighten out the crinkles in the newspaper. She scanned the page and Faye leaned over to join her.

"Nothing of great interest," said Faye, turning over the page, then moving on with the boys to look elsewhere.

Suddenly, Lucy gasped. With a tiny cry, she threw the page back into the pot.

"What was that?" Faye whispered loudly.

"It was awful," said Lucy, lifting the lid with some difficulty and slamming it back on the pot.

"What fun. Sounds Halloweenish," Noah said with a grin, but his grin slipped when he saw the real fear on Lucy's face.

Once Faye removed the lid again, the rest of the children struggled to see the newspaper. Faye took more thought now in reading the articles, but again, she didn't see anything really terrible. Neither did anyone else. At first glance, Jasper figured it was the awful photograph of a pinched-faced lady that had scared Lucy.

"Yes, that is a rather gruesome visage," Faye noted as Jasper pointed out the photograph.

"Horror!" Noah gasped, putting his arm before his eyes in mock terror.

"But what is that leather pouch doing here?" Faye asked. She looked at the article, which was from *The New York Times* and mentioned some awful woman and something in a tunnel. "And why was it wrapped in newspaper?"

"What does it have to do with anything?" Noah asked. "It's another bit of nonsense from those fellows."

"I want to go to bed," Lucy declared. She was chewing her nails and hiding behind her brother.

"We won't let the nasty lady get you, Luce," said Noah.

"You've weakened her defenses with that hooded stunt of yours," said Faye.

But Lucy shook her head.

"It's a photograph, and it can't come to life," Wallace said, putting his hand gently on Lucy's shoulder.

"Nothing comes to life, does it?" mumbled Lucy through her nails. Jasper took that hand and pulled it from her mouth.

As the others resumed their search, Faye straightened the page again, rewrapped it around the pouch, and closed the lid. With some effort, she turned the handle to lock the lid.

"I found the pie!" called Wallace from inside the pantry. Noah dashed ahead and carried out the remains of the prize. Soon, the pie took precedence over the crinkled newspaper and the clamber of the pot lid. Instead of nibbling her fingers, Lucy, whose formidable memory was able to shift to more pressing concerns than an old newspaper, joined with the others as they happily consumed the sweet tartness of the delicious dessert.

When they had finished every last crumb, they looked at one another, realizing clues of their deed were written all over their faces in bits of crust and caramel and juice-covered chins from the apples. Noah placed the dish in the sink, and Wallace wiped the table after Lucy and Jasper swept the crumbs from it. As the others tiptoed back to their rooms, Faye took one last look. Yes, the room looked exactly as they had left it—minus, of course, the apple pie. She left the kitchen and the odd pot, its useless contents forgotten by all except Lucy.

CHAPTER TWELVE

A Sign on the Horizon

OR

ALL HANDS GOING DOWN

Tired and overfed from their kitchen foraging, the children showed none of the usual enthusiasm for breakfast the next day—not even Noah, though he did muster some energy once he saw the hot, buttery pancakes. Lucy's eyes brightened, too, at the sight of iced buns, but Wallace, Faye, and Jasper could barely manage toast. Faye, in truth, looked positively green.

"I take it you found some treats on your adventures last night?" Miss Brett asked as Noah refused his usual seventh helping of pancakes and whipped cream. Trying not to smile too much (which she decided would be entirely cruel), she poured each of them a cup of tea. She added sugar and, to Faye's cup, a few mint leaves from a very small glass bowl next to the sugar. She passed a cup to each child.

"Sip this," she said kindly, handing Faye her cup. "The tea and the mint will help your belly."

Faye followed Miss Brett's instructions and, slowly, the green seemed to fade from her face.

Lucy reached over and added mint leaves to her cup. She stirred and stirred, looking up from her cup as she breathed in the scent of the mint. "I don't understand how something so lovely going into your belly can feel so horrid after it's made itself at home."

Noah nodded seriously. "I ponder that myself at times like this," he said, letting out an unexpected belch. "It seems wholly unfair, to be sure. And pardon me, of course."

Faye did not look as though a pardon was likely.

It was clear there would be no intense classwork today. Miss Brett suggested they make it an early day and break from lessons before lunch. She would read to them for a while, and then they would get some rest. They were thankful.

"But this is not a holiday," she insisted as the bedraggled crew marched toward their rooms. "Tonight, children, we're going to check on the moon. There's a waxing gibbous, and I want you to estimate when the moon will be full. We have the telescope set. I'll come fetch you all at six o'clock."

⟶►◄⟵

The sky was aglow that night. Following a good rest and a warm cup of cocoa, they were all up on deck, looking through the telescope. It was truly an amazing thing, to be able to see the stars and the planets and the moon. They could see shapes on the moon, as if there were mountains and valleys, just like on Earth. The sky was utterly cloudless, and seemed simply enormous.

"I wonder who lives there," Lucy said as she peered at the moon through the telescope.

"No one, I suspect," said Wallace.

"But you don't know that," said Lucy. "They could be ever so tiny or live underground, or even be the color of the moon itself. Maybe they can fly, or perhaps swim. I wonder."

"So, Miss Brett—you taking wagers?" asked Noah with a quick grin no one could see.

"Wagers on what?" said Faye.

"On who gets the closest in their estimations," said Noah. He had often stared up at the moon through the bedroom windows of the many homes in which he had lived. He had looked out and stared at the moon as he waited for his mother to return from some fabulous event. He knew that this moon was almost full.

Noah reached out a hand to shake, as if to challenge Faye.

"Noah thinks he knows something," Faye said, slapping his hand away. "As if we can't all tell the moon is nearly full."

"Look at the bright star!" shouted Lucy, pointing across the deck and over to the left.

Miss Brett looked up into the sky. "That's Polaris," she said, pointing up.

"Not up, but *over*," said Lucy, her finger wagging across, not toward, the sky.

Following the direction in which she pointed, everyone looked. There was indeed a very bright light, hanging low above the water. It was so low, in fact, that it seemed to be sitting on the horizon.

Miss Brett pulled the telescope around to face the direction of Lucy's star. But what she saw looked impossible. The star seemed to be growing.

"Jasper," Miss Brett said, trying to remain calm, "please call for one of the men in black."

———⇒●⇐———

By the time Jasper returned with the man in the captain's uniform, Lucy's floating star had grown in size, which meant, of course, that it had come all the closer.

"Down," the man said.

"Down?" Miss Brett said. "Should we go down?"

"Must be up to go down," the man said.

"Up?" Noah looked up. "Up where?"

"Up, must be down," the man said, with more emphasis in his voice.

"I ..." Miss Brett felt completely at a loss. "I'm not sure I understand. You want us to go up? Or down? Or—"

"It is up but down for up and down," the man said, beginning to prod them all toward the door to the stairwell. Since the stairs went up to the crow's nest, Miss Brett turned around to ask if they were to go up.

But at that moment, the man pulled a huge lever hidden behind a panel near the door. It had great, massive gears, and created a grinding noise that made the floor vibrate beneath their feet. Suddenly, from either side of the ship, two great, curved glass walls began to rise. They formed a shell clearly designed to encompass the entire ship. The glass must have been a foot thick, tapering to a thin metallic line at the edge.

Jasper realized at once what those magnetic edges along the side of the deck were for. "They're going to seal it with a magnet," he said.

"But how will glass protect us from a bomb, or whatever is coming at us?" Faye demanded.

"Probably not very well," Noah said. Touching the glass, he said, "Though it feels strong, and it certainly is thick."

"But it might crack just from the reverberations from an explosion," Wallace said anxiously. "It can't be to protect us against an explosion. It must be for something else."

After the shell sealed itself, the man pulled another lever, and a second shell, this time coming in a curve from one side, sealed it- self around the outside of the first shell. Miss Brett and the children heard what sounded like shutting latches throughout the stairwell.

And then, something happened that made Wallace nod in com- prehension. When it happened, they all finally understood what the man had been saying. The shells went up so that the ship could go down.

With a great lurch and groan, the ship began to sink.

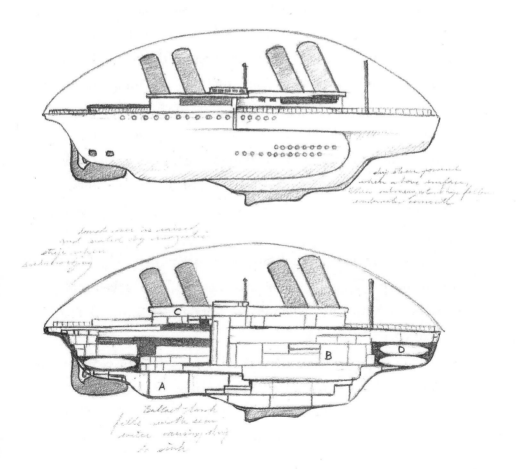

Faye could feel the tightness growing in her chest as the steel shell covered the thick glass window. It was not merely closing, but closing in around her. She felt a bit dizzy and slipped, reaching out and grabbing Jasper's arm. Jasper fell onto Faye, but caught himself on Noah's shirttail. Noah's shirt tore as he reached to grab Wallace, who was falling onto Lucy, who had grabbed Miss Brett around the waist and buried her face in her teacher's apron. There was a great muddle of arms and legs and cries, and one very large belch from Noah.

Luckily, no one fell down the stairs. And, except for Noah's shirt, nothing was damaged and no one was injured. In fact, Lucy, muffled as she was by Miss Brett's apron, was giggling.

"My tummy feels funny and I feel like I'm floating." Lucy was right. The descent gave them the impression that gravity was easing. This did not keep them from tumbling, and, in truth, created more chaos as feet misread the distance to the floor.

Tangled as they were, they all stared up and watched in shock as the water began to rise along the sides of the clear glass shell.

Within minutes, they were totally submerged. From their new position below the surface, they could clearly see fish as they came up to the glass.

"I can't breathe—" Faye gasped. Jasper pulled away from her, realizing he still held her arm. "No, it's not…" She looked at Jasper, who was blushing up to his ears. "…Not that. I'm feeling…I feel… I'm stifled. I—"

"Give her space!" Miss Brett said. "Faye, what you're feeling is claustrophobia. Just try to breathe easy. Here, sit down."

Faye felt like she was going to vomit. Or perhaps faint. Or both. She was furious with herself. What a weakling. What a lily-liver. But her anger only made her feel worse.

"Jasper, would you please bring a cup of water from the pitcher on the table at the bottom of the stairs? Faye could use a sip of water," said Miss Brett. But she could see Faye's fury. "You know, this is something most people feel at some point in their lives," Miss Brett said. "We *are* underwater, so it is not something to be—"

"No one else is collapsing like some feckless damsel!" Faye cried, wiping the sweat from her forehead.

Jasper handed her the water. She sipped. Then Jasper took her clammy hand and spoke softly.

"I remember once, I went for a ride in a hot air balloon," he said. "We were visiting my mother's family in France. The breeze blew through my hair and across my face. It felt like the wide-open world was all around me." In truth, this was something Jasper hardly remembered. It had occurred while his mother was in confinement, her lying-in period, waiting for Lucy to be born. Someone had taken him, though he didn't remember who. But Jasper did remember the feeling of being out in the biggest open world.

Faye closed her eyes. She imagined the breeze and the open space. And her breathing began to deepen and slow.

Wallace jerked. Out of the darkness came the sudden flash of a large blue fish swimming across the glass. "The light from the room is shining into the sea. The creatures therefore appear larger than they really are," he said, taking off his glasses and wiping them before returning them to his nose. "The glass and the water make them seem so." It was night, so there was almost no light outside—only what came from inside.

"Ralph would go crazy," Noah said, thinking of his dearest companion. "Silly dog. He'd probably give himself a heart attack trying to catch the fish."

Faye's breathing was nearly normal now. She opened her eyes and looked gratefully at Jasper. Suddenly feeling awkward, her hand still in his, he looked up, away from her. He was going to let go of her hand, but Faye squeezed his fingers before he released his grasp. That was enough for Jasper.

"It—it really is remarkable," Faye said, once she felt strong enough to speak and steady enough to look up from Jasper's face. It *was* beautiful out there. She watched, looking into the vast, dark, watery space.

Standing, her hand still on Faye's shoulder, Miss Brett allowed herself to marvel at the incredible ship. They were still sailing, but now below the surface of the water. She could feel the ship continuing slowly to descend, until finally it felt as though they evened out, perhaps only a few meters below the surface of the water. Surely the ship was now invisible from above.

Silently, they moved through the water like some great creature. The lights in the ship dimmed to near total darkness, so the glow from within the ship no longer illuminated the sea outside. But after a few moments, their eyes were able to capture some of the light from the moon above, and they could see shadows moving gracefully through the water.

The man in the jester suit appeared through the door. Miss Brett realized that she and the children were still standing, huddled, at the top of the stairs.

"Why did we have to go down?" asked Lucy. "Are we having fun or are we scared?"

The man did not answer.

"Is there danger?" said Noah. "Is there a reason we're down here, other than watching fish?" Noah waited, but there was still no answer.

"Should we go to our rooms?" Miss Brett asked. Looking around, she realized, too, that any light might make them visible. "Should we put out the lights up here?"

"Perhaps and no," he said. "The mirror reflects. No need total dark."

"You said..." And then Miss Brett decided she actually understood. "Ah, you meant perhaps, as in perhaps we should go to our rooms?"

But the man just looked at her, then turned and slid down the railing onto the deck below and out of sight.

"I don't want to go to my room," said Noah. "I want to see whatever crazy things happen now that we're a giant squid."

"We are not a giant squid," said Lucy. "Are we?" She looked up at Miss Brett, who could not help but smile.

"Leviathan, then," said Noah. "We are a giant underwater sea creature. Let's face it." He made a fish face, and Lucy laughed.

"Amazing, to think we're breathing in a ship underwater." Miss Brett stared up, wide-eyed at the scene just beyond the glass.

"Actually," Wallace said, also staring out at the deep blue sea all around, "submarines, of sorts, have been around since the fifteen hundreds, but it wasn't until almost the seventeen hundreds that the idea of controlling air pressure was introduced. The fluctuation of air pressure presents a problem, as pressure builds quickly after a rapid descent, so... but..." Wallace adjusted his glasses and his story, as his teacher clearly did not follow everything he was saying. "Real submarines, as we know them in modern times, have all been intended for war, and some have been successful."

"Are we at war?" Lucy asked, her fingers moving stealthily toward her mouth.

"No, I mean … this is something completely … well, it is differ-ent, however …" And Wallace had nothing else to say.

"Are we?" asked Lucy, looking from face to face.

"We're not at war, Lucy," said Jasper. "Just … just making sure we're not under attack."

"To guard us, sweet angel, just in case," Miss Brett added. "That's all. Nothing to worry about."

Without warning, they once again crumpled into a heap as the ship came to a sudden stop.

Then, just as suddenly, the engines went silent. Miss Brett pulled the children close to her, arms around them all. She knew that the glass was reflecting and that her arms could not do any-thing to protect them if there was danger, but she wanted them near. It was all she could do.

Then they heard it. Only because of the silence could they hear the hum of another vessel. They could feel the wake as another ship passed along the surface—a huge ship that sailed directly above them, lights blazing on all sides. They could even see the hull as it passed overhead, like a giant whale. They could feel the rhythmic churning of the water around the propeller below the ship. The si-lence was so eerie, and the boat so big. The silence, Miss Brett knew, kept them from being spotted. Was that Komar Romak above the water line? Had he found them?

She looked at the children and put her finger to her lips. Lucy smiled and giggled silently. She, too, put her finger to her lips.

It seemed like forever as the ship passed slowly above them. They could see the hull and, around it, a giant shadow as the ship belched black smoke that filled the sky above it. How could they hide like this in plain sight? How could the ship not see them sit-ting right below? The children and Miss Brett could even feel the rippling water rocking their submarine vessel as the ship finished passing overhead. Then, after several silent minutes, their own en-gines began to rumble anew. The boat began to move again. But now they sailed underwater.

Miss Brett let out a big sigh. Her whole body relaxed and she gave the children a shaky smile. Lucy seemed thrilled.

"We were hiding," said Lucy, knowingly. "And nobody found us."

CHAPTER THIRTEEN

CREATURE COMFORTS OF THE GREAT BLUE SEA

OR

THE SALUTE OF THE MYSTERIOUS MEN IN BLACK

If, in the morning, any of the children had interest in sitting up on the deck and taking in the air, they would have to find something else to do.

In truth, there was a bit of sun, but only the rays that cut through the water. The daylight brightened the ocean around them, and what they could see was truly amazing, until the distance faded into blue. The sea life that scooted, floated, and swayed around them made them feel as if they were in a strange land, a distant planet, or a magical world. But was it a world far enough away to elude the danger?

Creatures of all shapes and sizes and colors came swimming past, like huge tuna and several giants that looked like lumpy rocks gliding gracefully in the water.

"What are those?" asked Lucy, staring at the strange creatures.

"I know! Those are ocean sunfish," Noah said. "I saw one caught off the coast of Brazil."

"What did it say?" asked Lucy.

"It didn't say much," Noah said. "It was dead." Lucy's lip began to quiver. "But not *that* dead," said Noah quickly.

"Look, Lucy!" Jasper pointed and turned Lucy back to the window as an enormous school of tiny herring swam by, bathing the entire dome in a sparkle of silver fish. Some smaller, colorful fish swam alongside the ship, coming close as if to investigate this enormous glass-encased creature. More schools of tiny herring moved as one, and larger mackerel made shadows against the glass. Breaking up the silvery mass, a swordfish jetted by, headed for the surface. The children watched, eyes wide, as if they were observing an incredible underwater ballet.

"It is truly lovely, isn't it?" Miss Brett found that she, too, could not keep her eyes off the great glass ceiling.

She smiled, expecting the return of smiling, awed faces. But Jasper's face was shadowed not with awe, but with worry. This was not uncommon, and Miss Brett was quick to understand it. Why had they suddenly disappeared under the sea and, if they were hiding from danger, had they truly managed to escape it?

Quietly, she stood, leaving them to observe the underwater world. She had two errands to run. The first was to stop the man in the black frilly apron passing through the corridor at the bottom of the stairs.

"Excuse me!" Miss Brett called.

He stopped.

"Are we out of danger?" she asked. "That is, were we in danger? I mean to say that we were obviously in danger, but—"

"No but yes," said the man, who then turned to go.

Miss Brett caught his arm. "Excuse me, but that doesn't put me at ease," she said. "Are we ... will we be safe? Are we going to be safe?"

The man just stared back at her through his dark glasses.

But Miss Brett began to understand that the question she had asked was absurd. Safe? They were hiding in a giant ship beneath the sea from some unknown terror. Safe? "Are we out of immediate danger?" she asked, realizing that this was the best she could hope for.

The man seemed to consider her question. "Perhaps so," he said.

Miss Brett tried to search his near-hidden face for some other crumb of wisdom, some greater answer she knew was not there. She let go of his arm and straightened her skirt. She could feel a familiar lump in her throat. She swallowed hard to get it down.

"Can we have our breakfast up in the glass room?" she asked, smiling at his unsmiling face.

"Glass room?"

"Yes, the room up those stairs, where we can see the sea."

"Food," he said.

"Yes," Miss Brett said. "Breakfast. Can we have it served upstairs instead of in the dining room?"

"Crumpet," said the man.

"Pardon me?"

"Crumpet," he repeated.

"You mean for breakfast?"

"Potato," the man said.

"Hot chocolate?" Miss Brett said.

"Banana," the man said.

"And perhaps some orange juice." Miss Brett, her eyebrows rising of their own accord.

"Jelly," he added.

"And toast would be lovely."

Well, that went well, Miss Brett thought as the man left.

She then went on her second errand. When she found the closet of books, the door was unlocked. She opened it a crack, but then found she would need to keep it wide open to bring enough light into the room, because she had no lantern, lamp, or torch.

As she squinted in the darkness, she realized that she could only peruse the books on the shelves closest to the door. Even so, there were many she could see. There were thick books and thin books, tall books and squat books. There were books in English and French and Arabic, and books that were in a very strange language, neither Spanish nor French nor Arabic, that Miss Brett did not recognize. The books in that language, for the most part, seemed the oldest.

Curious, she pulled one off the shelf. Then another. She began to look at them, one after another, hoping to find a clue to the language. They had titles like *Istorja bikrija tal-Kavallieri mill-għira ta 'Rodi lejn Malta għall-grazzja Suleiman.*

"Istorja."

This could have been a woman's name. In fact, it was very close to her own name, Astraea, but with a very different spelling. She wondered if it could be the story of a woman.

There was a book titled *Tales tal-patrijiet sigriet ta 'l-isptar*, and one that seemed to be more of a journal that was called *Il-kavallieri fl-iswed.* There was one in handwriting so tiny she could hardly make out the words. It was called *Noti dwar il-battalja ta 'Transilvan-ja meħuda mill-ambaxxatur Ruman Qaddis, 1521*—and, if "1521" was a year, it was a very old document indeed. "*Ruman*," perhaps, meant "Roman," she thought, but the language was not Latin. There was another book called *Noi, i fratelli in nero*, and another, *Il-fratellanza ta 'niket.* It had a badly tattered cover, but one she thought once held an image in red and white.

Miss Brett looked at these old books (most of which seemed to be historical documents or journals from battles) and found, tucked between two larger ones, a beautifully illustrated book called *Il-poeżiji ta 'Muhabi*. "*Poeżiji*," she said aloud, feeling the word on her tongue. "Sounds like poetry. Perhaps it's a book of poems."

As she began to examine it, she felt that she was peering into something very ancient and treasured. This book was incredible. Each illustration was hand-painted—she could see the lines and feel the texture of the brush strokes. Though she had no idea what language it was written in or what meaning could be given to the poems—and they were indeed poems—the drawings were so delicate, so elegant, so beautiful, that she felt someone with great heart and understanding must have drawn them. The artist clearly loved birds, for they were depicted with large, wise eyes and strangely beautiful colors. There were other creatures, too, also painted lovingly.

And there were some illustrations of designs she could not discern. These were more geometric, almost as if they were technical drawings. She wondered if the artist and the poet were the same person.

As she came to the latter pages, she found that some were missing. This upset her—that anyone would harm such a thing of beauty as this book. Closing the book, she decided she would never know what had happened. How could she? She hesitated before placing the book back, carefully, on the shelf. She would return and borrow it later. The illustrations were something she wanted to show the children.

She now turned to the shelves with books in familiar languages.

There were books in English with translations. Some of the adventures of Sherlock Holmes were translated into French—next to copies of *The Strand Magazine* was a bound copy of *Le Chien des Baskerville* and *Le Rituel des Musgrave*. Sitting next to the Verne original, *Vingt mille lieues sous les mers*, was the translation she was looking for—*Twenty Thousand Leagues under the Sea*.

This was the perfect book, and she remembered seeing it on the shelf when she had previously selected another book by Jules Verne, *Le Tour du Monde en Quatre-Vingts Jours*, though she had only found the English translation, *Around the World in Eighty Days*. Her French was not as good as it had been when she was in school, so she preferred to read the English anyway. Miss Brett was sure that the children would love any book by Jules Verne, but *Twenty Thousand Leagues under the Sea* seemed a perfect choice, considering how they were traveling. (Of course, *Around the World in Eighty Days* was a fine choice as well. But they had already become so absorbed in the story that they had read it cover to cover, with Lucy begging for bits to be read again.)

Miss Brett took *Twenty Thousand Leagues under the Sea* from the shelf. Yes, this was exactly the right selection.

During the two days they had spent so far under the water, eerie light created strange daytimes, and the nights were filled with shimmering shapes passing before the portholes. On the third day, they felt the pressure in their ears and the shift beneath their feet. First it was the great rush of water, and then the sensation that gravity had just increased tremendously. Between the descent and the ascent, the difference was remarkable.

They had just finished breakfast, and were heading with Miss Brett to the "window deck," as Lucy had begun to call it, where, on arriving, they all buckled to their knees or, like Lucy, fell over flat onto the floor. Since they were on the window deck, they could see the rush of sea as the ship ascended, moving upwards at a fairly fast clip. Their rise brought all sorts of creatures sliding past the glass.

"A mermaid!" said Lucy, now lying on her back, pointing at a clump of seaweed.

Faye was going to disabuse Lucy of the notion that there was a mermaid anywhere in the ocean, but the look from Miss Brett urged her to refrain from anything that might stop Lucy from believing in fairies, elves, and mermaids. (Miss Brett often sent these looks in Faye's direction.)

With an ear-popping whoosh, the ship hit the surface, and bright sunlight poured down upon them. Shielding their eyes, the children got to their feet. Miss Brett helped Lucy, who clapped her hands together in excitement.

Then, with a loud groan, clank, and whir, the heavy glass shell began to open, slowly receding into the sides of the ship.

"It's so loud!" said Lucy. The noise was in direct contrast to the last day of utter silence, during which the ship's engines seemed to have ceased working, even as the vessel continued to move through the water as if pushed by an invisible hand.

Fresh salt air stung their faces. It was colder than it had been the last time they felt the air outside.

"Where are we?" Faye asked. She could see land ahead. There were two lumps of land on either side of what looked like an opening to a harbor.

"I know where we are," Noah said, excitedly, "and why it's been so quiet since yesterday. We're at the Strait of Gibraltar, and we've been riding the waves!"

"Riding the waves?" Faye was incredulous. "We've been below the sea, you twit."

"Riding the waves below the sea—the underwater current," Noah said, unphased. "The Strait has powerful currents beneath the water, flowing into the Mediterranean. We haven't needed our engines. This is awfully exciting."

But their conversation was cut short by something that, at first, sounded like the beating of sails against a mast, but the rhythm was almost musical and clearly deliberate.

"Is it down or up?" Lucy asked. Then, without warning, she hurried down the stairs.

"I'll get her," Jasper said as he raced after his sister. "Lucy, where are you going?!" he called as Lucy ran down the hall. "Don't just run off like that when we don't know what's—"

But then he stopped, almost knocking Lucy down. She was standing in the doorway of the costume closet.

"Someone has stolen the big things!" she said, pointing to the empty shelf where the large cloths had been folded. She reached into the pocket of her apron. "But it wasn't me."

"I'm sure no one's stolen them," Jasper said, taking her hand. Lucy's oddly guilty expression distracted him for a moment, but then the sound again brought him back. He listened, and now could only faintly hear the drumming. "Come on, let's go up on deck and see what the sound is, shall we?"

Brother and sister walked together back toward the stairs. As they came closer, they heard music. It was some string instrument, as well as a drum.

On deck, they found Miss Brett and the others staring toward the bow—the very front of the ship. When Jasper and Lucy reached the top of the stairs, they, too, stared at what they saw.

Standing in four rows, with seven in each row, stood the mysterious men in black. Each had, at his side, a strange and ancient sword. All stood staring out at the sea, as if entering the Strait of Gibraltar held some grand significance. Among them stood two drummers, one the man in the captain's dress. The man with the frilly apron was playing something that looked like a mandolin.

Then the drumming and the mandolin stopped, and they all began to sing. They sang in the most beautiful tone, like angels. It was a very ancient-sounding song, almost a hymn or a chant. The sound echoed as they passed through the Strait of Gibraltar, and the mysterious men in black seemed to sing back to the echo. The sun was bright in the sky, and the children did not look up, their eyes still sensitive to the light. A shadow seemed to wave over the men as they sang:

> *Ferħ huwa għal dawk li jaħdmu għal paċi!*
> *Ferħ huwa għal dawk li huma puri fil-qalb.*
> *Ferħ huwa għal dawk li huma veri li Suleiman.*
> *Xogħol għal dawk li huma għandhom jipproteġu d-dinja minn*
> *el Magnau el Magna mid-dinja.*
> *U dan se jġib paċi.*
> *Il-poeta ser ikollok paċi.*

"What does 'paċi' mean?" Lucy asked Miss Brett. "They say that an awful lot."

Miss Brett smiled an "I don't know" and turned back to listen to the song.

"I *will* know," said Lucy with a significant nod.

"Look!" Wallace whispered loudly, pointing up.

And for the first time, they all looked up and saw that the waving shadow came from a giant flag—in fact, two giant flags, raised high on the ship.

"The special cloths," Lucy whispered.

"They're flags," Noah said, just a bit louder.

And it was true. One was white with four black shapes, like swords or arrows, angled toward the center. The other flag was half red and half white. These flags, unfolded, were enormous. Two men stood on either side of each flag, holding them up by long poles. It took two men to hold up one pole, and they struggled against the wind.

"What do they stand for?" asked Wallace. "The flags. Are they from a country?"

"I don't know," said Miss Brett, but the question got her thinking. Were the flags from the country of the mysterious men in black? Or were they symbols of some order, some fraternity, some brotherhood?

"Do they come from somewhere far away?" asked Lucy. "Are they special?"

Again, Miss Brett did not know. But it was mesmerizing, listening to the song, watching these men all together, part of some mysterious ritual, singing in some mysterious language.

The song ended. All the men pulled out their swords and said something, which also ended in the word "*paci,*" and then they sheathed their weapons. They all bowed their heads, except for the men holding the poles on which the flags continued to wave. In a rather impressive, almost dance-like movement, the men seemed to weave in and out of each other's flag, until both flags were not only off their poles, but folded perfectly.

"Well done," Jasper said breathlessly.

"That was amazing," Faye said.

CHAPTER FOURTEEN

A Cozy Ride to Somewhere

OR

THE ALLEGORY OF THE CAVE

The odd performance of the mysterious men in black gave the children and their teacher much to consider. Was this a secret ritual? Were they a secret society?

"They're not masons," said Noah to Wallace's suggestion. "Masons have secret handshakes and rings. They don't wear bonnets and bunny ears."

"How do you know?" asked Lucy.

"Well, they just do. One knows this," said Noah.

"Whatever they are, they're protecting us against Komar Romak, aren't they, Miss Brett?" said Wallace.

"Oh, I get all overish when we talk of Komar Romak," said Lucy with a shiver.

"Well then, let's think about other things, shall we?" said Miss Brett.

But the children could not stop thinking about those two big questions: Who were the mysterious men in black, and were they protecting the children against Komar Romak? Or, perhaps more importantly, *could* they protect the children against Komar Romak?

Over the next couple of days on the Mediterranean, things felt different. Perhaps because they were closer to land than they had been in ages, they felt they had emerged in a very different place than where they had embarked. The water was bluer and milder, and the air more fragrant.

"That's Sardinia!" Lucy shouted as they passed the island. Lucy had been looking at maps. "And we're headed into the Tyrrhenian Sea, toward Italy."

It was early in the morning, the sun tiptoeing up into the sky. The air was cool. Wind in their hair, the children watched as they sailed into Civitavecchia—the Port of Rome, as it is often called. The ancient city was impressive, with its fort and its powerful history. The children scrambled to the deck as the ship pulled into dock. Miss Brett came up to meet them, letting them know it was time to pack up their things. She had been told they would be disembarking, or believed that was what the jester meant when he said, "Off! Get!" and made hand motions before doing a flip in the air and running off.

Soon, as they descended the gang plank, they heard the sound of a distant train. But carriages were waiting for them, and they climbed aboard one, while their bags were loaded onto another. After a very short ride, they came to the train station. There, they were herded onto a train. Suddenly, they had to run after a sprinting man dressed in a black conductor's uniform, with a black scarf over his nose and mouth and dark triangular glasses over his eyes. Quickly, the man led them from the very back of the train to the front, and then out the other side.

The children began to groan. "What was that?!" Noah gasped, clutching at a stitch in his side.

"Why on earth did he make us run that race?" said Faye, wiping her brow on the corner of her skirt. She pulled back her lovely hair and re-braided the plat that had come loose.

Miss Brett tried to catch her breath, too. She raised her hand to get the attention of a man in a black cap resembling the green one worn by Robin Hood. But she had not gotten enough breath back to demand to know why they were running around like lunatics.

The man in the black Robin Hood cap urged them into a separate train car that sat next to the train tracks. The train itself then took off from the station, leaving their car behind. Next to their car were two carriages, sleeker and more compact than the ones they had used before, though just as black.

A door opened at the back of their car. A slender man in a tall chimney pot hat and a waxed cotton cloak stood, looking in. He did not guide them out but, instead, raised a black rose to his barely visible nose. Then, almost as if he were suddenly aware of the waiting children, he cleared his throat and motioned the children into the first of the two carriages.

"Wait a minute," said Noah, closest to the door. "I—"

And with a *thwap!* the man with the black rose bonked Noah on the head with his flower. Too surprised to say anything, Noah hurried along. Lucy slid out after Miss Brett. She looked up at the man with the black rose.

"Don't be sad," she said, touching his hand.

The man looked down and gently touched Lucy on the head with the rose, then turned and walked away. Robin Hood left them, too, and climbed into the second carriage. A man with an impossibly huge top hat sat in the driver's seat of the carriage the children and Miss Brett entered. Inside seemed much roomier than the outside suggested. The seats were covered in velvet, and very soft. There were pillows thrown around the over-large seats. This was going to be a comfortable ride, no matter where they were going.

"I suppose we're going to Italy," Noah said, smiling.

"Well, aren't you the clever boy?" Faye said. "And do you think we'll be going in carriages?"

"I don't think we'll be going by train, if that's what you're asking." Noah smiled, and Faye just shook her head.

Lucy gave a shiver. The sweat from running had now cooled on her neck. She shivered again. "Brrr. Who took away the warmth?" she said.

"Roll up the window!" Faye said. Wallace scrambled to close the window on the carriage door.

"Light the brazier," said Noah.

Faye turned and said, "Don't be—"

"He's not!" Lucy said. "But there *is* a brazier!"

And sure enough, there was a small brazier stove attached to the other door of the carriage. It was slim, and almost flush with the handle, but was made of bronze both beautiful and ornate. It had dragons welded on the two front corners and other symbols and patterns around the base. There was coal already inside.

"Well." Faye reddened. "Light it then."

"Keep your hair on," Noah said.

With daggers in her eyes, Faye growled, "If you ever tell me to keep my hair on again, I'll take your flaming locks and—"

"Gadzooks, Faye, I'm getting it." Noah raised his hand, then leaned over to see how he could light the stove.

But the door flew open, and a man wearing a black fur cap, aviator goggles, and a thick balaclava was holding a flaming torch.

They all jumped back, away from the rather menacing-looking fur-capped man with the burning stick, but he was simply there to light the brazier, which is what he did. He then closed the door, and the carriage began to move.

Within minutes, the lot of them were taking off cloaks and getting much more comfortable. They found a hamper of biscuits that melted in their mouths, crepes stuffed with cheese, and pastries filled with dried fruits and nuts.

"This is so lovely," Lucy said, her mouth filled with biscuits. "It's as if it was made with almond milk and sweetened with flower nectar."

"Well, aren't you the busy bee?" said Noah. He buzzed at her. Lucy giggled.

In the hamper were a jug of warm honeyed milk and six cups. Miss Brett made sure everyone got their fill of the milk and the treats.

Feeling well-stuffed, cozy, and warm, the children were quiet as the carriage began to head up toward the mountains. The day was settling into afternoon, and they all watched the landscape begin to rise around them.

"They're like sleeping giants," said Lucy.

And they all knew what she meant. The afternoon shadows made the mountains seem to sleep lazily around them. Jasper smiled and took Lucy's empty cup. Her eyes were beginning to droop, and Jasper knew his sister was not going to fight closing them for a nap. He, on the other hand, was not yet ready for sleep. He looked out at the mountains as the carriage ascended through them. Jasper saw a deer and then, within a few short minutes, a fox and a badger. He almost woke Lucy, but he let her sleep. Surely, there would be more of these creatures if they were headed out into this mountainous unknown.

———⟫●⟪———

It was not a gentle arrival that woke them. It was not a slowing of the carriage or the bubbling of the River Tirino's water that opened their eyes. It was, instead, the harsh rearing of the horses, the sudden stop, and the driver's shouts that made them jump up and cling to one another.

"Out, *out!*" shouted the driver in the impossibly huge top hat.

It was now dark, and the children were forced from the carriage along a rocky path and into a crack in the mountain, which led into a dark cave. Lucy fell on the way, and the man swept her up and practically threw her into the crevice. She was too stunned to cry. Everyone was nearly knocked over by the bags that were thrown in after them.

Peeking out, the children saw the driver with the impossibly huge top hat urge the horses forward without a carriage attached. He stuffed a scroll of some sort into the bridle of one horse, then hurriedly attached the reins to both sides of the driver's seat. He turned a lever and sent the carriage, horseless, driverless, and passengerless, off down the road. The Robin Hood man, who the children had last seen entering the second carriage, then joined them in the cave. In the near-total darkness, they could see him place his finger to his lips and beg for silence.

And it *was* silent, except for the sound of the carriage trundling down the path and the occasional howl of an Apennine wolf.

Then they heard it. Something metallic. Something groaning and cranking. It was a vehicle of some kind, coming down the same

road. The children didn't need the finger on the man's lips to tell
them they had to be as silent as they could ever imagine being. Not
a single breath seemed to come from a single mouth.

The clanking and groaning grew louder and louder, until a
dark shadow, darker even than the darkness that surrounded them,
passed before the crevice. And then the sound got softer. Noah let
out a breath, but Robin Hood put his hand over Noah's mouth.

A second later came a terrible crash, and then a powerful explosion. The sky lit up with flames. They could smell the burning
in the air as the wind blew the smoke through the valley.

"What happened?!" shouted Faye, as angry as she was fearful.

The driver in the impossibly huge top hat turned and, silently
furious, gestured for her to be quiet. Faye's voice echoed in the still-
ness.

"They will come," said the driver in a whisper.

"Is that a good thing?" Noah whispered back, removing the
man's hand from his mouth.

Robin Hood looked at the driver in the impossibly huge top hat.

"Stay quiet," Robin Hood warned. "No shout."

"Was that, you know, him?" asked Wallace, meekly.

"You mean Komar Romak?" asked Noah.

"Well, of course he means Komar Romak." Faye looked at Noah,
who just nodded. "Well?" Faye turned to the driver in the impossibly huge top hat.

"They to come and take," the driver said.

"Do we want them to come?" asked Noah. He looked at Robin
Hood expectantly, then at the driver in the impossibly huge top
hat. Whether it was the slight hint of moonlight or his imagination, Noah thought he saw a nod coming from the driver. At least he

hoped he saw a nod.

Robin Hood went over and drew something from his pocket. He bent down and, scraping two stones together, lit a small fire from some kindling already piled on the rocky ground.

"Is this your home?" Noah asked, looking around. "Lovely, really lovely."

Robin Hood looked at Noah for a long second, then stood up and walked out of the cave. The driver with the impossibly huge top hat followed him.

With the light from the fire, they saw they were in a fairly narrow cave, but one heading deep into the mountain. They all moved closer to the fire—the air was decidedly chilly. Looking around the cave, they could see it was empty, except for rocks and dirt and a large clump, perhaps a sack, in the corner. Robin Hood came back to check on the fire, then left again. The driver did not return. It quickly became clear that everyone would have to wait here, for a while at least.

Almost immediately, Lucy began to doze. Miss Brett had been concerned that she would be unable. It was a testament to the strange nature of their lives that Lucy, having been thrown from a carriage into a cave before witnessing an explosion likely caused by the very man tearing their lives apart, could fall asleep amidst the low grumble coming from Noah, Faye, and Jasper.

Miss Brett, herself exhausted, covered Wallace, who was also losing the battle with his eyelids. She pulled the little ones closer. She glanced over at Faye's angry face and Noah's shield of buffoonery, which made Faye even angrier. Should she say something?

Miss Brett placed beside her three candles she had in her bag, though she was running low on matches. She pulled her cloak around the three of them, leaned her head on Wallace's, and, upon consideration, let the others battle things out themselves.

"I never said we should go after him ourselves," Faye said angrily to Noah. "I said we should do something to help ourselves instead of sitting here like a row of pigeons at a fox convention."

"I'd prefer to think of myself as an eagle," said Noah, chin in the air.

"Funny, I think of you as an idiot," Faye grumbled. "And you have no idea what I'm saying."

"I do, Lady Faye," Noah said. "I know exactly what you're saying, and I think you're an idiot to think that we, five children, should seek out and fight Komar Romak."

"Faye, it's not that we want to sit here and do nothing," Jasper said in an attempt to calm her. "But we have learned that our battles must be well-placed, and well-planned, and this is not a time when a battle from us is likely to help."

"So what should we do?" Faye was exasperated. She felt that she alone understood that they were in danger. It was as if everyone else was willing to wait for the axe to fall. Komar Romak was out there. He held the axe.

Jasper took a deep breath. "If we think about it—"

"What, Jasper? What I am supposed to think about?"

"Flern," said Noah.

Faye turned on him and opened her mouth, prepared to shout words that no lady should ever use. But then she thought about what he had said. Noah was probably acting like the fool he was, but if "flern" meant "all that one has learned," she had to agree. What had they learned? Komar Romak was impossible to stop, and there was far more to him than they thought. He seemed to be everywhere and nowhere. There was something about him that made a whole army of crazy men in black afraid of him. And their parents. And everyone. What was it?

No one had any answers. They didn't even have the right questions. But Faye and the others would know. And perhaps, once they did, they could fight him. But for now, Jasper and, yes, even Noah... they were right.

Faye took a deep breath. "Very well," she said, then turned over, closed her eyes, and pretended to go to sleep.

CHAPTER FIFTEEN

A CREATURE BUT NO COMFORT

OR

FAYE SKIPS TO THE LOO

With a shiver, Miss Brett was the first of the lot to wake. Neither Robin Hood nor the driver in the impossibly huge top hat was in the cave, but tea was prepared, and warmed biscuits sat in a pan near the fire. She warmed her hands on a cup of strong, sweet tea and looked at the sleeping children who were, more or less, in a pile on the floor. They reminded her of puppies, all cuddled together.

In the light, the large pile in the corner was now an empty sack. Robin Hood or the driver in the impossibly huge top hat had obviously stored blankets and cloaks in it. One of them had covered the children in the night. Wallace and Lucy were nicely tucked in on either side of her, sleeping soundly in warm blankets. Miss Brett pulled her cloak more tightly around her, trying to ward off the cold morning air.

She took her cup and walked to the opening of the cave, where a beautiful sight took her breath away. The sky was as blue as she had ever seen it. High in the mountains here, it felt as if she were closer to the heavens. There was a sweetness that lingered in the air, like the freshest of grasses and trees and flowers, watered by the purest of waters. She breathed deeply and found it strange that she could find this moment of peace amid all that was happening around her.

The driver with the impossibly huge top hat came around the path. He had a basket of pears and apples and what appeared to be almonds. He handed them to Miss Brett, then climbed up on a rock and stood there, like a sentry.

"Thank you," Miss Brett said. The driver did not appear to have heard her. Miss Brett brought the basket back to the cave. The children were just rising, though Noah's head was still totally covered by his blanket. Jasper was not among the sleepers, but Miss Brett soon saw him.

"This is amazing," Jasper said, emerging from a narrow crevice in the rocks. "This cave must have been used by the Romans. There are carved torch bases and inscriptions on the walls back there." He pointed behind him, where there was a carving of a bird with its wings spread wide. "There are urns, as if the Romans stored supplies in here. We really should explore. It's not too dark with a torch." Jasper had broken a straight stick and lit the end in the fire.

"Well, certainly there would have been Romans," said Noah, his hair mussed and his mouth yawning. "We are in Italy, after all."

Miss Brett smiled and began to fold the blankets. She glanced over and noticed that now only two candles were lying out. It was as she pulled up the last blanket that fear grabbed her by the neck.

"Where is Faye?" she asked, her voice forced through her tightened throat.

"She's..." But Noah found nothing as he rummaged beneath the blanket. Faye was missing.

———≫●≪———

"Faye!" cried Miss Brett, followed by the others. They had lit the two remaining candles, opting against flaming torches from the wooden sticks strewn around the cave. The wood was slightly wet, and the torches smoked too much for a crowded cave. Miss Brett, though, had her electric birthday torch. She handed it to Jasper, who held it in front.

"We have to stay together," said Jasper. "These tunnels twist and turn."

At first, in the tunnel, there was some light coming from the outside, and then, a bit farther, light came from a crack in the rocks above. From there, it was dark, and they were all very happy they had the candles and the electric torch.

Lucy clung to her brother's shirttail. He had thought about having her stay in the front of the cave, but his own fear of leaving her had kept him from doing so.

"I hear something!" cried Wallace.

They could all hear it. It sounded like groaning or grunting.

"She might be hurt!" cried Lucy. Reaching out, Jasper failed to grab his sister's arm as she ran ahead. And then, like ice in his veins, he heard a scream.

It wasn't Faye who was groaning in the cave—it was a huge, snarling, grunting creature with hooves and fangs that looked as if they could run a man through. And Lucy was right in front of it, her face bleeding from the cheek where she had slid into the rocks trying to avoid the beast. Jasper put his arm out to keep the others from rushing into the cavern.

"Don't move, Lucy! Don't move!" he cried, his voice cracking. He saw the blood on his sister's face and wanted to tear the creature limb from ugly limb. The monster snorted, and Jasper could feel the others squeezing closer.

Lucy looked up at Jasper and nodded, tears streaming silently down her face. The monster seemed to be sniffing the air, as if realizing there was more meat nearby. Jasper looked around for something to distract the beast, but there was nothing but the rocks and the dirt.

And then came a rock from behind him, flying through the air from Wallace's hand. It hit the back wall, and the monster jumped, turning its gaze from Lucy to the sound. Without even a thought, Jasper dashed forward, grabbed Lucy, and brought her back to the others. Tearing off his shirt, he quickly lit it on fire using the candle Noah held. To the others, he shouted, "Run!" He threw his burning shirt at the beast and ran after the others. They could hear a loud squeal coming from the monster, and the pounding of its hooves against the rocks of what seemed to be its lair. They all ran back through the maze of tunnels, guided by Wallace's torch and following Lucy, who clearly remembered the way out.

And then, with a *wumpf*, Lucy ran smack into something else. This time, it was not a giant monster. This time, the groans came from Faye.

"Where were you?!" cried Jasper. "You almost got us killed."

"What?" said Faye. "I...well, I—"

"Just run!!!" Jasper grabbed her hand.

And they ran. They did not slow down, even as they spotted faint light ahead.

"Let's get back to the main cavern," gasped Jasper, his side bursting with a painful stitch. "There are enough rocks scattered around to fill this entrance. If we block it, we'll keep that thing on the other side." And as soon as they reached the cavern, he began grabbing rocks and piling them atop one another.

Faye saw the scrapes on Jasper's arms, the bruises already ripening on his side, and she could see his lips, which were almost blue. It was cold, and he had no shirt. She grabbed a blanket, but he refused. It was too cumbersome, and they were rushing to get the rocks in place.

She pulled off the muffler she had around her neck and wrapped it around Jasper's. She knew he'd never agree to take her wooly cardigan and, if he had, it would have been terribly scratchy against his skin. The muffler would keep him warm enough until he was done. She gave him her hat, too. Then she set to work.

———⋙◆⋘———

It wasn't until they had filled the narrow crevice with rocks that Jasper wanted to hear what Faye had to say.

"Well, at first I had to, well, use the ladies' room," she said demurely.

"What ladies' room?" asked Noah, confused, but he shut up when Jasper elbowed him in the ribs.

"Then I had the idea that I might be able to explore—perhaps find a way out, like a secret exit if Komar Romak showed his ugly face. But then, when I tried…" Faye blushed. "I couldn't find my way back to—that is, I didn't find another exit." In truth, Faye had not really looked for an exit. Though she was not about to admit it, she had simply gotten lost, then panicked when she found herself in a small dark cavern off one of the tunnels in the cave. "I heard you all calling and I thought you needed my help. Then I came running."

The driver in the impossibly huge top hat entered the cave carrying a tea tray. Everyone turned at once, and a barrage of questions and accusations came his way.

"You didn't tell us there was a monster in this cave!" Faye said, glad for the distraction.

"A?" He seemed quite confused.

"A monster!" Jasper said loudly. "A huge creature with fangs and tusks and hooves. It almost killed us. It almost killed Lucy! What madness to leave us in a cave with something like that nearby!"

"What is?" the driver in the impossibly huge top hat said.

"The creature," Miss Brett said. "What did we see? What is it we saw?"

"You are boar," the driver in the impossibly huge top hat said.

"I am a what?" Miss Brett sounded shocked.

"Wild boar," said the driver in the impossibly huge top hat, who then turned on his heels and left the cave.

Gaping mouths, followed by dawning realizations, created silence in the cave.

"A wild bore? I didn't find him boring," said Lucy. "He was horrid. But he wasn't boring."

"No, sweet angel," said Miss Brett, with some relief. She was slightly red-faced, having been fearful of hellish beasts now entering their lives. She was glad to know that the creature was of earthly origins. She thought back to books she'd read with drawings of wild boars chased by hunters. She thought about her childhood and perhaps seeing one stuffed in a museum. Yes, now that she was thinking clearly, it had clearly been a boar. "The wild boar is indeed a fierce creature, but it's in the pig family. They are native to this area, I suppose."

"Well, if they are, that is the biggest boar I've ever seen," said Noah. "I've seen stuffed boar heads on the walls of a Swiss mountain lodge in the Alps, and once in the hall of a German count. None of those heads was anywhere near the size of that one. It must have topped five hundred pounds."

"Oh, well, yes, what a relief! We have nothing to worry about, now that we know the boar is not a magical creature," said Faye sarcastically. "I say, let's hope we're only passing through. We don't need to add wild boars to our list of threats."

"Why, Faye," Noah said in feigned shock, "you don't fancy living among the wild boars? Don't you have some boars in your palace, milady?"

"You are a bore, Lady Noah," she said, falsely sweet, "and I have to live with you."

"Well," Miss Brett said. Though she was relieved to know that they were not being pursued by monsters, she knew they were not out of danger. She tried taking another deep breath. She wanted to feel relief that the creature was away from them and they would all be fine. But her children were not going to be fine if that evil man was still in pursuit. Her breath caught in her throat. How could she protect them?

She placed a smile firmly on her lips. But her hand shook as she passed out cups of tea and biscuits. She took some of the hot water and poured it on a clean tea towel. She spoke gently as she cleaned Lucy's wound. "I think we all could use some sweet tea and, perhaps, some air. I went outside this morning and the view is lovely."

"Did you learn anything, Miss Brett?" said Faye, stirring sugar in her cup of tea, her hand still unsteady from her own ordeal in the cave. Faye was not good at being helpless.

Noah, on the other hand, had already discovered the biscuits and was helping himself to them, two at a time. His appetite generally tripled when he was anxious.

"No," said Miss Brett. "Only that it is beautiful outside."

"As long as the boar doesn't have any big brothers looking for him," mumbled Noah.

"The boars are not our only worry," said Jasper, thinking of last night's explosion.

"Too bad we don't have a wall around us," Noah said. "One tall enough to keep out Komar Romak as well as those wild boars."

———⟫•⟪———

By the time they were done with breakfast, they were calmer. Lucy clung to both Miss Brett and Jasper, insisting on sitting between them. Then the driver in the impossibly huge top hat urged them to follow him outside. Waiting there were two carriages. One had a pile of bags upon it. The other was empty, and the driver loaded the bags the children and Miss Brett had brought.

As they began to board, Miss Brett heard the sound of falling rocks, and jumped. But nothing hit the ground. Miss Brett looked up. The noise seemed to come from above them. Then there was a cry. It sounded like a scream of fear or sorrow—a throaty, gasping cry. It sounded human.

"Children!" cried Miss Brett, counting heads twice to be sure they were all there.

"Look!" Lucy pointed to the branch of a tree growing from a

craggy edge above the cave. On a bare branch sat a huge black bird.

"Aaaow!" came the bird's cry, sounding almost like someone being strangled.

"Come, children." Miss Brett ushered the children into the carriage. Her nerves were frazzled, and she just wanted them all together in a single carriage, close together and safe. She looked up toward the black bird before stepping into the car. A shiver ran up her spine.

She shook her head and looked up again.

The bird had flown off.

⟶≻●≺⟵

The driver of their carriage closed the door once they were all inside. Another man in a square cap and dark square glasses drove the pre-loaded carriage. He nodded, then took off the way they had come. The children boarded the carriage, and they headed down the way they had been going.

They were quiet for some time. Miss Brett handed out lap robes so each child could keep their legs warm on the ride. Looking over the side of the mountain, they saw a wreck of a carriage and a pile of burnt rubble. The remains were still smoldering—a sobering sight indeed.

Miss Brett had to turn away. She tried to keep those thoughts from filling her head once again. Monsters with tusks were the least of their fears.

Though she did not truly want an answer, she could not keep the question from rising in her thoughts: Was it indeed Komar Romak once again?

CHAPTER SIXTEEN

THE VILLAGE
OF SOLEMANO
OR
FIELDS OF BLACK

It was clear from the direction the carriage took that they were going back over already traveled ground and zigzagging through the mountains. The carriage had a working brazier, like the first one, and a hamper of treats for passengers as well. Exhausted from the preceding events, from crashing carriages to monstrous meetings, the children (at the urging of their teacher) took a rest. Miss Brett spoke soothingly, and Lucy was the first to close her eyes. Noah was next, but Wallace squirmed as if he could not get comfortable.

"I'm here, sweet angel," Miss Brett said, caressing the little boy's back.

"Miss Brett." Wallace did not know if he could ask this. "We're so far away from where our parents were. Do you think we will... are we ever going to..."

"I am sure they are fine. Look, Wallace, you know that these men have never hurt us." Miss Brett's voice was strong and reassuring. "They are surely protecting your parents, too." This seemed to bring Wallace some comfort.

"Was there something else?" Of course, there was something else, Miss Brett thought. There was so much else.

"Do you think those giant pigs are going to come near us again?"

"Now don't worry about that," she said with a smile. "A boy who won a battle against an evil villain couldn't possibly fear a pig, no matter how big its teeth." She kissed Wallace on the head and he, too, fell asleep. Miss Brett closed her eyes too. She hoped they'd arrive somewhere soon. It was getting dark early in these late autumn days. As she began to doze, she hoped they wouldn't be traveling into the darkness.

Only Jasper and Faye were awake.

"I'm sorry I wandered off, Jasper," Faye said. Jasper had been furious with her, and she did not like it. She had felt the weight of his anger and it hurt. The hurt was stronger than almost anything she felt—at that moment, it was stronger even than her anger toward the mysterious men in black. Her thoughts went from anger at him for being mad at her to true remorse for causing them all to go into the wild boar's cave.

"Well, it was not smart to go off like that," Jasper said.

"*You* wandered off into the cave," Faye said, but she said this without rancor.

"I did, didn't I?" Jasper said. "Then I'm sorry, too."

"Apology accepted," she said, firmly.

Faye looked over at Jasper and saw, in the fading afternoon light, that Jasper was smiling. Faye smiled, too, and leaned her head against the glass. With a deep sigh, she felt a weight lift from her shoulders. If things were right with Jasper, at least something in the world was right. Faye closed her eyes and, rather quickly, she, too, fell asleep.

Jasper reached and pulled Miss Brett's cloak across the sleeping others. He leaned over to be sure Faye's shoulders were covered. His hand brushed against her cheek, and she sighed again. He alone knew that there, in the darkening carriage, he was blushing.

———————

By nightfall, it was clear that they were not stopping. Likely, they were going to continue through the night. Only after Miss Brett begged the driver for a chance to throw off their lap robes and stretch their legs did they pull off the bumpy road onto a bumpier path and stop. By then, it was late, but the moon was bright and sparkled in the river water down below. They barely had a chance to notice how high in the hills they were before being ushered back into the carriage and, once again, heading off into the unknown. It wasn't long before they could feel the carriage descending the hills again.

When dawn brought a thin layer of light that settled like the mist over the valley, the children yawned the sleep out of their eyes. Coming through the mountains in the dark and then down again had not woken Wallace or Lucy, but Jasper woke with a start at every bump. As for Faye, she had been awake before the light made even a promise of rising. But now, the misty light made Wallace and Lucy stir as well. They were all awake—all except Noah, who continued to snore into Wallace's ear.

Miraculously, Miss Brett had managed to heat water on the brazier, and had made tea for the lot of them. She opened the hamper and found there were still some buttery biscuits. She assumed it was the aroma of the baked goods that brought a large snort from

Noah, and he sat bolt upright as if someone had called his name.

The carriage continued descending. There was just the hint of a coming winter. Hoarfrost covered the leaves on the trees, which, at that height, had seemingly frozen during the night. As they came down into the valley, they could almost see a line where the warmth began. It was definitely not cold enough for crystal dew down there. Instead, the leaves presented beautiful reds and oranges. Grape vines and olive trees blanketed the rolling fields.

"What a lovely fairytale," Lucy said, and she was right. The whole valley, pristine and elegant, lay before them. The trees, or at least those that changed with the season, still held onto their autumn colors. And the villages looked like something right out of a story read by Miss Brett.

"Look!" Jasper pointed to an old wooden sign that no one was able to read. There were several wooden plaques that once must have been signs, all nailed to a post and all with letters too worn to read. But on one of the wooden signs, there was an arrow pointing in the direction they had just turned.

The children felt warm in their woolen coats, and cozy under the lap robes and blankets that lay across their legs, but as the carriage turned onto the winding road that led up to the village, and the children clambered for window space, the covers fell to the floor, unnoticed.

Fields spread out, surrounding the hill upon which a castle sat, a village beneath it. A creek that seemed to follow the curves of the road ran down the side of the hill and through the fields below.

"A bubbling brook," said Lucy. "How lovely."

"I don't think you'd fancy a swim in it now, Lucy," Noah said, pointing to the tiny crystals of ice formed where the water met the banks. It was colder up here in the mountains. It became clear, as the carriage trundled along, that they still had a ways to go. The children all settled back into their seats.

As the carriage came around the curve of the mountain pass, the children could see the patches of farms and houses that marked the little villages upon the hillsides.

"Oh, this is beautiful!" exclaimed Miss Brett, who had never in her life been to such a magical place.

"I'd like Rapunzel to let down her hair," said Lucy, pointing to the tall tower reaching skyward from a castle that sat at the top of a very steep hill.

As they pressed along, there was a long gap without any signs of civilization. Here on the outskirts, many of the houses were in ruins, the walls of the towns crumbling. Then, for a while, the yellows and golds and reds of the autumn leaves, the winding sliver of water cutting through the valley floor, and the surrounding hills were all they saw. The road itself changed from flat stone to dirt. There were several forks that seemed to go nowhere or circle back onto the road they had traveled.

It was more than an hour before the next village came into view. In fact, this village was alone on the crest of a tall hill that sloped gracefully up toward the ancient wall surrounding it.

Looking in every direction he could, Jasper could see for miles, and there was not another village, or even a single farmhouse, in sight.

Turning back, Jasper could see, even from a distance, that this particular village seemed better cared for than some of the others they had passed. It seemed to sparkle in a way, as if the stone wall had just been built with fresh new stone.

"Now that is a city wall," Noah said. "That'll keep out the boars."

"Let's hope it does the same for Komar Romak," Faye added, under her breath.

The fields were in perfect alignment, and the houses, even the old farmhouses that peppered the hillside leading up to the surrounding wall, were immaculate on the outside. The whole area really did look like something straight out of a fairytale.

Looming high above the fields and vineyards, above everything in the village but the sky itself, was a castle. It was not huge, but it stood against the clouds like an ancient symbol of authority, looking down upon its valley, and upon the people that turned the soil, raised the cattle, grew the grapes, and harvested the olives. Although the gardens around the manor house were clearly tended with great care, the manor itself appeared empty, its halls likely silent but for the sound of the wind through the glassless windows.

The carriage made a left up a road that led toward the village—in fact, the only road that seemed to head serpentine through the village, the center of which was the castle or manor house. And it was then, as they came closer to the fields, that the children and Miss Brett saw the first signs of life. At the base of the crest were fields of green and vineyards laden with grapes on the vine. There they could see farmers working the land and harvesting the grapes. The five children watched as the farmers hoed and raked, trimmed and pruned, harvested and plucked.

And as the carriage drew closer, the five children and Miss Brett realized something all at once.

"It's them!" Lucy pointed.

The farmers working in the fields, pruning and harvesting, may have been working in most ways exactly like any other farmers, but they hardly looked like them. The farmer with the plow wore a black stovetop hat and a black feather boa. The farmer with the hoe wore a pair of black, fluffy earmuffs and a long, black, furry tail that stuck out of his black dungarees. The farmer feeding the chickens in the clutch wore a black leather jerkin over black hose and pointed black shoes, a flat black sun hat shading his face. The farmer plucking grapes from the vines was wiping his brow on ribbons that fell from his ruffled black bonnet. All wore dark glasses or goggles and were too busy working to pay any attention to the approaching carriage.

But the people in the carriage certainly paid attention to the farmers. How could they not?

"Is everyone here, you know, one of *them?*" Noah said.

The children watched the fields and the men as the carriage turned up toward the village. The houses were closer together as they neared the village wall. Jasper could see how these houses were built, with chickens kept on the ground floor and what was likely a kitchen above so that the birds would be warm in the winter and eggs could be easily harvested without going outside. As they approached the great stone wall that protected the city, Wallace adjusted his glasses.

"It really is one of those ancient walls that surrounded towns and cities in olden times," he noted, fascinated by the antiquity. "They built them to keep out intruders. They're extremely thick and strong."

"Only this village comes with its own marauding hordes," Faye said, pointing at a particularly large man wearing a huge black ribbon tied in a bow upon his shaggy head. The man held a particularly small brown bantam hen and stroked her head gently.

"Hordes, perhaps," Noah said, "but marauding? Why, that fellow looks like a gentle giant."

"If I were you, I would not be so trusting," Faye warned.

"Ouch." Noah cringed.

"What?" said Faye, eyebrow raised.

"If I were you? You'd rip me limb from limb and gut me before handing me back." Noah cringed again. "No, indeed, I'll be me on my own, thank you very much."

Faye often would have liked to rip Noah limb from limb, and might have done so then had two people not been sitting between them—mostly because she feared Noah was right.

"Well, you can have you all to yourself," Faye concluded. "I've had more than enough of you."

It was Noah's turn to raise an eyebrow.

The carriage came to a jerk of a halt. The driver began conversing with another mysterious man in black wearing a very tall pointed hat and standing in the road. Jasper looked at the great gate to the town ahead. The entrance was a huge archway, built into the great stone wall. Above the gate were two ravens, chattering away, unconcerned with the newcomers.

An ancient carving was visible above the gate. Jasper realized it was a written sign carved into the stone. Ancient as the sign was, Jasper could make out some of the letters.

"'VILLAGIO SOLEMANO,'" Wallace read aloud, sounding out the words. He, too, had been observing the sign. Beneath it were letters or symbols neither boy could recognize.

"It's the name of our new village, isn't it?" said Lucy with enthusiasm. "Only it's very, very old indeed. A very old new village." And she clapped her hands together and giggled. She then tilted her head and covered one eye with her fingers.

"What are you doing, Lucy?" asked Jasper.

"It's like Sole Manner Farm," Lucy said, now tilting her head the other way.

"What is?" asked Wallace, angling his head to see if he could see what she saw.

"It just is," she said. "In a way." Clapping her hands together, leaving behind whatever thoughts she had of Sole Manner Farm, she pointed up and waved at the two large black birds sitting on the stone wall. The other children soon forgot whatever Lucy was trying to say.

Presently, the carriage began to move again, passing slowly through the huge arch of the gateway. Jasper looked at the arch and noticed not only huge metal hinges, but, as they passed, giant ancient doors attached to them. The doors were opened to the inside and must have been two feet thick.

The carriage slowed even more as it passed through the gates. Next to the archway were stone houses built on either side of the entry. These houses were built right into the wall. Castle guards must have lived in those houses back in ancient times, thought Jasper. There was a strong sense of the past—a feeling that, somehow, little had changed here in hundreds of years.

"Look!" cried Lucy with a gasp. "It's a mysterious lady in black!"

Indeed, there was a woman in a black dress standing in a very small, square yard. She was surrounded by clucking chickens and held up an apron full of eggs. She smiled as the carriage ambled past her house. Miss Brett smiled back at her and marveled at the timeless sight. The woman could have stepped out of a painting from the Middle Ages. The woman's squinting, smiling eyes and crinkled nose, the black kerchief in her hair, and her thick, black, leather boots all brought to mind a peasant farmer from ages past— or, really, any age at all.

Two doors down, another woman was hanging up the wash. She, too, was dressed in a black peasant dress, with her hair in two long braids, pulled back in a black scarf. A woman in black dungarees was peeling potatoes next door to that house. All the women either waved or smiled and nodded as the carriage full of young inventors trundled slowly into town. The children waved and smiled back, Lucy the most enthusiastic.

Everyone was so friendly. There was a candlemaker, dipping long rows of strings into steaming vats of wax. They could see her work through her opened windows. It must have been very warm in that shop to keep the windows open on such a chilly morning. There was a shoemaker, hammering away in his own shop. He was, most certainly, yet another mysterious man in black, for he was dressed like a big black elf with star-shaped glasses clinging to the end of his long nose.

Next, they saw a butcher in a black apron, and then, a blacksmith. The blacksmith was outside, hammering at his anvil. The fire was blazing next to him as he stood and worked. The blacksmith wore a jerkin over a black tunic, like those worn in the Middle Ages, and had very large black protective glasses covering half his face and a balaclava over his neck up to his nose.

A small plump woman in a black skirt and white apron appeared in a doorway around the corner. She carried a saucer of milk that she placed on the ground next to the little bench. Lucy looked around for the kitties and was surprised when two rather well-fed ravens came and drank from the saucer like a pair of house cats. Smiling down at them, the woman stepped into the street, grabbed the corner of her apron, and shook hard. A plume of white billowed from her apron, and as it settled, they could see that her dress had not been black and white, but simply black. She had been covered in flour.

The scent of baking bread hit all the children before the woman waddled back into the bakery. In a few seconds, she appeared again with her hands full. She waved to the carriage as she handed a loaf of bread and some buns to an old shepherd near the potted cypress outside the bakery door. Smiling at his bounty, the shepherd, too, waved.

A few other women either opened shutters or stepped from shops and greeted the carriage as it drove slowly through town. At Miss Brett's urging, Faye joined the other children as they waved back, passing through the village and up a winding center road.

As they traveled, they noticed a single stone wall, not as grand as the city wall but still much higher than the low stone walls that separated land between farmers. There were stones missing, and vines growing over much of it. This wall ran from just above the town center up and along the path up the hill. It seemed to be the wall around the castle, or manor house, of the village.

"This must be a very grand place indeed," said Faye. "Did you notice the terraced garden?" Through small gaps in the wall, they could glimpse an enormous garden inside.

"Oh, I love grand places," said Lucy, her nose pressed against the window.

The carriage turned off the main road and headed through

a tree-lined drive, though it was quite overgrown. They came to a very majestic gate that rose high above the stone wall, beautifully and ornately welded with iron swans and swirls and flowers. The doors of the gate began to part, opened by a man wearing a long black feather in a handsome black hat, like that of a musketeer.

The path beyond led through the terraced garden, over two bridges—one above the olive orchard and one below it—and around a small pond. There, at the crest of the hill, surrounded by the gardens and orchards, was a great manor house, a *palazzo*, made of stone and marble. It clearly had been a grand manor, but as they came nearer, they could see that it had last been cared for a long time ago. The slate roof looked worn and green with mold and lichen. It was partially crumbled, and great chunks were missing from several gables. The elegant stained glass and leaded glass windows were filthy, and some were cracked. On the top floor of the towers were windows without any glass at all.

"Aaaow!" came a cry. Looking up, Jasper was the first to see the bird.

"It's rather disturbing, that cry," said Noah, shivering as Miss Brett had. Something about the old rotting manor house and the raven at the foregate and on the tower ledge made him feel a creep running up his neck.

The path that led right up around the side of this great house was overgrown with weeds, with a tree fallen across the paving stones. In some earlier time, it had been left to rot where it had fallen. But there was a stand of maples on the far side, and the red and golden leaves were beautiful on the branches. There were a few edelweiss still clinging to their stalks near the stepping stones. A huge oak stood in the circular lawn in the front of the house.

As the carriage came closer, the children could all see the elegant details. There were bas-reliefs, sculptures, coming out of marble panels spaced around the sidewalls of the manor. In the front garden, and as far as they could see along the side and into the back, there were statues and fountains, pergolas and gazebos. The statues looked as if they came from ancient Rome. It all seemed so sadly uncared for.

It must have been beautiful, Faye thought. It reminded her of her home in Delhi, only this place had been forgotten. Once, long ago, there must have been smoke coming from the chimneys and families playing in the garden. And those gardens, well, they could have been as beautiful as those at her estate. But, alas, no longer. There were dead trees and branches scattered around, outside, and on top of the wall. There were trees that might have been hit by lightning or simply fallen dead with age. In some places, there were trees growing out of those long-ago fallen trees, new life springing from old.

"Look," Jasper said, pointing at some engravings on wide marble steps leading up to the enormous front door. "Those are like the engravings in the cave." On the stairs, they could see ancient script and Roman numerals.

"That isn't Roman, though," said Lucy. "That looks like another language completely. Like by the sign for Solemano."

Beautiful calligraphy graced the base of a sculpture at the second level of the stairs. The sculpture seemed to have been destroyed, but the base was there, and the calligraphy was elegant, almost art rather than letters. There were also beautiful images of animals and birds—mostly birds, Jasper noted.

The carriage came to a stop in front of the grand entrance. The front faced a taller wall, which was covered in ivy and moss. The huge doors had stone lions guarding either side. *This could not possibly be where we're staying,* Miss Brett thought. But Jasper stepped out of the carriage, followed by Noah, both curious about the carvings. Miss Brett, Wallace, and Lucy just looked out of the window, staring up at the huge house.

"Don't go far, children!" Miss Brett called from the carriage. "We're likely to be off in a moment." As she gazed at these ancient ruins, she thought it was like looking at a living museum. She understood the desire to explore.

Faye wanted to see the gardens before they headed off to their new home. She stepped out of the carriage and walked across to the back veranda. Down from the terraced gardens were more than one hundred olive trees, gnarled and ancient, laden with olives. The steps themselves were cracked, broken as if from years of disuse. But there was an herb garden that, for some unknown reason, seemed to have been well tended.

Faye walked back to find Jasper staring up at the house. She looked up, too, and figured out where he was looking, but not what it was. Jasper was staring at a strange curved, metal tube that seemed to be attached to the old chimneys. What it was doing or, more likely, what it once did was not apparent. There were six or seven ornate curving copper vents of some kind.

There were also a few wind vanes attached to gears and copper piping that seemed to curve back into the wall. The vanes turned the gears, but Jasper could not figure out what this system of vanes and gears did. It was beautiful, he thought, in a strange and ancient way. When the copper was shiny and not dimmed by the verdigris, it must have been striking. The contraption certainly had been there a long time. As Jasper stared, he thought he could see waves of heat coming from the copper.

"Why are we stopping here so long, Miss Brett?" asked Lucy. "Shouldn't we be off to our home?"

"Perhaps they have the key to our house," said Miss Brett as she ran her fingers through Lucy's hair and smiled. Of course, the smile hid the fact that she had no idea and feared the worst.

Lucy looked up at the broken windows on the top floor. She clung to Miss Brett, chilled at the sight of open windows in this cold.

"Well, I'm sure we'll find out," said Wallace, trying to fit a smile upon his own face.

As if on cue, the great door opened, and a man in an outsized black beret, a black smock, and very floppy black shoes came out of the house, closing the door behind him. He bowed, comically, and opened the carriage door.

"Are we stopping here for something?" Miss Brett asked the man, remaining in the warmth of the carriage.

"You come," the man said.

"Come where?" Miss Brett said.

"Come," the man answered.

"Where will we be living, the children and myself?"

"This is the home," the man said, gesturing toward the ruin.

"I don't see how this is appropriate," Miss Brett said with false calm.

"Oh, Miss Brett!" cried Lucy, pointing to the broken windows. "It will be terribly cold in there. Please don't let us stay in the floors above."

The man gestured again and took Miss Brett's arm. Not want-ing to alarm the children, Miss Brett did not do what her instincts were begging her to do—pull her arm away and run with the children. Unlike their stay at Sole Manner Farm, here it would soon be winter, and a giant ruin of a house in winter was no place for children. She took a deep breath.

"I'm sure there is a ... a plan for us," Miss Brett said, lamely. She was, in fact, sure there was a plan. What that plan could possibly be, and whether or not she'd find it suitable, was a different story.

Miss Brett, Wallace, and Lucy descended.

There was an eerie feel to the place. Miss Brett drew in another deep breath. The air smelled sweet and fresh, with the essence of figs and a slight, pleasant odor of hay and horses. She thought of her childhood and visiting the countryside with her parents. Looking around, she soaked in all that surrounded her—the beautiful valley, the gardens, the history. Except for the fact that she and the children were supposed to live in a drafty, leaky old ruin, this place could be heaven.

"Jasper, Faye, Noah!" she called. "It appears that this will be our new home."

Faye turned toward her teacher. Standing out at the edge of the top tier of the garden, she briefly thought she had heard Miss Brett say they were to live in this rubble. She hurried over to find out what was actually said. She found Jasper and Noah standing next to Miss Brett with their mouths agape.

Faye was adamant once she realized she had heard correctly. "They're mad if they think I will live here."

The man in the beret now ascended the steps, carrying, on his shoulder, all six of their bags, piled higher than he was tall. He pulled from his pocket a key ring with what looked to be twenty keys and began unlocking the many locks placed on and around the door.

"Why did he lock it if he was going right back inside?" Noah whispered to Jasper.

Jasper shrugged. Had he ever understood the mysterious men in black?

Miss Brett and the children waited patiently. With the bags still balanced on his shoulder, the man now climbed up to the side window and used another key in a lock hidden in a secret compartment above the sill. He then turned the handle of the latch, and a stone by the shutters moved to reveal another lock that required another key.

"He cannot be serious," said Faye under her breath. "We could be here all night."

"Oh, I don't want to stand here all night," whined Lucy. "It will get so chilly and we'll get so hungry." She rubbed her tummy and made a sad face for Miss Brett. But then Lucy looked down the road, and her hand flew to her mouth in joyous surprise.

"Merhba! Benvenuti!" came a voice in the direction Lucy was looking. The others turned to find the baker, rotund but diminutive in stature, her hair in a flustered bun falling out from beneath a dark scarf. The woman's apron was filled with baskets promising delicious treats.

"Hello," Miss Brett said to the woman, who was now red-faced and perspiring from the effort of waddling up the steep, sloping road to the *palazzo*. "Please, let me help you with those."

The woman shook her head, kissing the teacher's outstretched hand rather than allowing it to take any of the baskets from her. "We had heard there would be an arrival," the baker said in very good English, though with a strong, distinct Italian accent.

"Really?" Miss Brett was surprised. People from the town had expected them?

"*Si*, yes, we have heard. We hear of the ship and the train and how you are to come. I have made sure that there is bread and biscotti for you in the *palazzo*." She smiled, then began to hand out iced buns to the children and Miss Brett.

"Sahha!" she said.

They all nibbled away at what was surely one of the most delicious treats any of them could imagine. They were famished.

"Rosie used to make the most delicious biscuits," Lucy said, suddenly thinking of the nanny they had left behind in America. Rosie had been the first to take care of Lucy and Jasper when they had found themselves in that house in Dayton. In fact, each of the children, suddenly without parents, had found a nanny—Daisy for Wallace, Myrtle for Noah, and Camelia for Faye—to care for them in the houses prepared for their arrival. They spent the weekends in those houses, away from Miss Brett and Sole Manner Farm. The houses were all joined together by a big backyard where they would have picnics and conduct science experiments. Rosie had made Jasper and Lucy's house a home, at a time when the children had been so worried about their parents.

Lucy's face fell. These new treats from the baker made Lucy wonder if they'd ever see those nannies again—or their parents. But the baker patted her head and squeezed her cheeks, which made her blush, distracted from her sad thoughts.

A shadow passed over Miss Brett's shoulder as a tall man in black silk pajamas and a back turban, high black wading boots, and a dark pince-nez emerged, pushing a wheelbarrow full of potatoes up from the field. The baker smiled and said something to him in Italian. Miss Brett was suddenly taken aback as it dawned on her that this strange man was in full sight of the baker. Their driver had been in full sight of everyone in the town. And there, in the field, the mysterious men in black worked like so many farmers. They *were* so many farmers.

It was then that Miss Brett realized the mysterious men in black were mysterious only to the children and her. None of the parents ever commented on their strangeness. None of the villagers seemed to think anything of these very odd fellows.

The baker, having finished handing out sweet buns, stopped the man in black pajamas as he tried to pass.

"You can't work in the field all day without a treat, ," she said, handing the man a bun. He stopped, took it from her, and swallowed it in one bite, then gave a short bow. The baker patted him on the head, then placed the basket with the rest of the treats in the wheelbarrow. "Bring these for the others, and be sure that you are drinking enough water. The air may be cool, but the sun is hot today. Sahha!"

"*Grazzi hafna*, Fornaio, also from the others," the pajama man said in a low, gruff voice. Even his Italian seemed to have a strange accent to it. He continued his task, to the nonplussed silence of the children and Miss Brett. The man scooped up the potatoes in his arms and dropped them on the front steps of the manor house.

The pajama man then turned and pushed the barrow back down toward the village.

The baker turned to Miss Brett and the children. "I am Signora Fornaio, dear ones," she said. "I am the baker." Then she shouted something and blew a kiss to the pajama man.

"You... you..." Miss Brett began after several seconds.

"You know those fellows?" Noah said. "They aren't strange to you?"

The baker looked at them and cocked her head to one side. "Know who?"

"The men in black," said Wallace.

"I fratelli in nero." She smiled.

"I fratelli in nero?" asked Lucy. "What does 'nero' mean?"

"Black, yes?" the baker said.

"Nero," Lucy said to herself.

"And you know them?" asked Faye.

"But of course I know them. As my mother, her mother, and all of my family have always known them. As everyone, *tutti*, here in Solemano."

Again, Miss Brett and the children stood in stunned silence. A whole village—generations of a village—knew the men in black? Spoke with them? Greeted them? Fed them sweet buns and biscotti?

"So..." said Noah, who had so many questions he just picked the first one he could think of. "Is this where they are all from? Are they Italian?" It would explain the strange accents, though the language didn't sound Italian.

The baker laughed. "You are the funny," she said. "*Italiani*, I think not."

"How long have they been here?" asked Jasper, when it seemed that something else must be asked.

"Oh, well, so many stories." She chuckled. "I am always the storyteller. Well, they, *i fratelli in nero*, have always been here." Then the baker considered for a moment. "Or, perhaps, not always. Perhaps, *non conosco*." She looked behind the five children and Miss Brett. Another old woman was walking up the road. This woman pushed a wheelbarrow containing a giant wheel of cheese.

"Ehi! Lattea! Signora Maggio, da quanto tempo i monaci, i fratelli in nero vissuto qui?" the baker said.

Signora Maggio stopped and greeted the children and Miss Brett with hugs and smiles. She gave Miss Brett a large chunk of white cheese wrapped in cloth. "Sahha!" she said to Miss Brett. "Che cosa si chiede, Doclea? What was it you asked?" she said to the baker.

"*I fratelli* , them in black, *da quanto*, from when are they?"

Signora Maggio seemed to consider, then nodded. "*Circa* 350 years."

The only sound then was Jasper swallowing the chunk of sweet bun he had bitten but forgotten to chew.

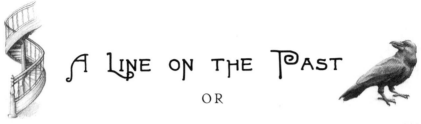

CHAPTER SEVENTEEN

A LINE ON THE PAST

OR

THE YOUNG INVENTORS GUILD MIND THEIR MANOR

"Three hundred and fifty years?" Jasper finally got his voice back as the chunk of bun passed, painfully, down his throat in one piece.

Signora Fornaio seemed to consider this. She looked off into the distance, as if she were counting years in her head. "Yes," she said, "about 350 years. Perhaps more. Perhaps closer to 450."

"That's an awfully long time," Noah said.

"Yes, and it is the way of Solemano," Signora Fornaio said, ruffling Noah's hair as he reached for another bun. "The village is about them."

"I fratelli in nero?" said Lucy, offering nibbles to a nearby raven.

"She remembers good," said Signora Fornaio.

"She remembers everything," said Jasper, proudly.

The baker pet the raven as if it were a cat. The bird closed its eyes and made that strange sound, like falling stones. "These birds are very smart. They know what is in the heart. Is that not right, *corvino?*" The bird chattered back.

The man with the outsized top hat returned from inside. He opened the door wide and gestured for them to enter. Signora Maggio handed him the huge cheese round. Then the two ladies kissed each of the newcomers on both cheeks. Finally, both ladies began to walk down to the village while the children and Miss Brett turned to go into the house.

As they reached the top of the steps, all six arrivals stood dumbfounded, staring at what was just inside.

"Oh, look! It's a fairy castle!" cried Lucy, who ran inside. And it was.

Even from where she stood, Miss Brett could see the fine curtains, the beautiful rugs and, unbelievably, the blazing fire in the fireplace. Jasper and Noah looked at each other, then at Wallace, who, too, nodded and smiled.

"It's brilliant!" Jasper laughed.

"Hey, why didn't we think of that?" Noah laughed, too.

"Maybe we did," said Lucy, following their gaze.

Wallace smiled. "I think Lucy may be right. It is possible that we are not the first of the Young Inventors Guild to have come to Solemano."

Miss Brett looked from one to the next. "What are you talking about?"

Lucy clapped her hands and came running out the door and down the steps. But the boys were transfixed by the ingenious contraption.

Wallace pointed up. "You can see the curve of the tubing branching off at the end," he explained to Miss Brett, "fanning out and returning to the wall—"

"And there," said Jasper, pointing to a fan of smaller pipes, "down into the floors. The gears likely turn by small turbines inside, which run from heat flow instead of fluid. The gears must turn something within the pipes, dispersing the heat and generating more."

"It's quite clever," said Wallace. "It functions in a twofold manner."

"Yes." Jasper smiled to himself. "It not only brings warmth back to the building, but it prevents anyone from seeing smoke coming out of the chimneys."

Miss Brett, out of curiosity, bent to touch the polished marble floor before the grand, sweeping stairway. It *was* warm! Not that she had doubted the boys, but it was such an amazing idea. It was a warm marble floor during what was soon to be winter.

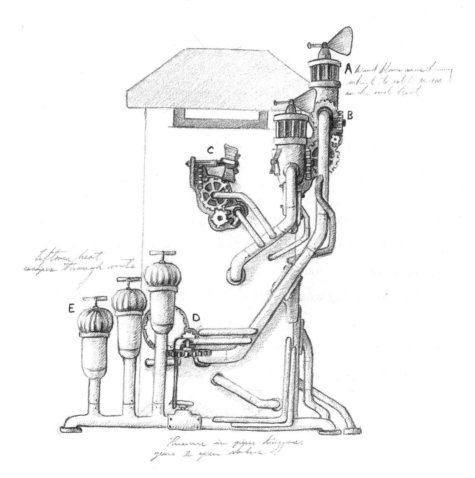

Lucy, back outside, ran to the side of the house and peeked down at the terraced gardens. The bird flew beside her, soaring up but always hovering nearby.

"They're splendid!" Lucy called. "It's like *Alice's Adventures in Wonderland!*"

The gardens were spectacular, or surely must have been in their golden days. The terraces were wide levels that descended from one to the next. There were four levels, each with its own tangle of vines or herb gardens or olive orchards or little ponds and bridges. The third level had what looked to be at least fifty small statues on pedestals throughout the garden. There was a crumbled archway that had once led to the garden. On the remaining piece of stone there were some indecipherable words. There even seemed to be a set of steps from one level to the next. The bridge between the olive garden and the garden of statues was much overgrown with vines.

Lucy stared in awe until a little gust of wind gave her a chill. She hurried to join the others inside.

"Come on, Mr. Corvino!" Lucy called to the bird. It made a chattering noise and flew up to the tower. The bird clearly was not interested in coming inside. Slightly saddened, Lucy waved to the bird and re-entered the house.

Inside, it truly was a palace. There were ancient Greek statues and velvet furniture. Beautiful tapestries adorned the walls. There was a fountain and jasmine growing in what seemed to be a glass conservatory attached to the large sitting room, facing the back of the house. The sitting room had huge windows that looked out over the village and the valley below. The six newcomers wandered, looking into the enormous dining room with its table long enough to sit fifty people comfortably. There was a chandelier that looked as though it could hold all five children. There was what appeared to be a ballroom and a morning room. And, to Miss Brett and the children's delight, there was a library.

The library had a beautiful wrought-iron spiral staircase that led to the upper stacks, which seemed to hold the oldest books in the collection. There were so many books that they'd never be able to look at them all.

There were books on history, geography, and music. There were books in every language they knew, and many they didn't. Jasper and Wallace found a section on science and invention. There was *Narrative of the Surveying Voyages of His Majesty's Ships* Adventure *and* Beagle, the four volumes of the famous expedition comprising Fitzroy's narrative and Charles Darwin's journals. Darwin's books, *The Expression of the Emotions in Man and Animals, Origin of Species, Insectivorous Plants to Worms,* and *The Descent of Man,* were there as well. There were works by William Clifford on mathematics. There was even a copy of Thomas Carlyle's *Sartor Resartus.*

Noah found a volume on music and math by an author he had never heard of. The pages looked fragile and yellow. Other books were so worn from use and age he could no longer see what was written on the spines.

Faye was almost certain one said "Galileo." She found two medieval collections of architectural drawings that made her heart beat faster. Several copies of different volumes of Leonardo DaVinci's inventions were there. Faye found some of his flying machine drawings, several of which she had never seen before.

Some books told of ancient castles and of kings and queens. There were books of poetry and art. There were loads of dictionaries, huge volumes with old script, including English-Italian, English-Spanish, English-French, English-German, English-Hindi, and, for some reason, English-Maltese and English-Basque. Miss Brett loved dictionaries. They were the gateway to cultures. They brought worlds together. Different worlds all in one place and, through many languages, you could find a common thread. She made a mental note to peruse them when she had a chance.

Several books were not in English or Italian at all, and at least one seemed to be in Arabic or Persian. One had a delicately hand-painted illustration of a raven on the cover. She could not understand anything within, but the book was exquisitely beautiful.

Miss Brett was glad to see that there was some literature as well—stories she could share with the children, including works by Charles Dickens, Robert Louis Stevenson, Rudyard Kipling, Anna Sewell, R. M. Ballantyne, and Lewis Carroll. Many were beautifully illustrated, with gilded pages and embroidered spines. Lucy loved the drawings from Lewis Carroll. On the shelves also were Jonathan Swift's *Gulliver's Travels* and Mary Shelley's *Frankenstein.* They even found a collection of the work of the Brothers Grimm, as well as a single illustrated story, "The Raven."

"We won't be reading that to Lucy on dark and rainy nights," Noah whispered to Jasper with a grin.

"Nor this," said Jasper, pointing to Edgar Allan Poe's poem of the same name.

There was, as well, a whole shelf of theatrical works, including volumes upon volumes of Shakespeare, as well as works by Marlowe and Ben Jonson. Miss Brett laughed to herself as she saw the title *Volpone* and thought, *Of course, that was . . . Corbaccio—the raven and the miser. Was that his name?* She turned the pages. It was then she saw another work, again with the image of the raven on the front. This appeared to be a book of fables, for each one was illustrated, and the stories were short. Basile was the author. How strange, she thought, putting it back on the shelf. So many books seemed to have ravens among their pages.

There was a groaning grumble, and everyone looked at Noah. Cheeks red, he said, "That was my stomach rebelling. It truly hates being ignored." Noah had come across a cookbook from France, which had sent a message to his middle.

"Oh, do we have to stop?" asked Lucy, nearly hidden by a pile of books. "I'd fancy a longer look around." She clung to a beautiful book of children's verses.

"Well, this is now our library, sweet angel," Miss Brett said. "We can come back anytime we like."

Tearing themselves away from the books was difficult, but Miss Brett's words struck home. This was their library, at least while they were here.

"I think exploring the kitchen might be our next adventure," said Miss Brett, putting books back on shelves and helping Lucy to close the book in her hands.

———⟶●⟵———

The kitchen was massive, and, again to everyone's joy, not empty. In addition to the huge pile of potatoes and the round of cheese, the kitchen held a familiar sight.

"Mr. Frilly Apron!" cried Lucy, who ran over to throw herself about his knees. He slapped his hands together in surprise. The frilly apron man had been rolling dough. He looked at Lucy as if she were a puppy that had peed on his shoe, his hands and face now powdered with flour. Lucy, now also covered in flour, smiled up at the man, who had no visible grin to return.

"Come, Lucy." Jasper took his sister's hand and pulled her off the floury frilly apron man and past the long farm table.

The man in the frilly apron took a ladle from the hook and opened a big pot of hot, richly seasoned potage.

"Oh, that smells lovely." Lucy hugged herself and rubbed her tummy. "I do suppose I'm famished as well."

Taking seats around the table, the children were all served a snack of warming stew, filled with roast fennel and pumpkin. It was not spicy, but it had wonderful, strong flavors. Some bread from the bakery was in chunks on the table, as were plates of olive oil.

When they were finished, Lucy thanked the frilly apron man with another squeeze. She had saved a bit of stew in the bottom of her bowl.

"I've left this for Mr. Corvino," she told him, and he nodded, setting her bowl aside.

They set off from the kitchen to explore some more—all but Noah, who found his way to a tin of chocolate biscuits. Faye pulled him from the tin just as Jasper had pulled Lucy from the apron man.

"Can we find our bedrooms, Miss Brett?" asked Faye as they came back together in the foyer.

"We don't have to sleep on the top floor, do we?" Lucy looked stricken as she considered her view earlier of the tattered remains of the upstairs windows.

"Of course not," Miss Brett said. "There are four floors, as I observed from outside. My guess is that we will find bedrooms on the second floor, just up there."

"Oh, may we see?" Lucy said, needlessly. "I'm ever so glad we don't have to sleep in the broken rooms on top. Oh, please may we go see?"

"Certainly," Miss Brett said, looking around. "I think I'll join you." She picked up her skirt and followed at a slower pace as the children ran upstairs.

Miss Brett noted how everything was meticulous and beautifully cared for inside. She was sure that the upper floors were specifically designed to make the *palazzo* look like ruins. Was there a passage to the upper towers? She would look to find out. If there was a door, she would ensure it remained locked, because it would likely be a dangerous place for the children to wander. The ground floor and the one above would be their home.

The bedrooms upstairs were as magnificent as the rooms downstairs. The first one looked as if it were designed for a queen. The bed was high, but seemed even higher, for it was on a dais, raised a step from the rest of the room. The four posters were very tall, and beautiful lace and silk curtains fell around the bed. Miss Brett's bags were placed neatly at the foot of the bed.

She looked around the room. It was lovely, with a beautiful bay window and a fainting couch covered in red velvet. The wall had several lovely paintings, one of a child in a garden and one of a bowl of red apples. She looked at the painting of the child. There again, almost hidden among the hedges behind the child, was a raven. There was also a rabbit.

She checked the drawers and found fresh sachets of lavender and pine. There was a large iron key hanging on the wall, too. This, she would find, fit no lock in her room. Looking in the mirror, she pulled back some hairs that had fallen astray and wiped some smudges from her cheeks.

"This must be your room, Miss Brett," Faye said, although she would have been happy having it herself. Peeking down the hall, she saw there were six more doors leading to six more rooms.

"Well, I am sure you will find plenty of space in this house, Faye," Miss Brett said, smiling reassuringly, noting how Faye was looking at the other doors. Faye found her bags in the room toward the end of the hall. It had red silks hanging from the bed. There was a drafting table, and some blueprints she had sketched when they were out at sea.

How did they get these? Faye asked herself, remembering that she had left them in the laboratory on the boat. It was thoughtful of the mysterious men in black to have brought them, though Faye would never admit this.

Miss Brett joined her as the others came to see. "I don't think you will need to share a bed with Lucy."

"Oh." Faye tried to smile, but it came out crooked and unbelievable, and she felt a little squeeze in her belly. She had thought that, once they got to their destination, she'd be sharing with Lucy again, as she had in the room back at the farmhouse in America. She had grown accustomed to the warm little wiggly girl. She would miss having someone else that near. But she would be fine alone. She had been alone most of her life.

Lucy slid her hand into Faye's. "Maybe we could share sometimes." Lucy looked up at Faye.

Faye smiled down at the little girl, who smiled back and then dashed to her own room.

The other bedrooms were just as beautiful. Each room had a big, comfortable bed, wall hangings to keep the cold out, and fires burning in the fireplaces. And they all had the children's bags waiting. Wallace's room, next to Miss Brett's, had a small chemistry laboratory right next to the window. Noah's room, in addition to a lab table with a large battery and workable engine components, had a large toolbox filled with gears and mechanical parts. It also had a music stand and a cabinet filled with sheet music. His violin had been tuned, polished, and placed on a stand.

Jasper's room had a table with a spool of copper wire, a battery as in Noah's room, and some of the drawings he had left on the ship.

Lucy's room was attached to Jasper's by a door. Her room was filled with picture books, drawings, and fairytales.

While the children were settling themselves in their rooms, Miss Brett walked past Faye's to the end of the hall, where the sixth door stood. She tried it, but it was locked. This was probably the door to the upper floors—stairs leading to the attic, most likely. She was glad it was locked, and she was determined it would remain so.

CHAPTER EIGHTEEN

THE GARDEN
OF THE BEASTS
OR
THE BAKER TELLS HER TALES

T he children took some time to settle into their spaces. Lucy
took some books from the library to keep in her room. After
tea and sandwiches for lunch, the children and Miss Brett set off
into the gardens, exploring the walled and terraced space attached
to the house.

On the topmost terrace, there were many little bridges over clo-
ver patches and beds of flowers, most of which were finished bloom-
ing for the season. The second tier had little creeks and ponds and
tiny waterfalls. Lucy was beside herself with pleasure as she ran
through the tunnels and over the little footbridges. At one point, she
climbed into the opening of a tunnel by the olive orchard. After several minutes of calling frantically, Jasper found her crawling out of
a small opening up by the garden just below the house.

"It's a secret!" cried Lucy, jumping up and down.

"Not anymore," Noah said with a laugh.

"I wonder," Jasper thought aloud. "I wonder where some of these
tunnels lead."

The third tier was the oddest. It was a maze garden, though the
hedge was very low, and it was filled with statues of all manner of

creatures. There were monkeys and elephants, bears and ravens, camels and coiled snakes. There were also unicorns and griffins and dragons. Each creature was perched atop a pedestal and seemed to gaze off in an odd direction, never looking at one another, never looking at the same spot.

"Look at me!" cried Lucy. "I'm trying to hide from the creatures, but someone is always watching!" And this was true. The others walked around the garden and found that, wherever you stood, there was at least one creature staring directly at you. It was a bit eerie.

"No!" came a shout from the orchard. A man dressed in a long black frock was carrying wood across the orchard.

"No what?" said Noah.

"No *kreaturi*," he demanded.

Faye wasn't sure she heard. "What are you—"

"No look! Stay out!" he called as he carried his wood out of the orchard and out of sight.

Having no idea what the man was referring to, the children shrugged.

"I suppose he didn't want us to follow him," said Wallace.

The fourth tier held the orchard. It was filled with gnarled and ancient olive trees, overgrown and intertwining. Soon, the children were climbing the twisted trees and running in and out of the tunnels and over the bridges. They found that the tunnels often intersected or led from one tier to the next, or back up to the house, or to a dead end, leading nowhere, or off into total darkness. The darkness was a bit worrisome, so the children tended to stick to places where they could see exits. They ran after each other and hid amazingly well. Lucy fell into a small, dried-out pond that was mostly moss and dirt, and when she reached under, she fished out an old coin. Lucy wiped it off and found the date: 1705.

"It's old," she said, handing it to Jasper.

"Perhaps not old for this garden," said Wallace, adjusting his glasses.

"Let's go down to the village," Miss Brett said after Noah, brushing against the wall of a tunnel, nearly collapsed the whole thing upon itself. "We don't have long before it's dark, and I'd love to have a look around."

So they walked down into the village. The walk was lovely. The ancient streets were made of stone, and the buildings were ornate and elegant, like buildings from a storybook. But the streets were nearly empty. Occasionally, a little old lady in a black skirt or a man wearing a black bonnet or a furry cap would hurry down the street, nodding at the children and their teacher.

"Benvenuti! Tutti, tutti!" called Signora Fornaio. "Come, I am here." Their noses, however, were already leading them toward her shop. She stood with a dish of milk that she now placed down outside her door. Two ravens hopped between her legs and began to lap at the dish. Down from the window ledge came another raven, who joined the others.

Inside the shop was a world of delights. Signora Fornaio offered them bombe alla crema and zeppole, which were fluffy soft pastries sprinkled with sugar on the outside and sweet cream filling on the inside. She had boconotto, biscuits made with almonds and chocolate; and chewy pasticiotti, like meringues with almond butter. She also had cinnamon biscotti with chocolate and nuts and honey.

"You are liking the gardens, eh?" The baker chuckled. "*Si, si,* such gardens. What are you thinking of *il giardino delle bestie?*"

"Of course, *il giardino delle bestie*," said Lucy. "I bet that's what it said in the stone in the garden when it used to say something. It's the garden with the lovely creatures, surely."

"I do believe you're right, Lucy," said Noah. "It's a very odd garden, isn't it?"

"Yes, very strange and very old. And very mysterious, yes?" The baker tapped the side of her nose.

"In what way mysterious?" asked Jasper.

"It's certainly a mystery as to why they'd put all those odd animal statues there," said Faye.

"Indeed," said the baker, but then she leaned closer and spoke softer. "But the mystery is the eyes."

Lucy's eyes were as wide as saucers. Wallace's were closed. *A story about eyes?* he thought. It sounded like a scary story. The others leaned closer to hear what Signora Fornaio had to say.

"It is said that the garden was built three hundred years ago on the ground of the old *palazzo*. There were much older statues in the garden, but they were removing them, leaving some of their pedestals for the new creations. It is said that the old *barone* shot all of the ravens and killed the wisdom, for ravens are the keepers of wisdom. They never forget. Then his house burned to the ground.

"The garden beasts," she continued, "were sculpted by a famous artist, young and very, very handsome, so that kings and queens loved him. He made the many beasts."

The children and their teacher were silent, leaning in toward the baker as if she were sharing a secret.

"It is said," said the baker, "that the handsome young artist was also a magician, but not the silliness with the hat. He does the real magic and studies the *occulto*."

"Occulto?" said Wallace with a gulp.

"Yes, the dark magic of the ages," said the baker. "And the beasts, it is strange how they are all facing not one another but always looking at you, no?"

The children nodded.

"Well, there is the reason for this." The baker beckoned them nearer. Their heads were almost touching as they moved in closer. "It is said that there is one place in the whole garden where there is not one pair of eyes upon you. Only one place where no creatures look upon you. If you ever find this spot, you will disappear."

At this point, the children were so close their heads were pressed against one another. Except for the odd gulp, there was silence.

"Well," said Miss Brett, clearing her throat, pulling back the stray hairs that had fallen out from beneath her hat, and patting the children out of their stupor, "that is quite a story, Signora Fornaio."

"No, *signorina*, not a story. Beware. It is that the *artista*, he who is also the *mago*, the magician—it is he who disappeared when the garden was complete."

—◄●►—

As the children and Miss Brett were leaving, Signora Fornaio filled their pockets with caggionetti and other delights. "I will save a few for my little friend, the shepherd," she said. And then she said his name, which sounded funny to the children. Signora Fornaio's accent was difficult enough even when they knew the words she was saying.

"Bezzomaffi?" Noah said, crossing his eyes.

"Mezzobassili?" asked Miss Brett.

"Mezzobaffi," said Lucy decisively. The others looked at her. Was she right?

Signora Fornaio smiled, placing some treats aside in a small basket.

As they watched, a tiny old man carrying a shepherd's staff came slowly up the road.

"That must be the shepherd," Jasper whispered to his sister. But Lucy was looking up at the sky. Above the shepherd, two ravens soared, chattering mournfully.

"Bene, bene. I was worried you might have been hurt," said Signora Fornaio as he approached.

"Tutti bene, Signora." The shepherd waved jovially, though it was clear he was a frail old man.

"I worry for him," said Signora Fornaio to the children. "His brother died last spring. So sad—such a good man. He loved the birds like they were part of his own flock. Now the poor man is alone with his sheep, always having to climb over the Forca di Penne passage every winter. I don't know what would have happened if I had not brought him in from the storm last month. He was shivering to the bone, *povero vecchio.*"

The shepherd greeted everyone as if they were old friends. His beard came down to his knees, and his feet were wrapped in rags. In fact, he was entirely wrapped in rags. The ravens alighted on the vines that clung to the ancient wall. They made the sound of falling stones.

"They're sad," said Lucy, looking at the birds. They were sad for the shepherd. Of this, she was certain.

"Per voi, vecchio," Signora Fornaio said, handing him the treats.

"Aspetta un secondo." She held his arm, begging him to wait a second, then rushed into the back room. She brought out a cloak—a
warm, woolen cloak. "This belonged to my beloved husband," she
said. "It kept him warm for many winters, *grazia di dio*. No," she said
as the shepherd began to refuse, "I have another that I save for my
son. This one is too small for the boy. It should keep another kind
soul warm this cold winter." She placed it on the shoulders of the old
shepherd.

He looked a bit nervous, then nodded. "Grazia, molto grazia," he
said. Then, taking his treats and his new cloak, he shuffled down
the street and disappeared around the corner. The birds cried out
and followed the old man down the road. The children watched this
strange departure.

Leaving the bakery and extending their walk, Miss Brett and
the children continued down through the village.

The shepherd must have taken his sheep over the hill to the
other side of the village, because they did not run into the little man
again. They did, however, watch the men in the field, and those harvesting the grapes and olives. They came upon an ancient chapel,
too. It was in ruins, the roof caved in and the walls crumbling. It
seemed to be one of the oldest structures in the village.

"Better not step inside," said Miss Brett, concerned that what
was left of the roof was unstable and could fall down upon them.
That said, she did notice that someone had been stomping around
in there. While the grass had grown through the floor, the path going into the chapel was well worn. She and the children could easily see inside.

Miss Brett could not help also noticing the still beautiful fres-
coes painted on the chapel's ruined walls. Along its inside were

scenes with angels, and scenes she thought could be of a garden, with, of course, ravens.

Through the alcove she could see, when she squinted, a scene that looked like monks together in battle. It seemed so strange, she thought, monks in black robes fighting with swords, along with some kind of dragon. She decided she must not be seeing the drawing correctly. Still, hanging behind those monks was a banner and it looked like the symbol on the flag from the ship.

As the final light of dusk began to fade, the children and Miss Brett headed back up to the manor house.

CHAPTER NINETEEN

SPIES IN THE DORMITORY

OR

WHERE THE CHILDREN WENT AT HARVEST

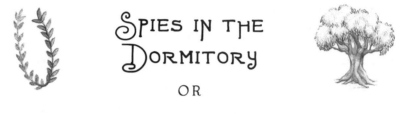

"What are they doing out there?" asked Faye as she waited for tea, standing by the big window facing the gardens. She was looking down at the olive grove.

"They've been at it all morning," said Lucy, coming over to join her at the window.

"They're harvesting," said Miss Brett, bringing in the tea tray. "Come help me lay the table, girls. We're on our own this morning."

"On our own?" asked Faye. "What do you mean?"

"All the men in black are helping harvest," said Miss Brett, laying the tea on the table and carrying the tray back to the kitchen. She passed Lucy the napkins and Faye the plates and silver. "They need everyone to help since the cold is setting in early."

"I want to help!" cried Lucy. "I want to pick the olives!"

"I think it's hard work," said Miss Brett. "Not that you couldn't do it, Lucy, but they need to have big, strong men who can reach the branches.

"All the men are out there?" asked Jasper, taking the tray of glasses as Miss Brett went to fetch the water pitcher.

"Every last one of them, apparently," Miss Brett said, carrying the pitcher to the table.

"Every last one of them?" Faye asked, slowing as she laid the spoons next to the tea cups. She looked over at Jasper, who had been thinking the same thing, though without the purely devilish grin that Faye sent in his direction.

"You are thinking of something," Noah whispered out of the corner of his mouth, placing the knives on the left side of the plates as Faye followed and, without comment, placed them correctly to the right.

"Of course I'm thinking of something, you dolt," growled Faye, grabbing the remaining knives from Noah's hand. "You think I don't think?"

"You know what I mean." Noah rolled his eyes, then waited until Miss Brett returned to the kitchen. "Jasper," he said, "what are you planning here behind our backs?"

"What's behind our backs?" asked Wallace as he and Lucy came in, carrying biscuits and jams.

"Look, you lot," Faye whispered with intent, "do not say anything. We'll talk after breakfast."

"We're not thinking of doing anything naughty, are we?" asked Lucy. "I really don't want to do naughty things today. I want to see the olive harvest."

"Naughty things?" asked Miss Brett, entering the room with a tray of the most scrumptious iced cinnamon buns.

"Oh, silly Lucy," said Faye with a laugh, "Noah is always naughty, but he will wait for his tea and not be naughty today."

"I..." But Noah could not argue. His teacup was already in his hand.

"If you bundle up warm, you can go to the olive grove and watch," said Miss Brett. "I'm so glad you're interested, Faye."

"Oh, we all are," said Faye, smiling a bit too sweetly for Miss Brett fully to believe. "We'll be sure to use the warmest gloves and hats and mufflers."

"Lovely." Miss Brett smiled back at her. "I'll get my own warm things on and—"

"Oh, you needn't bother coming out in the cold," said Faye. "We'll only be watching the harvest."

"Hmmm," said Miss Brett.

"Oh, do come with us, Miss Brett!" Lucy insisted.

"Lucy," scolded Faye under her breath.

"Well, Faye, I think I *will* join you." Miss Brett put down her tea cup and straightened her apron. "I think I'll come down as soon as I put the bread in the oven."

"Lovely," said Faye, throwing a glance at Jasper.

Noah pasted a falsely innocent look on his face while Jasper avoided her eyes. *Yes*, thought Miss Brett, *they are up to something.*

"What are we going to do now?" asked Noah, under his breath as they pulled the cold weather clothes from the closet in the foyer.

"I'm trying to think," Faye muttered. "We've got to be clever."

"You really think we're going to be able to do it?" asked Noah, hunting through the pile of mufflers to find the orange one he favored.

"Look," Jasper said, pulling on a boot, "all the men in black will be at the harvest. We can look around. It's not like we'll dis-

turb anything. We're just going to look for our missing notes—
and maybe some clues about all of this."

"There is something we're missing—something we need to
know that they're not telling us," said Faye. "Maybe something
we can use to fight Komar Romak." She would surely have tried to
search the men's rooms before on the ship, but it had been impossible to know when all the men would be gone.

But now, for the first time, the children had a chance to learn
for themselves where they could find their parents, what their
parents were doing, and why they were all here. With Miss Brett
joining them, though, it would be tricky.

Outside, the blowing wind made the chilly air chillier,
thoughbetween gusts of wind, it wasn't really so cold. Just the
same, Lucy rubbed her nose, insisting the tip was going numb.
She waved at a ruffled raven sitting on an olive tree branch. The
children and Miss Brett found a comfortable vantage point and
sat on the stone wall together. The men were busy at work as Faye
tried to think of a way to rid themselves of Miss Brett. After several minutes, it came to her.

"Miss Brett," Faye said, acting as if she'd suddenly remembered, "are you sure it's safe to leave the bread alone in the house?"

"What do you mean, Faye?" asked Miss Brett, now wondering
herself.

"Just that we don't want it to burn, and we *are* a bit far." Faye
again gave Miss Brett that overly sweet smile.

"Well," considered Miss Brett. Up to something or not, Faye
was right. "I suppose I should head back up. Just be mindful of
Lucy and Wallace," she said, climbing down from the wall. "And
mind yourselves, too. Don't get yourselves into trouble."

As soon as Miss Brett was safely back in the house, the five of them trudged down to Signora Fornaio's bakery to find out where, in fact, the men in black lived.

"I want to see the olives!" Lucy said.

"No one's stopping you," Faye said.

Lucy squinched her face and followed quietly. She didn't want to be left out.

When they got to the bakery, Lucy's face brightened. Signora Fornaio welcomed them, offering them each a brioche warm from the oven.

"Come have some chocolate," she said, pulling five mugs from the shelf and filling them with hot chocolate. She was mixing some vanilla into the whipped cream when Lucy, looking out at a pair of ravens eating from the dish, asked, "Why are the ravens here?"

"They've probably always been here," said Faye, eager to get to the more important questions.

"Only since three hundred, more close to three hundred fifty years, but before, maybe one hundred years before, they used to be many," said the baker, handing out the foaming mugs. "They come from Matthias Corvinus, the Raven King."

"Raven King?" asked Jasper, taking his mug gratefully after handing one to Faye and one to Lucy.

"He was a grand philosopher and lover of learning," said Signora Fornaio, "and he lives about 450 years ago. He had many books—you have some of these books in your house, I believe."

The children exchanged quick glances. Some of the books had belonged to royalty?

"He was known as the Raven King, and so, when some of his library was given to a nobleman in Napoli, family of his wife, they kept ravens at their palazzo."

"But then *le Due Metà del Male* killed birds and burned many of the books."

"Who?" Jasper was riveted.

"We say *the Two Halves of Evil*—a force you must not consider, because it is so terrible." Signora Fornaio pulled beads from her pocket and kissed them, mumbling a silent prayer. "But not even fifty years later, when the village of Solemano came to be known and the fortress built around it, they bring, too, the tradition of ravens."

"Do the ravens protect the village from evil?" asked Lucy. "The two halves of evil?"

"It is said that the black birds, *i corvi*, are the guardians," the baker said, walking to the window. She opened it and tossed out pieces of brioche to a waiting bird. "Ah, *bella*, my little *corvino* is truly my guardian, yes?" The bird chattered back as if to answer.

"Why did the library come here?" asked Wallace. If there was a raven king somewhere, why keep the library in this tiny village?

"It was a gift to the village of Solemano," said the baker, smiling.

Faye considered this. The village of Solemano made a home for the books of the ancient scholar king. And along with them came the big black birds and the strange black men. She shuffled forward, toward the baker. "So do the men in black keep books, too? In their rooms, perhaps?"

"In their rooms?" the baker asked.

"Where are their rooms anyway?" Faye asked, trying to sound

uninterested. "Do they live in the village?" She gestured to show she meant in the village proper, not outside near the fields.

"*I fratelli in nero* live in the big farmhouse at the edge of the vineyards," said Signora Fornaio, "and some have their rooms in the houses at the gates."

"The stone houses at the entrance to the village?" asked Faye.

"Si, bella. Why do you ask?" The baker, smiling, picked up the icing sugar to sprinkle on the fragrant brioche while they were still warm from the oven.

"Just wondering," Faye said, her voice slightly higher-pitched than usual.

⸺⸺

"There is no way we just can hunt through the farmhouses," said Faye as they hurried down the main road through Solemano. "They can probably see down to the vineyards from the olive grove, anyway, and the house is right there at the edge of the fields. We can't risk it."

"Well, perhaps someone can look elsewhere," said Wallace.

"We'll go to the houses at the gate to the village." Faye was clear about this.

Lucy ran to keep up with the others. In fact, Noah and Wallace were struggling to keep up with Faye's long legs and Jasper's fast gait.

"Are there two houses?" Wallace asked, trying to catch his breath.

Faye kept her eyes on the houses along the wall of the town. She came to the arched gate.

"Yes, of course. Don't you remember seeing them when we ar-

rived? I saw them." She pointed to the two houses on either side of
the arch, the ones Jasper had noticed that first day.

"Are we sure anyone lives in them?" asked Jasper. The one on
the left looked like it was missing some of its roof.

"Of course I'm sure," said Faye. "Guarding is what they do, and
these are guard houses."

"Well, that's good to know," said Noah. "They have houses on
either side of the entrance. That makes me feel safer."

"Really?" asked Faye, one eyebrow raised. "I'd say it's not too
safe right now, with no one home. Better for us, though." Not waiting for a reply from Noah, she went right up to the front door. It
was not locked.

Jasper was hesitant. "Faye, I'm not sure we should just rum-
mage through their—"

"Their *what*? They don't care about taking our things." Faye
was more pleading than angry. "They don't care about stealing
our possessions if it suits them, and I just want to see if they can
offer us any clues. I don't want to steal anything. Unless we find
something of ours—and then it's not stealing."

"I suppose they don't usually worry about people stealing
from them," said Jasper, relenting. "Everyone in the village knows
them and wouldn't steal."

Faye pushed the door open. But the room was empty—no furniture, nothing at all.

"It doesn't look like anyone lives here," said Wallace, relieved.
Being there made him anxious.

"And it doesn't look like there's anything here to steal," said
Noah, looking in the room. "You're out of luck, Lady Faye."

"What?" came a thundering voice from above.

There, at the top of the stone steps leading up to the top of the wall, stood the man in the Robin Hood hat.

"What?" he asked again.

"What?" gulped Faye. "We were just walking in town, and—" But Robin Hood turned away, facing out over the wall.

"Well, clearly, they don't keep the place unguarded," Noah whispered loudly.

The children casually walked back out.

"Let's try the other one," said Faye, heading to the other stone house.

Noah rolled his eyes and followed.

"Hello?" called Faye in a quiet voice as she stood by the door. If someone was asleep or busy, the children might still have a chance to search without waking them. But if someone was there and awake, she didn't want to appear to be breaking in. No one answered, so they silently entered the second house.

The room was fairly bare, though not empty. There were no elegant carpets or drapes or chairs or tables. The room was furnished with seven beds. Each bed had a small wooden table beside it, little more than a box, and a candleholder with a single candle. There was a small gray rug at the side of each bed. A basket of bread and a flask sat by the door.

On the tall walls, there were two paintings and several old tapestries. On one wall, there was a large flag, like the black and white one on the ship. But this flag looked very old, its edges frayed and worn.

The paintings, too, seemed very old. One was of a man with a crown of olive leaves, long blond hair, and a fur-trimmed robe. On one arm sat a raven, and next to his chair were books, piled high atop a table. In the raven's mouth, there was a coin. At the bottom of the painting was writing too faded with time to read. But they could read "MCDLXXVII," written in fancy script. The children knew this meant 1477.

The other painting was of a man in a giant turban. He, too, was fair-haired. Unlike the other man, who was clean-shaven, this man had a reddish moustache and trim beard. There was an olive tree in the background, and seven ravens sat upon the branches, each with a book in its mouth. They stood very stiff and tall, unlike the other bird in the other painting, who seemed almost alive. At the bottom of the canvas was something written in beautiful script in another alphabet. It, too had a date: "MDXXXII," or 1532.

"Who are they?" asked Lucy.

Wallace walked over to the painting of the man with the raven. "That must be the Raven King," he said. "It says 'Matthias Corvinus Rex' on the frame. 'Rex' meaning king, of course." Wallace moved closer and stared up. He took his coin from his pocket.

"What are you doing, Wallace?" Faye groaned. "We don't have much time."

"It's my coin," he said. "Or like my coin. Look." He pointed to the coin that, in the painting, was in the mouth of the raven.

"Why would that be your coin?" asked Faye, doubtful. "What would this raven have to do with your lucky coin?" But she couldn't deny that, from what they could see of the coin, it was very like Wallace's, if not exactly the same.

Wallace looked down at his coin. Faye did, too.

"I don't understand." Wallace turned the coin in his hand.

"And the birdies—the black birdies are in the paintings, too," Lucy said, pointing to the bird with the coin in its mouth. "Everyone in the painting has the same dresses, but in his own way, and no bonnets."

"What?" Noah looked at Lucy.

Faye, however, looked up from the coin with a new understanding, "You know, Lucy, I think you're right. Those birds of yours seem to be guardians—very familiar guardians."

"They are!" cried Lucy, who then giggled. "They are! They're the men in black, only smaller and with wings."

"Exactly," said Faye. "I think there is a connection between the mysterious men in black and the birds. It's as if the birds are an artist's impression of the men, or something like that."

"What about Wallace's coin?" asked Jasper, who had been considering all of this in quiet confusion.

"The coin is a key to something," Faye said. "And it must have been for ages and ages, too. This painting wasn't done yesterday."

"Well, we can't wait until tomorrow," said Noah. "Let's get on with it and get out of here."

They all got to searching. They looked under beds and behind the tapestries. The tapestries had interesting images of monks in gardens and farms. There were animals and scenes from country life. Some of the colors, mostly reds and oranges, were a bit faded, but the pictures were sharp, intricately sewn, and beautiful. But there seemed to be no personal items—nothing to reveal anything about the men living there.

"Look here!" called Noah. He had found a doorway hidden behind a tapestry.

He slipped through it and the others quickly followed.

"Wait, it's dark!" cried Lucy.

"She's right." Wallace tried to straighten his glasses in the dark—someone's elbow had knocked them askew.

But before anyone else could complain, they came to another tapestry and walked out into light. They were in a small room that had high windows catching the fullness of the sun. There were hooks, upon which hung, in three neat rows, twenty-one black cloaks. There was a small table with a lamp upon it. Faye walked over and pulled open the drawer. In it were several large, ancient keys. There was a box as well—a small wooden box. Faye opened it, but it was empty.

"Maybe it held another key," said Wallace.

"Maybe it was the key to everything," Noah said.

"You think it was?" asked Lucy, her eyes wide with wonder.

"No," said Jasper. "He's only teasing, Lucy. We've come to the men in black's dressing room. That's all."

"Their mysterious dressing room?" Noah asked.

"Very well. Their mysterious dressing room." Jasper shook his head.

"Well, there must be something here," said Faye, looking through pockets and feeling inside sleeves.

"There is," Jasper said. "Their flags, their farm, and their robes—look at this place." Jasper gestured around the room. "And the ceremony on the ship. These men are in some kind of order."

"A mysterious order?" said Noah.

"They are part of some *mysterious* order," Jasper said.

"But what order?" asked Wallace, feeling his coin in his pocket. "What does it mean—this place, and the ravens, and my coin?"

"Do you think we might find some explanation in our books?" said Jasper. "We certainly have an excellent library. Signora Fornaio said it came from the Raven King. Will there be answers among those pages?"

"*That*," said Faye, "is something we are going to find out."

———————

After poring through volumes in the library, they could find many poems and references to the Raven King, but nothing helpful. They found one massive reference volume that had a painting of the Raven King on the cover. It was faded and scratched, but they thought there was a coin in his hand, though Lucy insisted it was a lemon sherbet. It didn't matter, though, since the book was in Old Hungarian, which no one—not even Lucy—could understand at all. Deciding the library was not going to help right then, they put the books back where they found them.

Back in the sitting room, Faye and Jasper discussed whether to be honest with Miss Brett.

"Do we tell her or not?" Noah whispered to Jasper and Faye as they headed over to the hearth. Miss Brett was sitting and having her tea, reading and looking out the window, enjoying the scent of the jasmine growing in the pots on the table sitting in the sunlight.

"I say we tell her," Jasper said firmly. He did not want to lie, nor did he see a reason to do so. He was glad when Faye nodded.

Miss Brett's reaction had been much as they expected. "Goodness," she said, and then was silent. What was she supposed to think? "Well, I'd have to say that it was not smart to go snooping around someone else's things. Would you like someone doing that to you?"

"No," said Faye, "but those men don't seem to be bothered by rummaging through *our* things. Or bothered about stealing from us—like the notes from our journal. Or shuttling us around. I *would* have felt bad, only they do it to us all the time."

Miss Brett sighed. It was true. The mysterious men in black did rule their lives, move them around, and take what they pleased from the children and from her. She had not forgotten her lost diary. Miss Brett softened her stance. "Very well. Did you find anything?" she said. "Did you learn something important?"

Faye told Miss Brett about the painting with the raven eating Wallace's coin.

Miss Brett sat and listened. When they finished telling her, she was silent, thinking deeply about all of this. In the silence, Noah, Faye, and Jasper exchanged looks of concern. Was she upset with them? Was she worried? Miss Brett seemed to be miles away. Then she turned to Jasper, Faye, and Noah and asked for them to go and sit with Wallace and Lucy, who had been warming by the fire. She needed time to think.

She breathed in deeply, looking over at the delicate jasmine growing safely inside when the cold outside would freeze the life out of the flowers. Safety, for them, was not so simple.

Who were these men? If they were some brotherhood, some order, did someone send them to watch over the children? She looked out at the village below. Solemano and Sole Manner Farm were both places of refuge, but who had been the one to decide where they would be taken? Clearly, something very ancient was at work. Something was happening that had its roots back in time. But when? And why? Miss Brett shook her head. These were not answers she could give, or even questions she could ask, because there was no one there to respond.

Looking beyond the fragrant flowers, she could see the clouds.

The day's weather had become increasingly nippy. In fact, it was more than nippy. It was cold. She looked at the orchard. Those mysterious men in black were lucky they had harvested the olives when they did.

She quietly wished the children had harvested more information.

And she wished she could give them something to ease their minds—or at least something to distract them.

CHAPTER TWENTY

Adventures in a Winter Wonderland

OR

A VERY COLD WAR INDEED

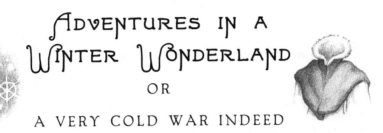

"Come, wake up!" shouted Lucy, running from room to room.

"I'm coming, Lucy!" cried Miss Brett. She sat up in bed, throwing off her covers. She practically stepped into her slippers as she ran from her room.

"Lucy!" cried Jasper, running down the hall. But Lucy was no longer there.

"Where is she?" called Faye, rushing out without a dressing gown.

Wallace and Noah sleepily emerged from their rooms.

"What is it, Lucy?" Miss Brett, now wide awake, feared danger. Was it an intruder? Could it be the horrid Komar Romak? She ran toward the little girl's voice.

"Look!" shouted Lucy from within the curtains of the wide window in the sitting room, her voice muffled by all that fabric.

Nearly stumbling down the stairs, Jasper hurried, followed by Miss Brett and the others.

He grabbed the edges with Noah and they pulled back the great curtains. Lucy squealed and grabbed Jasper's hand. Jaws dropped.

"Goodness!" cried Noah, with a gasp.

Wallace, too, gasped, and Faye stood silent, unable to speak.

This was not a fearful response to terror. It was a response to the incredible magic they saw before them. The whole of Solemano, which just the night before had been brown from the cold and the dead fallen leaves, was covered in a blanket of white.

"It means Christmas will be coming any day now!" Lucy twirled with pleasure.

"Christmas would be coming, whether it snowed or not, Lucy," Noah said, looking over to Faye, sure she would agree, as she was never in the mood for nonsense.

But Faye did not. She stood there as if in a trance, staring out into the deep whiteness.

"Faye?" Noah reached out to touch her arm but changed his mind. He shrugged and scratched his head, looking at Jasper. Then Noah began to mimic Lucy, jumping up and down and clapping his hands together.

But Jasper knew. He knew that, at that moment, Faye was feeling inside exactly what Lucy was feeling inside and out. He did touch her arm.

"It's the first time you've seen snow, isn't it?" Jasper asked.

Faye turned to Jasper. Her beautiful green eyes shined against the brightness from the snow outside. She had a smile of pure bliss, and looked, for once, like a little girl—a beautiful little girl.

"It's just…" she began, but then she stopped and turned back to look again.

"Lovely," Jasper said, looking from Faye to the winter wonderland.

"But it *is* lovely," Lucy said as Noah continued to tease her, "and it means there will be a real Christmas. When it's lovely and snowy, Father Christmas will be happier and want to come. How will he know where to find us if we don't leave footprints in the snow to track us?"

"What?" Noah laughed. "You are the funniest thing, Lucy."

"I am not," insisted Lucy.

"You did write to Father Christmas to let him know we were here, didn't you?" Noah asked. Lucy, worried, shook her head, and Noah looked stricken. "You had better do it quick, or he might not know where we've gone!"

Miss Brett put the kettle on, then came into the sitting room from the kitchens to watch the children. She warmed herself by the fire burning in the hearth as Lucy worked on her letter to Father Christmas. Noah was making suggestions.

"You can ask for a camel. Camels are very traditional."

"A baby camel?" Lucy asked, wide-eyed. "Oh, that would be lovely."

"Yes, indeed," said Noah. "And a flock of geese. And an elephant—a white baby elephant, like Faye's."

Jasper, meanwhile, wondered what was happening in this part of the world 350 years ago to explain the men in black whose chambers the children had explored. Three hundred and fifty years ago, Michelangelo had been around, and Leonardo da Vinci. And the Ottoman Empire was nearing its peak. Less than a half century before that, Copernicus had made the sun the center of the solar system. The plague had been in Europe for two hundred years. None of these things seemed directly related to the mysterious men in black. He looked over at Wallace, who was staring at his coin, turning it between his fingers. Clearly, Jasper wasn't the only one wondering how these pieces fit together.

"Goodness!" Miss Brett looked up from her book—she had found a book of Italian grammar and was determined to learn some Italian—as the smell of cinnamon began to waft into the room. She jumped out of her seat. "I've forgotten the kettle!" She ran into the kitchen in hopes the kettle hadn't burned.

"I know what she needs for Christmas," said Noah, slyly.

"Oh, please tell," whispered Lucy.

Noah grinned, tapping the side of his forehead.

"Noah is trying to knock something out of his tiny mind, Lucy," said Faye, braiding her hair as she stood by the fire. "Things often get stuck in there."

"All right, young inventors, I say breakfast before snowmen," Miss Brett said, coming back into the room.

"Did it burn?" asked Wallace, slipping his coin back into his pocket.

"No, I managed to get to the fire before all the water boiled away," Miss Brett said, coming in with a tray of tea things. She set the tray on the table by the wide sitting room window so they could look out at the snow while indulging in the sticky cinnamon buns and almond biscotti.

"Look, the sun is making everything sparkle," said Lucy, pointing at the tiny crystals of snow, dazzling in the sky.

Faye stopped mid-step, her eyes reflecting the dancing light. Jasper led her by her elbow to the table and, to keep her from falling, moved a chair to catch her as she sat without taking her eyes off the snow.

Wallace let the others sit down before him. He took Miss Brett by the sleeve.

"Um, Miss Brett," he said in his quiet voice. Something was wrong.

"Yes, sweet angel, what is it?"

"I . . . I'm not very good in the snow," he said. "I get cold, and my glasses get foggy, and . . . I . . ."

"Well, you're from New York," Miss Brett said. "You're one of our snow experts."

Wallace fidgeted with his glasses. "Yes, I certainly have been around it. I'm sure my father would be happier if I was better around it. It's just that I get cold, and—"

"You'll be fine." Miss Brett smiled, patting him on the back gently. "We will make sure you have extra woolens and the warmest socks. And you'll come right in the minute you want. It's not something to worry about. It's quite lovely, and fresh air will be good for you. Just see how you feel once you're outside."

Wallace nodded and, quietly, sat at the table with the others.

While Noah stuffed his face, Faye sat there, stirring her tea, staring out the window. Jasper finally took the spoon from her and put her hand on the cup. Faye took a sip, never removing her eyes from the view.

Jasper looked at her and smiled. It was so lovely to see the Faye she kept hidden under all her prickly layers. Jasper didn't want to say anything that might cause a retreat. She was, at that moment, finally escaping the ominous and ever-present darkness that followed them. He turned away, in case she discovered him staring.

"I do believe we have found something to silence Lady Faye," said Noah.

And the moment was lost. Jasper had to admit that, sometimes, Faye was right—Noah could be a complete fool.

"Leave her be, Noah," Jasper said softly.

"Are you coming to her defense? Are you her knight in shining armor? Is that what you wish yourself to be?" Noah didn't mean this to be cruel, but it stung Faye out of her trance, and it stung Jasper, too, because it was true.

"I don't need a knight in shining armor, Noah," Faye hissed. "I don't need you or Jasper." Faye turned back to the snow, but the moment was truly gone. She knew, too, that she had said something she did not mean. She turned to Jasper to say she was sorry, but he had gone. She turned back to scold Noah, but he, too, had gone.

"He doesn't mean it," Miss Brett said, her hand on Faye's shoulder. "It's just his way."

Faye forced herself to nod in acceptance. "Just his way"? She thought about that as she went to fetch her warm clothes. Who did Miss Brett mean? Could it be Noah, annoying and pestering as a way to cope with whatever made him sad or nervous? Or Jasper? Could she have meant Jasper's way, reaching out to her because he cared? Faye didn't want to ask, so she decided to pick between them. She silently made a choice and somehow felt flushed when she did.

———

Dressed in their warmest clothes—Wallace was wearing double layers—the children spent the morning romping around. They built snowmen, snow angels, and snow ravens. Jasper and Noah threw snowballs at one another. Wallace managed to hide behind a large drift and avoid the entire snowball duel.

Faye was blissfully happy at this incredible new experience. Snow was amazing. She touched it and rolled in it. She followed Lucy's lead, sticking out her tongue and catching flakes. She completely ignored the ruckus the boys were making.

It was the snowball Noah threw at Faye that brought Faye out of her serenity.

"You blasted idiot! You did that on purpose, hitting me in the face." Faye, snow down her back and inside her coat, was wet, cold, disheveled, and quite furious when they came in for lunch.

"Of course I did," said Noah, shaking off the piles of snow that had fallen down his own collar. "I thought you liked the snow. I wanted to help you get better acquainted with it. Hey!" Noah leaned back, nearly falling off his seat as Faye stood up, shooting daggers with her eyes. "See, that's the problem, Faye. You don't know how to make nice."

Faye was turning scarlet. She knew she should let it go, that Noah was being silly, and that, like earlier, it was just his way, but that last comment had hit her where it hurt most. She was not very good at being a friend, and she hated being bad at anything.

"You ruin everything!" she cried at Noah. In a rage, she pulled her arm back, but Miss Brett caught it before it made contact with Noah's face. But it was as if the slap really had hit him. His face fell when he saw the expression on Faye's. While he was able to hitch his smile back on, inside he felt bad. He hadn't meant any real harm. Faye, on the other hand, had.

"All right, you two," Miss Brett said. She had put down the tea tray and, holding Faye's arm, gave them both a warning look. "No more of this nonsense. Noah, learn how to tame your tongue. Faye, you know that Noah has a problem teaching his tongue to stop wag-ging. Both of you, be aware of yourselves. You are not alone."

Faye gulped. "Yes, Miss Brett."

"Well," Noah said, arms akimbo, "I do need to housebreak that part of me."

"Too true," said Jasper with a friendly pat on Noah's back and a nod to Faye.

"Very good," said Miss Brett as she served hot, thick soup and fresh bread. They had bowls of olive oil, sprinkled with coarse salt, to dip the bread in, as well as fresh butter and tapenade. "And hon-estly, I think it's pretty funny that five brilliant young inventors are throwing snowballs. I am sure, Faye, that you could invent some-thing to throw them far more effectively."

"Far more effectively than Noah, certainly," Faye said, glowering.

"I meant more effectively than having a war like this," said Miss Brett.

"Oh, we shall have a war," Faye said.

"Oh, yes, let's do it!" cried Lucy, throwing a bit of bread into the air. Noah caught it in his mouth and nodded emphatically.

Miss Brett was glad to keep the children inside for the rest of the day. While tempers were heating up, the temperature outside was dropping. Wallace was suddenly much more interested in snowballs than he had been earlier. The afternoon and evening, up to dinnertime, was spent deep in invention, Faye and Lucy on one side and the boys on the other. After Noah casually sauntered over to ask for a spanner, and Faye threatened to hit him with one, the girls took a panel screen used for arc-welding and raised it as a room divider. These were enemies at war, with secret weapons in the making.

"It's got to be able to throw some whoppers," Noah said quietly, as he and Wallace pored over sketches. The three boys had devised a rotating arm, using one of the giant soup ladles from the kitchens. Using a second gear that Jasper rigged, Noah was able to pull back the arm and wind a rubber band tight enough to throw a snowball with extreme force.

Faye had used the remaining soup ladles for their device. She had five, attached with wire to a central gear.

"But where do we get all the snowballs?" asked Lucy.

"That's it!" Faye jumped up and kissed Lucy on the head. "If we add a trowel or some other sort of small shovel in-between the ladles, we can make snowballs that continually drop into the flinging arms, and we won't have to worry about making enough! It will make its own supply."

And so they worked, after supper and well into the night, until Miss Brett demanded that they head off to bed.

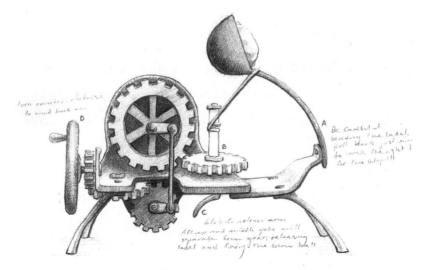

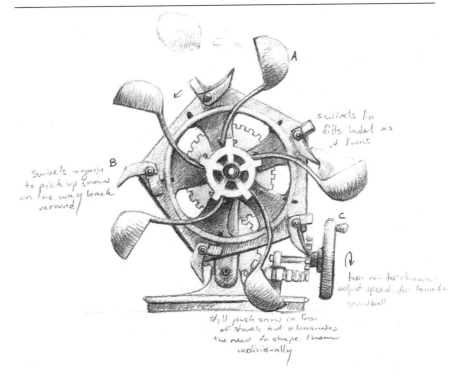

After breakfast, carrying their weapons well-concealed under old blankets they found in the pantry, the children set out onto the terrace and down to the gardens.

Noah and Jasper headed for the mound on the south side of the garden.

"Come along, Wallace!" Noah called. Wallace was coming down behind the girls.

They had agreed that they would use the lower terrace to avoid breaking a window if an errant snowball was blown off-course. It was not the easiest walk down. The girls took the north side and found the biggest bank of snow.

But before they could begin, on the road, Faye spotted the little shepherd using his crook to help him along the snowy path that the horses had carved into the road. Three ravens circled overhead. At that moment, they looked like vultures to Faye. They were horrid, bothering him like that, crying and cackling. Faye called out to greet him, and the man raised a shaky crook.

"The poor little man," Lucy said, her voice muffled, since she'd slid her chin under her muffler to keep it warmer.

"Sir!" Faye called. The shepherd turned and waved again. "Wait!" Faye rolled up the blanket that covered the girls' snowball machine. Getting as close as she could to the snow-covered wall, she tossed the blanket over to him. He reached up, the birds scattered, and the blanket hit the little man square in the face and knocked him onto his rear end. Faye was startled and stood frozen, but the little man quickly laughed, brushed himself off, and, with no small effort, managed to get himself to his feet.

"Grazie!" he called, and bent to pick up the blanket. The birds swooped and cackled again.

As Faye stood distracted, Noah made a snowball and hurled it at her. But Faye, oblivious, bent down to pick up her machine, and the snowball sailed over her head and into Wallace's face as he moved slowly down the path behind Faye. He fell down on his bottom, startled.

The shepherd burst into laughter, clapping his hands. Then, still laughing, he bent over and, with two cloth-covered hands, formed a snowball. In the spirit of the moment, he threw it, but his frail, shaky arm did not offer a good launch, and the snowball simply rolled off his fingers and landed on his foot. He laughed all the harder.

He blew kisses at the children and, still giggling to himself, wrapped the blanket Faye gave him around his shoulders and tottered down the hill toward the village.

But Faye looked not at the shepherd, but over at Noah, who was busy setting up their machine. No, this would not do. "He's going to have to sweat a little," Faye muttered to herself. "Even in the snow, I'll get him to sweat."

Then, Faye said to Lucy, "No, this isn't the right spot," loud enough for the boys to hear. Wallace had finally made it over to Jasper and Noah, and all three boys watched as Faye picked up the machine and trudged to the east side by the steps, Lucy waddling behind her. The boys had no choice, since they were now aiming at nothing and were completely vulnerable to Faye's attack. Grumbling, they pulled up their machine and moved over to the west side.

"Not enough room," Faye said, pretending to be quite serious. The girls moved again, and the boys followed suit.

After three more changes of position, Noah fell to his knees, and Wallace decided he might be dressed too warmly. He considered just sitting down until Faye had settled on a single spot.

"Come on, Lady Faye," grumbled Noah. "Just pick your position and get on with it."

"It's a woman's prerogative to change her mind," said Faye in a sing-song voice. She was happy to be wearing Noah down. More important, *she* finally had the chance to annoy *him*.

At last, when the ache in her arms was greater than the pleasure she got from taunting Noah, Faye settled behind the very first mound—always her intention—and winked at Lucy. They dug a space where the machine could sit, but still rotate easily and pick up the snow as it turned.

"Comrades," Noah said to the boys, "it is clear that negotiations have failed. It is time for war."

And so the battle began.

WHAM! Faye had ducked just in time. There was no question

that the boys' invention could throw harder and farther. *WHUMP!* Faye was knocked clear off her feet by one that caught her in the shoulder.

But the machine Faye and Lucy built was relentless. For every one super-snowball coming from the boys' machine, the girls' invention could throw ten regular ones, which it did until the boys were nearly buried in snow. With a *RATT-A-TATT*, Wallace was walloped and fell on his behind.

The boys were running out of soft snow within reach. "Man the machine, Wallace!" cried Noah. "I'll get more snow."

"Me?" Wallace, fallen, was sitting right behind the machine.

"Just imagine their machine is Komar Romak's head," whispered Noah.

KAHBLAM! Noah, too, was knocked over. Jasper, meanwhile, had an armload of snow he delivered to Wallace before he was pelted from behind. Even through the mufflers covering his ears, he could hear the cheers of his sister. It stung more than the snow down his neck.

With a crash, a shot from the girls broke off the lever that launched the boys' catapult.

"We did it!" cried Lucy.

Faye was jumping up and down.

Wallace smiled, now determined to go down fighting. He pulled the rubber band that was now hooked around one of the ladles and launched a snowball by hand. The result was a stray snowball that landed a few feet from Noah. It didn't matter. Quickly, he refilled the ladle, and then again.

"Get 'em, Wallace!" cried Noah, rolling in the snow and laughing.

"Hooray for Wallace!" Jasper cheered, laughing too.

Wallace adjusted his foggy glasses, took aim, and fired again and again. He only stopped when, with one last load, a missile hit the girls' speed machine and knocked it over.

Lucy continued to jump up and down—or, rather, she waved her arms up and down, since she was unable to move much at all. "We won!" she cried. "We won! We beat those silly boys!"

"Lucy!" cried Jasper in mock indignation, though it did bite to hear his sister include him among the "silly boys."

"Oh, not you, Jasper," she said.

"Me?" Wallace asked.

"Not you, Wallace, either." Lucy felt sorry she had said it.

"Oh, so you mean me?" Noah demanded, making a ridiculous salute in which he pretended to poke himself in the eye.

"Yes, oh, yes, Noah, you are the silliest of boys," said Lucy.

"I believe *we* won," declared Noah, now so covered in snow he had something of a white beard.

"Never!" said Faye. "You were all down by the time you knocked us over!"

"But we did knock you over," said Noah, slipping and falling.

Even Faye laughed, knowing the girls had beaten him, no matter what the boys said. Even so, Faye suddenly felt a certain warmth toward Noah, especially when he got up and immediately fell back into a snow bank.

Jasper reached out a hand to help his comrade back to his feet. Noah teetered and looked as if someone had put his legs on backwards. He walked up to Faye and made a sad face, then raised his eyebrows.

"You are the silliest boy, Noah," Faye said, with nothing but laughter in her voice.

"Truce?" he offered.

Faye smiled. "Truce." And then he tried to lick her nose.

Faye's hand went out. "Don't push it," she warned with a growl. Noah, his tongue shooting back between his frozen lips, winked. He then crossed his eyes and fell back into the snow. Faye laughed again.

With that, Noah rolled over and stood up, groaning.

"Well, I can just be thankful that your snowball machine doesn't shoot anything but snowballs," he said, slipping as he barely managed to stand. Faye considered what Noah said. It shot snowballs, but that was not the only thing it *could* shoot.

Noah lumbered over to Lucy and picked up the little girl, who squealed with delight. "Me hungry," he grumbled like a hungry giant. Then, upon reflection, he realized he *was* hungry, and he carried her all the way to the house, grunting and groaning and saying things like "bones of an English maid" and "delicious fingers and toes" and "very nice on toast." Wallace and Faye followed close behind.

Jasper looked out at the beast garden. With the leaves all gone, winter gave the impression of having cleared away some of the bramble, he thought. Maybe this was the time to see if the magician's story was true. They would have to be careful and cunning, but it would be fun to try. Unless the mysterious men in black were hiding something else, what trouble could there possibly be?

CHAPTER TWENTY-ONE

THE MAGICIAN'S SECRET

OR

WHAT THE BEASTS WERE HIDING

Jasper had been thinking about it all night. How could they figure out the beast garden's "blind spot," as he thought of it? The others, too, seemed interested in the idea. After a late breakfast the next morning, the children went about hunting down all the string and twine they could find in the house.

"What are you children up to?" Miss Brett asked.

"Just an experiment," said Jasper, for it was, after all.

"What kind of experiment, Jasper?" asked Miss Brett.

"No hydrochloric acid, Miss Brett," he said. "It's more of a geometry project."

"And perhaps an experiment in physics," said Wallace.

"Very well, sweet angels," she said. "Be wise, though, won't you?"

Yes, they'd be wise. But they hadn't yet been wise enough to figure out what was going on around them. It was exhausting to live every day in the depths of a mystery they did not even begin to understand. The mystery of the beast garden was another story. That, at the very least, had a specific question: How can one find the place in the garden where none of the eyes of the beasts are upon you?

Jasper wasn't sure he believed the part about the disappear-

ance. He figured it was something simple. In a place in the garden
where no beasts looked at you, out of any line of vision, you simply disappeared to the beasts. And figuring out where was in the
children's power. It made sense. It was science. Whatever they discovered, at least it could be a good distraction. Jasper wanted to set
aside fears of Komar Romak and missing parents and focus on solv-
ing another mystery. It was a puzzle, and Jasper was good at puzzles.

Somewhere, deep down inside, perhaps he believed that, if they
could solve the secret of the beast garden, maybe they could find
the answers to their own mysteries.

Discovery of the single disappearing spot in the beast garden would depend on their excellent sense of geometry. Miss Brett
heard words and phrases like "x axis" and "y axis," "vector" and
"graphing," and knew vaguely what they meant in terms of mathematics, but how they were going about the whole experiment
seemed remarkable to her. Then again, everything they did was
remarkable—almost.

"Noah," said Miss Brett, "would you please refrain from balancing that gherkin on your forehead?"

Once they were dressed, in much less outerwear than the day
before—it had warmed substantially since then—the children
carried their string and twine out through the garden and down
to the third terrace. Jasper and Noah carried the small ladder they
had found in the cupboard under the stairs. They decided it might
come in handy. It was just after nine o'clock, and the sun cast shadows to the west. In the beast garden, against the fallen snow, those
shadows were very creepy indeed. It was as if they were hiding
something—something they might not want to share.

Getting down to business was not as easy as Jasper thought.

There were still vines and bramble to contend with under the fallen snow. They were able to remove some of the bramble and pull it to the side of the garden. They pulled back vines using the short ladder. Once they got done, they could really see all the statues, and the paths around them all were clear.

Finding the x and y axis between two beasts was not conclusive, since it did not always allow for a second set of points beyond where one could see a third or more beast, also looking in the same direction. And then there was the z-axis, since the beasts were not all the same size and the young inventors were working in three dimensions, not two. There always seemed to be pairs of eyes upon you.

"I'd say we really are addressing physics as much as geometry, Jasper," Wallace said as he tied a string to the nose of an alligator balanced on its tail. He took the string and, his eyes staring back at a hyena on its haunches, made a loop around the hyena's baton. Wallace then walked slowly along the line, watching the eyes of the beasts as he went. A raven with a monocle was in the way, so Jasper included him along the trajectory. He then looked around and found that he was still in the line of vision of not only a hippopotamus and a winged horse, but also a monkey in a feathered cap—and then, once again, another raven.

"This is impossible," moaned Faye, trying to untangle her string from Noah's. They had run into one another between a warthog and a baboon with a pair of angel wings.

Jasper climbed up to the terrace above. From there he could see the garden as a graph, the creatures' faces offering a starting point for the vectors. *Yes,* he thought, *I can see the intersection of lines and where . . . yes, where it is possible . . .* "Everyone!" The others looked up.

"I think we…Lucy!"

"You are Mr. Twinkle Toes, and you are Chubbily Boo," said his sister, running through the garden giving names to the animals. "You are Flinty and you are Jingly Mittens and—"

"Lucy!" called Jasper. "I need you."

"Yes, Jasper?" Lucy turned. "I'm naming my new friends."

Jasper closed one eye and measured with his thumb. "The others have their strings to tend, so I need you to listen, Luce. I need you to stand over by the dragon." He pointed down.

"By Twinkle or Mr. Squilly Wings?" There were two dragons, after all.

"I don't know the names you've given them." Jasper didn't mean to sound cross. "The one over by the hedgehog, beyond the raven with the balancing scales."

"Mr. Squilly Wings," said Lucy.

"Never mind, Lucy, I'll get Wallace or—"

"I want to do it, Jasper! I can do it, I can!" cried Lucy. She hurried through the more deeply packed snow to stand next to the taller of the two dragons.

Wallace, Faye, and Noah, finished with their measurements and string-checking, climbed up to stand next to Jasper, who eyed and measured.

"Very well. Right. Now come toward the elephant—no, away from the hedgehog. Stop! Now step back towards the griffin. Stop! No, you've gone too far."

"You're not being very nice, Jasper!" Lucy whined, taking baby steps away from the griffin. She waved at the griffin who, in turn, looked as if he were waving back. "Goodbye, Mr. Kingsley," she said, waving still. "Goodbye."

And then, quite suddenly, she disappeared.

———⟩•⟨———

"Lucy!" cried Jasper, trying to move fast through the thick white mounds. The upper garden was still high with snow.

"Lucy!" Faye called.

And the lot of them clambered down and ran to the spot where Lucy had been. She simply was not there.

Jasper was silent. Panic filled his lungs and he could not breathe. He thought of the artist, the magician, and how he, too, had disappeared, never to be seen again. Sick to his stomach, Jasper began searching frantically. "Lucy!" he cried. The birds above them seemed to echo his cries.

From the house, Miss Brett had been watching the children. The maze of string looked like a complicated mathematical problem on a white sheet of paper the size of a garden. She'd watched Jasper calling down to his sister—and she'd watched, in horror, as, in a blink, Lucy simply disappeared. The teacher had grabbed her cloak as she ran out the garden door, still wearing only her slippers on her feet. She could hear the cries of the children as they searched.

"Lucy!" Miss Brett added her voice to the cacophony. By then, the children were all in utter panic. Wallace was unable to speak, and kept taking off his glasses and wiping them with his gloves. Faye was shouting for Lucy and fighting back tears. Noah, too, cried out, his voice cracking from fear and cold.

Jasper, however, felt the heavy weight of grief upon his shoulders. He had been cross and demanding. Now Lucy was gone, and not a trace of her could be found.

Jasper wiped his face as a few tears raced down his cold cheek. "Wait. Quiet," he said. "We're making too much noise."

"Jasper's right," said Faye, who, too, wiped the tears from her stinging cheeks. "We couldn't possibly hear Lucy if she was calling back."

Jasper raised a finger and shouted, "Lucy!" Then, silence—no one made a sound. Only the cry of the ravens overhead could be heard. Jasper fought back hot tears again. "Lucy!" he cried. Then the birds, too, stopped chattering.

Silence.

Jasper's shoulders began to quake. Great guttering tears streamed down his face. He muttered, "I should have put a rope around her waist . . . I . . . I should have had someone hold her, or . . ." But he couldn't finish.

"Jasper, you've done nothing wrong." Faye came to him, her hand on his back. "We'll find her. She's here. Somewhere."

"Don't blame yourself for this," Noah said. "None of us could imagine she would have disappeared into . . ." What? Another world?

"Children." Miss Brett forced calm into her voice. "We will continue to look. We can't find her if we sit here."

Jasper nodded and, again, called his sister's name. He walked around the garden calling her name, and everyone listened silently.

Nothing.

"What if we repeat what we did?" said Faye. "What if I stand where Lucy was and we try to reenact the whole thing?"

"We've looked. She's not there," Noah said, dryly.

"Then we can find her—"

"Or lose you, too," Noah said.

"It's worth a try!" said Faye. "At least I'd be with Lucy so she isn't alone." Her voice caught in her throat.

Determined, Faye took the end of the twine. She grabbed it and tied it around her waist. Then she unrolled it a few feet and handed it to Noah. "Jasper, go back up there and give me the exact information you gave Lucy."

"Are you sure you want to do this?" Jasper asked, hoarse from calling his sister's name.

Faye looked directly into Jasper's eyes. She leaned closer to him. "Yes, Jasper, I'm sure."

Jasper nodded and squeezed Faye's hand. Would this be the last time he ever saw her? Would she, too, disappear forever, like the magician? Like Lucy?

Trying not to think about such things, Jasper climbed back up onto the terrace wall. Noah held the end of the twine. Wallace and Miss Brett stood in the garden to be near Faye, just in case.

"Ready," said Faye. She looked up at Jasper.

Jasper nodded. He closed one eye and measured in his head.

"You need to be about three paces closer to the hedgehog. Now a bit to the right. Now back, toward the griffin. Closer. It's right about there."

"Here?" Faye asked, standing still, her eyes closed.

Nothing happened.

"I suppose it's not that far to the left," Jasper said. Was it? Was that the right spot?

Everyone looked up at Jasper.

"Maybe you need to—" But Jasper's words were whipped from his lips as Faye, who had started taking tiny steps around that area, simply disappeared.

Noah grabbed for the twine, but it snapped with a tug. "No!" he cried.

Miss Brett cried out, too. She stood in shock, her arms reaching out to nothing. Faye was gone.

Jasper jumped off the wall and ran down to the others. *No*, he thought. *No, no, no, no!* Jasper had lost Faye, too.

"Wait!" cried Noah, who still clung to the broken twine. "Look!"

Jasper followed Noah's finger as he pointed to the base of the griffin statue. There was a small dusting of stone, smaller than sand, around the base. It was as if stone had been ground against stone. From a tiny crevice in the stone, through no visible crack, came the torn end of the twine.

"But that's impossible," Wallace said in almost a whisper. The stone looked solid, as if it had not moved in three hundred years. Yet, out from the corner came the twine and something had rubbed against the stone to make the dust.

Jasper reached for it as if it were a lifeline. He ran his fingers over the edge of the stone. Then he called, "Lucy! Faye! Shout as loud as you can!" And he listened. Nothing. Then he cupped his hands against the stone and shouted the same thing into it. He put his ear to the stone and listened.

Tears once again came to his eyes, but they were blessed tears of relief. A very faint sound came from the rock—the sound of the two girls calling out from wherever they were. "If you can grab a rock or something, bang it against the stone wall! Or ceiling!" Jasper didn't know where they were trapped, below or above—though the pedestal couldn't really hold them both. They had to be underground.

In a few seconds, everyone could hear it: the distinct sound of stone hitting stone.

There were great cheers from the beast garden. Jasper still clung to the twine. He called into the stone again. "Are you both okay? Hit the stone once for yes, twice for no."

There was a sharp clack. A single clack.

"Are you in another world?" asked Noah.

"Are you underground?" asked Wallace. "I mean, did you fall very far?"

Two clacks.

"Can you see anything? Is it dark?" Miss Brett looked at Jasper, who looked back so hopefully that she felt a speck of relief herself.

One clack. Jasper thought for a moment. "Is it a small space? Or a tunnel? Sorry, is it a small space?"

One clack. Then two. Then one.

"I don't think they know," Miss Brett said, wisely. "If it's dark, they might not be able to tell."

"Are you hurt?" Jasper asked.

"They said they were okay, Jasper," Miss Brett said kindly.

Two clacks reassured Jasper. He wanted to ask again, but knew that stemmed only from his fear and relief wrapped up together. Jasper stood and looked at the pedestal. He had not let go of the end of the twine. He stomped his feet around the ground there.

"You're tempting fate, my man," warned Noah, grabbing Jasper's hand.

But somehow, they had to trigger whatever it was that had opened to swallow up the girls. It had been so fast, opening only long enough to pull the girls in. Yes, that was it—it had opened so fast.

"I think I know what we can do," Jasper said. He explained his plan. He then kneeled back down and spoke into the pedestal. "We are going to get you out. Stay still and move away from … whatever it is you came in through—the door or the gate or the opening."

One clack.

With lightning speed, Jasper grabbed Noah, and the two ran up to the house. They took a tall ladder from the storage room and carried it back to the beast garden. Under Jasper's arm was an electric torch.

"Now, the position of the twine suggests that whatever opened did so from the northwest corner, and from this direction." Jasper pointed to where the opening must have occurred and showed everyone the twine. They all agreed.

Turning the ladder on its side, the boys positioned it against the bottom of the pedestal. Using a brass-topped wrought-iron pole in the frozen hedge as a fulcrum, they balanced the ladder so that it teetered.

From there, Jasper was able to get the ladder to hit the ground anywhere. He could pull it back and forth and move it from left to right. Out of harm's way, Noah stood on one side of the ladder and Miss Brett and Wallace on the other side, Jasper at the end. They all held tight. Jasper began beating the ground with the ladder, simulating the stomping of feet or the baby steps taken by both Faye and Lucy. Tap, tap, tap—but no luck.

"We need more weight," Jasper said.

Noah grabbed a fair-sized chunk of the stone wall that had crumbled a century ago. With a great heave, he perched it on the end of the ladder. This made the tapping much more difficult, but Jasper was so determined he hardly noticed the enormous weight.

Tap, tap—Jasper tapped the ladder around and around the area, everyone ready to shove the ladder in if they found the magic spot.

And then it happened. They found it. The spot that was the trigger. The disappearing spot. Jasper pushed, and the bottom stone of the pedestal gave way.

"Push!" cried Jasper, and they shoved the ladder without even thinking about what they were doing or where the opening had occurred.

"We did it!" cried Noah. Other world? Bah. Centuries of fairytales put to rest with some good string and good physics. And a strong ladder, clearly. Science was the magic of the age.

The ladder, much taller than any human, had wedged itself into the opening so the mechanism could not shut. They rushed over to see what the mystery of the beast garden really was. And yet, standing there, they still weren't exactly sure. It was a doorway and, somehow, the weight upon a single spot on the ground triggered the mechanism. The ground somehow tilted down, and the pedestal, more than a foot thick, tilted in, explaining how the twine got stuck in the stone. But the doorway seemed ancient—older than the beast statues. Did that mean it was here before the artist?

"Lucy! Faye!" cried Jasper.

"We're here," came a voice from the darkness.

"Yes, we are somewhere!" cried a smaller voice.

"The opening isn't wide enough," Jasper said, groaning as he tried to wedge his shoulder through the crack. Pulling out, he grabbed a chunk of stone. Together, with the others, they managed to wedge three large stones between the ladder and the pedestal so that the mouth of the opening was large enough to climb in or, for that matter, climb out.

"Quick, the electric torch!" said Jasper, easing the ladder down what was clearly a chute of stone.

Miss Brett flicked the switch on the torch and handed it to Jasper. Taking cautious steps down the rungs of the ladder, Jasper eased himself into the darkness.

<hr/>

Jasper had to slide himself down the last few feet, for the ladder was not quite long enough to reach bottom. He found himself in a dark cave that proved, instead, to be a tunnel. At least, it once had been a tunnel. Jasper raised the electric torch and could see a pile of rubble that blocked what must have once been a passageway. How far it went, or where, were not questions Jasper cared about at the moment. He raised his electric torch.

Huddled in a ball was Lucy, clutching Faye, both of them covered in lichen, moss, and dirt.

"Jasper!" cried Lucy, who flung herself around her brother. Jasper held her so tight she wiggled and coughed before he was willing to loosen his grip.

"I thought I'd lost you," he said, tears again trying to fight their way down his cheeks.

"But I was just here," said Lucy. "I wasn't lost." Lucy looked in her brother's eyes and, with her dirty-mittened hand, she wiped the tears from his cheek.

Jasper looked at Faye. He stood and walked over to her. She looked shaken, her eyes hollow. "I don't know how to thank you," he said. Without thinking further, the two embraced.

"Me, too!" cried Lucy, who nudged her way in-between them. For the first time since breakfast, Jasper laughed. And the girls joined him.

"I'm going to come down, too!" called Noah. "It sounds like much too much fun!"

"Don't, Noah," said Jasper. "I don't know how safe it is. The ladder could break under the weight or the stones could give way. We'd better get out. Lucy, you first."

"Yes, please," said Lucy, as Jasper lifted her to the ladder. She climbed the rest of the way.

"It's snowing!" cried Lucy. Jasper thought her voice sounded miles away.

"Jasper." Faye spoke in almost a whisper. In the light of the electric torch, Jasper could see fear in her face.

"What is it?" he asked, as she stared behind him.

"I think . . ." She gulped. "I think I know what happened to the artist."

Faye pointed behind Jasper. He turned, lifting the electric torch to shed more light. There, on the stone ground, was the crumpled skeleton of what must once have been the great artist—the sculptor-magician, who had disappeared so long ago.

CHAPTER TWENTY-TWO

THE TONGUES OF SOLEMANO

OR

LANGUAGE OF THE PAST

The snow did not let up. It fell harder through the night and, in the morning, the doors of the house were impossible to open, blocked by great drifts of snow. Faye opened her window to breathe in the snow-filled air of the early morning. After the whole experience in the beast garden, she treasured every crisp, cold breath. Finding the skeleton of the artist had been a shock. And afterward, when she and Jasper looked around, they had found the bones of other animals, including the skeleton of a wild boar and the carcass of a raven. Whoever had built the secret door had not considered the possibility that it might claim innocent victims. Or, perhaps, they had.

As Faye breathed in the cold, the whole village was silent. Even the birds had gone quiet. The sun was obscured, so the light was not very strong. The snow was still falling hard, and everything, everywhere, was white. Faye smiled to herself at the thought of the mysterious men in black covered in white snow. Would they now be the mysterious men in white? Or would the snow melt right off them? Surely, Signora Fornaio's ovens would keep the snow melted on her window and fill the chilly air with sweet, warm smells in the morning. Faye thought, for a moment, of the little old shepherd, and she hoped he was safe and warm somewhere. Signora Fornaio would have seen to it.

With a strong gust, the wind sent a waft of snow and a brutal chill into the room. Faye leaned back in and shook the snow from her hair, then quickly closed the window. She shivered. Going to her wardrobe, she pulled out her warmest jumper and put it on over her nightdress. To that, she added two pairs of stockings and a woolly hat before she left her room.

"I don't think we're going far today," Wallace said when Faye came into the dining room. The others were already watching the snow fall. The fires were lit in the two largest fireplaces, in the dining room and sitting room, and a brazier was lit in the foyer. The whole first floor felt warm and cozy.

"A day inside would be good for everyone," said Miss Brett.

Faye's face fell. It was thrilling, all this snow.

"We can work on lessons and read," Miss Brett added quickly. "I will read. It will be nice by the fire."

"If the snow stops gushing, can we see all the powder it's left us?" asked Lucy, looking longingly out the window. "I so want to make snow people and snow angels and snow lumps."

"Snow lumps?" Noah looked up from the stack of magnets he had been piling carefully atop one another.

"Yes, lumps made of snow," Lucy said.

"Hmmm," said Noah, lifting an eyebrow. "I probably could have guessed that, given enough time."

But the snow did not let up. It snowed hard through the next afternoon, and the one after.

"What if it was all sugared icing?" Lucy said several times a day.

By midday following, the sun finally came out. The whole of the valley was truly a winter wonderland.

"Oh, please, can we go outside?" said Lucy. The children all nodded. All except Wallace, that is, who was not quite sure about the idea.

"Well, I did want to go down to the bakery and see how Signora Fornaio is doing," said Miss Brett. "But I don't see how we're going to make it with all this snow."

"I know!" called Noah from the cupboard under the stairs. He held up a pair of snowshoes he had found among the other things stored there.

There were four pairs of snowshoes. Wallace opted to stay and read. He had found a book on Sir Isaac Newton that he did not want to put down. The others all set out to the village. Lucy sat on Jasper's shoulders, which made him feel as if he were going to become hunched forever.

What normally took about seven minutes took the explorers nearly half an hour. Hats were blown off and had to be retrieved. Shoes slipped off, which led to stumbles, and more stumbles. They all had to dig Lucy out of the snow when she plunged headfirst off Jasper's shoulders, after Noah accidentally slipped and tripped Jasper, knocking him into Faye. Jasper had, in fact, only just gotten Lucy back up onto his shoulders. She had been slipping lower and lower down his back until her feet were dragging along the ground. Miss Brett had offered to take Lucy, but Jasper insisted that he carry his sister.

When they finally got to the road from the manor house, they found more of a path to follow into town. Someone had been riding horses through the village, but the path was very narrow and difficult to navigate.

"We need to invent something to clear these roads," Jasper said, trying not to tip over in his snowshoes.

"They have those rotary plows on trains," said Noah. "I've seen them in Canada."

"If we can apply the technology to a carriage," said Faye, "and make a road plow—"

"Well," said Miss Brett, trying desperately to hold up her skirt, which had become intensely heavy with all the icy frost attaching itself to her hems, "for now, let's just manage to keep from falling in a snowdrift."

With many a misstep, they managed to get to the main road through the village. From there, they could smell the bakery and the delicious treats that waited inside. Outside the shop was a large horse with a small sleigh. The horse had the end of a focaccia in its mouth. One of the ravens stood beneath, catching crumbs in its beak. Lucy greeted both the horse and the raven. Shaking off their snowy clothes, the five visitors entered the bakery.

"Buongiorno, Signora Fornaio," said Miss Brett. "Quello che un giorno di neve!" She had just taught herself the Italian word for snow, *neve*, and was excited to use it.

"Merhba! Benvenutti!" cried Signora Fornaio. "And your Italian is growing, *Signorina*."

"Grazie, Signora, e il sopracciglio profumo delizioso." Miss Brett smiled. But Signora Fornaio burst into laughter. "Oh, dear, was that not right?"

"I do not know," said Signora Fornaio, through tears of laughter. "You tell me my eyebrow smells delicious." Signora Fornaio had to wipe her eyes. "We are so glad you come!" From out of the kitchen came another small, round woman the children and Miss Brett recognized as the cheese-seller. She carried two large bundles, then went back into the kitchen for one more. Jasper and Noah quickly took the bundles and followed the cheese-seller to the door. They helped her load the bundles onto her cart.

"Well, that is a big load of treats," said Lucy. "Someone must be very hungry."

"Signora Maggio brings Christmas caggionetti to her sons," Signora Fornaio said.

"Her sons?" Faye wondered, as they all did, if her sons were mysterious men in black living in the village.

"Yes. Two boys lives in Rome," said Signora Fornaio. "Two are *fratelli* in Malta, *fratellii nero*. She brings the bundles for the sons to bring their brothers." She, the children, and Miss Brett followed Signora Maggio outside.

"Signora Fornaio makes the best caggionetti in all of Abruzzo," said Signora Maggio as she climbed into her sleigh. "From when they are babies, they love her."

"You will check with the post carriage for the package from my son?" Signora Fornaio asked.

"Of course, *amica*, I will get your package. It is not yet Christmas, though." The cheese-seller put her hand on Noah's shoulder to hoist herself up.

"Sometimes it comes early," Signora Fornaio said with doubt in her voice. "That big white carriage always comes through weather."

"Of course, my friend. For the wonderful pleasure you bring

my sons, I would do anything. Paci lid-dinja." The sleigh took off.

"I would be happy for news from America," Signora Fornaio said. "My son is there for almost one and a half year, and he writes me every few weeks. Still, it is long." She pulled a small handkerchief from her pocket and showed Miss Brett. "It is from a very important company in America, in New York City, made with real American cotton. The American cotton is so better, it is said. And you see here. There is an 'F' embroidered."

"For 'Fornaio,'" said Miss Brett.

Signora Fornaio blushed. "For *Favilla*, my name, or, *onestamente*, what my husband always called me."

"Is your son one of... them?" asked Noah.

"The *fratelli in nero?*" she asked with some surprise. "Of course he is not. But we have all lived together for so many generations, it is long forgotten that they are not like others. Many stories are told of the *fratelli in nero*—many stories of the heroes and villains. *Si, si,* you will hear stories." She laughed, her whole face glowing with warmth and kindness.

"What did she say?" asked Lucy of Signora Maggio. "Paci lid-dinja. That wasn't Italian." While Lucy did not speak much Italian, she did always remember what she had learned. And she was acutely adept at recognizing accents and the sounds of words.

"'*Paci lid-dinja*,' we say here," Signora Fornaio said. "It means, 'Peace to the world.' We have always said that here."

"In what language?" asked Lucy.

"Maltese." Signora Fornaio smiled.

"Maltese? Why Maltese?" asked Noah. "It isn't the native tongue anywhere in Italy that I know."

"It is tradition, for hundreds of years. Like '*Sahha!*'"

"That's not Italian?" Noah had been so pleased he had learned a word in Italian.

Signora Fornaio shook her head and laughed.

"But why Maltese?" Noah asked again. "I still don't—"

"Oh, yes!" said Lucy. "It's—you remember! Malta! How amazing, it's like the boat—"

Lucy was cut short by a noise from behind the counter. Another large bundle emerged from the kitchen, followed by none other than the shepherd. He was so tiny, the big bundle hid him from view.

"There you are, *il mio amico!*" Signora Fornaio said. "I thought you fall asleep in the kitchen."

"I do for *bambini,*" said the shepherd. "The canella, cinnamon, and the sugar caggionetti, with the cioccolato and nocciole, hazelnuts, too."

Miss Brett gladly took the bundle. It smelled divine—the chocolate, cinnamon, and, though he hadn't mentioned them, almonds. "We were worried about you, Mr. Mezzobassi," Miss Brett said. "It has been so cold, *tempo molto freddo,* and so much snow."

"Ah, *il pastore,*" Signora Fornaio said to the shepherd. "You almost froze, *congelato,* but I saw you. *Il* shepherd has slept in my kitchens, and helps me bake the many Christmas goods."

"That is so nice." Faye somehow felt much happier knowing the little old shepherd had a place to be. To Faye, he seemed all alone, and so did Signora Fornaio. "We're glad you both have company." It reminded her of her own loneliness back in India—her own desire to have at least one friend.

"And there are just two weeks before *Natale*—Christmas," Signora Fornaio said. "But only a few days before something else very special." With that, she looked at Lucy. Lucy looked up, beaming.

Jasper's heart sank. "It's your birthday, Lucy!" he said. "Fifteen December! Little Lucy will be seven." With everything else going on, he had forgotten.

"Oh, *Signora*, I'd really love to have a lovely birthday cake and some other delicious treats." Lucy clapped her hands together, her eyes as big as saucers.

"Well, we will bake you one," said the baker. "The most delicious birthday cake in the world."

⟶•◦•⟵

On the way back to the house, Noah offered to take the bundle from Miss Brett. She gave it to him, but with an eye of suspicion, and warned him about sneaking nibbles. Noah looked guilty and knew he'd never get away with it. Distracted from the smells of chocolate and almonds, he told them about Christmas in Vienna.

"We had an advent wreath on the door, and we added a candle for every night up to Christmas. It was wonderful to have something every night—like ticking off days on a calendar, I mean. When I was small, that sort of thing was important. Vienna was amazing during Christmas—the best food of anywhere."

"Jasper always made Hortensia wait until after my birthday to put up decorations for Christmas," said Lucy, smiling at her brother. "That way I had my own special day that wasn't squashed into a day before Christmas."

"Bad luck having a birthday next to Noel," said Noah.

"Actually, it's rather good luck," said Jasper. He smiled at his sister, and she hugged him and clung to his arm.

"Well, that shouldn't keep us from collecting pine twigs to make a wreath," said Noah, who picked up a perfectly bendy branch from a pine tree. "We can put it up after Lucy's birthday."

Lucy clapped her hands and smiled up at Noah. He bowed deeply, then put down the bundle to help Lucy climb onto his back. He galloped all the way back home.

CHAPTER TWENTY-THREE

What Did Not Come in the Post

OR

SIGNORA FORNAIO MISSES HER PACKAGE

"Why did you ask about the words?" said Jasper as they sat warming at the hearth while Miss Brett fetched the hot chocolate from the kitchen. He handed Faye another twig he had cleaned of dead pine needles.

"Because I knew it. 'Paci,'" said Lucy. "You all know it." She passed Noah a little bow she had made from a piece of red ribbon.

"What do you mean, we all know it?" asked Faye, handing Noah the braid of twigs she had made from those Jasper gave her. She turned back toward the fire to warm her hands again. Somehow, she was still chilled from outside. It did not make her happy that her constitution kept her from fully adjusting to the cold.

"Peace," said Lucy. "Like on the boat."

Everyone exchanged glances. Then a slouching Wallace sat up from the floor. His face said "Eureka!" and he adjusted his glasses with enthusiasm. "During the flag ceremony on the ship," he quickly said. "Lucy's right. They said the word '*paci*.'"

"And you remember that?" Faye said, doubtful.

"Yes, I do," said Wallace. "It made me think of my pocket, and..."

He trailed off. What he meant was that he thought of his pocket and the coin that lived there.

Miss Brett came into the room from the kitchen. In her hands was an empty plate waiting to be filled. "Noah, where is the bundle from Signor Mezzobassi?"

Noah's heart sank. "I—I must have left it in on the ground when I picked up Lucy, or when we started collecting twigs for the advent wreath. We were climbing up the snow bank by the road and I put it down to… I'm so sorry."

Miss Brett didn't want to scold him. She could see his pained expression. Noah suffered at the thought of food anywhere other than his stomach. "Well, not to worry," she said. "I'll get some buns from the kitchen for tea." She took the tray to fill in the kitchen.

"Oh, how sad," said Lucy. "And Signor Mezzobaffi made them just for us. Can't we get them? Can't we run back and see?"

But the snow had begun anew, and with a vengeance. It was like a sheet of white outside the door. They could look for hours and never find where on the journey the bundle could be, for it surely was under the snow by now. And, more of a concern, it was getting late.

"Sorry, sweet angel," Miss Brett said. "It is almost dark and much too snowy. We can have a look tomorrow."

Lucy humphed with her chin in her hands.

Soon, Miss Brett returned with a tray of cups and the lovely basket of biscotti and sugared buns she had baked the night before.

"Sahha!" she cheered to their health, smiling broadly at Noah as he reached for a bun. She looked at the wreath that was now adorned with ribbons, pine cones, and braids of pine. "The wreath is beautiful, Noah. You all made such a lovely addition for Christmas."

"We'll need candles," said Noah between bites. But before he could get another bite in, he yawned an enormous yawn, then shook his head as if to shake off his sleepiness.

"I'll look in the kitchen for some small Christmas candles. There must be some around."

Miss Brett looked at the other faces around her. Lucy's eyes were drooping. Wallace was turning his coin in his fingers and seemed deep in thought. Jasper tried to stifle a yawn but failed. Faye pretended to stretch, but she was herself yawning.

"Okay, everyone. While the men make our supper, I thought I'd read to you the story of Sleeping Beauty." She could tell the children were set to relax. This was an excellent time to get in some reading.

"Does it have swordfights and dashing escapes?" asked Noah.

"Well, perhaps a bit," said Miss Brett.

"And heroic conquests and daring heroes?" he added.

"Well, in time, yes, heroes triumph," offered Miss Brett.

"Well, good, because I really am tired of losing and hiding and running away. I want to hear about heroes defeating evil." Noah stretched out on the sofa, his arms beneath his head as if he hadn't a care in the world.

"I actually agree, Noah," said Faye. "I could use some triumphs, too. No heroes running away."

"I don't want to run away. I want to stay here and wait for Mummy and Daddy," said Lucy. She looked at Jasper, who tried to smile and nod. Then Jasper looked at Miss Brett, who had a worried, sad look about her.

"Will Mummy and Daddy be with us for Christmas?" Lucy asked Miss Brett.

Noah slipped a bit, his feet falling from the armrest. He hadn't been thinking about his parents and Christmas. He recovered quickly, though, looking to Miss Brett for an answer.

"You think they will?" he asked, hopefully.

Wallace looked up from his book. He could feel his heart jump at the idea.

"Stop! I don't want a false promise," Faye said. "And Miss Brett can't promise anything. She's in the same situation as we are."

Miss Brett didn't say a word. She agreed with Faye—no false promises, and no guessing games. Instead, she cleared her throat and picked up a lovely large volume. They all gathered closely. She knew the story of Sleeping Beauty by heart. This was a good thing, too, for the book, *Il Pentamerone*, was written in Italian. And she recognized the name Talia, given to the princess.

Miss Brett showed the children the book's illustrations. "This is a story about good people overcoming bad things thrust upon them," she started. "It's the story of a kingdom long ago."

—————⟶●⟵—————

Just before dawn, Jasper woke suddenly. Loud noises, shouts, and the crashing and clanging of bells filled the air. The noise jolted Wallace out of his sleep. Noah jumped up and fell out of bed. Jasper ran into Lucy's room. She was still asleep. Miss Brett, Faye, Noah, and Jasper nearly collided in the hallway.

"What was that?" Noah asked sleepily, rubbing his elbow where it hit the floor. "Is the house on fire?"

"Don't even joke about that, you fool," Faye growled, sniffing around for smoke.

"No, look. Down there." Wallace pointed down, past the village

walls, into the field. There *was* a fire blazing through the mist, reflecting brightness from the white all around. There were people
running and shouting.

"It's the post carriage!" Jasper could see more clearly as the rising sun lightened the sky. The yellow post carriage had smoke billowing out of its back door. But the danger seemed to have passed.
The flames had died down. The continuous buckets of water from
the villagers did the job.

"Should we go down to help?" asked Wallace as he adjusted his
glasses.

"I think we'd just be in the way now," Miss Brett said, honestly.
"It looks like the fire is out. I don't see what we could do."

"I don't get it." Noah scratched his head. "Did it explode? What
could make it do that? Wasn't it emptied in the afternoon? There was
nothing in it that could catch fire."

"It *was* emptied," Jasper said. "Signora Maggio went down to
look for Signora Fornaio's package. I wonder if she got it."

"I don't think it came," Miss Brett said. "She told me that when
she came by to ask about Lucy's cake." Signora Fornaio had stopped
by just a short while after supper.

"Well, there must have been something in the carriage that
caught fire," said Wallace.

"Or someone lit it on fire," Faye said, darkly. "Someone who is
trying to find us."

"Why?!" Wallace blurted, fixing his glasses, which were slightly askew. "It can't be him."

"Could it?" Jasper looked at Miss Brett.

"I just don't know," she said.

Back in America, there had seemed to be a reason Komar Romak was after them: the aeroplane. But why was this terrible man coming after them now? True, he had come after them in that contraption when they were on the train to New York. Then in the middle of the ocean—had that been him again? And in the mountains on the way to Solemano? Was he the reason they had been forced to hide in the cave? No one gave them a straight answer. No one ever did. But it did seem as if Komar Romak could be anywhere at any time.

"It was probably just a tipped-over oil lamp," Miss Brett said, herding the children back into their rooms. "Let's try to get some sleep, all of us."

"Sleep?" Faye could not think of it. "I want to know what happened."

"It's foolish to go out in the freezing cold to see why the mail carriage caught on fire," said Noah. "Only a fool would even think of doing that."

"That's you, then," said Faye. "I didn't say we should go out. There has to be one of those men in black around here."

"Sweet angel," Miss Brett said kindly, "let's try to rest, and we will certainly learn what happened in the morning."

"It's already morning," grumbled Faye, who happened to be right.

"Well, try," Miss Brett urged. "For another hour or so. It's just now breaking dawn."

But Faye felt that she could not rest until she learned some answers. Maybe it was just a lamp tipping over. That happened all the time. And weren't the mysterious men in black there to guard them? But why, then, did she feel as though they were in as much danger as before, or more?

Jasper could see it on Faye's face. Something was wrong and they did not know what it was.

"Let's all just try," Miss Brett said.

And with that, they all headed back to their beds, where all but sleepy Lucy and snoring Noah lay with eyes open until the sun broke through the morning mist.

CHAPTER TWENTY-FOUR

FAYE'S ALMOND ADVENTURES

OR

A GRIM DISCOVERY BEFORE THE FETE

Signora Fornaio was as mystified as the children about the events of the early morning and did not know how the fire had started. Miss Brett and Faye discussed it with her later in the day, having come down to help bake Lucy's cake. They shared a cup of tea and some biscuits and talked about the fire. After they circled around the events several times, coming up with no answer, Signora Fornaio declared, "Now, we bake."

It was an interesting afternoon. Faye soon became overly excited by everything, going into detail about raw eggs versus cooked eggs and how the heat affects the physiology of the egg. She explained the chemistry of baking powder, the effects of shortening on flour, and loads of other things that were either completely ignored by or totally lost on her audience. Signora Fornaio could not have understood a single word Faye had to say about egg albumin or bicarbonate of soda. Miss Brett didn't understand the science, but she understood why Faye was rambling on like that. This was Faye, worried about the fire and worried about danger. And this was also Faye's way of tackling something she could not do. Faye was brilliant, yes—but she was not a baker.

"Faye," Miss Brett said kindly, cutting the girl off mid-sentence, "we are so pleased that you are with us here, but you need to be firm when you cream the icing. Watch." Miss Brett took the spoon that Faye had been poorly using, and showed her how to put some muscle into smoothing out the lumps of butter and sugar floating in the cream. Faye's face reddened, and she took the spoon in silence. She wrenched the chunk butter from the sugar so hard, a large glop of icing flew in the air, hitting Signora Fornaio right between the eyes.

Faye gasped. She was mortified. But Signora Fornaio crossed her eyes and saw the icing slide down her face. She licked it off as it came to rest on the tip of her nose, laughing all the while. Faye could not help but laugh, too. She thought of all the servants at her home in Delhi. Did they have this much fun together in the kitchen?

"I am so happy you distract the worry, Faye. You make me have so many laughs." Signora Fornaio giggled, finally catching her breath. "Only our little *pastore*, our little shepherd, can do worse. He's always knocking everything down when he helps. How so little a man can make so big the problems, how he can knock down boxes from the high shelves, I do not know. Every one of them falling open on the floor." She laughed again. Faye's face burned. She felt sorry for the little old shepherd, but she did not want to be compared to him in clumsiness.

After several attempts to find something Faye could do without causing damage to the kitchen or those in it, they discovered she was excellent at using the mortar and pestle to grind the almonds for marzipan. They put her to work until her hands were red from grinding, but Faye felt she was able to prove herself in the kitchen, even if the job was just like something she had done many times in her father's laboratory.

———————

Later in the morning, Miss Brett and Faye returned to the house to let Signora Fornaio put the final touches on the cake (and to remove Faye from the kitchen), and to help the boys distract Lucy so they could decorate the dining room for the party. On the way, however, they came across a sad discovery.

"There's something wrong with that raven," said Faye. The bird was leaning over on an opened wing. Miss Brett went over to it. The bird's eyes stared blindly, frozen open where it lay. Another bird was near it, also beyond help.

"They look as though they're sleeping," Faye said. Farther along the path, they discovered three furry bunnies. The bunnies were dead.

"They look so sweet," said Miss Brett.

"Do you think they starved?" Faye asked.

But the bunnies' fur was thick and fluffy, not ragged, as it would have been had they been malnourished. And the ravens were well-fed, too. Miss Brett had noticed the remnants of the bundle they had left on the path. These birds and bunnies had likely eaten it.

"Most certainly not." Miss Brett looked closely. "They may have frozen in the night. It was quite cold last night and they may have gotten stuck outside. Perhaps there was a sudden drop in the temperature."

"Well, I am so glad Lucy didn't come with us," Faye said.

Miss Brett picked up the cold little furry creatures. "Let's get them off the path so Lucy doesn't have to know."

Faye picked up the birds in her mittened hands. She had complained about the curious birds, but it was so sad to see them like this. She followed Miss Brett, and they carried the animals to the far edge of the road, by a stand of trees.

"We can't bury them in the frozen ground," Miss Brett said. "But we can leave them out of Lucy's way and bury them under the snow." The soft snow made light of their grim burden.

When they finally came to the gardens, Miss Brett and Faye found Lucy sitting with a whole collection of snow people.

"Jasper said it's my birthday and I can make as many snow people as I want," Lucy said as she put a tiny head on yet another tiny snowman.

Miss Brett motioned to Faye. "Hey, Lucy," Faye said, "can I make some little snowmen with you?"

"No," said Lucy. "But you can make some snow birds and snow puppy dogs."

"Maybe we can make some more over on the other side of the garden, too," Faye said, pointing toward the wall of the garden that would keep the soon-arriving Signora Fornaio out of sight.

"I was making some snow birds for Mr. Corvino," said Lucy, looking up into the sky, "but he hasn't come over to play yet this morning. He must be busy in his own garden."

Faye thought of the birds and the bunnies. "I'm sure you're right," she said, not sure at all, "but we can make some friends for him anyway."

So the girls stayed outside and made snow birds and snow dogs and snow people, some snow horses, and a few snow sheep. Faye made a snow shepherd to stand by the snow sheep. It made her think of the little old shepherd, whom she hoped Signora Fornaio would bring to Lucy's surprise party.

———————

"*Surprise!*" they all shouted. Lucy's wide-open mouth quickly turned into a very big smile. There, in the dining room, were the most beautiful decorations. There were paper angels and little candles. The mysterious men in black had made tiny fairies with wings made of lace. Faye looked at the fairies closely. Such delicate work, such care. This surprised her as much as anything she had seen them do. There must have been a hundred of them all over the room. There were paper flowers, and a table set for a queen. Lucy was in heaven.

"Wait until you see the cake," Noah whispered in her ear as both of them reached for the tiny finger sandwiches, Lucy's favorite. She saw Signora Fornaio beaming at her, but the little old shepherd had not been able to make it. Lucy reminded herself to save a piece of cake for him. And one for Mr. Corvino the raven.

"Sahha!" called out Signora Fornaio, and everyone offered the same cheer.

While the children celebrated, Miss Brett approached the man in the frilly apron. "I'd like to know about the postal carriage," she said softly.

"Fire burn," he said, refilling the plates with miniature brioches and petits fours.

"I know it burned," she said, a bit short. "The alarm woke us in the night. I want to know if it was an accident, or if it was ... if it was *him.*"

"They maybe," he said.

"Maybe?"

"It could only be, perhaps," he said.

"Are we safe?" She was certain this conversation would not go well.

"For our lives," he said, walking back into the kitchen with the empty tray.

Holding the kitchen door open for Signora Fornaio, the frilly apron man retreated when the cake came out.

"Eight candles," Noah said. "Seven, plus one for good luck."

Lucy held her breath and wished with all her might. *Please*, she wished, *please let it be so for Christmas.* And then she blew.

"I hope she wished for Komar Romak to disappear," whispered Noah to Jasper.

"No wish is going to make him go away," Faye whispered over Jasper's other shoulder. "It would be like trying to protect mice from an invisible cat."

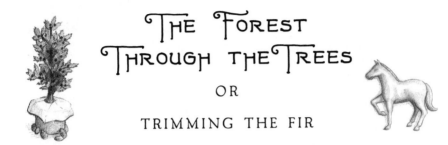

CHAPTER TWENTY-FIVE

The Forest Through the Trees

OR

TRIMMING THE FIR

After Lucy's birthday passed, thoughts turned to finding a tree for Christmas. Wallace wanted to stay back and work with his magnets, so Lucy, Faye, and Jasper went with Noah, more for the adventure than for the expectation of actually finding and felling a tree on their first outing. Any tree they might find would have to be quite small, for they had only one small axe, one shovel, and one trowel to dig away the snow—hardly the tools of professional woodsmen.

"In England, people sometimes have small trees in their rooms," Jasper said. "Or at least that's the way it was when Queen Victoria was young."

"Actually, she had one in her room, but nobody else did," said Lucy. "But it would be lovely to have a little tree in my room."

"I do not fancy cutting down six trees," Jasper said.

"What do you mean, 'cut down'?" asked Lucy, mortified. "I only want to bring them in for Christmas. Then we can set them free back in the forest."

Jasper and the others looked at each other.

"Um, Lucy..." But Jasper did not want to be first. Faye put her hand on Jasper's arm and nodded.

"Lucy, we need to explain something," said Faye.

The conversation went on as the children trudged through the snow, into the small wooded area next to the village. There were more fir trees than they could count, and because the trees grew fast, cutting them *was* necessary. But there was no explaining that to Lucy.

"But what if a bird is living in it and has built a little nest?" she said, anxiously. "Oh, we mustn't take down the home of a little bird family."

"We won't take a bird's home," said Noah quickly. "But they'll all be living in tenements if we don't clear a bit of space for them." He smiled at Lucy, who seemed reluctant to understand what everyone else was saying.

"In theory, and in fact, Lucy, we are helping the forest," said Jasper.

But Lucy began to cry every time they selected a tree. Faye was anxious that they might run into dead birds and bunnies, so she kept directing them away from the road. Finally, Lucy allowed them to dig up a tiny tree that she carried all the way back and planted in a little pot, for the earth was still frozen and it couldn't be planted in the ground. It was quietly decided that Faye, Jasper, and Noah would go without Lucy and find the perfect tree sometime the following week. Lucy and Wallace could work on making bigger rare earth magnets or building more snow creatures.

As they trudged out of the forest, they heard a loud chopping. They could not see anything from where they were.

"Is it a snowman?" asked Lucy, looking around.

"Why would a snowman make that sound, Lucy?" Noah tried to keep a straight face. "Why would a snowman be out here making any sound?"

"A snowman is only out in the snow," Lucy said. "He wouldn't make that sound if he wasn't."

Noah looked cross-eyed at Jasper, who stifled a laugh. But as they continued walking, the sound got louder.

"It must have scared the birds away," Lucy said. She had not seen a single raven.

What was it? What could be making that sound? As they climbed over a snowdrift, they discovered what the sound was, and who was making it. And it was not a snowman.

The children came across four mysterious men in black. They had felled a large fir, and were about to fell an even grander one. They watched as the majestic tree began to lean.

"Oh, please come back as a beautiful swan," said Lucy, closing her wet eyes.

The others simply looked at one another for a moment before looking back at the great falling tree.

"Why don't we head over there?" said Jasper, pointing away from the tree-cutters. "Is that Mr. Corvino I hear?"

Lucy jumped up and down and ran in the direction Jasper pointed. Without a word, Noah and Faye knew they were saving Lucy from having to wish any more trees into another existence.

⟶►●◄⟵

Lucy named her tree Bertram. It was a tiny red juniper with tiny red berries clinging to its tiny branches. She made the tree a little bed of stones and tinsel. She kept a small tin cup of dirt in-side to warm it for the tree. "When I feed sweet little Bertram, I'm sure he'd be happy if his dirt was lovely and warm. Then it will be like warm crumpets or hot chocolate." She sewed some small piec-es of fabric into a small cloth she called "wee Bertram's blankie" and surrounded the pot with little pine cones she had collected around the front steps. "So he doesn't feel lonely when I'm not with him, the little darling." Lucy was worried that they had taken the tree away from his mummy. When they made the wreath to put on the door of the house, Lucy made a tiny wreath for Bertram out of paper and green ribbon.

It was almost Christmas. Christmas brought with it thoughts of family. Those thoughts weighed heavy on the Young Inventors Guild. For Lucy, it weighed heavy on Bertram as well.

———◆———

"Oh, my! It's lovely!" squealed Lucy, She quickly covered her mouth with her hands. She didn't want to wake the others. She didn't want them to think she was a baby.

Lucy had woken early that morning. It was almost Christmas and she had been waking earlier each morning since her birth-day. She was excited about Christmas, but sometimes bad dreams woke her early. She'd wake in the morning with her fingers near-ly bleeding from chewing her nails. She took special care to hide them from Jasper.

But that morning, there were no bad dreams. She woke and was certain she could smell Christmas in the air. And she was right. Christmas was standing, right there, by the sitting room window. It was thirty feet tall, and when Lucy came down the stairs, she stopped in her tracks. Mingled with the smell of jasmine was the smell of Christmas pine. Right there in the large bay window was a beautiful Christmas tree, the biggest Lucy had ever seen.

There were tiny candleholders from top to bottom, attached to almost every branch, but the decorating had only just begun. On the rug by the hearth, there were baskets of pine cones and tinsel and nuts. There were boxes scattered throughout the room containing mysteries ready to be solved. Lucy ran down the stairs once she could get her feet moving.

"It *is* lovely," said a voice from the big comfy chair. Lucy turned to find Wallace. Wallace had been up since dawn. Like Lucy, he had been getting up early these pre-Christmas mornings. Like Lucy, his dreams had often kept him awake.

"You startled me, Wallace," Lucy said, her hand on her heart.

"Sorry," Wallace said.

"What's in the boxes?" asked Lucy.

Wallace's face flushed. He had peeked into the boxes, but felt a bit guilty for doing so. "Um, well, it looks to be a grand selection of tree trimmings."

"Oh, how wonderful." Lucy ran over to the boxes and pulled open the first one she touched. From the paper wrapping it, she took a lovely, hand-carved horse. It was very small and fit into the palm of her hand, but it was so intricately cut, she could see the lashes upon its eyelids and a little smile upon its lips.

Inside the box were more animals—camels, reindeer, sheep, goats, dogs, cats, and even a boar and a beaver. Lucy set them up on the floor and began to play with them. Wallace reached into another box and found tiny carved mice, but mice dressed like people—as farmers, knights, princesses, and clowns. Lucy and Wallace began to play with the animals and the mice-people. Each of these creatures had a little looped ribbon tied to the tops of their heads. They were ornaments for the tree.

"Well, it certainly did arrive." Miss Brett descended the stairs, thrilled to see the children happily playing with the tree trimmings. She had asked the mysterious men in black about having a Christmas tree delivered.

"Always twenty-three," the frilly apron man had said.

"Twenty-three Christmas trees?" Miss Brett was struck by the idea of this strange tradition.

"Twenty-three it will be," said the man in the large beret. "It is always the way."

Miss Brett opened her mouth, then waited to see if she'd be able to arrange this information so that it made sense. *Aha*, she thought. "So the tree will arrive 23 December?"

"It is so," the frilly apron man had said, as the other men nodded.

"I'd like to have trimmings, too," Miss Brett said. "Candles, braids of berries and glass, tinsel, and—"

"We have trim," said the floppy-hatted man. "We have the hands we make."

Miss Brett nodded, though she was not sure what he meant. She was sure that she and the children would be able to make some trimmings if the men did not bring enough festive things to brighten the tree.

But as Miss Brett stood there, watching Lucy and Wallace, she found her heart pounding with pleasure. The trimmings appeared to be as beautiful as any she had ever seen. She bent and picked up a tiny wooden mouse, no bigger than a real mouse, dressed like a princess in a gown. Every detail had been carved, including the sparkle in the princess's eye, and the gown was made of the finest silks. Whoever made this ornament was a master craftsman.

"Will you look at that!" Noah was now coming down the stairs, followed by Faye and Jasper.

Within moments, the boxes were all opened, and the trimmings were finding their way onto the tree. Jasper showed Faye how to make pine cone stars and string them with ribbon. Noah was busy making funny scenes with various ornaments he pulled from boxes. He had a glass raven sitting on the head of a wooden rocking horse. He managed to take a small wrapped present for Faye and hang it upside-down, a small lace angel sitting upon it.

"Noah," Miss Brett gently scolded. Noah smiled, but left the arrangements as they were.

In one box, there were long strings of colored glass. There were also balls of thread, and Miss Brett went into the kitchen to get a bowl of red juniper berries the children could string along the thread. In another box, she found a collection of very fragile ancient flowers made of silk and paper. She recognized these from stories she had heard of the earliest Christmas trees in Bremen, Germany, back in the sixteenth century. She also found a smaller box, inside one filled with tinsel, that was made of wood. This box contained an odd selection of small crosses and small wooden squares painted in red and white, or black and white, and seemed familiar. She had seen these designs before.

"Look," said Faye, carrying a large plate piled high with beautiful marzipan biscuits. Each was shaped like a tree or snowflake, or a little angel. And each had a small wire through the top so it could be hung on the tree.

"Oh, may we eat them?" asked Lucy, who found she was suddenly very hungry.

"I think these are for the tree," said Faye. "But there appear to be some lovely butter biscuits with marzipan stars coming out of the oven now." Faye tried discreetly to wipe the crumbs from her lips and her pinafore.

Miss Brett watched as the children, taking a break from their decorating, went into the dining room. She quickly ran upstairs to collect an armful of wrapped gifts that she brought back down to place beneath the tree. She then joined the children and found beautiful iced cakes and butter biscuits covering the whole table. There were biscotti, with almonds and chocolate, and caggionetti, filled with cinnamon sugar. There were pasticiotti so light and fluffy that the sweet treats melted on the tongue. There were loaves of hot bread coming out of the oven, butter melting on slices Miss Brett held in her hand. She reached into her apron pocket to take out a cloth, and found she had accidentally brought one of the little black and white ornaments to the table.

"Look, it's the flag," said Lucy, pointing to the ornament.

Miss Brett suddenly remembered where she had seen those designs. "Of course," she said aloud. "The flags on the ship."

"Of course," said Noah.

"Would you put this on the tree, Lucy?" asked Miss Brett, handing the ornament to Lucy, "I'll break it if I carry it around, and it looks old and fragile."

As the frilly apron man entered the room carrying a plate of hot crumpets, Lucy lifted up the little flag. "Is this your flag, Mr.

Frilly Apron?" she asked. "It's lovely."

The frilly apron man set the plate on the table, stood suddenly very still, and placed his hand over his heart. He bowed his head, mumbled something, then left the room.

"I suppose that's his way of saying yes," said Noah, who was much more interested in the biscotti than the wooden flag.

"Perhaps he misses his mummy," said Lucy, staring at the flag. "Perhaps his mummy is back where the flag is and he misses her because it's Christmas and he won't get to see her and have Christmas dinner with her or his daddy."

"I don't think he was sad." Miss Brett placed some irresistible pasticiotti on Lucy's plate. "I think he was remembering. Perhaps the flag is from somewhere far away, and he was showing his faith and respect. Sometimes people see flags as a thing to honor, as if it was the very place itself."

"But Mummy doesn't have a flag and Bertram the tree is lonely without his mummy and daddy and ... and I'm sad about Christmas," said Lucy, tears welling in her eyes. "Jasper, where is Mummy? Why can't we have a bit of a rest from being afraid and hiding in caves and have Christmas with our families, too?"

Even Noah put down his crumpet. The man in the floppy hat came in at that moment and stopped when he saw the silence around the table.

"Oh, please, can't we have our mummies and daddies for Christmas?" said Lucy to the man. "I don't mind if I have no other presents. I only want to be with Mummy and Daddy and ... and ..." But she broke into sobs.

"Don't cry, Lucy," Jasper said gently. Faye and Noah, too, came to comfort her. Wallace tried to keep his own eyes from tearing, and Miss Brett reached out and the five children came to her. She held her arms wide so she could embrace them all.

"Please let our mummies and daddies come for Christmas!" Lucy cried again.

No one heard what the man in the floppy hat said before he placed the plate of oranges on the table and turned to go back to the kitchen.

CHAPTER TWENTY-SIX

A CHRISTMAS OF SURPRISES

OR

WHAT THEY FOUND IN
THE CHAMBER BELOW

"Where are we going?" Faye demanded for the tenth time. But there really was no answer other than "down" or "across" or "yes" or "not." She considered refusing to go any further, but the indignity of having one of them pick her up and carry her like a sack of potatoes kept her from standing still.

Christmas Eve had been a series of odd events. Everyone had been discussing what they might possibly be having for Christmas Eve dinner. The children's families had different traditions, if they had any at all.

"We always have our big feast on Christmas Eve, " said Noah. "When mother is in town and we actually celebrate."

Miss Brett had been making notes and reminding herself of recipes all morning. She assumed the mysterious men in black would be there cooking when she headed down to help in the kitchen. It was odd that there were no smells of turkeys or roasts or apple pies. She went to the pantry for her apron and was surprised to find the kitchen dark and the ovens cold. Might they be cooking elsewhere?

She rehung her apron and joined the children, who were assembled together at the front door. Then, as they lit the last candle on the wreath, Miss Brett turned around and was startled to find Robin Hood suddenly behind her. In the odd way of the mysterious men in black, he told her to be sure the children dressed warmly.

"I was going to set the table for Christmas Eve dinner," she had said.

"No setting," she was told.

"Why?" she asked, not willing to allow the children to miss Christmas Eve. "Are we going somewhere? Is there a plan for Christmas Eve? Where will we be taken?"

The answer was simply, "Yes," and she was left to prepare for whatever was in store for them. It being Christmas Eve Day, she and the children were all dressed in their nicest frocks and trousers, coats, and shirts. Miss Brett had hoped that, whatever was going to happen, they would have some celebration of the holiday. They pulled the warm woolies from the cupboard under the stairs. There were three fur muffs for Lucy, Faye, and herself, and warm, woolen gloves for the boys. The snow had fallen early in the day, but by the late afternoon, the mysterious men in black had shoveled a path and no more snow fell upon it. The walk into town would be easy, if that was where they were going.

It was not yet getting dark when the children and Miss Brett headed out into the cold, led by two of the mysterious men in black who had suddenly arrived at the door. One was tall in a wide-brimmed hat, and the other was thin and wore a beret. "Robin Hood" must have gone somewhere else.

"I'd much rather stay by the fire," said Wallace with a shiver. The others felt the same. Why were they heading off into the cold outdoors instead of having a lovely, comfortable Christmas Eve at the *palazzo*? Miss Brett could not answer this question, but hoped the answer would be worth the journey.

They headed down the road toward the village. Signora Fornaio's bakery was dark. No fabulous smells came to them along the road, and there was no stray raven drinking from an empty saucer. They all hoped that the baker was with the little old shepherd, or someone who would share the holiday with her. Miss Brett silently hoped, too, that the package from Signora Fornaio's son had finally arrived from the United States, and that a new postal carriage had brought it to her before the holiday.

But there were no signs of anyone. The whole village seemed to be closed up. Miss Brett decided everyone must be with their families. This made her feel sad for the children, who were not to be with their own.

"Mr. Corvino must be away for the holiday," said Lucy, looking up at the empty sky.

They walked in silence for several minutes, right through the center of the village, then down toward the fields, now vast beds of white. They followed the men in black as they turned from the road onto the small path that led to the tiny, ruined chapel.

"This is getting even stranger," Noah said through his warm balaclava. "I hope we're not expected to sit in a frozen ruin for Christmas Eve."

But from the looks of it, this was exactly where they were headed. The man in the wide-brimmed hat pulled open the creaky, broken gate. He stood, waiting for the others to enter. Reluctantly, they did. Luckily, there was a path into the chapel, so they would not have to trudge through the deep snow surrounding the place.

They followed the man in the wide-brimmed hat, stepping

over the crumbled threshold as he did, stepping around a hole in the floor as he did, bending to get through the arched doorway as he did. The beautiful vaulted ceiling was still there in some places, but much of the roof was gone, and in the gaps they could see the sky above. Snow filled the scattered pews, and drifts and wafts of snow were in the recesses and the rafters above, one of which was broken. A single raven sat on the broken rafter, chattering like falling stones. Still visible in the main room were frescos painted on the walls. The frescos depicted scenes in fields, with friars or monks dressed in black cloaks. Interestingly, Jasper could swear that some of the monks wore strange hats. Perhaps it was just the cracks in the walls that made the monks appear that way.

"Look at that," whispered Faye.

Jasper looked at one of the paintings and saw a group of monks, their heads bent, standing around a flag of white and red, as well as a flag of black and white.

"Recognize the flags?" said Faye, knowingly.

Jasper did recognize the flags. There was damage to the wall, but he could see, clearly, a man standing next to them. He had a close-cropped beard and a huge white head-dress.

"He must be their leader," said Noah.

"Maybe he's a bishop or something. This is a chapel, after all, and those are monks," said Faye.

Faye made sense, Jasper thought.

The raven in the rafters let out a screech. Jasper looked from the fresco and realized that he, Noah, and Faye were standing alone in the snow-filled chapel.

"Where did they go?" Jasper tried to keep a note of panic from his voice.

"They were just here," said Noah, looking around everywhere.

"Lucy!" Jasper called, his voice strangely muffled by the snow, his throat suddenly tight.

"Yes, Jasper?" Lucy said, her head popping out from a door Jasper hadn't seen.

"Oh—I just thought you might like to see the painting," he said sheepishly. He didn't want her to think he was worried.

"Well, don't dawdle," she scolded. "Come along, you three."

They quickly followed her through the archway.

The man in the black beret led them from the main room into a side room. It must have been the vestry, for the remains of an ancient robe still hung on a hook against the wall. There were other hooks that were bare. Jasper, Noah, and Faye followed Lucy up to what seemed to be a blank wall with a long crack from the broken ceiling to the crumbling floor. Lucy pushed against it, and it turned.

"I had to come back for you," Lucy said, again sounding very bossy. Jasper looked at Noah, who simply raised his eyebrows. Faye looked cross, until she really thought about the absurdity of Lucy scolding them for messing about.

"Sorry, Lucy," Jasper said, trying not to laugh.

"Well," the tiny girl said, "don't let it happen again."

⎯⎯➤◆◄⎯⎯

They next found themselves in a small room that once must have been the scriptorium—the room in medieval times where monks would write. There were still a couple of broken tables scattered around the room, and a small alcove in the back. There had been frescos painted from floor to ceiling, but now they were too faded really to see. Very faint, though, was the blue that may have been a sky, and some chips of green and gold. Dead vines and bramble were stuck all over the opening, but there was a cleared space at the center. The mysterious men in black led the children through this opening.

"We're not all going to fit in there," Wallace said as the men entered the little space.

First, Noah headed in and, looking around, found he was alone. Looking carefully in the dying light, he saw that against one wall was a large crack. He peeked over and saw light coming from inside. Because there was no other option, he stepped into the crack and, to the others, simply disappeared. Faye, then Jasper, entered and followed him.

When Miss Brett entered the alcove, Wallace and Lucy clung to her hand. She held them tight, as a sudden fear filled her heart. Once again, Noah, Faye, and Jasper were not with her. Where were they? Over the months, she had developed a little tic—a small ache, almost—when any of the five was not in her sights, or was somewhere she did not know. The smallest of worries—the tiny thought that the mysterious men in black were leading them into harm's way—tried to make itself known in her thoughts. But as she looked closely, she saw the light from the crack, and she decided, come what may, she would go into that space. After all, Faye, Noah, and Jasper were already there.

Holding Wallace and Lucy close to her, she, too, entered.

Immediately, bright light came from torches of fire placed along the walls of a tunnel. They were in some sort of passageway. Ahead, Lucy saw the wide-brimmed man, Faye, Jasper, and Noah. Without saying a word, the man continued through the tunnel.

Several times, they came to forks where other tunnels seemed to intersect. The man in the floppy hat seemed to know the way without hesitation. Silently, they all followed.

The walls of the tunnel were stone. Along the way, they all noticed some carvings and writings. Whatever language the carvings were in, the children could not read them. Wallace noticed a small circular carving that recurred three times along the tunnel walls. They passed what looked like a chute of some kind, something that might once have been used to send coal or some other sort of supplies down into the tunnel. It looked old and unused.

After several long minutes, during which it felt as if they were walking in circles that slowly spiraled downward, they came to a large set of doors. The doors must have been ten feet high, with huge iron hinges and a set of gears that was surely a locking system. Along the center, between the two doors, was a thick metal astragal. While it is not unusual for a set of doors to have an astragal—the strip or folded molding often found between two doors—it was unusual for the astragal to have a rounded groove running up its center. Perhaps it was decorative, thought Faye, running her finger along it. It was smooth where almost everything else was rough.

Wallace, too afraid to move forward, noticed a round carving on the right-hand door. It looked familiar to him. It was like the carvings he had seen along the passageway.

"Lucy!" said Jasper as his little sister ran up to the door and knocked. The sound of her knock was a tiny whisper. The door must have been so thick that no sound could penetrate, not even a knock.

The wide-brimmed man looked down at Lucy. She looked up at him and, as only Lucy could, seemed to understand his wordless gaze. She stepped back into Miss Brett's skirt and clung to her teacher, her eyes never leaving the mysterious man in black.

The man reached up and pulled a small metal tong from the hinge of the door on the left. He inserted it into a small hole in the door on the right, and a click sounded. He then turned a small metal bar that, in turn, flipped open a small hatch in the center of the door on the right. He flipped the hatch door, which then turned a gear that turned another gear and opened another hatch a bit lower than the first. Inside this hatch was a key.

The key fit into the first hatch, and from that snapped an opening in which there appeared to be an iron dragon or bird carved in the center. The man pulled out the dragon or bird, and it swung on a hinge. It was this hinge that allowed the dragon to become a knocker. Hitting against the iron frame, it made a loud *clang* that echoed through the entire passage.

"Now, that's handy," said Noah, his ears ringing.

Not more than a moment later, great grinding and clanking could be heard as the doors began to open. Miss Brett could see that the doors were more than a foot thick. She reached around and pulled Wallace and Lucy near her. She grabbed Noah's shirt collar and pulled him closer, too. Jasper and Faye stood staring at the door, neither one within her reach.

Suddenly, Miss Brett wanted to run. She wanted to take the children and run as far as she could. The urge was strong enough to make her feet tingle. Gulping, she stood firm, holding the children close. The doors opened wider until the gears and grinding came to a halt.

In front of them was a huge room. It looked like something from a medieval castle. On the left was an enormous wooden table, set beautifully with festive ornaments. At the far wall, on the right, was a giant fireplace. A roaring fire glowed from there, warming the whole room. Not far from the fireplace was a beautiful, ornate bird perch. On it sat a shiny black raven. The bird began chattering the moment the children entered. Across from the fireplace, against the corner, was a giant tree, resplendent with candles and tinsel and trinkets.

"It's the tree," said Lucy, staring up at the amazing tree. It was the second tree they had watched the mysterious men in black cut down. "And look, a raven!" she cried, pulling the bird from the perch and hugging him close to her body. The bird, strangely, did not object. "You look so much like Mr. Corvino. He must be your brother. I miss him. He's been away for days." Lucy snuggled against the bird's breast. Faye and Miss Brett chose not even to look at each other.

There were tapestries and carpets to help keep the cold stone from chilling the air. There were large velvet chairs and sofas around the fire. There were hallways leading off on either side of the fireplace, and from each side of the room. But there was no one else in the room—no one, that is, except a tiny, ancient lady sitting in a chair, warming her hands at the fire. She did not seem to notice the children's arrival.

Miss Brett, still flanked by her charges and finding it difficult to move with them surrounding her, managed to step toward the woman. She could hear the old lady mumbling to herself, as if she were continuing a conversation she had been having before the other person left.

"Oh, yes," she was saying, "I do love a good meringue. And Christmas pudding. Don't fight over the biscuits, children, and don't nibble on the treacle tarts, yes? Oh, yes, indeed, doesn't stop them, does it?"

"Excuse me," Miss Brett said softly, not wanting to startle the old woman. But the woman did not seem to hear her. She continued to prattle on about puddings and sweets and children.

Miss Brett cleared her throat. "Excuse me," she said louder. But still, the old woman did not respond. Miss Brett turned around to ask the mysterious men in black what was happening, but none was in sight. The men had gone, leaving only her, the children, and the tiny old lady.

Lucy broke away from Miss Brett and ran to the lady. She touched the old woman's cheek. The woman turned toward her and smiled so broadly, it lit up her entire face.

"Isobel," she said in recognition. "My sweet Isobel."

"I'm Lucy," said Lucy.

"Then we must feed you if you are hungry," the lady said.

"I..." Lucy began, but then something took her breath away.

The sound of laughter was the first thing, but it was what followed the laughter that made all the children cry out.

Walking together, dressed in their Christmas best, came their parents.

CHAPTER TWENTY-SEVEN

An Uneasy Feast

OR

THE PROMISE

The Drs. Modest, Dr. Banneker, the Drs. Vigyanveta, Dr. Canto-Sagas, and the beautiful Ariana stood before them. Miss Brett moved back toward the door to give space to the children and their parents.

Lucy ran to her parents. "Mummy! Daddy!" she cried, and allowed herself to be scooped into their arms. Jasper, quite nonplussed, slowly walked over to them. He wasn't sure how to react. They were there and they were fine, but the ghost of the terror he felt when he thought they had died still lingered in his heart.

Noah took a moment to register that his mother was there, too. He shook his head, then ran to her.

"Noah, my boy." His father joined them in a hug.

Wallace's father didn't give Wallace time to approach. He rushed over and lifted his boy in his arms. "Look at you. I could swear you have grown in just these months."

Faye still stood by the door. Her parents stood together by the hearth. They were smiling at her. They were standing there, smiling and expecting her to come bounding over and jump into their loving arms.

"How could you?" Faye said quietly, almost to herself. She shook her head. "How could you?" she asked, a bit louder.

"Darling," her mother said. "Darling, don't be like that. Not on Christmas."

"*Marmelo*," her father said, "come to us. We have been missing you."

"Really, you've been missing me?" Faye could feel the hot anger rising in her cheeks. Now the others were noticing as well. "You've been missing me? Maybe if you have been missing me, you'd send a letter or come for a visit or in some other way *let me know you were alive*!!!" Tears streamed from her face.

Jasper had reached his parents, but had yet to fall into their embrace. Between the thrill of seeing them and the walk toward them, something had happened inside him. He had been unable to speak for the lump in his throat, but he felt the words Faye spoke as if he had spoken them.

Noah turned to his parents. "Why didn't you get in touch?"

"I'm always in touch," Ariana said. "I send you cards from every place I go."

"I'm sorry, son, but for us, it's difficult," his father said.

"It's ... difficult for you?" Noah took this hard. "You mean because you didn't come to visit us? Because you didn't know where we were?"

"We knew where you were, son," Dr. Ben Banneker said. "We know you are living in the *palazzo*."

"Yes," Tobias Modest said, looking at Jasper. "You are so clever, Jasper. All of you are. The snowball-throwing machines and the magnets..."

"*C'est vrai*," said Isobel Modest. "It is—"

"You knew what we were doing and where we were living, but you didn't bother to let us know?" Faye was incensed. "You even knew about the snowball machines? Did you ever wonder if perhaps we might worry, or wonder if you were being held captive or been killed or were suffering somewhere? What if *we* had disappeared and *you* didn't know where we went?!"

"I disappeared," said Lucy, who had been so busy being embraced that she had not heard a thing.

"You disappeared?" asked Dr. Isobel Modest. "*Ma foi, cherie,* how did you disappear?"

"What is the matter here?" asked Dr. Banneker in his booming voice.

"*Oui,* Jasper, what is this?" Dr. Isobel Modest turned to her son.

"Didn't you ever think we might be worried?" asked Jasper. He was not sure how to think about this. Had his parents been so thoughtless? Had they truly not cared?

"Why would you be worried?" asked Ariana, caressing Noah's face.

Noah closed his eyes and soaked in the pleasure of his mother's touch, but it didn't prevent him from asking, "You didn't wonder whether we were afraid?" He looked at his father because, after all, Ariana really did not have anything to do with this.

"Son," his father began. But upon looking into Noah's eyes, Clarence Canto-Sagas dropped his head. "No, we didn't consider that you might be worried."

This admission seemed to shake Faye from her fierce indignation, and her face fell. But she was still angry—very angry.

"Yes, Faye," her mother said, "we simply didn't think that you would be worried. We were so busy being worried about you."

"Worried about us? *We saw you killed!*" Faye shouted. "You let us think you were killed, blown up, on the train! Not worried? Are you mad?!"

"Now, that is not the way a young lady speaks to her mother, *marmelo*," Dr. Rajeesh Vigyanveta said.

"We did what was best," insisted Dr. Banneker.

"Well, that was bad form," Jasper said, finding his strength and determination. "We are not simply possessions to be bandied about, tossed, and stored away at whim."

"What—what—" His father hesitated. "Utter nonsense to think we..."

"I want to know now," said Faye. "Are you being held captive?"

"Captive?" Her mother looked at her father. "Raj?"

"Such nonsense, my little *marmelo*," said Dr. Vigyanveta.

"Well?" demanded Faye. "Are you free to go?"

The adults all looked from one to another, as if speaking silently among themselves. None was willing to look into the eyes of one of the children.

Dr. Banneker cleared his throat. "Well, it's not as simple as that. Being free to go is not exactly an appropriate way to—"

"Father." Wallace pulled back from his father's strong embrace. "The question is not a difficult one."

"Yes, Wallace, it is," Tobias Modest said. "We are bound by— well, something like an oath, or a deep... a long... serious... well..." He faltered.

"Maybe they made a promise," Lucy said. She was anxious. She didn't like the idea of parents being attacked by their children. She didn't care that she had been heartbroken when her parents were missing or that she missed them terribly. She was afraid that the others might make her parents go away again.

"Yes," Dr. Canto-Sagas said, wiping his forehead. "We have, indeed, been a part of a promise that was made long ago."

"A promise to keep us believing you were dead?" Faye demanded.

"No," Dr. Banneker said loudly. "Not that, but we must—"

"Why can't you tell us why?" Faye was no longer just angry. She felt miserable to be left behind and pushed away. "Why?"

"Because . . ." Faye's mother put her hand on her daughter's shoulder.

"Because they cannot tell you anything for your own safety and protection," Ariana said, a touch, just a touch, of sarcasm in her voice. "Because danger and sinister, hidden truths fill the rooms in which they find themselves detained. Because if they don't stay, the world may collapse and . . . and . . ." But Ariana's angelic voice broke and she put her handkerchief to her lips. Her husband and son embraced her as she shook her head in silence. Noah looked into his father's eyes and saw pleading.

"I think," Noah said, still looking at his father, "I think we need to remember this is Christmas."

The parents all nodded and, looking at each other, seemed relieved but also guilty.

"You will make a promise to us," said Jasper. "A promise that you will not abandon us."

Isobel gasped. "*Mon cher*, we never—"

"Yes, you did. Promise you won't do that again," said Jasper.

"We promise, son," said Dr. Banneker. "And I respect your demands."

Jasper nodded in appreciation, but did not let up. "You will be in touch with us—"

"Whenever possible," Dr. Banneker said. "There are times—"

"Whenever possible," said Jasper.

Faye opened her mouth, but then realized it was over. She could not fight this battle—not now. At that moment, she just wanted her parents to hold her. She looked up at first her mother, then her father. She leaned into her mother's shoulder, and her mother and father both surrounded her with an embrace.

"We love you," Noah's father said, then looked to the other children, too. "We are sorry you have been brought into all this."

Miss Brett had been silent. Still standing near the doorway, she kept herself from accusing the parents of neglect and, thus, abuse of the children they supposedly loved. She herself would never have treated her own children this way. But she held her tongue. It was not her place to speak for the children, and besides, they were doing an excellent job speaking for themselves.

"Miss Bird," came the booming voice of Dr. Banneker as he leaned toward the tiny old lady. "May you lend me the favor of your arm?" She did, and he walked her over to a comfortable chair near the fire.

"Why, thank you, Benjamin dear," she said, patting his hand. "Yes, it has always been hard for you children."

Dr. Banneker's smile faltered, but he was quick to return it when Miss Bird smiled at him.

———

"Where are we?" Faye finally asked as the children and their parents, recovered somewhat from the intensity of their initial confrontation, settled into comfortable seats around the fire. Faye's mother caressed her daughter's hair, and held Faye's amulet in her hand. She looked at her husband, who returned the look. Both showed concern.

Faye felt the necklace around her neck. She had been quick to notice that her mother might ask for it back. But her mother let the amulet fall back into place. Faye looked over at Lucy and Jasper and saw their mother looking at their bracelets too—small things that brought them comfort, things the children clung to when they had little else from their parents.

Faye looked around the room and wondered again where they could be.

The ceilings were high, and the room very large. Across the room, on the other side of the table, was where the kitchen must be, because the parents had carried dishes from there.

"We are deep in the ground," Dr. Banneker finally said. "The whole of the castle was built into the mountain."

"There's a castle built underground?" said Lucy, fascinated by the idea.

"I think we're in it," Noah said.

"But where are the men in black?" asked Faye. It did not escape her notice that not a silly black bonnet nor a pair of black bunny ears was in sight.

"They must be cooking in the kitchen," Jasper said.

"Not tonight," said Dr. Canto-Sagas. He smiled, looking toward the kitchen.

"Because it's Christmas?" asked Faye. "They celebrate Christ-mas?"

But a clucking and a clatter came from the kitchen. "Saints preserve us," someone said, "there best be some hungry bellies in this room."

The children turned, and there, coming toward them, carrying all manner of dishes, were four people the children were very happy to see, though utterly surprised to find.

"Rosie!" cried Lucy and Jasper together. And the others, too, jumped up to see their own nannies from back in Dayton.

"Well, you don't think they could do a Christmas without your Rosie, do you?" Rosie hugged Jasper and Lucy in her strong, fierce arms. She smelled of nutmeg and cinnamon, and the children were well-crushed in her grasp.

"The nannies are making Christmas dinner tonight," Dr. Modest said. "It's tradition."

"Tradition?" said Jasper.

"Oh, yes," came the voice of the tiny old lady by the fire. "We have always used fresh butter when we make the apple pie."

"Miss Bird." Dr. Banneker, standing, placed his hand gently on the old woman's shoulder, bending down at the knees so he was not speaking down to her. "May I bring you a cup of hot chocolate?" He spoke in his loud, booming voice, and spoke so she could look at his face.

"Oh, that would be lovely, Benjamin," she said, patting him on the head as if he were a child. "Such a thoughtful boy you are."

"Boy?" Wallace said, grinning. "She called my father a boy."

Faye's father jumped up to get the back cushion Miss Bird had accidentally lost.

"You are a sweet boy, too, my ickle Rajikins."

Faye burst into laughter. "She called my father 'ickle Rajikins'!"

Dr. Rajesh Vigyanveta laughed, but blushed nonetheless. "Of

course she did. To her, we are all still the children she knew."

"She knew you all?" said Faye.

"The golden children." Miss Bird giggled to herself, tapping the side of her nose. "The gilded children."

"Of course she did, dear," Dr. Gwendolyn Vigyanveta said. "Well, not all of us. I met Miss Bird once your father and I . . . well, after we were married. But your father did." She looked around the room. "And all of your parents, too," she said, then quickly looking at her husband. She was relieved when he patted her hand.

"Yes, dear, that is fine," Rajesh Vigyanveta said gently to his wife. This seemed to relax his wife. But it had the opposite effect on Faye. This was the woman who had been one of the youngest, most powerful minds in science? That was before she married. What happened to her?

Noah looked up. He opened his mouth to correct Faye's mother. But why bother? He knew the great Ariana could not have been a member of this childhood group. She was a chanteuse, an artist, not a scientist. But he had not known this about his father. This involved more than individual scientists, stolen from their lives. He and the other children were brought together because their parents were already part of something.

"Miss Bird was our teacher," Dr. Tobias Modest said. "All of us. She taught Benjamin, Isobel, Clarence, Raj, Louisa, and N—"

"Louisa?" Noah said. "Who's Louisa?"

"My mother," Wallace said, adjusting his glasses and sticking his hand back into his pocket. "I mean, Louisa was my mother's name." He looked up at his father. "Father?"

"She was with you all, too?" Noah asked, eyebrows raised.

Dr. Banneker looked from Dr. Isobel to her husband, and then to the Drs. Vigyanveta. He looked at his son and the other children.

"She was a brilliant scientist," Dr. Banneker said, a sadness in his voice. "And ... well, yes, Louisa, your mother, we knew each other from the time we were—"

But he was cut short by the sound of pots and pans clanging loudly in the kitchen. There was a roar, like an angry bear, then a lot of clucking.

"Don't you try that with me, you!" came Rosie's voice. "I've put the right amount of ginger in the recipe and I shan't have you adding your crazy numbers to it."

"Madame," came a retort, "there were only six pieces, and there were seven in the other batch. You cannot expect anyone to—"

"Thems were smaller pieces, Nikola. You get your interfering hands out of my pie. Saints preserve us."

"Ah, yes, and Nikola," said Dr. Tobias Modest, smiling as he spoke.

With a flourish and a stomp, the tapestry on the other side of the dining table flew back and, to the surprise of all the children, out stepped the very strange man they had met before the train exploded, and then in New York.

"Nikola Tesla?" Lucy said with surprise.

"He was your schoolmate?" Wallace adjusted his glasses.

"Well, Nikola was one of us, yes," Dr. Rajesh Vigyanveta said. "Not a school chum, no."

"*Was* I, Rajesh? So you no longer consider me a member of the fold? Am I no longer a mind worthy of your consort?" Nikola Tesla huffed his way past everyone and, after sweeping imaginary dust from the chair with his white handkerchief, seated himself stiffly across from Miss Bird by the fire.

"Nikki," Dr. Banneker said soothingly, "you have always been one of us. We are honored you came to share the holiday with us here."

"Hmph," said Tesla, shimmying his feet in a shuffle, trying to turn away from them all the more.

Ariana, graceful as a ballerina, swept across the room and placed a hand on the back of Tesla's chair.

"Nikola Tesla, your name reaches throughout the world of intellect, beyond the world of the mundane, into the mind of all who seek to understand the universe. Anyone who has come to know you must surely love to hear of your wondrous discoveries and inventions." She smiled the dazzling smile that brought kingdoms to her performances. Nikola Tesla blushed and, inch by inch, toe by toe, moved his legs back around the chair so he was facing the room. She offered him her hand and, unlike with anyone else, he took that hand and, his pale face now pink, brought his lips within nanometers of her hand.

"That's a good boy, Nikola," said Miss Bird. "Don't go sulking when there are so many people who want to play."

"Miss Bird, for your information, I was not—"

"Always a bit huffy, that one. I never," Miss Bird said, leaning aside to tell the others. "But what a genius." She looked up at Miss Brett, who had moved closer to the fire. Miss Bird took Miss Brett's hand. "You are so kind, dear, so caring with the children," the old lady said, a twinkle in her kind eyes.

Miss Brett flushed and bent down to speak closely to Miss Bird. "You were the teacher of the children?" she asked.

"Oh, yes, I taught them, though sometimes I felt they were teaching me."

"I know the feeling," Miss Brett said, smiling.

The children exchanged looks among themselves.

"Well, it'll be getting cold if yous aren't at the table to eat it," said Rosie, her hands on her hips. "Now." She pointed toward the dining room.

"Yes, ma'am," Dr. Banneker said, jumping up as if he had been scolded. Wallace could not help but smile to himself. His father was acting like a little boy. His big, strong, powerful father was, in some real way, scared of the nannies and Miss Bird.

Both Dr. Banneker and Dr. Modest helped Miss Bird from her chair and to the dining table. Dr. Canto-Sagas and his wife helped her into the seat at the head of the table, which Dr. Vigyanveta pulled out for her, and which Nikola Tesla dusted with his ever-present white handkerchief. The children watched as their parents fussed over the elderly lady. And the children, in turn, each imagined Miss Brett as an elderly lady, and how each of them would adore her and fuss over her.

"How I love roasted sweet potatoes," Miss Bird said, and no sooner were the words from her lips than she found each of her boys trying not to burn his fingers on the hot sweet potatoes. "Stop this nonsense," she said, taking the potato held by Dr. Canto-Sagas. "You sit and eat. And the lovely teacher, come sit by me, my dear. We have so much to share. On my left, dear, so I can see you with my better eye."

Miss Brett blushed, feeling honored to be so asked. At the far end of the table, Clarence Canto-Sagas sat on Miss Bird's right, then Noah, then Ariana. Jasper sat next to his mother and Lucy between her parents. Across the table, Dr. Banneker sat beside Miss Brett, and Wallace next to him. Faye tried to avoid sitting next to her mother, but was unsuccessful. Rajesh sat next to his wife, and Nikola Tesla sat across from Lucy.

Wallace looked into his empty plate, finding it hard to look at his father. Jasper felt that things were still too unresolved for his liking, and found the plate of fish very interesting, for it allowed him to look away from Lucy, who was beaming, sandwiched between her parents.

Noah succumbed to the caresses and embraces of his mother. He basked, helplessly, in her presence, his father somewhat abandoned on Noah's other side. Clarence Canto-Sagas smiled affectionately at Miss Bird. Faye sat between her parents and tried to shed herself of the anger that still burned inside her.

———→●←———

There were soups—rice and chestnut, roast vegetable and orzo. There was a roast on either end of the table. There were four terrines of potatoes—mashed, roasted, baked, and sweet. The sweet potatoes had been crusted with a brown sugar, salt, and butter rub, so that they were sweet and savory at the same time. They practically melted in your mouth. There were gravies and sauces and relishes and butters. There were big loaves of hot, fresh bread and small plates of salted olive oil for dipping.

There was a whole smoked salmon, sliced very thin, its head garnished with parsley. It being obvious that the fish was a fish, Lucy declined a serving. "Oh, I couldn't eat the sweet little fishy," she said sadly. "It was somebody's friend once."

There were sausages and crisp onions, and trout almondine. Noah took a giant helping of the roast boar and Faye continued to shoot him dirty looks, which did not keep him from making comments about eating the boar before it could eat them and snorting piggishly as he chewed. Lucy nibbled sausage, blissfully unconscious of its origins. Every plate was sumptuous. Nikola Tesla, picky though he was, did not turn down a single dish offered at the feast, though he cleaned his fork after every bite and talked nonstop of his death ray.

"Theft, I tell you. I am certain someone gazed upon my death ray and stole it." He wiped the side of his hand after pounding it on the table.

"Stole it?" asked Jasper. He glanced over at Noah, who had raised his eyebrows in suspicion.

"Stole it by looking at it?" asked Noah.

"Stole it, yes, with the mind. Someone's mind stole it, I am sure. The blueprints felt different," he insisted.

"How does it work?" asked Wallace, genuinely interested in the device from a scientific point of view.

"It uses a ferrous mercury alloy as the ammunition, first of all," Tesla said in a near whisper.

"And that is a powerful choice for ammunition?" asked Noah, doubtful.

"It can blow a hole through a wall—even slice a cow in half," Tesla said, wiping a phantom speck from his tiny moustache.

"Oh, never do that," said Lucy, who leaned back so her mother could slice her roast beef. "Never cut a sweet, furry cow in half."

Jasper shot Noah a glance.

"Wallace, you take a big helping," said his father. "Put a little hair on that chest of yours."

Miss Brett could see Wallace shrink next to his father.

"Then there are my lightning balls," continued Nikola Tesla.

"Lightning balls?" asked Noah, his eyebrows raised.

"And you know exactly of what I am speaking. My lightning ball was the brilliant invention you saw on the train. I call my invention the Fire Sphere of Death, or Sphere of Atmoselectronic Power, or the—"

"AtmoSphere?" suggested Noah.

"What?" said Tesla, indignant.

"The AtmoSphere." Noah smiled. "Kind of a catchy name, yes?"

"What is this silliness?" grumbled Nikola Tesla. "My Spheres of Death are beyond any—"

"Yes, we know," Faye said. "It's what you used to make us think our parents were dead."

Tesla had not spotted the waving arm of Dr. Canto-Sagas, begging him not to speak of this.

"We did that explosion for your own safety," he said. "What of it?" He shook his napkin and pushed his food around with his fork.

"What?" Faye was indignant. "For our own safety? You allowed us to suffer and believe our parents were blown to pieces for our own—"

"This is why I have no children," said Tesla. "This and the horrid things that come down from their noses. Why would I want to have such whining creatures with no sense of propriety and self-preservation?"

Faye stood up. "We have a sense of—"

"Faye!" said Jasper. This was going nowhere. "Please, Faye. It's Christmas."

Faye sat back down. She sat quietly until the anger subsided. She would not spoil their evening. But she would also not let this rest, either.

When the main meal was finished, sweets and puddings followed in droves. There was treacle tart and apple pie, pumpkin cake and biscotti. There were meringues and marzipans, frangipane, chocolates, and custards.

"Would anyone like this frangipane with apricots?" asked Lucy, holding it up. "I've eaten three and would very much like this one, too, but—"

Faye couldn't bear Noah eating yet another. She stood up and reached over, as Jasper reached and Wallace leaned over as well. Their arms all bumped at once, knocking Lucy. Again, it was as if an electrical shock passed through them. Jasper felt a tug in his wrist, Faye from her neck, and Wallace through his leg. Lucy dropped the tart and wrenched her hand back.

"Oh!" cried Ariana, who reached for her throat. Then, recovering herself, she looked around the room.

"I understand, dear lady," Nikola Tesla said, fanning Ariana with his kerchief, believing she had been as appalled by the dropping of the tart as he had.

"What happened?" asked Noah, mid-bite.

"It happened on the train, only not as strong," Faye said. "It must have been static electricity."

"Or the electrical charge from the frangipane," said Lucy, picking at the fallen treat. "It is electrifyingly delicious." And into her mouth it went.

Ariana, collecting herself, reached for a handkerchief to delicately dab at the perspiration on her upper lip. Lucy watched her, wide-eyed. Ariana smiled and, with her graceful fingers, brushed away the crumbs in the corners of Lucy's mouth.

Electrical charges? Wallace considered this. It was true, the charge seemed stronger than on the train. Faye, Lucy, Jasper, and Wallace had all been near one another before tonight, many times. But somehow, that evening, around the table with their parents, something happened. Could there be some strange electric or magnetic or electromagnetic charge among them? He might be able to explain the coin, for he had been working with magnets, but what about everything else? Was something changing? Getting stronger?

———◦●◦———

By the end of the meal, everyone had been exceptionally well fed. Noah had to be dragged away, reaching for a last custard, a last biscotti, or a last caggionetti. Ariana was worried the boy might burst. Lucy took one more meringue and wrapped it in her napkin.

The parents, teachers, and Nikola Tesla repaired to the hearth. The nannies joined in for some after-dinner conversation, bringing along trays of tea and brandy.

"Just a little Christmas nip," said Rosie, taking a brandy and handing one to Miss Bird.

"I'd fancy a look around," Faye whispered to Jasper, wanting neither tea nor brandy. "What, for example, is down those halls?" Faye pointed to the four halls that led from the main room. "Can you hear it?"

Jasper strained to listen. Yes, there was something. A humming. Was it music? It sounded like one low, humming voice.

"Come on, Jasper," said Faye. "Let's explore." She would have wandered off on her own anyway. She even thought of sneaking off so her parents might have to wonder where she was. Somehow, the moment had never seemed right, but now, with the music, she had to explore.

"Oh, yes, let's do explore," said Lucy. But then she looked anxiously at her mother and reached for her hand. "Maybe—maybe I'll stay here to be sure they don't go away."

"Good luck with that," said Faye. She looked at Wallace, who seemed so tiny sitting next to his father.

Lucy tugged at her mother's arm. "Please don't go away right now, Mummy. I'm—"

"*Ma cheré*," said Isobel Modest, "we are here and will not go anywhere... without letting you know."

With slight trepidation, Lucy let go of her mother. Isobel looked from Lucy to Jasper. "Je vous promets, mes enfants. I promise you both."

Initially, the children realized they had to trust that promise. They had no choice. But Lucy chose to test the promise and came running back to her mother's arms moments after leaving. Then, seeing her mother still there, she hurried off to catch up with the others.

CHAPTER TWENTY-EIGHT

A Black Gathering

OR

THE MYSTERIOUS MEN IN BLACK IN BLACK

"Let's go there first," Lucy said, pointing to the hallway on the far right. The archways offered nothing but darkness beyond.

"Why?" asked Faye.

"It's where the singing is coming from," Lucy said. The others could tell now that the music was louder in that direction. It was the sound of Gregorian chanting. So the children entered the passageway gingerly, carefully, slowly.

Farther down, there were small flame torches mounted to the walls, as they had been in the tunnel, invisible from the main room. With the dim torchlight in the passageway, their path was not total darkness. Still, with the chanting, there was a haunting feeling as they approached.

Lucy slipped one hand into Faye's, and her bracelet, on the other arm, into her mouth. Faye squeezed to let Lucy know she was there.

After listening to the different doors, the children determined that it was the third door on the right side. Without a doubt, the voices were coming from the room beyond.

"Open the door," Noah said, standing deliberately behind Faye.

"Oh, isn't that brave of you," Faye said.

"I think we should leave it closed," Wallace said. "I mean, out of respect for whoever is singing." He was shaking a bit, but tried to hide it. He had shoved his hands into his pockets, grateful his lucky coin was there.

"If we open the door just a bit, we can see what's going on," Faye said. She had to peek. She touched the handle of the door and turned it slightly. It was not locked. "Shhhhh," she said.

Noah leaned over Faye, with Jasper just below him. Wallace and Lucy bent below Faye. Slowly, Faye turned the knob and pushed the door open. She opened it only a few inches, but it was enough.

The room was smaller than the dining room, but it, too, had tapestries and tall ceilings. In the room were gathered twenty mysterious men in black—at least, the children assumed they were mysterious men in black. All the men wore dark robes, like monks, instead of their usual strange costumes.

"It's like it was on the boat," whispered Noah.

Faye carefully, and silently, closed the door again. Somehow, it felt wrong, looking in on them. Somehow, it felt wrong, even cruel, to disturb them.

"Let's go," said Faye, but Wallace was looking at his pocket. He could feel the coin inside it moving, as if to get out. Faye walked off to try another door.

"What is it, Wallace?" asked Jasper. Right then, the coin stopped its strange behavior, and Wallace didn't feel like mentioning anything. He followed the others down the hall, but every other door was locked.

"Let's get back before they miss us," whispered Jasper.

"Oh, I don't want Mummy to miss us," Lucy squeaked.

They turned around and headed back the way they came. They quickly slipped out of the corridor and into the room of adults. Conversation had not been altered by the departure or arrival of the young inventors. In fact, within moments, it was clear to Faye that the children had not been missed by their parents at all. Had the parents even noticed they weren't there? Was life better for them without children, who were a bother and a distraction? No, the parents were all deep into their discussion. Was she surprised? Faye took a deep breath and bit her tongue. No, she was not surprised. She was hurt, but not surprised.

Faye sat sulking for several minutes after that. She found herself sitting next to her mother, who sat listening intently to something her father was saying. Suddenly, Faye felt she had been there before—déjà vu. Her mother sitting meekly at her father's side, looking up at him, hanging on his every word.

Faye looked from one to the other. She could not decide who she was angrier with. Her father was so full of himself, telling everyone about something he had done—something brilliant. Faye looked at her mother, who was smiling that bovine smile with her big green eyes gazing adoringly at her husband. Then her mother turned those eyes on Faye and gave Faye that same weak, cowish expression. Her mother was a genius, or she had been.

But Faye could not remember her mother being any other way. She remembered her mother being even worse—never speaking, very thin and ill, always ill. Gwendolyn Vigyanveta had been the youngest graduate of the Annex, the first woman to be admitted to actual classes at Harvard. She was a rising star in science, yet she let her husband run her life. Faye's mother couldn't even make a decision without her husband's approval. What had happened to her?

Faye would never be like that. She would never let a man make all the decisions and sit quietly as he did so. Never.

Miss Brett brought a plate of biscuits over to Faye. "Here, sweet angel," she said, then she leaned close to Faye's ear. "I know this is hard," she said in a whisper. "But you need to let yourself forgive them, even a bit at a time." Faye did not take a biscuit, so Miss Brett placed one on Faye's saucer and handed the saucer to Faye.

Faye took it, reluctantly, and held it without eating. She bit her lip, still watching her parents. She knew Miss Brett was right, but not entirely so. No, she would not forgive. She placed the saucer on the table and stood up. She walked over to the corridor across the room, but her stiff departure was barred by a wrought-iron gate. She had not seen it, shadowed in the dark. It would not open, even as she shook it, but she noticed the strange grooves that ran around it and up around the archway.

Then she turned and walked to the next passageway. It, too, was barred. Feeling her face flush, Faye turned back to the last corridor. Without a passing glance at the parents, she marched toward the last passageway. Here there was no gate to bar her way.

Faye took a deep breath and walked into the darkness.

Soon, she was standing in the dark, without even the singing to serve as excuse or direction. She inched further into the hallway, but here there were no flaming torches, however small. There was only dark and cold as she moved away from the entrance. It felt tight and close. Were the walls closer than she thought? Were they getting closer as she walked? Faye's chest felt tight. She shut her eyes tight. No, she would not call for Jasper. She tried to catch her breath, but it felt as if her lungs were suddenly made of stone.

"Faye?"

Faye heard the voice calling softly into the darkness. She saw Jasper standing at the entrance. She wiped the sweat from her brow. Even in the chill, she was sweating. Gulping down what air she could, she closed her eyes again.

"What is it, Jasper?" She tried to sound relaxed.

Jasper stepped into the darkness and, as his eyes adjusted, he saw Faye sitting on the stone floor. He sat down next to her.

"I just can't accept it all as easily as everyone else," she said. "I can't stop being angry."

"It's funny," said Jasper, thoughtfully. "You see yourself as weak when you need a friend. It must be exhausting, trying to keep your chin up all the time. Your power to fight is the thing that makes you battle-weary, Faye. It's all right. Really, it's all right."

"What should I do?" asked Faye, suddenly holding tight to Jasper's hand. She tried not to resent the crack in her voice. She felt the chill of the sweat on her skin and wished she were sitting by the fire instead of here with her stockings and skirts on the stone floor, clinging to Jasper's hand.

Jasper stood up, letting her hold onto his hand. She stood up, realizing that she had been clutching Jasper's hand, but she didn't let go. She was grateful that she didn't have to come stomping into the room all alone. He had saved her from humiliating retreat.

Together, they went back to the warmth of the hearth.

CHAPTER TWENTY-NINE

A PRICKLING FEELING THIS WAY COMES

OR

WHAT WALLACE FINDS SHOCKING

Back by the fire, Miss Brett and the parents were deep in conversation. Miss Bird snored in the comfy chair, and Nikola Tesla muttered to himself by the fireplace.

The children sat either on the rug, on cushions, or on the armrests of their parents' chairs. Wallace's father patted his leg as an invitation, and Wallace climbed up to sit in the big man's lap.

"It really is good to see you, son," his father said, pulling Wallace into a bear hug. "You got that coin? I mean, for good luck?"

Wallace smiled. "Yes, Father," he said. "I never let it out of my pocket."

"I knew it would be safe with you." His father smiled. "Because we could all use good luck, right?"

"I love it because you gave it to me," said Wallace. "I'm not one to believe in either luck or magic."

"Of course you're not," his father said, grinning more broadly. "You're my boy. You're a scientist."

Wallace threw his arms around his father's neck. His father wrapped those big strong arms around him. It felt so good to be near his father. He felt so safe.

Rosie came waddling in, carrying a big box with the name "Thomas J. Smith" on it.

"Crackers!" cried Lucy. "Christmas crackers!"

Lucy jumped up and down, and the others couldn't help being excited, too. Soon, small explosions were going off all over the room. Jasper and Lucy each pulled an end of a green- and blue-colored cracker. With a *pop*, Lucy squealed with delight and grabbed the foiled chocolate.

Wallace, meanwhile, smiled, leaning back against his father's chest and clasping his coin in his hand. He felt so secure holding it, feeling the comfort of the familiar warm metal against his palm. And it *was* warm, he thought. In fact, it was not only warm, but it seemed to be vibrating.

Wallace looked around the room at the others. Everyone seemed consumed by the festivities. Everyone was focused on the Christmas crackers.

Maybe it's just all the excitement, Wallace thought. He looked over, and Lucy was wearing her bracelet, as was Jasper his. Faye held the charm on her necklace, just as Wallace clutched his coin.

With an impulse he could not explain, Wallace held his coin out and walked over to Jasper. He brushed his hand past Jasper's arm, as if by accident. He could not be absolutely sure, but he thought he felt the coin in his hand quiver as he passed. Jasper jolted back.

"Hey, Wallace," Jasper croaked, rubbing his wrist. "You gave me a start. That was—well, that was really weird. Have you hurt yourself? Are you all right?" Jasper scanned Wallace's startled face. Wallace, quickly slipping the coin back in his pocket, looked down at Jasper's arm.

"Yes, I...I was looking for...something," Wallace mumbled, completely absorbed in his thoughts. Then Wallace walked past Jasper and toward the fireplace. He knew what he wanted to do next, but he didn't know why.

He walked over to Faye and, trying to look relaxed, took the coin from his pocket and raised it, as if to show Faye.

"I've seen your coin, Wallace." She smiled, then suddenly grabbed her throat. "Ouch!"

Wallace quickly withdrew his coin and shoved it deep into his pocket. "What happened?"

"You, no, it...I don't know, but you must have done something." Faye rubbed her throat, where the charm lay against it. "It must have been an electric shock. Don't shuffle across the carpets, Wallace," she said. "You know better than that."

"I...I'm sorry," Wallace said, though his mind was racing. Suddenly, he felt as if the coin was an imposter. What was it doing? It was as if his coin was attacking his friends. Nothing like this had ever happened before. Or had it? Trying to think back, Wallace considered that maybe, just maybe, the electrical events on the train had done something to his coin. Or was it even his coin?

He took it from his pocket when he was a safe distance from Faye. It was indeed his, as surely as the train that had exploded had not been their train or...or...he did not know. Something was different. Something had happened to the coin, but when? Yes, something happened, or was happening.

A large hand closed around his. Wallace looked up into the eyes of his father.

"Father," Wallace said. "Father, there's something strange about the coin. Something—"

"Keep that safe in your pocket, son," he said quietly, as if he didn't want anyone else to hear, "and don't let it near the others." His tone was serious and pleading. Then he cleared his throat, as if he'd caught himself. He smiled. "That is, don't let anyone drop it down a hole or . . . well, keep it close, right? Don't want to lose it. Maybe it's best if I take it back . . . after all this . . . to keep it safe."

But Wallace pulled his hand back and returned the coin to his pocket. His father opened his mouth to argue, but didn't. Wallace could feel his father's arms grow a bit tense, as if he was trying to keep Wallace safe within them.

But why was everyone using the word "safe"? *Were* they safe? Wallace still didn't know, and that scared him.

"We have some gifts to exchange, dear," Ariana gently said to Wallace, placing her hand on his shoulder.

Wallace turned around, but his father kept his arm around the boy's shoulder. Wallace nodded to Ariana, who had pulled her hand back. She smiled, but Wallace wondered if he had given her a shock, too. It was as if everyone who touched him got jolted. He looked up at his father. *Not everyone*, he thought. *Not everyone.*

———◦◦◦———

"Oh, these are lovely," said Lucy, again and again, as she ran her fingers over the beautiful red and gold ribbons from Ariana. The children were admiring their gifts—a small leather tool pouch for Jasper, a set of handkerchiefs embroidered with her name for Faye, a bismuth crystal for Wallace.

"That is beautiful," said Faye, admiring the strange iridescent metallic lump in Wallace's hand.

"Bismuth is fascinating," said Wallace. "It's the most diamagnetic of all metals. Remember, I was working with it on the train. It can create a strong reversed magnetic field—"

"Well, beauty can often be repulsive," said Noah, nodding at Faye, who ignored him but handed the bismuth back to Wallace.

Lucy, who had eyes, now, for no one but Ariana, was digging in her apron pockets. "I have a gift for you." She pulled out the old handkerchief she had taken from the ship.

Ariana looked at it queerly and, for a few moments, looked back at Lucy. "Thank you, Lucy. I guess you must have found it somewhere."

Lucy smiled and went back to her ribbons.

Another round of tea was served, but things were certainly winding down. Lucy began to snore softly, leaning on her mother's shoulder. Miss Bird had long ago fallen asleep by the fire. Miss Brett realized it must be very late.

"Are we to spend the night here?" she asked the parents as a group, not knowing which of them would have an answer. "Unfortunately, I didn't pack any—"

"Not," came a low sharp voice. It was the man in the floppy hat. He had entered the room, coming from the passageway by the fireplace.

"Pardon?" Miss Brett had not heard the word, only a sudden grunt from the man.

"We go," he said.

"Oh, well . . . I suppose we need to wake—" But the man cut off Miss Brett. He simply picked Lucy up and tossed her over his shoulder.

The others, who were no less exhausted, but had only managed to stay somewhat awake, stood up to go. Slowly, they marched toward the huge doors. But Wallace stopped. He turned and ran into his father's arms.

"I . . . I don't want to go," he whispered, trying to keep the tears from coming down.

"Now you be strong," his father said. "You be a man, and—"

"But he is not a man," Miss Brett said, trying to keep control of her voice. "He is a boy, and he needs his father to understand that." She knew her face was reddening, but she held her ground. She had been there, holding this little boy almost every night after arriving at Sole Manner Farm. It was not fair for his father to demand so much of him. "Wallace is brave and strong, and you need to see that."

"Well, I only meant . . ." But Dr. Banneker could see his mistake, written all over the face of his little boy. He held his son tight. "You *are* brave, Wallace. And I am so proud of you."

——◦◦◦——

"Where are you going? Will we see you?" Jasper reached for his mother's hand.

"Of course, *mon cher,*" she said, squeezing his fingers, "We will not be . . . far."

"Of course, we'll see you," said his father.

"Will we see you . . . tomorrow?" Noah asked, looking into his mother's eyes.

His mother smiled, averting his gaze. "Dear, I'm off to New York. My friend, Enrico Caruso, performed *Rigoletto* in November. I met him in London and wired the Met immediately. I could hear something magic in that voice. He performed with Marcella Sembrich, as I was otherwise engaged. She is fabulous, though, and no one was disappointed. She is the queen of the Met after all these years. So, where was I?... Yes, I'm off to New York to record with Enrico."

Noah barely listened. He didn't care about Caruso or the Met. To him, these were simply the familiar details of yet another departure.

"When will you be back?" he asked. He looked up and into her eyes. She looked back and, for the first time, he detected something. Was it fear? Was it sorrow? She touched her beautiful necklace and seemed to pull herself back together.

"Back? Um ... back here?" She looked at her husband. Noah could see his father, with the tiniest movement, betraying the fact that he was secretly shaking his head. "I don't know if I will be back here soon, but we have ... we will ... there's something. I forgot to give you your present ... well, goodness, Noah, don't you worry." Reaching into a fold in her gown, she brought out a small silk bag and handed it to Noah. He opened it and found a small brass compass.

"When you look at it, you can know in which direction to find me. Then you can send me kisses and I will feel them."

Noah looked up at his mother and forced a smile between two tear-stained cheeks. He would rather have had one more hour with her than any other gift she could offer. He looked down at the compass. Yes, he'd rather have her than anything in the world.

Ariana kissed her son on the top of his head, then pulled him to her. "I love you, Noah," she whispered. "I love you so."

And for Noah, this was music to his ears.

"This is taking a lot longer than when we came," said Faye as they walked through the tunnels. She realized they had only the light from Miss Brett's electric torch. Faye looked around. "We must be going the wrong way. Where is the man with the lamp?"

"Was there another way to go? Did you see a second tunnel?" Jasper didn't remember. Neither did anyone else. "The man has Lucy."

"Faye." Miss Brett stumbled into Jasper, who had stopped. "Sorry, Jasper. Sweet angels, the direction back is the same as the direction there. We're just tired, and ..." Suddenly, she looked around as her torch began to fade. Where was the man carrying Lucy? She shook her electric torch and flicked it back on again.

"We're lost," Faye groaned.

"No, we're just ..." What they were, besides lost, Jasper had not yet decided. "Okay, we just need to go back the way we came." But the light from Miss Brett's torch shined into two passageways behind them.

"Which way did we come from?" asked Faye.

"Lucy would know," said Wallace quietly.

"We're going to need a better guide than our memories," said Noah.

"Hello!" called Jasper. "Lucy!"

"Shhh, you'll wake her," Faye said. "They've got to be right behind us ... or in front of us."

This meant that standing still would either bring Lucy closer to them or take her farther away.

"I'm sure we've just ..." Miss Brett looked around. Had they gone the wrong way? Was that possible?

"Sorry, I ... I don't want to wake her but ... we must find them." Jasper felt a bead of sweat coming down his brow. *Stop it*, he thought.

The man had not taken off with Lucy. They'd simply taken a wrong turn.

Deciding on a tunnel to take, they followed it right into a dead end. Then, quickly turning around, they hurried along, but found themselves not back where they had come from, but cornered by a pile of rubble.

"Is that moonlight?" Noah pointed to what may have been a crack in the top of the tunnel.

"Or a reflection of the electric torch?" wondered Wallace.

Clearly, the tunnel seemed to veer and then fork at the bend. They continued down one tunnel, but found that way also blocked by rubble.

"Did this just happen? Did the rocks just fall to block us?" Wallace said, adjusting his glasses. Were they now trapped down there?

"We would have heard it," said Faye. "And there would be dust in the air."

So they traced their steps back once again and tried the other way. Here, they found themselves in another long, dark passage. Miss Brett's torch was dimming. She shook it once again.

"This can't be right, either," said Noah, taking a few steps back and looking in both directions. Pulling his new compass out of his pocket, he looked at it in the gloomy dimness. "I wish I knew what direction to find."

They kept walking. The brick in the tunnel turned to stone. They passed a chute much like the one they had seen earlier. But the walls changed as they walked. Soon, the walls were covered with drawings and carvings. Again, they saw men in cloaks depicted as a group. There were carvings of birds and animals, too. And there was writing. It seemed to be Latin.

"This must be an older part," said Wallace.

"Does that say 'Galileo'?" asked Jasper, trying to see faded script in the flickering light.

"No, that's impossible … right?" But Noah did not sound so certain.

The carvings were nothing they had seen before—nothing, except for one thing Wallace noticed, right above an etching of a bird. He pulled his lucky coin from his pocket and held it up to a carving in the wall.

"It fits," he said. He slipped the coin into the carving. There was a strange noise, like a moan or a hum. Wallace pulled the coin out and the noise stopped. He looked at the coin again. It was ever more a stranger and, once again, warm to the touch.

"We've got to get back to the underground castle," said Jasper. "Then we can retrace our steps." But he had noticed what Wallace had been doing. It was not something he would forget. And, soon, he would be glad for that.

Suddenly, there was a *pop* and the light went out. But in the darkness, they could see a shadow and dim light in the tunnel ahead. It was coming toward them.

"You are where," came the anxious voice of the floppy-hatted man, appearing at last with a lamp in his hand and Lucy, asleep, over his shoulder.

"Well, if we knew that, we wouldn't be lost," Noah said.

The man turned, and everyone followed quickly behind him. Wallace cast one look back, wondering if he'd ever get a chance to examine that wall again.

CHAPTER THIRTY

THE MISSING MISSIVES

OR

NOAH'S POST COMES ALONE

After Christmas, Miss Brett and the children set about making bundles to be delivered to Signora Fornaio for the shepherd. It was Boxing Day, and the children were pleased to pack sandwiches, mittens Miss Brett had sewn, and a bottle of wine she had taken from the kitchen coffers. Signora Fornaio embraced them for their kindness, and they all walked home with armfuls of treats.

January brought more bitter cold. Miss Brett was so glad the children had liked their knitted gifts, but with the exception of Lucy and her bunny doll, they did not use them much for the first few weeks after Christmas. They spent much more time indoors. Wallace was experimenting with a bit of the bismuth, floating all manner of metal objects using magnetic levitation. He also assembled a few more electric torches, adjusting the electro-magnetic dynamo to retain more power. Lucy was playing with the Christmas ornaments and making clothes for them out of her ribbons.

Jasper and Faye were trying to devise a more portable design for her snowball-throwing machine. They worked long hours perfecting it, which was easy, given endless ammunition. Faye had not forgotten Noah's comment that he was glad the machine fired only snowballs. This shooter could have another use should Komar Romak find them again. So she and Jasper fortified the new, smaller machine. They'd slip outside to try it whenever they could.

But that wasn't the only thing they were doing outside. They had also started investigating, and hunting around, and taking short excursions to see if there were any other places in the forest, or on the other side of the stone walls, where the mysterious men in black might have left clues to their secrets.

After Christmas, Noah had been quieter than usual, so much so that even Faye was concerned. But now he was in better spirits. A bundle of postcards from his mother had come. He had shared some of the adventures with the others.

One, from December 30, said, "Terrible fire in Chicago, so I shall be off to New York (almost directly west of you)." Another, from January 11, said, "Heading to Moscow for Anton Chekhov's new play. It is colder in New York than it can possibly be in Moscow. It is a record! (Will be northwest of you)."

These postcards brought Noah a sense of calm and pleasure. He would take out his compass and smile to himself, sending silent love in those given directions. Much to Miss Brett's delight, he had taken up his violin again. She enjoyed the hours spent listening to the haunting melodies wafting through the halls as she perused her Italian grammar books.

Wallace spent time in his room with the magnetic spheres and his bismuth crystal and had created a bismuth alloy using a chunk of the metal he already had. On this morning in January, Noah stood by the large sitting room window and played the violin. Somehow, the music made Lucy hungry, so she went to ask Miss Brett if it was time to go down to the bakery.

Wallace was up in his room. He had been thinking about the painting with the raven and his coin. He had been thinking about the carving in the tunnel and how his coin was suddenly behaving strangely. He wondered, as he moved his coin and watched it react with the bismuth and his magnets. It was spinning, as if someone had turned it.

As he noted this, there was suddenly an ear-splitting screech from the kitchen. Wallace jumped up and Noah suddenly stopped playing.

"I think the water has boiled," Noah said cheerily, heading into the kitchen.

Miss Brett, followed by Jasper, Faye, and Lucy, ran after him into the kitchen. Sure enough, there was the kettle, and it was whistling all by itself.

"I thought it was a good idea, Miss Brett," said Noah, feeling confident about his invention. "Happy Christmas, a little late. It's the steam that causes the whistle," he explained, "so when it boils, it steams, and when it steams, it whistles. Ergo, no burnt kettles."

From the top of the stairs, Wallace, heart pounding, could hear the whistle stop screeching, and then Miss Brett calling from the kitchen. It was time to have a warming cup of tea before heading down to the bakery. Wallace ran back to his room to grab his coin. He would never leave it behind. As he watched it spin, he realized he did not know what his coin was made of. He suddenly wanted to analyze it, but knew he'd have to wait until he had the time. He pulled the spinning coin from the magnetic field and put it back in his pocket. Then, rushing back, he grabbed one of the magnetic spheres and his bismuth crystal and the alloy and put those in his other pocket.

Soon, the children and Miss Brett were leaving the house, and Jasper and Faye were speaking to each other in silent glances.

——➤●◄——

As the others headed to the bakery, Faye and Jasper split off and walked down to the chapel. Again. Since Christmas, along with the forest and surrounding areas, Jasper and Faye had been exploring the chapel for answers. They'd peruse the mosaic and feel the walls for secret levers, sometimes even climbing up onto the broken walls. They looked in vain for the secret entrance, only to find a stone wall where they had thought the entrance to the tunnels had been. Faye was determined, and frustrated, but Jasper secretly thought that this was probably for the best. They would never have found the way back through the maze of tunnels.

Today, though, they did find the little old shepherd there in the chapel. He was all alone, sitting on a crumbled stone wall, singing to himself. The poor little man, Faye thought. She immediately felt the urge to search. She wished she could have found the entrance to the tunnels, because they would surely be a safe place for the shepherd. What if a storm hit suddenly? Or a sudden drop in temperature, like the one before Lucy's birthday that killed those poor creatures? If the shepherd knew the secret entrance to the tunnels, he'd be able to go inside. Faye thought of the secret door in the beast garden, too, but that would be a tomb more than a shelter.

The little man smiled through his scruffy beard. He climbed down from the wall and began a slow walk away from the fields. He must be heading back to his flock, Faye thought. She hoped he had some food and a place to stay.

331

Faye didn't know why the little man made her feel so sad. But he did. It tugged at something in her heart, watching him walk away. He was cold and all … alone. He was alone. Faye felt the rise of that feeling. Yes, she knew what it felt like to be alone. Back in her home in India, with all the riches and servants, she had always felt alone. But at least she had not been cold.

She followed Jasper as they hurried towards the bakery to catch up with the others.

⎯⎯⎯►●◄⎯⎯⎯

Presently, Miss Brett, Noah, Wallace, and Lucy arrived at Signora Fornaio's. The bakery seemed oddly quiet. Outside, there was only an empty plate of milk and no ravens. When they walked inside, it seemed to be empty. There was only one candle lit in the front room. This was odd. It worried Miss Brett. Signora Fornaio was always there when they arrived, singing and forcing sweets upon the children. But she was not at the counter.

"She isn't here?" said Wallace.

Where could she be? "Signora?" Miss Brett called. Signora Fornaio would not just leave a candle burning.

It was then they heard it: a whimper from the back room.

"Signora?" Miss Brett called again. "Are you all right?"

Signora Fornaio waddled out from her kitchen. Her face was drawn, and her cheeks, usually rosy with pleasure, were red and streaked from tears.

Miss Brett quickly stepped around the counter and put her arms around the baker. She could feel the woman shaking, her breath coming in stutters as she tried to control her sobs. Miss Brett noticed that she seemed thinner. Had they not noticed? Suddenly, this strong lady felt truly frail. Miss Brett held her closer.

"*Signora*, what happened?" Miss Brett said softly, caressing the baker's back. It was several moments before Signora Fornaio could speak. And then, she did so between great, gasping sobs. Noah stepped back outside and urged the others to do the same.

"It feels rude to stare," he said in uncharacteristic awkwardness as Faye and Jasper appeared, spotting the baker's shoulders shaking. But they pushed past Noah and went inside. Wallace adjusted his glasses and stepped out to stand next to Noah. They waited outside the tiny bakery.

Lucy went right up to Signora Fornaio. She put a hand on the baker's arm.

"Don't cry, Signora Fornaio. We love you," she said, leaning into the baker's skirt. Signora Fornaio reached down to pat Lucy, but it did not stem her sobs.

"For days I wait. For weeks I hope. It is past Christmas, and Antonio has not sent me a package," she said. "He send me a birthday gift and a letter in June, and I receive one more in August, written in July, but that is all. This is not like my *figlio*—my Antonio. This is not like my *bambino*." She blew her nose like a trumpet into her fancy American handkerchief.

"I'm so sorry," said Miss Brett, putting her hand on Signora Fornaio's shoulder. "Could there have been a problem because of the fire in the postal carriage? Perhaps something else happened to a different carriage."

"No, it was Signora Maggio who was there before and saw that no package had come," she said, her English breaking as she fought tears and tried to speak. "Later, Mezzobaffi said he check for me, but

I forgetted to tell him that Signora Maggio already, she check. I am so fearing that my little friend, *il pastore,* the shepherd is hurt from the fire, but he come back. So worried."

"Perhaps the weather," said Miss Brett. "The weather can hold up the post for months. Or perhaps there is so much because of the holiday, so many packages, I . . . I don't want you to be sad. I am sure—"

"Don't you worry for me, *mia bella,*" said Signora Fornaio, taking Miss Brett's hand and kissing it, forcing a smile between her tears.

With Signora Fornaio refusing to hear any more sympathy, she gave them some loaves of bread and warm iced buns.

As they hurried out the door, Signora Fornaio rushed after them with a small bundle.

"*Per favore,* can you give this to the poor shepherd? It is so cold in the field, and he works so hard all the day. Please—it is biscotti and warm milk," Signora Fornaio said. Miss Brett told her she would be glad to bring it to the poor shepherd.

As they ambled up the hill toward the field, they came upon Mezzobassi, who was now standing in the field with his staff in his hand, clearly chilly and tired. The walk from the chapel must have worn him out. The old shepherd took the bundle with gladness, looking out toward the hillside where his flock must have headed. Then he devoured the warm biscuits and sweet milk as he walked.

"Poor man," said Miss Brett. "Poor Signor . . . um . . . shepherd. Oh dear, to be so old, and have to live off the land, alone but for his sheep."

"He must make money in the spring, with lambs and wool," Jasper said.

"How many sheep does he have?" asked Lucy.

"Well, I don't know," said Miss Brett. At the moment, no sheep were visible at all.

"It's terribly cold," Lucy said. "Shouldn't we ask him to come to the house?"

Miss Brett called after the shepherd. He looked around, then back at them. *Poor dear,* Miss Brett thought. *His hearing is clearly not very keen.* "Would you like to come inside?" Miss Brett said, clearly and loudly.

"Mio?" The little shepherd seemed to be amazed that anyone would have considered him worthy of an invitation. He dusted off his ragged arms, as if he was sprucing up for the event.

This made Miss Brett all the more adamant. "We'd really love to have you."

"Yes, it will be lovely," said Lucy.

Mezzobassi looked down into his hands and shook his head.

Miss Brett smiled. "Why don't you come?"

"It won't be any trouble. Mr. Frilly Aprons, he's one of the mysterious men in black, and he will make lovely sandwiches, and Signora Fornaio will bring sweets and cakes and delicious treats," said Lucy.

Mezzobassi shook his head, laughing. "Non, grazie. So beautiful, molto bella, gentile." He smiled.

"Won't you come?" Lucy asked again.

But the shepherd again laughed, shaking his head and wagging his finger. He took out another biscotti and waddled off, a lone raven circling overhead.

Miss Brett's heart sank. *Poor thing,* she thought as she watched him go.

CHAPTER THIRTY-ONE

The Baker's Son

OR

WHAT LUCY KNOWS NOW

The next morning, Miss Brett and the children again walked down the hill to the bakery. They were getting some sweet buns for breakfast, but mostly, Miss Brett was worried about the baker.

Before they even arrived at the door, they could hear banging and a volley of Italian that no one could understand and, from the tone, it was probably for the best. Signora Fornaio looked terrible. She had clearly been crying all night. But she was not crying now, and she had a fierce look in her eye.

"It's your son," Miss Brett said, coming around the counter. "Have you heard something?"

Signora Fornaio shook her head, shaking her fist in the air. "Monello sconsiderato! That thoughtless, inconsiderate scoundrel."

Miss Brett didn't know what to say. Clearly, the baker's worry and fear had transformed itself into anger. "If there's anything—"

"Oh, that boy!" cried Signora Fornaio. "Always *istigatore*! Troublemaker. Always *egoista*, selfish! He is always wanting more, wanting bigger. He wanted to be in the big cities, to have the fine clothes. He fought Mario, the welder's son, because he wanted the girl. That is how my beautiful, *mio bello*, how he is having the scar right across his eye like this." She drew a line with her finger across her left eye. "My Antonio and I were so thankful he did not lose his eye."

Lucy gasped, her hand flying to her mouth.

"What is it, Luce?" Jasper asked his sister in a whisper. Lucy shook her head, tears filling the corners of her eyes.

"Lucy? Are you all right?" asked Miss Brett. Lucy shook her head, then suddenly turned and ran out and up the road to the *palazzo*.

Faye hesitated, looking at the baker who was wiping her eyes,

"Go, *bella*. Go to her." The baker waved her hand for Faye to go.

Faye nodded, though she felt bad about leaving her. Noah followed close behind. They hurried to catch up with Jasper, who had run after his sister. They caught up at the stone wall by the chapel.

"What is it?" asked Noah. "What happened back there?"

But Lucy just shook her head, tears streaming from the corners of her eyes.

"Lucy, please, what is it?" Jasper asked.

Lucy shook her head all the harder.

Jasper took a deep breath. He hugged his sister and let her cry. Then he pulled her back and looked her in the eyes. "You need to tell us, Lucy," said Jasper, trying to be comforting but also growing a bit impatient. "If you don't, we can't help."

"But no one can help!" she cried. "It's the article. I read it in the article."

"What article?" asked Jasper, catching her hand as her bracelet went to her mouth. "When did you read it? This morning?"

"On the boat," said Lucy, sucking in her breath as tears flowed down.

"An article on the boat?" Noah scratched his head. "There was no article on the boat."

But Faye suddenly remembered. The newspaper from the kitchen in the boat. Lucy had read something in it, and made a huge racket when she did. *What was on that page?* Faye thought. *What did it say?* There was something about a tunnel and a wealthy woman. Something about a hydroscope . . . "Was it the hydroscope?" she asked.

"No, the *real* article!" cried Lucy.

"The real article?" Faye tried to remember what else was in the paper.

"What do you mean?" Jasper asked.

Lucy looked up. "You read it, too. All of you."

Faye thought. There was something else. "There was a story about a lady—"

"Not the lady, not the hydroscope. It was about the man, the Italian man . . ." And Lucy broke off crying again.

"What Italian man?" asked Faye. She didn't remember anything about an Italian man.

"The man they found in the tunnel," Lucy managed between sobs.

Faye remembered the tunnel. She also remembered something was found in there. With Lucy's photographic memory, Faye had no doubt she was right.

"What did it say?" asked Noah.

And Faye remembered. "He was dead, wasn't he?"

Lucy buried her face in her brother's coat.

"What else did it say, Lucy?" Noah asked. "Why is it bothering you now?"

Lucy just shook her head. When it seemed Lucy could breathe more easily, Faye leaned over and wiped the tears from the younger girl's face. Clearly, Lucy had put something together—something that might be very important. Faye took Lucy's hand and looked her straight in the eyes.

"Lucy, take a deep breath and tell us what the article said," said Faye. "We need to know."

Lucy took a deep breath and nodded, her breath catching in her throat. "It said that a man, an Italian man, in his twenties, was found in a tunnel. They ... they knew he was Italian but it didn't say how they knew but they did. They said ... they said it. He was ... he was dead and de-com-posing—I mean, in advanced de-compo-si-tion. He was stabbed and stabbed and stabbed, nine times, six times in the back and once in the tummy and twice more in his breast ... and the stiletto had markings—strange signs on its handle. I don't know what a stiletto is, but it was murderous-looking, the newspa-per said."

Noah shook his head. "But it doesn't mean anything to us. I mean—"

"It was him! I know it!" Lucy cried.

"Him?" Then Noah figured it out. "You think the man was Anto-nio Fornaio?"

Lucy nodded, sniffing back tears.

"But Luce, how—I mean, why now?" Noah tried to be reason-able. "What does this have to do with the baker's son? You read this weeks and weeks ago, and you never thought to connect it to Signo-ra Fornaio then. Why now?"

"I ... I didn't know before." She sobbed.

"But what do you know now?" asked Jasper.

"The scar," she blurted out between sobs. "The newspaper said he had a scar across the eyelid on his left eye."

CHAPTER THIRTY-TWO

A Box of Sadness

OR

THE ARM OF THE SHEPHERD

"I do not understand this," Miss Brett said as she poured hot chocolate for the children. She looked outside at the snow, once again starting to fall.

Sitting by the fireplace in the manor house, the children tried to tell her about the newspaper article found in the kitchen on the ship.

"I hardly remember reading that bit," said Faye, trying to think back.

"Lucy does," said Noah with a humorless smile.

"Lucy remembers everything," said Jasper, stroking his sister's hair. Lucy had fallen asleep in Jasper's lap. After he had gently taken the bracelet out of her mouth, her stuttered breathing seemed to ease.

No one spoke, but they all knew something bad was happening, and somehow, Antonio Fornaio was involved. Was he working for the men in black? Or, infinitely more worrying, was he working for Komar Romak? Did the baker's son do something to displease his masters? Had they killed him? Why was that article kept on the ship? Did the men in black know? Had they been involved? Once again, there were so many questions and so much doubt. Should they trust these strange men, or should they fear them? A knife with strange markings could easily have come from these men.

These questions hung in the air and circled around and around, over and over as Miss Brett and the children stared into the crackling fire.

Suddenly, there was a harsh knock upon the front door. Lucy sat up, somewhat dazed. "Is it morning?" she asked, groggily.

Miss Brett went to the door. It was Signora Fornaio.

"Signora," Miss Brett began, but Signora Fornaio stopped her. She was not crying, but the marks of her tears were like red scars down her cheeks. She looked resigned, but shrunken, like the weight of the world had pressed down upon her. Closing the door, Miss Brett noticed a drift of snow wafting in. It was really snowing now.

"Signorina Brett," Signora Fornaio said, her voice full of strength and will. She walked over to Lucy and bent down to meet her eye to eye. "La bella Lucia. I know that you know something. Something about my Antonio."

Lucy looked up at Miss Brett, panic on the little girl's face.

Miss Brett started, "I, we...I—"

"Or perhaps, you believe something," Signora Fornaio said, standing back up.

Miss Brett opened her mouth but said nothing. She closed her mouth and looked down. She could not deny this. Signora Fornaio turned to Lucy.

"Cara, Lucia," she said, "it is you with the head that holds every-thing. *Per favore*, Lucia, *cara mia*, tell me what you believe."

Lucy flew into Signora Fornaio's arms. She didn't want to say.

She never wanted to say. And Miss Brett considered this much too big a thing to put on the shoulders of this little girl.

Miss Brett removed Lucy gently from the baker, and Jasper took his sister in his arms. Miss Brett took Signora Fornaio by the hand and led her to the settee, sitting next to her, holding the old woman's hand all the while. In a soft voice, Miss Brett told Signora Fornaio what they knew. Signora Fornaio listened in silence, an occasional tear escaping from her often closed eyes.

When Miss Brett had told her all she could, Signora Fornaio opened her eyes and nodded. She seemed suddenly to summon strength from within. She pulled a package from her cloak. It was small, about the size of a tinderbox or a square bar of soap, and it fit into the palm of Signora Fornaio's work-worn hand.

"This Antonio left with me," she said. "He told me his mission was very secret and he was going to be a rich man in America. But he said that I must never tell anyone, especially *i monaci in nero, i fratelli in nero*. This I wanted to disagree, but he begged me. He gave this me and tell me that I must keep it for him and never open it until he writes to me. But he has not written and I fear..." She wiped her eyes with the corner of her apron. "I fear he will not be writing to his mama anymore."

"You mustn't say that." Miss Brett took her hand. "We don't know ...we..." But Miss Brett knew what the clues meant. She knew that, in all likelihood, the man in the tunnel was the young Fornaio. "Where did your son get this package?"

Tears welled up again in Signora Fornaio's eyes. "It could be, but I don't want to believe." She blew her nose. "I fear it is my fault, but... I don't see how... I... bring him for help me, to clean, to prepare ...but he... he may be take it... maybe... but no... *non capisco... non è possibile…non può aver tradito il suo popolo…"* She was speaking to herself, mumbling in Italian, shaking her head, tears falling hard.

"Signora—" Miss Brett began, but Signora Fornaio stopped her. She put her hand to Miss Brett's mouth and shook her head. Then Signora Fornaio handed the package to Miss Brett. She turned to leave.

"Wait, Signora, I can't take this—"

"You must," Signora Fornaio said.

"Should…should I open it?" Miss Brett asked.

"I wish you would," said Signora Fornaio. "But if it is the reason my son has been killed, I never want to look upon it."

She stepped outside and walked down the steps. Not wanting Signora Fornaio to be alone in her sorrow, Miss Brett grabbed her winter cloak and rushed to the door to follow. But through the door, Miss Brett could see Mezzobassi, the shepherd. He was standing outside, his hand on his friend's shoulder. He looked up at Miss Brett and waved. Miss Brett waved back, nodding that she understood Signora Fornaio would be in his hands. The shepherd then offered Signora Fornaio his arm, and the two of them walked slowly down the road toward the village.

The snow was falling like a blanket, and almost immediately, the two little people disappeared in the deep whiteness.

"It's really turning into a storm," Noah said, looking at the wind twisting the trees.

Miss Brett looked out the window toward the village, trying to see the two walking. She could see nothing—nothing but white.

CHAPTER THIRTY-THREE

A Black Discovery

OR

WHAT THEY FIND INSIDE

Miss Brett looked at the package in her hand.

"Open it," said Jasper.

Miss Brett carefully pulled back the plain paper covering the package. Inside was a simple wooden box. On its exterior was a faded carving, like petals of a flower. Tied around it was a length of twine. The twine held a folded piece of paper to the top of the box. Miss Brett untied the twine and opened the paper. It was a letter, written in Italian. At the top of the writing paper was a drawing of a black bird. Miss Brett placed the letter aside and opened the box. Inside was a soft cloth, perhaps silk.

"Can you move back a bit, sweet angels," she said. The children were clumped around her, blocking her view of her own hands.

She slowly unfolded the cloth, only to find another cloth. This one was strange and seemed to be lined with lead. Whatever was in there, she had no idea. She untied and unfolded the lead-lined cloth. They all leaned over to take a look.

In the box was nothing but a small orb made of shiny, almost iridescent, metal. It was larger than the magnetic spheres, but still would fit easily into the hand of a child. But it had a strange reflective, almost glowing, quality. It was not like any metal the children had ever seen.

Noah reached in to touch it, but Miss Brett grabbed his hand.

"We don't know what it is or what it does," she said. Then, carefully, using her apron as a protective cover, she touched it herself. It did not react in any way. She dropped the apron and touched it with her finger. Nothing. She took it out of the box. They all crowded around closer. She placed it on the table. The orb did not move. It did not make a sound. It did not react in any way that betrayed its mission, if indeed it had one.

"What is it?" asked Noah.

"It's an orb," said Wallace.

"It looks very much like our magnetic spheres," said Jasper, "but it almost glows."

"It might contain bismuth, or something radioactive," said Wallace.

He took out the sphere and the bismuth he had in his pocket and handed them to Noah, who placed them next to the orb, but the metal orb in the box did not react. Wallace then reached for the orb, but Miss Brett stopped him. She picked it up, using the edge of her apron. She didn't want them touching it in case it was made of something toxic.

"Could this be the thing that was so important?" said Jasper, incredulous.

Noah pushed the orb slightly with the edge of the bismuth crystal, and it moved slightly, then stopped. It was, as far as they could tell, simply a orb.

"Maybe the note says something," said Jasper.

Noah put the orb back in the box, and Miss Brett picked up the note.

"Can you read it?" asked Noah.

"I've only been learning Italian for two months, Noah," Miss Brett said, "and, as the incident with the eyebrow has taught us, I am not fluent. Lucy is much better at—"

"No! I don't want to look!" Lucy covered her face with her hands.

"Well, it is obviously from Antonio, and written to his mother..." She scanned the letter, looking for familiar words. "And he says '*morto*,' which means—"

"Dead,'" said Lucy, biting her lip.

"I think he says that he must be dead if she is reading this, or, I suppose... '*Se fossi*' means 'if I was'... '*vivo*,' 'alive'... that if he had been alive, she would not be reading this... or something like that. '*Camera di un migliaio di lingue*'... I don't understand that, but I think it says 'room of a thousand languages,' but that makes no sense. Let me see... '*in pericolo*,' someone is in peril or danger. He... it says he has betrayed someone... '*tradimento*,' 'betrayal'... '*benefattore*,' 'benefactor'... he has... I think... '*pauroso*'... fear... of..." And here Miss Brett sucked in her breath.

"What is it?" asked Jasper.

"It says—"

But Miss Brett was interrupted when the door flew open and a man in a black bonnet, black-laced pantaloons, and a large, hooked shepherd's staff walked in. Although he wore a fierce expression on his face, the rest of his attire made him look like a big Bo Peep in mourning.

"Where has it?" he asked.

"What?" asked Miss Brett, not sure whether she should hide the box or not. She casually covered it with her handkerchief.

"Has he been? Did he know?" Bo Peep looked what could best be called fearful.

Miss Brett was flustered. "I am sorry, but I don't—"

"No!" he shouted. Then, he turned toward Jasper and pointed, menacingly. "You…what has?"

"Me?" I don't know what you mean." Jasper moved back from the man's pointing finger.

The finger moved to Faye. "You…where? He has been?"

"Do not point your finger at the children!" Miss Brett was now not only afraid, but quite angered. "Who? Who are you talking about? Does who know what?"

"Yes, tell me!" he shouted.

Lucy started crying and hid her face in Jasper's arms.

Miss Brett had had enough. "Look, you, I want some answers. Did you kill Antonio Fornaio? What is going on here?"

Bo Peep stepped back as if he had been hit.

"Antonio?" he said quietly. "Does she know?"

"She? Antonio is not a she," Noah said. "Antonio is the baker's son."

"That's not who he means, Noah," said Faye, her eyes narrowing as comprehension dawned.

Miss Brett seemed suddenly to put the pieces together. Signora Fornaio had not known before tonight—but *he* had. "Yes, she knows. Oh, you horrid, horrid—"

"No, not we—" But he didn't finish. Instead, he turned on his little black boots and ran out the door.

Miss Brett stood with her mouth agape. Through the window, she watched the man run, his laced pantaloons billowing with each stride, his bonnet flapping on his head. He grabbed the man in black who was shoveling snow from the path to the garden, then ran back to the house, dragging the man along. The man Bo Peep brought with him wore a brimmed hat with black feathers trimming the edges, and what appeared to be a black suit made of feathers. He looked at the children, then at Miss Brett. He pulled his feather boa from his face. They could see his quivering chin.

"It was me," he said, dropping into a chair, his head falling into his hands.

CHAPTER THIRTY-FOUR

WHO DID WHAT

OR

CONFESSIONS AND DISCOVERIES

In an instant, Miss Brett began to formulate plans. She ran various scenarios through her mind, quickly altering and revising. They would have to pack their belongings, but that might take too much time. Instead, she considered just grabbing the children and running. The problem was, she didn't know where to run. Could she run to the underground castle? There must be more to it than that one room. Possibly that was where the parents were at work, but she had no way of knowing for sure. And she had no way of finding their workplace, either. More likely, they'd wind up lost forever in those tunnels, ultimately joining the unfortunate artist.

Whatever she was going to do, she was going to do it now. They had murdered the baker's son. The feathered man had just confessed. She could no longer allow the children to be with these murderous men in black. She felt so betrayed. She had trusted them, or had at least begun to. Could it be that all the mysterious men in black were evil? Or was just this feathered man?

But when the feathered man looked up, she was taken aback. She saw no evil. She saw no anger. She saw no murderer. What she saw was profound sorrow, the deepest sorrow that eyes could reveal. Something was wrong, Miss Brett could see. This man could not have meant to kill Antonio Fornaio. Collecting herself, Miss Brett steadied her voice.

"You didn't want to kill him then, did you? Was it an accident?" Then she remembered that Antonio had been stabbed nine times. "Or self-defense?"

He looked at her in horror. "Kill Antonio? I am not. I find him."

Now she was utterly confused. "I ... I'm sorry, I didn't ... What did you say?"

"I find Antonio. Dead." From his shaking shoulders, she could see the man was now weeping.

Miss Brett didn't know what to say. The feathered man looked up at her. She could see how miserable he was, even through his dark glasses and huge moustache and beard. Looking at him sitting there, wringing his hands and shaking his head, she knew there were tears hidden in his eyes. She felt sorry for him. He was in pain. He was hurt. He was *real.* It was the first time she had even considered one of these mysterious men to have any human attribute whatsoever.

The feathered man looked down again, hanging his head, eyes on the ground. She put her hand on his shoulder. He began to sob. She patted his shoulder and waited patiently. He hiccupped, then seemed to collect himself.

"Antonio bad boy. He *hafna inkwiet*—trouble. He worry to us," the feathered man said.

"He ... *ideat ħżiena*. His ideas bring sorrow," said Bo Peep, who had been standing in the doorway, quietly sad and thoughtful.

The feathered man looked up at Bo Peep. He spoke in a language unlike any Miss Brett had ever heard. It was not Italian, that was for sure. She realized these men, when they spoke English, were certainly not speaking with Italian accents. What on earth was it?

"Tell us what happened," said Faye. "What is going on here?"

"Not know to say," said the feathered man.

"To say what?" asked Noah.

"I don't want to know what happened in the tunnel," insisted Lucy, covering her ears.

The feathered man looked at Miss Brett.

"Please tell us," she said quietly, placing her hands over Lucy's ears to further deaden the sound.

"Antonio," said the feathered man. "He in, and I wait."

"For who?" asked Noah.

"Say not say," said the feathered man.

"He told you?" asked Lucy, pulling her hands and Miss Brett's away, then quickly replacing them before she could hear the answer.

"Told him what?" asked Noah, scratching his head.

"Not know we knew."

"Knew what?" asked Faye.

"Yes," said the feathered man.

"Yes, what?" asked Noah.

"Yes, knew we he do," said the feathered man.

"Do he what?" asked Noah.

"What was he doing?" asked Jasper.

Miss Brett's hands no longer over her ears, Lucy decided to give up trying to hide, since she could hear through her hands anyway. "He was doing bad, wasn't he?" she said. "Antonio did something very bad and you were trying to stop him."

"So bad." The feathered man shook his head, looking down.

Bo Peep shook his head, too. "Antonio want. He want free. Riches. More than more."

"Heart gone," the feathered man agreed.

"Lost and break," Bo Peep added.

"Not to know. Never back. She heart so," said the feathered man.

Lucy shook her head. "So sad."

Bo Peep and the feathered man, too, said, "So sad."

"What was so sad?" asked Noah, looking from one to another.

"What was sad, Lucy? Explain," demanded Faye.

"Antonio broke his mother's heart," said Lucy. "She never knew—he was never coming back."

"And give away," said Bo Peep.

"To who?" asked Lucy.

"Them," the feathered man said, bitterness in his voice.

"Them?" Noah asked.

"Komar Romak," said Bo Peep and the feathered man at once.

"Komar Romak?!" said Miss Brett and the children all at once— except Lucy, for whom this was obvious.

"They," said Bo Peep.

"After too long, I go dark," said the feathered man. "The knife with them—"

Bo Peep said something, and the feathered man stopped. He took a deep breath. Lucy covered her ears again.

"The nine wounds," said the feathered man.

"Nine?" asked Noah, holding up his fingers.

"Yes!" cried Lucy, who saw Noah's fingers. She uncovered her ears and explained, "That's what the newspaper said! You went in there, into the dark tunnel, but they'd already come and ... and ..." But she couldn't say it, and she hid her face again in Jasper's arms.

"Seven spirit, back and gut. Two then," said the feathered man, "in the heart. Always two."

"Is?" asked Lucy, looking up.

"Yes," Bo Peep said.

"What?" asked Noah.

"It's a symbol," said Lucy. "But I don't understand it."

"The number of wounds?" asked Faye.

"Yes, and the two. It means something that there is always two." Then Lucy looked up at the men. "It is, isn't it? It's the symbol."

Bo Peep nodded. The others did not need to ask this time. It had to be Komar Romak.

"I go him, not dead," the feathered man said. "I . . . I move. He cry out. Pull me. Tear my cloak. He try me. Komar Romak map. Map to Abruzzo, to Solemano. He want the . . ." He said something they did not understand. "Komar Romak knows. Komar Romak want it," he said. "Komar Romak say but no. Antonio dream. Antonio wrong. Too late. But Antonio. He not to Komar Romak. Not to any."

"He bring word," Bo Peep said in a voice full of worry. "The children. They come. It mean the move. Must us."

The feathered man reached into a pocket in his feathered jacket. He pulled out a torn, wrinkled, folded piece of paper. When he unfolded it, they could see that it was a map. Or, that is, it was a part of a map—a map of Italy.

"What is this?" asked Miss Brett.

"Antonio hand. Map, tear it," the feathered man said. "This is part. Maybe more."

"What does that mean?" Wallace asked.

But the feathered man just shook his head.

Miss Brett and the children stared at these two men. They had explained more than any man in black had ever explained before. But none of them but Lucy was entirely sure what had just been explained.

"It was Antonio who made the meeting with that Komar Romak, wasn't it?" asked Lucy.

Noah shook his head as if to get the words out. "Not him," he said.

"Not him," said Bo Peep.

"Not him?" squeaked Wallace, who was cowering behind Miss Brett.

"Not," said the feathered man.

"Him," said Bo Peep. "Never the him."

"I ... we don't understand," Miss Brett croaked, her throat suddenly dry.

Lucy squirmed out of Jasper's grip. Her face was pale, but she spoke clearly.

"Yes, we do," she said. "Antonio didn't want to just be happy. He didn't want to be a man in black. He wanted lots of things—not hats and frocks, but *things*. I think he wanted to be a big rich man and a show-off, and he made a deal with Komar Romak, who somehow got to him."

"But Komar Romak didn't come here." Miss Brett was anxious. "They said, 'Not him.'"

"Not *him*," said Lucy. "Komar Romak."

"Lucy." Jasper tried to get her to come back to him, but she didn't. She went over to the feathered man and put a hand on his shoulder.

"Int imdejjaq," she said.

"What?" Noah asked.

"Lucy?" Jasper gawked.

"It's Maltese," said Lucy. "I was just telling him I knew he was sad."

"I don't even want to know how you know Maltese," said Noah.

"I only know a few words," said Lucy. "There was a book with translations."

"But what about Komar Romak?!" shouted Faye. "The only thing that matters is if Komar Romak is in Solemano. Is Komar Romak here?"

"Is," said Bo Peep.

"How?!" cried Noah. "It's insane! We were in caves and blew things up and hid and ... it's impossible. How?"

"I don't know how," said Lucy.

"Map," said Bo Peep. "Pieces of map."

"But that wouldn't tell him where we were," said Faye.

"Did Komar Romak know of the village?" asked Miss Brett.

"He must have," said Jasper.

Feathered man started to say, "Not—"

"Just stop!" Faye said. "It was Komar Romak who set fire to the post carriage. Komar Romak was after Antonio's box."

Feather man nodded. Bo Peep, too.

"We must ask Signora Fornaio if she saw anyone strange with her son," Miss Brett said, standing tall and speaking with authority. "We must find out if she saw anything that might lead us to Komar Romak, or at least let us know whether he was here."

Bo Peep said, "Not—"

"Shut up!" cried Faye. "Whatever you are taking about doesn't matter now." Faye looked pleadingly at Jasper, then Miss Brett.

"Well, we can go ask Signora Fornaio," said Miss Brett. "And we can warn her."

"She must be up at the bakery, at her home," said Faye. "The shepherd came and walked her down."

"Shepherd?" The feathered man stood abruptly.

"Yes, you know—the little old shepherd who is always around," said Faye.

"He brought his sheep over the Forca di Penne passage this winter," Miss Brett said. "He's been sharing his pecorino cheese with Signora Fornaio, and ... you must have seen him."

"We have no more shepherd," Bo Peep said, "and no sheep."

"Yes, you do," insisted Faye.

"No sheep," said Bo Peep.

"Sheep?" Lucy said. "I'd like sheep. Little ones." She would have liked to see some fluffy little sheep.

"Of course, he has sheep," Noah said. "He's a shepherd."

"Sheep?" said Bo Peep. "Where sheep?"

"Where sheep?" asked the feathered man.

"Well, he keeps them ... he brings them over, or ... he ..." But Miss Brett trailed off, as it dawned on her that she had never actually seen his sheep. The others must have. "You've seen his sheep, haven't you, children?"

"Of course we have," Faye said with assurance.

"I wish I had," said Lucy. "But I never did."

"Yes, you have, many times. You just don't remember." But the moment Faye said it, she knew that couldn't be right. If anyone had remembered, it would have been Lucy. Faye thought hard. Had she ever actually seen any sheep?

"I don't think we ever did." Jasper looked at his sister. No, they hadn't seen any at all. A shepherd with no sheep?

"No sheep, no shepherd," said the feathered man.

"But he has been around," Noah said. "He's hard to miss."

"He's very little and very old," said Lucy.

"No sheep and no shepherd," the feathered man said again. "The shepherd of Solemano dead. Dead last spring."

"Well, that's just not true," said Faye, but she was getting nervous. No sheep? "The sheep must have been on the other side of the passageway and we just didn't see them."

"Dead." Bo Peep spoke louder now.

"It's his brother," said Lucy. "Remember? Signora Fornaio said the shepherd's brother died in the spring."

"No brother," said Bo Peep. "No family. Alone."

"He was not alone!" said Faye. "He's a sweet old man and his brother died and . . ." But Faye took a breath and realized that she simply did not know the truth.

Miss Brett felt a bead of sweat on her brow. *No, this is impossible. Surely the sweet old shepherd poses no threat,* she thought. *There must be some misunderstanding.* The mysterious men in black were simply not understanding what she and the children were trying to say.

"Listen," she said calmly, "you must have seen him. He has been around. Signora Fornaio has been taking care of him, giving him food. She even had him help her in the bakery. He made buns for us and—" With a sickening jolt, Miss Brett suddenly gasped. She looked at Faye, who seemed to have had the same thought.

"The bundle," Faye said, softly going pale. "The ravens and the rabbits."

"What rabbits?" asked Lucy. "What ravens?"

Faye looked at Miss Brett. She nodded. They had to tell. So she explained about the ravens and the rabbits. "They must have died from eating the treats," she said. "They were poisoned."

"It can't be." Noah was shaking his head again. "If I hadn't dropped the bundle..." He trailed off.

"Not Mr. Corvino." Lucy's eyes filled with tears. "Please untell me."

Faye turned to Lucy and grabbed her arms, looking the little girl straight in the eyes. "Lucy, think hard. Whenever we saw the shepherd, was one of the men in black ever there?"

Lucy gulped down her tears and thought. "Well, he was near, sometimes, but never right there. And we asked him to come to the house and he almost came. But he didn't want to come once I told him that Mr. Frilly Apron was making sandwiches."

"Was he purposely avoiding them?" asked Faye, looking at Jasper.

"It can't be," he said. Then he looked to Miss Brett. "Can it?"

Miss Brett didn't want to think so. Signora Fornaio had a habit of feeding strays. Could her warmth and generosity have blinded her to danger? No, it simply could not be so. "Perhaps the shepherd was an unknown brother of the old shepherd—and perhaps the bunnies did die of the cold," said Miss Brett. "We cannot immediately jump to conclusions. Remember, we believed these men guilty of murder only minutes ago."

Noah stood up and let out a deep breath. "Okay, what should we do?"

"Let's go down to the bakery. If the shepherd is there, we'll ask him some questions. Signora Fornaio will have an answer for these fellows. She'll be able to explain. We need to speak with them," she said, feeling slightly more confident. "If the shepherd has been around for the last few months, he may have seen something, too."

⟶➤●◄⟵

Miss Brett led the way out of the manor house, and the others followed. They all walked quickly down the hill toward the bakery. Bo Peep called out in their language, presumably Maltese, to other mysterious men in black who were in the village. Three ran down toward the wall and through the gate to the farmers in the field: a man in black jodhpurs and a black fuzzy jumper; one in a black coverall and a large black hat with earflaps; and a man dressed in black farmer dungarees. The man Miss Brett and the children thought was the little old shepherd held a bundle in his arms, but a blanket on top fell off as he walked swiftly toward them. He was carrying a little lamb.

"Look, there's one of the shepherd's little sheep," said Lucy, pointing. As they grew closer, they could see it was a very thin young sheep, shivering in the cold. It couldn't have been bigger than a spring lamb grown through the fall. Her wool, matted and filthy, was an unusual shade of apricot.

There was a sense of relief. Miss Brett sighed heavily. That sweet old man could not have been other than what he seemed.

"No," said Bo Peep.

"This sheep we find," the feathered man said, picking up the blanket that had been covering the sheep and tucking it gently around the little creature. "We bring him back from spring."

"What do you mean?" This made no sense to Miss Brett.

"Sheep of dead shepherd," Bo Peep said. "All color the same."

"She we find last night," said the feathered man. "Caught in branches, tree fall down."

"Sheep many dead, over Forca di Penne," Bo Peep said sadly. "Many dead from cold, many dead from knife."

"Shepherd, too, dead," the feathered man said. "Dead from fall.

But maybe other kind of dead."

"Where is the shepherd? The other shepherd?" Noah said. But no one had an answer.

"There's his staff," said Jasper, walking over to the stone wall. He leaned over and picked up the large, carved stick that the shepherd always carried. It was heavy and more finely carved than he had thought before, although he had never had a good look at it, or lifted it, since the shepherd always had it in his hand and Jasper had never been that close to the man. Jasper took it along with him, forgetting to put it down. He only realized he still held it as they approached the bakery. A pair of ravens whined their guttural cry as the group approached. They were very agitated and circled round and round. An empty plate sat in the snow outside the door.

"Signora Fornaio!" Miss Brett called at the door. There was no answer. She knocked, and the door creaked open. Miss Brett looked at Bo Peep with fright. "Signora?" There were no sounds from within. The lamp in the shop front was not lit. "*Ciao*, Signora Fornaio. Are you here?" Still, there was no answer. She touched the door and noticed that the glass in the window had a thin crack running from bottom to top.

Miss Brett pushed the door open. She gasped, stifling the scream that rose in her throat. She threw out her arms to keep the children from entering, but she was too late, and Lucy slipped under her arm, followed by Wallace.

"Signora Fornaio!" cried Lucy. "*Per favore!* Please be all right!"

The bakery was in shambles. The baskets were overturned, the biscuits crushed on the ground, the breads torn apart, with flour covering everything. The ravens landed in the doorway and began hopping around the bakery, crying and chattering.

"Signora Fornaio!" Faye called desperately. The others called as well.

Jasper again realized he still held the staff. Climbing over the counter, he started to hand it to Bo Peep. But the moment he handed it over, he grabbed it back. On the top of the wooden gnarl, he noticed a particular engraving. Could it be?

It looked like a very ornate "KR."

Bo Peep noticed it at the same time.

Jasper ran his hand over it. No, it could not be. It mustn't be.

"But it couldn't be him," said Jasper. "This guy was short and frail, and Komar Romak is tall and skinny, and the shepherd was old, and he—what was his name again? I can never remember."

"It was a funny name. Italian," said Wallace. "Mezzobassi?"

"Mezzobaffi," said Lucy, who was looking through the baskets, hoping to find Signora Fornaio sleeping beneath them.

"Mezzobaffi?!" said the feathered man, Bo Peep, and the other men in black with a collective gasp.

"Yes," Wallace said. "That was the name."

Immediately, the men in black began conversing in their language. Without understanding a word, the children and Miss Brett knew something was very wrong.

"What is it, for goodness sake?!" cried Miss Brett, who was beyond frazzled. She, like Lucy, had begun to search through the wreckage. "What does it mean?"

"It is the name. What means the name," Bo Peep said solemnly.

"What does it mean?" asked Noah, swallowing hard.

"Name means," the feathered man began, looking at his brethren. "Means 'half-moustache.'"

CHAPTER THIRTY-FIVE

TROUBLE IN DOUBLE

OR

HOW TWO MAKES ONE

Had this been said, one friend to another, it might have been funny. The absurdity of this statement, under other circumstances, might have brought giggles and laughter. But the children had learned that things are not always what they seem. Just as a man in bunny ears can make your blood run cold, things can always be seen in a second way.

"But that is not his name," insisted Miss Brett. "It is Mezzobassi."

"But she called him Signor Mezzobaffi the very first day," said Lucy. "I remember."

Miss Brett had gone quite pale. "It's him, isn't it?" she asked. "That's what you think. Somehow, Signor Mezzobaffi or Mezzobassi is mixed up with him."

"Not him," said Bo Peep.

"Komar Romak," said Faye, uttering more a gasp than words.

"It...it cannot be." Miss Brett went as pale as the snow. It was not possible. It was simply not possible that the sweet, frail old shepherd was this monster.

"Yes," the feathered man said. "It means."

Noah just stood, shaking his head. Jasper reached for Lucy, who fell into his arms. Faye's mouth went dry. It was as if her thoughts were flipping back and forth between two realities—one where the shepherd was the shepherd and the other where he was not. Miss Brett tried to deny it, but more and more clues and facts were chipping away at the security wall she had built in her heart, around the children she loved so much.

"But... but... how is it possible?" Miss Brett tried to ask the men. "The Komar Romak we know looks nothing like this man. Nothing at all."

"But the other," said Bo Peep.

"What other?" Jasper asked.

"Komar Romak," said Bo Peep.

"There's another?"

"No," said the feathered man.

"No, *what?*" demanded Faye.

"There is only the one, and the other," Bo Peep said.

"So there are two?" Noah scratched his head.

"Two what?" asked Miss Brett.

"Komar Romak," said the feathered man and Bo Peep.

"There are two Komar Romaks?" said Jasper in disbelief.

"That makes one whole moustache, if you put them together," Noah said, to everyone's pointed looks.

"There are two men with the name Komar Romak?" asked Miss Brett.

"No," said the feathered man.

"But you said ..." Miss Brett could not understand what they had said. Nothing was making sense. In fact, everything made less and less sense with every word.

"There are always two," said Lucy. "I remember in the farmhouse when Komar Romak disappeared the first time. They said that there were always two. But we only saw one."

"Two, always. It has always been so," said the feathered man. "For as long."

"As long as what? Solemano? For 350 years?" said Noah, sarcasm in his words.

"Yes," said Bo Peep, without any sarcasm. "No."

"And not," said the feathered man. "Only know this."

"Only know what?" Noah had been joking. What on earth were they saying?

"From 350," said Bo Peep. "Before is story."

"The story goes back more than 350 years?" Wallace asked.

This time the men simply nodded. It was the first time the mysterious men in black had made sense, and they hadn't actually said anything.

Wallace's jaw dropped, and his mouth remained silently open. Lucy looked thoughtful, but Faye, Noah, and Jasper looked at one another with the same thought.

"That is insane," Faye said, speaking their collective minds.

"There is always two," Bo Peep said. "Forever, always two. Komar Romak.

"For all, all, all those years, there has always, always been the evil of Komar Romak," Lucy explained, "and Komar Romak is a pair."

Noah raised his eyebrows.

"Komar Romak isn't a man. Komar Romak is two," said Lucy, looking intently at Noah.

"But that's crazy," said Noah. "Isn't it?" He turned to Miss Brett.

"I don't know," she said. "If there is some force, some kind of... something, and that is where Komar Romak is from, I suppose there could be some continuous, some historical ... something evil that has remained..." But what?

"Insane," said Noah decisively. "Utterly insane."

Somehow, though, Miss Brett felt some tiny grain of understanding—an understanding that told her this was not merely someone bent on theft or assault. This was something much bigger, and much older.

"It wasn't the aeroplane," said Faye quietly, almost to herself.

"What?" Noah turned to Faye, who was staring ahead, as if seeing something for the first time.

With dawning comprehension, Faye looked at the others. She said, "It wasn't the aeroplane. It never was the aeroplane. We were wrong. We only thought ... he wanted our invention because we were so clever. But we were wrong. Remember? He never mentioned 'flying machine' or 'aeroplane' or 'flying' anything ... or ... or anything like that when he came to Sole Manner Farm." Faye looked at Miss Brett. "He didn't, did he, Miss Brett?"

"No, he didn't," Miss Brett said.

"But if not the aeroplane, then what?" asked Faye.

Bo Peep looked down.

Swallowing and finally getting a voice, Jasper said, "You mean this is real? Komar Romak is 350 years old?"

"No one is 350 years old," said Wallace, recovering his senses. But he threw a furtive glance at Miss Brett, who shook her head reassuringly.

"Komar Romak so long," said the feathered man.

"Longer," Bo Peep said, nodding.

"Is..." Miss Brett felt like a fool to ask. "Is he human?"

"Not he," Bo Peep said.

"Fine. Is *Komar Romak* human?"

The two men looked at one another. For Miss Brett, their exchange took far too long. "This…this is absolutely absurd! Are you asking us to believe that Komar Romak is some kind of a—"

"Yes," both men said.

"Yes, he's a devil? A monster? Not human?"

"Yes, but no." Bo Peep looked at Miss Brett and nodded. Then the men exchanged looks. They clearly thought this made sense.

"Yes, but no *what*?" Miss Brett's snow-white face now flushed red.

"Komar Romak, human, evil, devil," said the feathered man, "but always human."

Miss Brett took a deep breath. "But you are still telling us that… that he, sorry, Komar Romak can change?"

"Always Komar Romak and two," said the feathered man forcefully.

"One and the other," said Bo Peep.

"Is how it is," the feathered man said.

There was silence for a moment. And then they heard a faint groan. It shook them all back to where they were and what they were doing here.

"Signora Fornaio!" Faye cried. She rushed to the other side of the counter and tore through the breads, broken jars of flour, and wrapping papers piled on the floor. Miss Brett hurried over to help.

Under the mess on the floor, they found Signora Fornaio. She was covered in flour and crumbs and broken glass. She seemed to try to move, but could not.

"She must have been attacked. Maybe someone hit her on the head." Miss Brett felt the back of the baker's head and found blood.

Bo Peep pushed through and knelt down beside the baker. He felt her wrist, then her forehead, then leaned over and picked up Signora Fornaio as if she were a rag doll. He brought her out to where the little table was. Faye grabbed a pile of aprons and napkins, which the feathered man laid out so she would have a soft place to rest.

There was blood coming from Signora Fornaio's mouth and nose. Her lips were as white as her face. Miss Brett stifled a gasp when she saw blood all over the front of the baker's frock and apron. The ravens were now squawking loudly on the other side of the door.

The baker groaned again. She was trying to speak.

"Don't try to talk." Miss Brett tried to keep her voice from shaking. "Just rest. We'll ..." But what they were going to do, she didn't know.

"I am dying," the baker said in barely a whisper. Her mouth moved again, but no sound came out.

"No!" cried Faye, tears falling from her eyes. "Please, Miss Brett, we have to help her!"

"Oh, please!" cried Lucy. "Miss Brett, help her. Mr. Bo Peep, please!"

Jasper held his sister. Noah put his hand on Jasper's shoulder.

Wallace had begun to cry silently. He turned his lucky coin over and over in his pocket.

"I ... I ..." But Miss Brett could not speak. She was helpless, and did not know what she could do. She bit back tears, and screams, and terror.

"I must speak," Signora Fornaio said in the near silence. "My son ... he ... you must return it ... it must go back ..."

"What? Return what?" Noah wiped the tears from his eyes.

"It does not belong to him," she managed, then coughed as more blood spilled from her lips. She looked at Bo Peep, then at the feathered man. "They must … it belongs to you … *gli inventori gilda*, the Inventors Guild." She looked hard into Bo Peep's hidden face. She spoke softly in what must have been a mix of Italian and Maltese. Then she looked from Miss Brett to Bo Peep. "They must bring it down … down … to the room … *posto speciale* … special place … down … *la camera … la stanza di un migliaio di lingue* … thousand languages … under … now … *palazzo in basso* …"

Then she coughed again, and looked back at Bo Peep. She said something to him—something in a language the children and Miss Brett did not comprehend. Then, trying to focus her eyes, she looked at Faye. "So *bella*," she said. "Astraea, *bella*." Faye remembered that Miss Brett's first name was Astraea.

"What happened?" said Jasper, wiping his face with the back of his hand. "Can you tell us what happened here?"

"My fault … my son … I take him … he know … make … safe … it is safe …" She was mumbling. It was not clear whether she could hear anyone.

"Did you see who did this?" Faye wanted answers. And she wanted revenge.

"You must take care … the shepherd … not …" She coughed. Miss Brett wanted her to save her strength, but she could see the life ebbing out of the kind and gentle woman. "You …" And her words got softer and softer. "It is them now … to take care … of … the … world." The last word was almost silent.

Her eyes became unfocused, her mouth went slack, and she closed her eyes for the last time.

CHAPTER THIRTY-SIX

A Breach of Manor

OR

LUCY FINDS THE RABBIT HOLE

"No, it can't be." Faye couldn't stop shaking. She could not believe what had just happened. She would never be able to remove the image of the dying baker from her mind.

Wallace had turned silent, his eyes full of tears. He vividly recalled his mother's death. Now, he simply could not speak.

Noah continued to shake his head. It simply could not be. He wanted to shake the scene from his view. He wanted to stop it, to keep her here, to stop her from going. Tears stung in the corners of his eyes.

Miss Brett still held Signora Fornaio's head in her lap, tears falling into the baker's hair. She noticed there were specks of dough caught among the strands of hair. Miss Brett gently released them and adjusted the crumpled ribbon. Miss Brett felt the desperate need to restore some dignity to the baker who now lay helpless in death. Miss Brett, too, felt helpless. She had held Signora Fornaio as the baker took her final breath, and there had been nothing the teacher could do but watch her friend slip away.

They all remained there, silent save for the tiny whimpers coming from Lucy, who was burrowed into Jasper's cloak, the cold from the open door filling the once warm, bountiful bakery. Never again would the kind Signora Fornaio bring them her smiles and gaiety, her baskets of treats and warm embraces. Life would never again be the same in Solemano.

Miss Brett pushed away a lock of hair that had blown across Signora Fornaio's face. She looked down into the face of the kindest of women, one who could never turn from a stray without offering it kindness. Suddenly, Miss Brett looked up. No—Signora Fornaio could never turn away a stray.

"I don't understand," said Noah. "Was she telling us to take care of the shepherd?" Noah looked to Miss Brett for answers.

"No, she was not, Noah. She was warning us. She was warning us to take care and beware," said Miss Brett. She stared as Bo Peep bent over and, gently, took Signora Fornaio into his arms and out of the bakery, the feathered man behind him. They exchanged some words, and Bo Peep handed the baker to the feathered man. Then, like a sentinel, Bo Peep stood at the door of the bakery.

Lucy huddled with Jasper, but when Miss Brett stood up, she ran to her teacher, desperate for mothering arms. Jasper stood there alone for a moment, then looked over at Faye, who was still shaking with grief and fury. Jasper reached for Faye's hand. She pulled away, not even looking at him. The image of the crumpled baker seared her eyes, burning rage into her heart.

Jasper stood alone in his grief. He hung his head. He felt defeat-ed.

Miss Brett stood, using the shepherd's staff to keep her steady. She clung to it, rubbing the top knot, as if it were the only solid thing in the world. Noah's hand on his shoulder brought Jasper into focus. He looked at his friend, then noticed the staff in Miss

Brett's hands.

"The staff," Jasper mumbled to himself, remembering what had caught his attention before. "It has a 'KR' carved in the top. He might have found it, but more likely it was his."

"But that's impossible!" Faye cried through her tears, shaking her head. "We all know that he was tall and—"

"There are always two," said Lucy, wiping her eyes.

"It's true," Jasper said, "which means we can never guess what Komar Romak looks like."

Miss Brett gasped. The children turned.

She had rubbed rather hard on the staff's top knot, and somehow turned it. The knot clicked. It popped up, and she pulled.

Out came a strange knife, with odd markings. It was long and narrow.

It was a stiletto—a knife with a long, narrow blade. The blade was covered in blood.

It was then they all heard the screeching. Running out to the window at the front of the bakery, Noah looked up toward the manor house. A circle of ravens were screeching in the sky, flying round and round above the house.

"Something's wrong," said Noah.

There was no time to wonder why or anything else—whether the staff really belonged to the shepherd or if it had been used by Komar Romak against the little old man. The birds could mean only one thing—someone had entered the manor house grounds.

"We have to get up there!" Faye's loud voice quaked.

"Go up there?" Miss Brett was hit by the idea of heading into danger.

"Now!" cried Jasper. "We have got to get up there now!"

"Signora Fornaio's box!" said Faye. "We can't let Komar Romak have it!"

"What can we do?" Noah gulped.

Jasper pulled the door open and Bo Peep turned to face him.

"We must get up to the house," said Jasper. The ravens—"

"The ravens know!" Lucy said, pulling at Bo Peep. "They're the keepers of wisdom!"

Bo Peep nodded, hiked up his skirt, and ran toward the house. Jasper ran after him. Faye followed. Wallace looked at Miss Brett.

"We have to get the box to safety." Miss Brett pushed the staff's knot, and the knife fell back into the top.

"How? Where?" Wallace knew the answer as soon as he asked it.

"We have to take it down to that room in the under-castle, imme-diately!" Miss Brett took Lucy's hand.

"And we have to make sure no one else is thinking the same," said Noah, without a trace of humor in his voice.

⎯⎯►●◄⎯⎯

Running up the road to the manor house, the children and Miss Brett were slower than Bo Peep, but not by much. They all fought against the snow and the cold. The circling ravens were still screeching. The two ravens from the baker's place soared and swooped overhead, crying like mourners. The children and Miss Brett moved as swiftly as they could. The wind bit into their cheeks as they trudged, but they knew what they had to do.

"We'll grab Antonio's box and head back to the hidden Christ-mas room." Miss Brett felt she sounded a bit like Lucy, but she really didn't know where that secret place was or what to call it. It was some secret castle built into the mountain, but where the entrance was, or if there was another way in, she had no idea. She hoped they'd be able to find the way in and hoped the weather wouldn't turn and make it impossible to get there.

"The entrance was missing when we last looked," Faye told her teacher, who had raced to catch up.

"Well, we'll just have to look harder." Miss Brett knew her voice lacked warmth, but there was no way around it. They had to act fast.

"We'll find it," said Jasper with determination. "We have no choice."

"But we don't even know what that orb does," Noah said.

"It doesn't matter," Jasper said, trying to keep his calm. "If Komar Romak thinks it's important, then it must be important."

Where was the entrance? thought Miss Brett. She only knew that it had been beneath the chapel. Maybe the castle had a chapel above it. Perhaps it had been built by Templar Knights or medieval renegades, escaping from something. She wondered if the children's parents were there, or if they, like the children and herself, had simply been brought there for Christmas dinner. The parents said they were near, though, and they certainly had never been seen in the village.

Still, what she did know was that the children had to get themselves and the package back to that room. A fortified room was the only place where they could be sure it would be safe from the threat of Komar Romak, and it seemed to be what Signora Fornaio wanted. She had been clear—the room of a thousand languages. That was where they had to take the box, wherever that room might be.

As soon as they got to the manor house, they could see that the

wall had been breached—someone had tried to enter. The front door was opened. Bo Peep stood, waiting for them.

"Not enter, for me," insisted Bo Peep. The children waited in the doorway. Carefully and silently, Bo Peep entered the house. The children and Miss Brett stood silently, trying to listen. They could not hear anything but the cries of the ravens outside. There did not seem to be anyone inside.

"Did they leave?" whispered Wallace.

"Perhaps," Miss Brett said. "Wait here."

Lucy squeezed her teacher's hand. "But Bo Peep said—"

"I'm only going there," said Miss Brett, pulling her hand from Lucy as she gingerly walked toward the table just inside the entrance hall. Her heart was beating fast as she tried to keep her panic in check. The crumpled handkerchief was still there, but would the box be there, too?

"We need to stay quiet," said Jasper, as Lucy whined. "In case someone is upstairs."

Miss Brett stopped at the table. She pulled the handkerchief and, with great relief, found the box where she had left it.

"Hiding something in plain sight is sometimes the trickiest place to hide it," Noah said.

"And if something is missing," said Miss Brett, returning to the children, "it's usually under something else."

"Good thing our invader didn't know that," said Noah.

They could hear doors being opened and slammed.

Finally, Bo Peep returned. "I have searched. Still fear."

"Well, we need to collect some things," insisted Miss Brett.

"Two." Bo Peep pulled a pocket watch from his apron. Two minutes.

"Now we must hurry, children," Miss Brett said as they and Bo Peep ran toward the stairs, Lucy whining and whimpering at Miss Brett's skirt. Miss Brett brought Lucy to the fire, which was low but still warm. Lucy, she could see, was terrified.

Faye came over. "I'll sit with her," she said. "You collect anything we can use to help get into the castle. And anything we can use to defend ourselves."

Miss Brett nodded. "Give me the first minute."

"I'll take the second," said Faye, nodding back.

Jasper reached the top of the stairs, where Bo Peep stood watch. "Keep an eye on them," Jasper said. "The only way in is down there."

Bo Peep's eyebrows rose above his dark spectacles. Jasper ran toward his room. On his way, he passed Miss Brett's, where the teacher grabbed a handbag—something, perhaps, to put the box inside.

Jasper looked at his teacher. "Lucy's bunny doll."

Miss Brett kissed the boy on the head. He was ever the thoughtful brother. "I'll get it," she said. She handed the bag to Jasper. She ran to Lucy's room to get her bunny doll. "Put anything else we might need in the bag and meet us downstairs."

Jasper needed some things from his room. As he ran down the hall, though, the box began to quiver, and shook more and more as he got closer to his room. What was happening to it? He wanted to open the box. But for now, he had to ignore it. One minute was all he had.

Once in his room, Jasper's mind raced. He wanted to grab string, wire, and a few tools he might need, but there wasn't time. What could he use? He couldn't think. Then he recalled the electric torches. He grabbed one sitting on his nightstand and threw it in his bag. As he ran from the room, the box seemed to calm. Jasper continued into the other rooms, retrieving a torch from Faye's room and Miss Brett's birthday torch, which she had left behind.

"I couldn't think of what to bring. I didn't have time," said Wallace as he rushed down the steps, adjusting his glasses. "I just grabbed a torch." He had welded a metal ring around his own new electric torch so that it hung from his neck on a string. "And a couple magnets and a few extra bulbs." He had the magnets and bismuth in his now rather bulging pocket. He put the bulbs in the pocket with the coin so they wouldn't get crushed. His mind was racing, trying to think of what else to bring.

Downstairs, Faye grabbed the snowball machine, which sat by the window. She put it in the carpet bag she found hanging on a hook by the door.

"That?" Noah said.

"It's a weapon now." Faye tried to sound sure of herself.

"Then I wish we had ten," Noah said. Faye nodded, appreciative.

"We need more torches," Wallace said, suddenly turning to head back upstairs. "It will only take me two minutes to assemble—"

"No time," growled Bo Peep, now at the bottom of the steps. "Must go."

"Come, children." Miss Brett tried to sound calm.

"Hey, stand back," Noah told Wallace as they started for the door. Wallace looked crestfallen, but Noah winked and pointed to the compass. The magnets were keeping his compass from giving an accurate reading. Wallace nodded and understood.

Jasper reached for Lucy's hand, but she ran to their teacher. The little girl followed Miss Brett, clinging to her skirt, not wanting to open her eyes, because that would mean everything was real and

Signora Fornaio was dead. Jasper looked down at his hand, holding no one. He swallowed hard.

Noah looked over at Lucy and looked at his compass. He knelt down so he could speak to Lucy face to face.

"Lucy, will you be in charge of this?" he asked, his voice serious and meaningful. "We'll need the compass. I think you should carry it."

Lucy nodded and clung to the compass as if it contained all the answers they needed.

Noah gave her a big hug and kissed her cheek. Faye saw this and felt an odd affection for Noah.

"You're a good man, Noah," said Faye.

Noah felt the lump in his throat. The ice queen had a real heart, he decided. Faye was indeed human.

<hr />

Outside, the wind seemed crueler. Though the snow was not falling as heavily, the wind seemed to get in-between every thread on every hat, scarf, and overcoat. Bo Peep used his crook almost like an oar, pulling himself against the wind. They were heading through the gardens. "If anyone is watching, they'll know where we're going if we just head down the road to the chapel," Jasper said.

They edged around the house and began the climb down through the terraced gardens. Wallace and Lucy each clung to one of Miss Brett's hands. Wallace was not going to let go of her. Miss Brett could feel the strength of his grip. *He cannot afford to lose anyone else*, she thought.

At the beast garden, Lucy dropped her bunny doll.

"Wait!" she cried, and let go of Miss Brett.

"No!" cried Bo Peep.

"Lucy!" cried Miss Brett, who had been holding Lucy by the arm. But then it was too late. Again.

"Lucy!" cried Jasper as he reached for the little girl but missed.

"Miss Brett!" cried Wallace, still clinging to her hand.

"Wallace!" cried Faye, as Wallace vanished before her eyes.

It all happened in a flash, as if by magic. Miss Brett, Lucy, and Wallace had all disappeared.

Jasper grabbed the crook from Bo Peep's hand. He leaned into the pedestal. "Can you hear me?!" he cried, rapping Bo Peep's crook against the stone.

"They can hear you," Faye said. "We could before and it makes a very big difference."

There was a faint sound from below.

"Don't move. We're going to try to find a way in there." But Jasper, picking up his electric torch, did not know how.

CHAPTER THIRTY-SEVEN

FEAR OF SMALL PLACES

OR

WHAT BECOMES LOST IN TUNNELS

Lucy slipped slowly down Miss Brett's skirt, landing with a soft *plop* on the floor of the cave.

"Give me your hands!" Miss Brett called out in the dark. The space smelled of dirt and age, of roots and stone. She had only a glimpse of their prison, but she could see that on one side was a pile of rubble. If there had been a tunnel, the way out was blocked, perhaps by a collapse as long ago as centuries.

Lucy felt for her teacher's hand. Wallace adjusted his glasses, which had been hanging from an ear, although, in the dark, he could see nothing anyway.

"Wallace?" Miss Brett called. Then she felt his hand in hers.

"I can't find my bunny doll!" Lucy cried.

Miss Brett felt around on the floor, her hand brushing over what were surely the dry bones of a small animal, long dead. Then she felt the doll. She handed it to the little girl.

Lucy snuffled, clinging to the doll. Then she gasped.

"And I've lost Noah's compass!" She began to cry anew.

"I'm sure we'll find it when they come for us, sweet angel." Miss

Brett caressed Lucy's hair until the little girl was calmer. Then she turned her head back toward the pile of rubble, her mind at work. She couldn't see it well in the dark, but she wondered if they could somehow get through it.

"Is that a tunnel on the other side of the fallen rocks? Did you ever go through it, Lucy?" Miss Brett asked. "Do you know? Was it open the last time you were here?" She could feel Lucy shake her head. Miss Brett's hopes fell.

"Wallace," Miss Brett said, suddenly remembering. "Your electric torch."

Wallace shook his torch and flipped the switch. Light filled the space. Miss Brett felt relief—but only for a moment. With a small *pop*, the light went out.

"It's the bulb," said Wallace. "I have more, but I can't see to replace it."

"Can you try in the dark?" asked Miss Brett.

Wallace considered this. Yes, he could, but then if he dropped the bulbs, they'd be entirely out of luck. "I'll try, but it might take a while."

"We're in no hurry, sweet angel," Miss Brett said.

There was nothing to do but sit in the dark. And wait.

———⊰●⊱———

"Why?" Faye didn't even try to keep her voice down as she and Noah raced after Jasper, nearly dropping the torch she held in her hand.

"Because we need his help!" Jasper called back, chasing after Bo Peep.

"We could do it like last time," said Faye, reaching out for Jasper's arm but missing.

"There isn't time," said Jasper, determined. "It's not like last time when we were playing in the garden. We're up against Komar Romak." They did not have time to figure out the magical spot and retrieve Lucy, Wallace, and Miss Brett from the garden of the beasts—not with Komar Romak around here somewhere. They had to enter another way and, as they ran to follow Bo Peep, they assumed that is where they were headed.

And then Jasper stopped, having nearly run past the chapel. Faye almost crashed into him. Noah knocked her over as he plowed into her, slipping as he tried to brace himself against the collision. Glaring at Noah, Faye righted herself using his head, knocking him back onto the ground.

"He went in there." Jasper pointed and began climbing through the ruined entrance.

"Why?" asked Noah, following Jasper and Faye.

"The tunnel," Jasper said. "I wonder—"

"Yes!" Faye whipped her head around. "That's it! Or it could be."

"What?" Noah rubbed his bottom as he stood.

"The tunnel, the one hidden in the beast garden. One side was full of rubble, remember? It was blocking a tunnel." Faye and Jasper both looked up at the manor house and followed the possible path the underground tunnel might take.

"It's got to be the same one!" said Faye, commanding it to be true.

But when the three children entered the chapel, Bo Peep was nowhere to be found.

"Where did he go?" Noah asked as they all looked around.

"He must have thought we were right behind him." Jasper, too, was looking around the room.

"How can we find the entrance?" Noah followed their gaze.

"We've got to try," Jasper said, heading for the archway. Once again, Noah followed Jasper and Faye.

"It's got to be the same one!" Faye insisted.

They went immediately to the vestry, the small chamber off the main room of the chapel. They looked around at the fresco paint‐ings, the broken rafter above, the archway that separated the famil‐iar pieces of the ruined chapel. There was the blank wall—the one that had taken them into the tunnels on Christmas Eve. But the wall now was really just a wall. The crack that had run lengthwise was not even visible.

"Do you think that, maybe, *all* the tunnels are connected?" Noah said, scratching his ear.

"It would make sense," said Faye. "There must have been a secret passageway, built by the people who built the manor house."

"Or before the manor house, in ancient times," Jasper said, con‐sidering the ancient carvings in the tunnels. He felt along the wall but could not find the trigger to open the door.

Noah pulled something out of his pocket. It was his compass. "Lucy dropped it before she fell in the hole," he said. He faced the compass towards the manor. "The collapsed tunnel in the beast gar‐den faces southeast, right, Faye?"

He indicated the direction, and Faye nodded. She remembered from when she was down there.

"That's northwest of where we are." Noah turned. "This means … yes, they could be connected. If we find the entrance, we can take another reading inside the passageway and see if we can find the same collapse." Jasper was touching the walls in the alcove. There had to be a button or a lever or a switch. There had to be something that opened the chapel wall.

A loud chattering came from above. A raven landed on the broken rafter. He flapped his wings and, as usual, it sounded like clattering stones.

"Get out of here, bird!" cried Faye. But the bird flew down and hopped, flapping his wings and chattering as if yelling at Faye. "What?" Faye demanded. "What do you want?"

Not expecting an answer, Faye jumped back as the bird hopped up to the broken edge of the archway. It flew to the fresco and back to its perch.

"Is it trying to land on the wall?" asked Noah. But the bird did not seem to try to land—only to scratch against the painting. It did this three times before Noah looked more closely at the fresco on the wall.

As Faye carefully ran her fingers over the walls in the archway, Noah carefully examined the fresco. The bird was screeching now, hopping and flapping. Noah stared at the painting of the monks where the bird had scratched. And that was when he noticed the flags.

"That's it!" he said. He pushed the red and white flag. They heard a click, but the wall did not open.

"Look for another flag like that!" Faye cried. "There must be a second button or lever."

"It's here!" called Jasper. They had not noticed before, but next to the blank wall, pushed out from the faded fresco, was another painted flag. Next to the flag was a black bird. The first click had somehow exposed this flag. Jasper pushed it, but nothing happened. Faye felt it then. Instead of pushing, she turned it.

The wall cracked open.

———◦◦◦———

In seconds, Faye held the torch Jasper had retrieved from her room, and they were in the tunnel. Within moments, they could no longer hear the chattering of the raven in the chapel. They came to a split in the tunnel, stopped, felt along the wall, and noticed the round impression.

"That's the place where Wallace fit his coin."

"It can't be," said Faye. "There wasn't a fork in the tunnel where he found it."

"There must be more than one," said Noah.

"If only Lucy was here, she'd remember which way to go." Jasper pined for his sister, but he knew she was with Miss Brett, and that gave him some relief.

"No, she wouldn't," said Faye. "Lucy was asleep when we found the collapsed tunnel."

Noah looked at the compass. "That way is northwest." And they followed.

After many twists and turns, they finally came to another fork in the tunnel. One path turned sharply to the left. The other was more or less straight. Again, Jasper saw the round impression. It had to mean something, but he couldn't imagine what it was.

"I know we did not make any sharp turns when we came down at Christmas," said Faye, who seemed so sure that the boys went along. "This is a different passageway. When we found the collapsed tunnel, it was when we didn't follow the man carrying Lucy." So they remained on the straighter path, hoping they'd be able to have another choice soon.

A few minutes later, they came to another fork, this time with three different tunnels, all of which seemed to be rather straight.

"Now what do we do?" asked Noah.

"We need to try one and hope it's right," said Jasper. "We can always head back and try again if we have to."

"We'll start here, then," said Faye, pointing to the tunnel farthest to the left.

"Take this," came a deep voice.

Noah jumped.

It was Bo Peep, pointing down the tunnel farthest to the right.

"You nearly scared the life right out of me!" cried Noah.

"Nice job, leaving us there on our own," Faye said.

"I am here," Bo Peep said.

"We see that," Jasper said. "But where were you?"

"Yes," Bo Peep said. "Now I go."

"What?!" Faye and Noah shouted at once.

"I go to get," he said, then disappeared into the darkness.

"What is he getting?" asked Noah.

"It doesn't matter," said Faye. "This is the right way." They continued on down the third tunnel. The ground was smoother, and soon, they passed some kind of stone chute.

"Wait!" Jasper stopped, bringing the torch closer to the wall of the tunnel. Again, there were strange carvings and drawings on the wall. But one in particular caught his attention. "This *is* the path," he said with absolute certainty.

"How do you know?" asked Faye, looking at the carvings.

"Because this is where Wallace fit his coin," Jasper said. "This has to be the spot. I remember he put the coin to the wall and it made a noise, like a hum. This spot has scratches on it from when Wallace was trying to get it out."

"I wish we had the coin," said Noah. "When it hummed in the wall, it seemed like it had a purpose. Maybe it was opening something."

Jasper felt along the wall. There were no cracks or grooves, and nothing here to give them a clue as to what that coin might have done.

"Well, we don't have the coin," Faye said matter-of-factly as they continued down the passageway. Again, they came to a split. "So where to now?"

Noah checked the compass. "That's northwest," he said, pointing down the passage on the left.

Faye shined her torch but the light sputtered. She shook the torch and the flickering light came back, but not as brightly.

"I'm worried we're going to lose the torch. Wallace has the extra bulbs." Faye shined the light down the passage again.

"Right, yes, I remember. If we go down here, there's a fork, and the other way is blocked by rubble." Jasper was running now, the others right behind him.

As they ran, Faye almost tripped on some rocks in the middle of the path. With a sputter, her torch went out.

"What do we do now?" Noah asked in the darkness.

"I still have—look!" cried Jasper, pointing in the darkness. Nobody could see his hand, but they could see the tiny cracks of light coming from the far end of the passageway.

"Does that mean we're getting close?" asked Noah, hopefully.

But close to what? Jasper didn't feel like they were coming to the collapsed tunnel yet. No, it was farther—but how much? With the dim light, they didn't need Jasper's torch, and as their eyes adjusted, they managed to avoid some of the rubble littering their path.

"This is it," Jasper said, and he knew he had to be right. As if retracing their steps back up the tunnel they had found on Christmas, they walked cautiously toward what they hoped would be a blocked passage. And there, in front of them, was the pile of rubble. Through the rocks came the thin streams of light. Then the light went out.

"Lucy!" cried Jasper. There was no response.

"It might be miles of rubble," Noah said, rubbing his head.

"There was light coming through, you idiot!" yelled Faye. "It can't be miles."

"Lucy!" Jasper cried louder.

Noah put his fingers in his mouth and blew an ear-splitting whistle. Faye covered her ears and kicked his foot.

"Ouch," he said. "We need to make noise so they can—"

But there was a noise. In fact, it sounded like an ear-splitting whistle from the other side of the rubble. Someone was there and was whistling back.

⋙•◦•⋘

"You can uncover your ears, children," Miss Brett said, though both children had already done so. She wiped her fingers on her skirt and adjusted her hair.

"Wow, Miss Brett," said Wallace. "You sure can whistle."

It usually made Miss Brett feel a little funny, whistling the way her father had taught her, but she was very glad she had not forgotten how.

"I hope they heard that," she said. Silently, she hoped that it was

Noah's blasting whistle she'd heard, and not that of someone from whom she would rather be hiding. Wallace had managed to replace the bulb in the torch. He had been shining it at the pile of rubble, and just after he'd turned it off to save the bulb, they'd heard the faint sound of a whistle. Now, they heard nothing.

"How will they know for sure we're here?" asked Lucy.

"When I say three," Miss Brett said, "we are all going to yell, 'We're over here!' Okay?"

And on the count of three, they did.

———⟶•⟵———

"That is ridiculous. I'll go," insisted Jasper. What was Faye doing? She was terrified of closed spaces and here she was, demanding to be the one to crawl through the rubble.

"Get out of my way, Jasper," said Faye. "Please."

"She's my sister, and I want to—"

"Please!" cried Faye, gulping back the tears already coming down her face. Then, quietly, she begged, "Please, Jasper."

"Faye," Noah said, trying to reason with her, "you can't—"

"I can do it!" she shouted, beads of sweat already forming on her face. She pulled off her bag and shoved it at Noah. "I have to do it. I'm no good to anybody if I can't help when someone is most needed."

Jasper opened his mouth to argue, but stopped. He understood. Faye needed to prove that she could overcome her weakness. But it was his sister in there.

"Okay," Jasper said. "But there's no harm in taking turns. Maybe … maybe you can start and I can take over, after a while."

Faye nodded. She swallowed hard and felt her anxiety ease,

knowing she'd be able to get out if she needed to escape. But she was determined. She would not fail.

In a few minutes, Faye, clutching tightly to her still non-working torch, had slithered into a small opening at the top of the rubble. There was almost no room at all as she pulled rocks out while she crawled, passing them back down the tunnel. Jagged edges scraped her belly and tore her skirt, but what was worse was the warm, damp smell of her own breath. It felt like the only air she could get.

Sweat burned into her eyes. She kept moving, but the nausea was fighting for a place in her gut. She found she needed to catch her breath every few feet. The urge to turn back—back to air, to space—was enormous. Even while walking through the tunnels, she had felt moments of panic, and now she was in a tiny crack in a pile of rocks. It was a nightmare, but when she thought of Lucy and Wallace and Miss Brett, she pushed on.

Again, she heard a whistle, but this time from much closer on the other side.

"Can you hear me?!" she called.

"Yes!" came the voice of Miss Brett.

Faye pulled rocks out and passed them back through the crevice to Noah and Jasper. She tried to shake the torch she still held. She flicked it on and it worked again, a beam of light shining outward.

And then Miss Brett saw the small beam of light shining through the rocks. She could see the torch Faye had by her side as she dug.

"I see you!" cried Miss Brett. And with the light, she could also see where to dig.

—⟫●⟪—

"Maybe they *are* all connected," Noah said as he threw loose stones away from the space where Faye had crawled. "And if the tunnels are all connected to some network, there's got to be a passage between the underground castle, or whatever that was, and our house. The passage through the beast garden *must* lead up to the house somehow."

It was then they heard the sound of falling rocks.

"Is the tunnel collapsing?" asked Noah, covering his head.

"Let's hope not," Jasper said. "But let's hope the tunnels *are* all connected. Then we can get back out of here, one way or another."

"And we will need one way," Noah said. "One way, and maybe another."

—⟫●⟪—

It took a while longer before Faye could reach her hand through the crevice and feel Miss Brett's fingers on the other side. Faye hung her head and felt the warm moisture fill her eyes. Then, it was only a matter of minutes before she was able to actually climb through.

"I've made it!" Faye called back as she was embraced by the three she found on the other side of the rubble. Faye was shaking and took a few moments to catch her breath.

"You are so brave," said Miss Brett, fully appreciating what it took for Faye to climb through that small space.

Faye stood in the space where she and Lucy had once fallen, and looked around. Now she could find her breath in the very place where she had felt her chest clenching before. After the crack in the rubble, this space felt wide open.

It was a strange space. There were carvings on the wall, and even what had once been a shelf carved into the rock. It seemed ancient, as if from Roman times.

"I want to show you something," Faye said quietly to Miss Brett.

As Lucy and Wallace began climbing back through the crevice, she shined her torch and showed Miss Brett the body of the artist. Looking closer, they could see what remained of his clothes. The body, more a skeleton or a mummy now, faced away from the hole. His head lay at an impossible angle, as if he had fallen down the hole, headfirst, and broken his neck. His capotain—a tall, almost cone-shaped hat—was crunched and bent but still on his head. The ends of his shoulder-length hair showed from beneath it.

It was so strange to see a skeleton arm and a mummified face with hair that seemed almost alive. A very gray ruff that had once been white still adorned his neck. It seemed so fragile, as if it would crumble if touched. His jacket was ornately embroidered in pale pinks and yellows. There was a cape nearby, as if it had either been torn off his shoulders or, if merely slung over his back, flung from the artist in the fall. It had deep green and blue stripes and gold trimming.

"Look." Faye pointed to the artist's sleeve. There were splotches of colored paint staining the edges of his doublet.

"He was an artist after all," Miss Brett said.

"He was young and handsome when he died," said Faye. "But he disappeared and, eventually, no one looked for him. His story lived on, but no one remembered him as a person."

There was something so sad about that. It was a tragic story, the young artist with so much to live for who came to such an untimely end. He had been loved by kings and queens, yet he met his end alone in a dark and ancient hole.

"The baker's son died in a tunnel," said Faye, thinking, too, of how Antonio would one day be forgotten. Would Signora Fornaio?

"Far from home and those who loved him," said Miss Brett. She wondered about the artist. Someone had doubtless mourned when he disappeared.

"We might never have known about either one," said Faye. "These deaths, these mysteries…"

"You children brought them to light," said Miss Brett, her hand on Faye's shoulder. "You did a very good thing."

For a moment, the two of them stood there in silence. Then a few stones fell from the pile of rubble.

"We had better go," Miss Brett said to Faye. "We have paid him our respects. We will remember him."

CHAPTER THIRTY-EIGHT

FOLLOW THE SHIVERING ORB

OR

THE UNLOCKING OF CLUES

After Jasper had helped Miss Brett, the last to come out on the other side of the rubble, everyone brushed themselves off, turned, and started back through the tunnel. Almost immediately, they heard a rumble. Looking back, they found the path that Faye had carved was no there longer. The rocks had caved in upon themselves.

Faye gasped, staring at the rock.

"You made it," Jasper said.

But suddenly, the rumble grew louder—more than mere rocks falling in the tunnel.

"Was that an explosion?" asked Wallace.

"The rocks didn't fall by themselves," said Noah.

Lucy began to whimper.

"We've got to get moving," said Faye, urging everyone onward. "We've got to get to the room of a thousand languages."

"Here, Lucy." Noah handed her the compass. "We need to be heading east—southeast, actually—but mostly east."

"I won't lose it again, Noah," she said from inside the hug she was giving him. "I promise."

Noah gave her a squeeze back. Another rumble shook the walls.

"Let's go," Jasper said, handing Miss Brett her torch.

With Lucy in the lead, they continued back along the passage. They passed the walls of brick and stone, the symbols and writ-ing—Galileo's notations again. They followed the twisting and turning passages until they reached another fork.

"Which way, Lucy?" asked Noah.

"I'm not sure," said Lucy. Noah could see in the light of Miss Brett's flickering electric torch that the needle was going crazy. Miss Brett again shook the torch, but apparently the bulb was not very strong. Faye pointed her torch at the compass.

"Wallace, move away," Noah said. "Your magnets are making the compass go wacky."

But Wallace was already far from Lucy, and still the compass was quivering madly.

"It must be near," said Jasper, taking the torch from Faye and shining it ahead to see if he could see anything down the passage. He could not.

"Wait," said Lucy, taking a few steps down the passage, then a few steps back. "It must be this way! The needle starts shaking harder...and now it's starting to spin!"

Soon, they were moving down the passage, the needle spinning fast.

In the light of Faye's torch, they all leaned over and stared at the compass needle, and then they ran. Sometimes they could see, but then the shadows overtook them as Faye's electric torch flickered out again. Was there something wrong with the torch besides a bad bulb? After Lucy slipped and fell over an unseen rock, they slowed to a safer walk.

"I've got mine," Wallace said. He shook and then flicked on his torch. He handed it to Jasper, who traded him Faye's. "I can replace the bulb when we're safe somewhere. I've got one more." Wallace just hoped that the problem with Faye's torch was only a weak and burned-out bulb.

And then suddenly, right in front of them stood those huge doors, like giant, ancient guardians.

Miss Brett looked up in awe at their sheer size. Thicker than most walls, and carved in iron and wood, the doors were truly enormous.

It was then that two things happened.

First, the compass stopped quivering.

And suddenly, Jasper himself began to quiver.

Well, actually, Miss Brett's handbag, which Jasper had over his shoulder, began to quiver and shake.

"What is that?" asked Faye, moving slightly away from Jasper.

"I think it's the box," said Jasper. He pulled off the sack and removed the box. It was shaking. "Should I open it?" he asked Miss Brett.

"Yes!" shouted Faye. Then she looked at Miss Brett. "Don't you think?" Miss Brett nodded, and Faye was glad.

Jasper opened the box.

Whatever they thought might happen, they were wrong. What actually happened was utterly unexpected. At first, Jasper was a bit wary of picking up the orb. Shaking, it seemed to have come alive, and Jasper imagined it might open up a mouth and bite him. Still, he gulped and plunged his hand into the box. He caught the shivering orb in his hand. It felt like holding a tiny, metallic bunny rabbit or baby chick. He picked it up out of the box and then, without warning, the orb jumped (if an orb can jump) right out of his hand.

Jasper felt he had dropped it. But when he reached down to pick it back up, Jasper found himself chasing after the little orb. He tried to stop it with the staff, but the orb kept moving into the darkness, rolling toward the giant door. Noah tried to catch it, then Faye, but the rolling orb slipped through fingers and dodged grabbing hands. It rolled and rolled in a straight line. It rolled right up to the door.

Then, it rolled *up* the door.

"Hello? Is ... um ..." Noah began, but he couldn't even say the words.

The orb rolled up the long, metal astragal, the strip that ran between the two halves of the double door. This astragal, as they had noticed before, had a strange groove in it, and now, as they watched this bizarre orb defy gravity and roll up the astragal, the mystery of the groove seemed apparent. It was made for the orb. It rolled up to the place where the key had been inserted, then stopped. It began to vibrate again, and this somehow triggered the unlocking mechanism. The door was opened.

⟞•◆•⟝

Gingerly, the children walked through the doorway. Jasper reached out for the orb, which seemed to jump, still shivering, into his hand. Faye led the way with her torch, but somehow imagined they would find the fire lit and the candelabra glowing next to the hearth. This was indeed the Christmas room, but it was not the way they had left it. It was neither warm nor festive. There was no fire in the hearth, no scent of cinnamon and butter in the air. There was no bird on the perch. There was no gramophone playing Handel's *Messiah*. There were no parents around the fire or nannies carrying food. Now, the room smelled of stone. It was cold, dank, and silent, as if it had been this way for hundreds of years.

Miss Brett went over to the fireplace and picked up a dusty silver tinderbox that sat on the mantle. Within seconds, she had lit the dried wood remaining in the fireplace. The resulting fire was small, but it provided some heat and light. Jasper looked down at the orb in his hand. It really did feel like a tiny animal. It seemed almost to have a heart, beating fast and furious, as if it were in a panic to escape. Noah stepped over, shaking his head.

"It really is the strangest thing." He touched the orb in Jasper's hand and, suddenly, the orb stopped shaking.

"Well, either it likes me and I've calmed it down," Noah said, removing his hand with a jerk, "or I've killed it."

They all watched the little orb, now unmoving, in Jasper's hand. But a few seconds after Noah moved away, the orb began to quiver again. The quivering grew stronger, and the orb seemed to be tugging away from Jasper's hand.

Where did it want to go? Jasper had an idea.

He remembered the strange, darkened hallways from their Christmas visit. He remembered that two paths had been locked, and Faye had told him that there were strange grooves along the sides of the iron gates. They had also come to doors at the end of the passageways they had explored. These doors, too, had been locked. But so had been the door they had just passed through. Did they lock behind you when you passed through? Would they be trapped?

It didn't matter now. Jasper walked toward the first passageway, with the door behind which they had found the chanting men in black. The others followed, Faye close behind. The orb began to quiver more forcefully. As Jasper bent down, the orb rolled from his hand and down into the darkness. He shook his electric torch and flicked it on.

"Quick! The tinderbox!" cried Faye. Noah quickly ran back to grab the tinderbox from the mantle. He lit the two torches hanging in the sconce. Once the torches were lit, the passageway had enough light, and Jasper switched off the electric torch as they ran after the rolling orb. They were all aware that the electric torches now had only one bulb each. They needed to save the bulbs when they could.

The orb came to the end of the passageway and, as before, rolled up the doorway into a small, round indentation. Again, as with the big doors, this door unlocked. Faye took a hold of the door handle and opened it.

What they found was a set of stairs going up into darkness.

"If this is a way out, it might be a better option than heading back into the tunnels," said Jasper. "We could use another way out."

"I'm worried about the box," said Miss Brett.

"You're right, Miss Brett. Once we get the box put away safely," said Jasper, "we can head up there and perhaps find a different way back."

"We need to get the box to safety,"

"We need to bring the box to this 'Room of a Thousand Languages,' but we don't know where that is," Jasper said.

"We should try one of the other passages we couldn't enter Christmas Eve," Faye said.

"Perhaps the orb works on the same principle as our magnetic spheres," Wallace said as they followed Faye to the passage on the right. The orb quivered strongly in Jasper's hand as they neared the barred gate. "It reacted to the metal bar on the door. It was reacting to various things." Wallace pulled one of his magnetic spheres from his pocket. He placed it on the ground. It did not move. "Though I suppose there must be more to it than that."

Jasper set Antonio's orb on the ground. Unlike the magnet, Antonio's orb ran up the locking mechanism on the bars. It fixed itself inside of the indentation that seemed to be made for it. Then Miss Brett, Lucy still clinging to her skirt, pulled. But the gate did not open. Noah tried, too.

"Why isn't it working?" Faye growled.

Wallace, too, was mystified. He, Faye, and Jasper all reached for the bars at the same time. Miss Brett did as well, and Lucy reached up to hold the hand Miss Brett was not using. And then, suddenly, Wallace, Faye, Jasper, and Lucy were thrown back by a blast of electricity. Standing up, they looked at one another, and almost everyone's hair was standing on end—just as on the train, and in Nikola Tesla's laboratory.

"What on earth?" Noah laughed. Only he and Miss Brett remained unaffected.

"This is not funny, Noah Canto-Sagas," barked Faye, brushing herself off and trying to bring her floating hair back down from the air.

"We look funny, though," said Lucy. She felt her floating braids and left them where they were.

Wallace picked up his glasses and stood back up. He went to examine the lock on the bars. Then he saw it—some odd-shaped grooves along the astragal of the gate. One shape was flat and round, and had some markings on the inside. He pulled his coin from his pocket. Yes, the markings were the same—only in reverse, like an impression in clay. His coin would fit directly into the shape in the metal.

He looked at Jasper, Lucy, and Faye. Faye wore her necklace. Jasper and Lucy had their bracelets. He thought back to Christ-mas Eve and how his coin had reacted to their tokens. Maybe it was something in the metal alloy, or perhaps there was some strange magnetic field around the orb. Maybe there was something else—something to do with this place. Could it be? Were these things used for this lock? His coin? Was it made for this?

Wallace stood tall, tried to feel brave, and stepped back over to the bars. He placed his coin in the round groove.

There was a loud click.

And the gate opened.

CHAPTER THIRTY-NINE

The Room of a Thousand Languages

OR

A BIRD IN THE HAND

Miss Brett led the way through the gate. She now held Wallace's electric torch, and Lucy clung to her ever more closely. The passageway was long, and there were many doors on either side. The doors were made of thick steel.

Miss Brett tried the first door. It was locked. Jasper tried Antonio's orb. It jumped from his hand to the astragal, and there was a loud click. The door opened, but it led nowhere. On the other side was simply a stone wall. They tried this again on the other side. Again, nothing but a wall.

There were seventeen doors. When they reached the seventeenth, they found a tall door made of wood. Jasper ran his hand around the edge. There was nothing metallic that he could feel. He offered Antonio's orb a chance to do its magic. But the door did not open with it. The orb, in fact, did nothing.

"Look." Wallace pointed to the round impression on the wood of the door. He stepped up and placed his coin into that circular space. The door unlocked, but did not fly open. Faye reached out to pull it at the same time as Jasper. But both of them nervously stopped before actually touching the door.

"Why don't I open it?" Miss Brett said. She reached over and pulled the handle. It opened.

Lifting the electric torches up to spread the light, they could see that the room was something of a storage space.

"There's a lamp here," Wallace said, placing his torch on the table. Miss Brett came over and picked up a tinderbox sitting next to the lamp. She struck the match and lit the lamp. Wallace flicked off his torch. They could now see the room all the better. There were wooden crates lined up on great wooden shelves. It seemed that the room went on and on, shelf after shelf, row after row. There were wooden crates but, upon investigation, those were full of papers and journals and notebooks. Some of the papers looked ancient. There were even some scrolls stacked neatly on the shelves farther back from the door.

Then there was a click. Behind them, the door closed. Faye ran back to it and and reached for the handle, but there was no handle. She banged on the door but only made a quiet thud. It was thick and strong, and seemed barely to feel her fist.

"I can't open the door!" she said anxiously.

"Don't worry. Wallace's coin must open it from this side, too," Noah said. But there was no symbol for the coin inside the room.

"Well, we have to find a place for this box before we leave any-way," Jasper said. "We can figure out how to get out once we find a place for it."

"At least we're safe in here," Wallace said. "Aren't we?"

"Of course we are," Miss Brett said, nodding, though a bit too quickly. It was fine to think that, and likely, it was true. She went over to the shelves and picked up a few of the papers.

"We need more light," Miss Brett said, shining the lamp along the walls. She found a candelabra against the far wall. She lit it and the three others she found at intervals and above small wooden desks.

Now they could see most of the room. Indeed, it was a big room, with materials piled high on shelves. Some of the piles were bound into notebooks, and some pages were loose. The notebooks were not bound like books, but more like leaves of paper tied with ribbons into a booklet, as if they went together in a collection. Miss Brett leafed through some pages and realized quickly that not only could she not understand the language (most of which seemed to be Latin, but with many notations in numerous other languages), but she could not understand the diagrams either.

She picked up some other pages, only to find still more languages and diagrams. Faye went over with her electric torch and looked at what Miss Brett had found.

"Amazing," said Faye. She began to peruse the shelves, examining both loose papers and the bound booklets. Miss Brett observed that Faye was paying particular attention to the bound pages. She began to mumble to herself, as if she were adding numbers. She walked back and forth. Miss Brett knew the girl was figuring out something. She would occasionally exclaim, "It couldn't be so!" or "What is this? How could it be?," then return to her investigation.

In fact, all the children were reading through the pages and surely understanding the diagrams in ways Miss Brett never could. The room was silent, except for the sound of shuffling papers.

Suddenly, Faye looked up with a grin on her face.

"Look at this!" she said, holding up a page. "This is a fascinating design for an electrical ... wait ... it describes ... a circuit that could extend through a wide area. And this, the next few pages . . . But—" Faye held the papers, and Miss Brett placed the lamp on a desk in the middle of the room. "But that's impossible. Electricity hadn't been discovered. These pages are from 1560, and . . . but it's impossible. It says it's William Gilbert's *De Magnete, Magneticisque Corporibus, et de Magno Magnete Tellure*. But . . . but William Gilbert wrote that volume on electricity and magnetism in 1600! I know, I've read translations of it, we've read it, we've discussed it, we've argued about it. I have seen the original, and . . . this is a crude version of the diagrams in his magnum opus. This is the early work of William Gilbert, the man who defined and, essentially, discovered electricity!"

"And magnetism," Wallace said.

"Fine. But this . . . what . . . how . . . what is it doing here? What is *this* doing here? It was written in 1560."

"He was born in 1544," Wallace noted. "That means—"

"He was *sixteen* when he wrote this," Faye said, her mouth remaining open.

Wallace moved over to where Faye was standing. "That's long before *De Magnete* was published."

She handed the work to Wallace and picked up a bound collection of papers nearby. She looked at them for a few moments before she squealed—a very un-Faye-like thing to do. "Do you recognize these?!" she cried. "Look—designs for a telescope and notes on experiments with pendulums. The year is 1573, and . . . this is the work of a nine-year-old Galileo!" In the top corner, there was a notation, but it was not very clear. The only word Faye could read was "*iuvenes*," which she knew to be Latin.

Lucy began to look at some papers on the lower shelves. It is there she came upon a bronze box. It was decorated with six wheels. She tried to open it but couldn't. Then she saw that it was signed.

"Jasper!" she called. "Look! I found a Pascaline machine!"

"You mean Blaise Pascale's adding machine?" Jasper came over and looked. This machine was signed by Pascale, and dated 1640.

"His adding machine wasn't presented until 1645," said Lucy. "He was a big old kid when he made this computer."

Jasper saw that, next to the machine built by Pascale, there were notes and other writings, clearly by Pascale as well.

"Look at this!" Noah stuck his arm out from behind a shelf. He went up to Faye, holding a long, two-pronged fork. He tapped it on the shelf, then placed it against Faye's cheek.

"Stop that… Wow!" Faye was amazed that it vibrated so deeply.

"It's a prototype of John Shore's tuning fork," said Noah. "It's engraved with his name and the year 1709."

There were whole sections of unbound papers next to small, bound stacks. The papers were well tended, so none was greatly cracked, or even dusty or musty.

"It's amazing to see so many inventions and look at papers from so many inventors we have never even heard of before," marveled Faye.

"What's possibly even more amazing," Wallace said, moving back to the older shelves, "is the number of famous inventors and scientists we *do* recognize. Some of them we've read and studied. These things were invented by them, but before they're known to have invented them. Some were invented when they were so young—!"

"And look at this!" said Noah, holding another collection of papers and leafing through them with great excitement. "This one has diagrams of some kind of centrifuge—an invention to remove water from wetlands to allow for farming. And in these same notes, there are drawings that show some kind of submarine vehicle." Noah looked around. "I wonder if our amphibious ship is in here somewhere."

Jasper had walked over to Noah to see the work in his hands. "Look," said Jasper, "there are other designs! There's a giant crossbow, and some other weapons…I think…this…this can't be!"

"But it must!" Noah said, excitedly. "*Look!* Look at the signature!"

He pointed to a scribble of a signature, but for anyone who knew it, it was clear: Leonardo di ser Piero da Vinci. The year was 1464, two years before da Vinci was sent away to apprentice as an artist. A notebook was nearby, dated 1483, but there were no direct notes from da Vinci—only strange mentions of Edward and Richard, in the month of April, and something about the Tower of London.

"Fourteen eighty-three was a terrible year," Noah said, looking through more papers. "The Spanish Inquisition established their general council. Lots of executions, tortures, murders, and mysteries—all over Europe, in fact. Hey, I remember now—Edward and Richard in the Tower of London. That's King Edward V and his little brother. Edward was twelve, then disappeared—most likely killed by his uncle, Richard III. We all know this story, yeah?"

"It's a very sad story," said Lucy. "And he was a very lumpy man, that bad uncle, and they used to put his name on walls."

"Lucy is right, in her own way," Jasper said, looking up from his investigations. "We used to see posters for the play in London. And he was described as a hunchback. Remember, Miss Brett? You read to us from *Richard III.*"

"This is some strange library," Noah said.

"Is it a library?" Faye asked no one in particular. "Or some storage facility for precious papers? Or both?"

"This place must be why there are all those strange language dictionaries everywhere," Jasper said. "Someone had to be able to translate all this, if need be. And no one could possibly know all these languages."

"So much is in Latin," Faye said, picking up another notebook, "but almost every notebook has notations in other languages, too. Some are clearly Arabic or Persian, and some . . . I have no idea. I did see some pages in Tamil and something that might have been Basque, but—"

"That's it!" cried Lucy. "Camera di un migliaio di lingue! La stanza! From Antonio's letter! And from Signora Fornaio! This must be the room of a thousand languages!" Lucy clapped her hands together.

Everyone looked around with even more depth of intent. This was to be the safe place for Antonio's box.

"We need to find the special place," Miss Brett said. "Antonio's orb belongs somewhere here."

"I've found some random notes," said Jasper from up the row, pointing to a pile of papers. The year was 1840, and there were notes, in addition to diagrams and scientific equations, regarding a tragic affair on the island of Rhodes. One note said, "Comme 16eme siecle et Suleiman." Jasper could tell what it meant: that something happened in 1840 that had previously happened in the sixteenth century.

"Is there nowhere we can hide this dratted orb?" Faye said from among a pile of blueprints.

"It's hard because this place is so amazing," Noah said, picking up the tuning fork once again. "Look! The death ray! I bet that's Mr. Tesla's death ray."

Sure enough, the item leaning against the back wall near the shelf was exactly how Mr. Tesla had described it. Near it was a partial box someone had started building to house the strange weapon.

Though Miss Brett could not find a place for the orb, she did find a space for something else that was clearly special. As she wandered farther to the back of the room, the manuscripts seemed to get older. Miss Brett walked to the last shelf, near where Faye was looking. She placed her electric torch on that most distant shelf. It seemed to be slightly apart from the rest and was relatively empty. In the center, however, was a beautifully bound book. The cover was embossed leather, with gold leaf and silver beads pressed into the leather. In the middle was a faded flower, and there were black birds painted along the edges. The birds were so delicate and perfect they looked as if they could fly away.

For a moment, Miss Brett felt unsure she could touch the book. With great care, she opened it and found the pages covered in beautiful calligraphy and full of colorful illustrations. She recognized it: It was an older version of a book she had seen before. "*Il-poeżiji ta 'Muhabi*," she said to herself. Then, she called, "Come look at this, children!"

The children came over.

"Oh, it's lovely," Lucy said with a gasp.

As the children perused the book, Miss Brett noticed an ornate box on the shelf below it. She hadn't seen it at first, because a crevice was carved into the shelf that held the box. Like the book, the box was alone on its shelf. Inside were sketches and notes and a scroll tied with a golden string. There were also many pages that looked like written verse—poems, in a language that seemed to be Arabic or Persian.

This box was special. Miss Brett knew that it must be some-thing important among all of these important things. She replaced the notes, closed the box, and ran her finger over the beautiful carv-ings on the front. Then she noticed the carving in the center. "It's beautiful," said Miss Brett. "This is such a lovely flower, like the one on the book."

"And something like the faded carving on the box from Signo-ra Fornaio," said Jasper quietly, suddenly looking more closely.

"It's beautiful. I think it's made of mother of pearl." Miss Brett carefully untied the string on the scroll. She unrolled it gently and opened the parchment.

"It doesn't seem like a flower to me," said Lucy, still looking at the carving. "Flowers aren't so flappish and feathery. It looks like a bird. Three wings of a bird, dancing in a circle."

"What?" said both Jasper and Wallace, looking up

"*What* what?" asked Noah.

"What did you say, Lucy?" asked Faye, coming from around the corner.

"Look at this," Miss Brett said, pointing to the parchment—or, rather, two pieces of parchment, for there were two rolled together in the box. Like the book, they were written in beautiful calligra-phy. On both parchments were two stanzas. The first was in Ara-bic or Persian. The second, Miss Brett could read the letters and, though it was in another language, she was fairly sure the language was Latin. She had studied Latin in school, albeit a long time ago. She had a flutter in her stomach, because she knew the third word meant "bird" and she was fairly sure she knew the first two words. It began, "Inusitatus rotundum avis."

"That's Latin," said Jasper, who was almost as sure as Miss Brett.

But still he asked, "Lucy, do you know what it means?"

Lucy looked at it, then her eyes lit up. "Strange round bird," she said.

"Children, do you mind reciting that bird poem for me?" Miss Brett asked. She wanted to see if the words matched. Following with her finger, while trying to remember her Latin, she listened and read.

The children recited:

> "Strange round bird with three flat wings,
> Never ever stops when it shivers and sings,
> Never to be touched even if you are bold,
> Turns the world to dust and lead into gold.
>
> Three are the wings, one is the key,
> One is the element that clings to the three.
> Turns like a planet but it holds such power,
> Clings to itself like the petals of a flower."

CHAPTER FORTY

FINDING THEIR WORDS

OR

THE YOUNG INVENTORS GUILD

1872
1845   *1483*
1790
1738   **1573**
1740

"This is it—the poem your parents taught all of you," Miss Brett said, looking up from the parchment.

"Of course it is," said Lucy. "We just spoke it."

"No," Miss Brett said, excitedly. "It's the poem on this parchment."

"On the parchment?" Noah looked at the Latin verses.

"Do you think it has something to do with this engraving?" Jasper looked even closer at the odd symbol.

"It might," said Noah.

"It must," said Faye. "It must have something to do with the poem. Maybe the poem really is a clue."

"A puzzle," said Jasper, who had wondered about this before.

"Yes, like a puzzle," said Faye. "But we don't know what it means."

Everything in the box was in a language none of them could read. Jasper considered: What were the three wings? The key? The element? Did they refer to something real?

"We can ask our friends," said Lucy. They knew she meant the mysterious men in black.

"Fine," Faye said. "You just do that, Lucy. Then we'll be even more confused."

"Let's just find where that orb goes and figure out how to get out of here," Noah said, picking up a notebook that lay on a shelf closer to where Jasper had found the reference to 1840. "I'm beginning to feel a strange tingle up my spine."

"I know what you mean," Jasper said with a shiver. It was as if the shelves themselves were telling a very strange story. Somehow, it was his story—and their story.

"Yes, I agree," said Faye. "We could get lost in these works forever and still never understand."

Lucy scurried over to Jasper and grabbed his hand. "I don't want to get lost," she said to her brother.

"I won't lose you," he said.

"She said it was in a special place," said Miss Brett, her mind settling back to the words of Signora Fornaio. "*Posto*—that means place, and she said 'special.'"

"Hold your hats—wait just a minute here," said Noah. The journal he held had a date on the front page. It said, "Vienna, Early Spring (but too late), 1827." He picked up a journal farther up the row. It said, "Paris 1790."

"Seventeen-ninety," he said aloud.

"The year that the first patents were issued in the United States of America," Wallace said. He had a vast knowledge of patents.

"And things were going on in France, too," Jasper said.

Miss Brett said, "That would be the French Revo—"

"I think—" Faye said suddenly, but whatever caused the look of amazement on her face clearly kept her tongue from working. Frantically, she searched through the papers on the nearby shelves. She then went back to look at the journals. "I…I don't believe—"

413

"What is it, Faye?" said Miss Brett, who came out from where she was searching. "What have you discovered?"

"It's them," said Lucy, knowingly. "I mean, *us*." She held a journal she handed to Jasper, which he read in silence.

"These bound journals, or pages," said Faye, "are like Lucy's journal. And if I'm seeing it right, they seem to come in installments, about every thirty years or so."

"The journals are all written by children," added Wallace, perusing the pages, "or very young people, at least."

"And they're written, in part, by the geniuses we know," continued Faye. "Some we don't know, but some of these writers are famous geniuses who were children when they wrote them."

Wallace adjusted. "The notes here on Edward and Richard from 1483 are connected to someone's notes on the parachute..."

"That would be Leonardo da Vinci, most likely," said Noah.

"...and then 1545," Wallace continued, "the year of the sinking of the *Mary Rose*—I remember that from history lessons with you, Miss Brett—and 1573, a huge year of battles and wars. And then, here, 'Edinburgh, Late Autumn, 1738.' Look!" Wallace handed the journal to Miss Brett.

Miss Brett looked at the paper. "That's an interesting diagram, but I'm not sure I—"

"Goodness! *Look*," said Faye. She took Lucy's journal from Jasper. Its date was 1790. On the cover of the journal, it said, "Le Livre de la Guilde des Jeunes Inventeurs." On a journal that said "Amsterdam, Mid-Summer, 1740," it said, "De Jonge Uitvinders Guild." On the journal from 1827, it said, "Aus der Gilde der Junge Erfinder." And on the page from 1872, it said, "La Gilda per Giovani Inventori."

"I know," said Jasper, looking at Faye in wonder. And there, on the top page of the journal from 1738, the one Faye had handed to Miss Brett, it said clearly, in English, "From the Pages of the Young Inventors Guild."

"These are the dates we know, from the green Young Inventors Guild journal—Naples in 1872, Amsterdam in the mid-summer of 1740, Edinburgh in the late autumn of 1738. These notes were kept in our journal, weren't they, Lucy?" Faye could not believe what she was seeing.

"Yes, these are the notes we found ourselves," said Lucy.

"Could it be that these notes, taken from that journal, have been protected by the mysterious men in black for hundreds of years?" Jasper asked, looking at the others.

"Those fellows protect it all?" Noah asked.

Could it be?

Jasper felt it was all at the tip of his mind. "Think about monasteries, about how they always kept their records," he said. "Think about the chronicles we've seen and read." Jasper was thinking of the books he had found most interesting in the library at the manor house—*The Anglo-Saxon Chronicle*, a history of ancient England, and the book on the Venerable Bede, the monk historian. Then there was the one on the Bayeux Tapestry, created in France in the 1070s, which depicted the events leading up to the Norman Invasion of 1066 and the Battle of Hastings.

These were details of history that would have been lost without scribes keeping them safe. Protecting history, protecting information, was what they did. And it wasn't just the stories of kings and wars and big events that were intriguing. Daily records of the weather, food, and farming were kept, as were accounts of major wars and battles—kept by monasteries in Britain from before 1066. Some of these records were still being kept. You could pull out a page and learn what someone did on a given day. Sometimes they detailed monastic rituals and the power of silence. These mysterious men in black were men of few words and strange rituals. They were an order of brothers. And, it seemed, they were keepers of history.

"The cataloging and the care of records…" said Jasper. "I think what those men are…" But he hesitated.

"What do you mean?" said Noah. The mysterious men in black were clearly more than archivists.

"I think they have all these records—all these papers, diagrams, inventions—for a reason. They're keeping them safe, like an order—like some regiment of guards. And they've been doing so for a very long time. Whatever brought the mysterious men in black together, it must have been a long time ago. They seem to be guarding this place and, who knows? Maybe a lot more. Maybe secrets we can't imagine."

"It must be true," Miss Brett said, almost falling into a chair that was, luckily, right behind her.

Yes, Jasper thought, it was right to leave the box here, in this room, somewhere. But he knew there was something missing from this story—some bit of information that would be the key to understanding. But understanding what?

"Did anyone else notice that the shelves go back in time, the farther from the door?" Wallace was looking at the shelf next to him, then the one next to that, slowly stepping back, checking that this was true.

Faye gave Miss Brett the paper she had been holding and ran

up the rows, looking frantically through the shelves and coming to the last shelf, the one closest to the door. Then she jumped up and down as if she were Lucy.

"Our notes!" she cried. "Here are the notes we kept back in America!"

"Of course," said Lucy, unsurprised. "I told you they were safe."

The others hurried over and, sure enough, there were the drawings of Noah's engine, Jasper's propeller, and the other diagrams they had made.

"What does this mean?" asked Wallace, holding papers in his hand. "What does any of this mean?"

Miss Brett looked at the shelf, and there saw another box: a small box sealed with a pink ribbon. Somehow, when she saw it, she knew exactly what was in it. While the children looked through the Young Inventors Guild pages, Miss Brett took the box and discreetly opened it, turning away from the children. Yes, she was right—it was her diary.

A series of emotions flooded in, each knocking the other aside. She felt angry, triumphant, worried, embarrassed, angry again, and then guilty. The men in black had taken this from her and put it here, in good faith and for safekeeping.

Miss Brett knew what she had to do. She had to do as she was asked by her dying friend. They must leave everything here.

"What should we do, Miss Brett?" said Wallace, feeling anxious.

"Well...I think we need to put the papers carefully back where they were," Miss Brett said. She put her diary back in the box, retied the ribbon, and put it back on the shelf.

"I want to take the journal," Faye said, glaring as if to dare anyone to say otherwise.

"Faye," said Jasper, "I think it should stay."

Faye stepped back. She felt a sting of betrayal. "You do, do you? And why is that?"

"Because this is the room where it has been safe," he said. "If there is any place that is safe, it must be here. And we must believe it, because Komar Romak is here in Solemano. We're running for our lives again, and we can't risk bringing anything from here out into danger."

"Jasper, I don't believe you," said Faye, wounded—partly because he didn't back her up, but mostly because she knew he was right.

"Believe me, Faye," he said, gently. "You must believe me."

"We need to have it with us. It belongs to us. We've got to be able to get this door—!" Faye pushed against the door, but it did not move.

Jasper shook his head. "Put the journal back, Faye."

Faye didn't.

"Just put it back on its shelf," Jasper said. "It clearly belongs here, with the other work."

"But Antonio's box! That wasn't safe!" said Faye.

"Signora Fornaio must have had the key. Maybe she came to clean or something, and Antonio must have tricked her." Jasper reached out to Faye.

"Sweet angel," Miss Brett said. "Put the notes back. I am sure we can ask to see them."

Faye opened her mouth to argue, but she knew they were right. Contrary to her nature, Faye did as she was asked.

"We cannot leave with anything from this room," Jasper said. "We have to find—"

"It's here!" Wallace called from the other side of the room.

Rushing over to him, they saw a small, square, opened wooden crate. In it was a wooden box, unpainted, but lined with blue velvet. The box was very old, and had markings where its contents had rubbed away the blue velvet lining it.

There was an impression in the velvet—the outlined shape of the box in Jasper's hand. This was where Antonio had found the box. It was from here that he stole it and started all of the terrible events that followed.

"It was cruel to deceive his mother," Noah said, thinking of Antonio.

"We don't know exactly what happened," said Wallace, not wanting to think about a son betraying his mother.

"She trusted her boy," Jasper said, "and the brothers in black trusted her. It must have broken her heart to know she had unwittingly betrayed them."

"She trusted too much." Faye hid the tears welling again in her eyes again. "She trusted that blasted shepherd."

"So did we," Miss Brett said.

"We were fools not to notice," said Noah. "He always seemed to slip away or suddenly appear. No wonder. And we didn't think it strange he never had a single sheep?" Noah thumped his forehead. "What brilliant children we are, eh?"

"It doesn't matter," Jasper said, taking the box and putting it in its place. "We've done as Signora Fornaio asked."

"Enough. Let's get out of here," said Faye, heading for the door.

She pushed the door, but it did not move. She continued to push. "We must get out."

"We don't know how," said Jasper, joining her. The door was as solid as a wall.

"It's got to open somehow!" yelled Faye, pounding her fists against it in frustration.

And then it opened.

There, on the other side of the door, stood a very ruffled Bo Peep. They all blinked at one another. Then Miss Brett noticed the arm.

"You're injured!" cried Miss Brett. His arm was bleeding and his hand sliced deep.

"Must go," he groaned. Holding up his skirt with his good hand, he turned, limping slightly.

"Is he out there?" asked Faye.

"Not he," said Bo Peep, not turning around.

"Yes, yes, we know he's a they and whatever. Is Komar Romak out there?" Faye reached out to stop Bo Peep, but he kept walking down the long corridor.

As Jasper followed the others through the door, he couldn't get the idea out of his mind. Wallace's coin. Antonio's orb—he had said it himself. The coin was a key, wasn't it? And the orb? It was an element, a catalyst, something that caused a reaction. A key. An element. He ran it through his head as they went down the hallway: *Three are the wings, one is the key, one is the element . . .*

CHAPTER FORTY-ONE

Travails in the Tunnels
OR
A STAIRWAY HOME

They made it to the main room and ran to the big door. They pushed, but discovered that the door would not move.

"Okay, Bo Peep, open it," Faye said, panting.

"No," said Bo Peep.

"What do you mean, 'no'?" demanded Faye.

"Danger," said Bo Peep. "No go room. Stay." And he ran off down a hallway, shutting a gate behind him.

"Are we trapped in here?" Wallace asked, adjusting his glasses.

Lucy grabbed Jasper's hand and began to chew her bracelet. Jasper reached out and touched the door.

Suddenly, without warning, there was a loud thump. They all jumped back. It came from the door.

"Get back here, Bo Peep!" yelled Faye. There was no answer. Faye ran toward the corridor he had disappeared into, but found the locked gate blocking her way. She shook the gate. "He's gone."

"Gone?" Wallace gulped.

"What did he do?" Faye asked. "Did he make that sound?"

"No," said Jasper. "I don't think it was him—" There came another booming thump. Jasper moved farther away from the door.

The thump definitely came from the other side. But those doors were so thick, surely nothing short of an explosion could have passed through with even the slightest of sounds.

Again, a *boom*, as if someone was trying to ram the door. The door didn't move, not even the slightest—but for how long would it be safe?

"Is it Komar Romak?" cried Lucy, squeezing her brother's hand.

"No, I ..." But Jasper couldn't lie to her. *Yes*, he thought. *It has to be Komar Romak.*

"We have to get out of here some other way," Noah whispered.

"But Mr. Bo Peep told us to stay!" cried Lucy.

"Someone wasn't trying to knock the door down then!" said Faye. "We have got to get out of here."

"But how?" Wallace looked around, terrified. "How did Mr. Bo Peep get out?"

Jasper realized: the stairwells. But looking at the halls, he could see all of the gates were now closed. Jasper looked back to the hallway. Could he run back and get the key? Antonio's orb was the only hope.

"How would you get back into the room?" asked Faye, who could see Jasper's thoughts written on his face.

"Try the magnet!" shouted Jasper to Wallace. Then, softer: "Please, Wallace."

Wallace removed his little magnetic sphere from his pocket and rolled it toward the iron bars. Nothing. He moved it a bit closer. Still nothing. Wallace stood up and brought the magnet to the gate.

Then he could feel it. With it tugging at his hand, Wallace placed the little magnetic sphere on the floor. It began rolling—all the way to the passageway at the right of the hearth. With a small clang, it hit the gate. But there it sat.

Wallace looked up anxiously at the others. He tried to coax the magnetic sphere up, but it stuck—hard. Wallace turned his coin in his pocket, over and over. It felt warm against his hand.

Then he had an idea. He took the coin from his pocket and placed it against the iron panel on the gate. Then he moved the sphere along the astragal. He gave it a push and it rolled up.

They all watched. But the sphere soon slowed down, and then it stopped, sitting still in a groove in the bar.

"No," said Faye, feeling defeated as the banging from without grew louder.

But Wallace scanned the wall and the iron gate. It had to be there, he thought to himself. Yes, it must. Feeling around, he began to grow doubtful, until he touched a round carving on the actual metal gate itself. Remembering his electric torch, he shined it on the carving. Yes, he was right. He felt it in his bones. He placed the coin in the carving. Then he removed the bismuth alloy pellet from his pocket and pushed the bismuth against the magnet, as if he were sweeping it up the door. With a forceful brush of his hand, the bismuth repelled the magnetic sphere, which slid up and looped around the gate, then rolled into a hole where a lock might have been—right below his coin. Then the coin itself began to turn.

There was a click, and the gate was open.

Then—another *boom!* Only this one was louder.

"Let's go!" cried Miss Brett, picking up Lucy and grabbing Wallace's hand. "Now!" The others followed. They ran to the doors that led to the stairway.

"It's that door." Lucy pointed to the door Faye had opened.

Faye passed Jasper her torch and her carpet bag and pushed

with both hands. She grabbed the knob, and though it was hard to turn, she managed to open the door. But this time there were no stairs on the other side.

It was a room, and it was huge, its ceilings high, and once the torches were all switched on and focused, they knew immediately what they were seeing. Miss Brett put down Lucy, searching the walls of the room for another door.

"That's impossible," said Noah, standing with his mouth wide open.

"Since when is anything around us possible?" said Faye. "But it happens, doesn't it?"

"It was the right door!" cried Lucy. "I know it! I remember!"

"What is this place?" asked Miss Brett.

"It's...it's a giant laboratory." Faye looked at the rows of burettes and test tubes, the cauldrons and the basins, the mortars and pestles, and...and some things even she could not name.

"The stairs turned into a laboratory." Lucy sniffed. "I'm sorry."

"Don't worry. We all make mistakes," said Noah.

"But it's not a mistake," insisted Lucy. Then she bent over and picked up a gold and red ribbon that had fallen into a corner on the floor. She recognized it instantly. "This is Mummy's," she said, looking at the others for answers.

"I don't see a way out." Miss Brett saw only stone walls.

"Why would this be here?" Jasper asked no one in particular, looking at the ribbon in Lucy's hand.

"This must have been their lab," said Noah. "Don't you think?"

"Likely," said Jasper. He put Faye's torch and bag on the table, running his hand along the row of test tubes.

"You'd think they could have told us," Wallace muttered. He was hurt. His father had been so close. All of them had. But no one had let the children know.

"Who cares now?" said Faye, stifling the mix of anger and fear she felt. "We've got to find another way out."

Suddenly, another *boom*!

"We have to get out of here." Jasper reached for his sister.

Wallace quickly grabbed a handful of metallic pellets from a box and put them in his coat pocket.

"Let's move." Miss Brett led the children out of the room.

They closed the door to the laboratory.

"We have to try another door," said Faye, already heading back toward the big room and checking other doors as she ran. They wouldn't budge.

Noah went back to the door at the end of the passageway.

"That's the one we just left, idiot!" cried Faye.

But Noah had already pulled it open.

It was a staircase again.

"The stairs came back!" cried Lucy.

"That's not possible," said Noah, his hand still on the doorknob.

Faye pushed past him. "And once again, I say, what is?"

Up the stairs they ran, Noah leading the way through the dark, Miss Brett coming last, closing the door behind her. Faye shifted the carpetbag with the snowball machine on her shoulders, and Wallace came up behind them. Lucy stopped partway up, anxious and scared.

"It's too dark," she whimpered.

Miss Brett shook her electric torch and flicked on the switch. Light filled the path, and they could dimly see the long stairway twist to a landing ahead.

And suddenly, with a *pop*, the light went out.

"Oops," Noah said.

"We can't use more than one torch at a time," Jasper said, forging ahead. "Faye's is starting to flicker again. That makes only two and a half left. We'll use the torches only when we really need them."

They had gotten a good look, so heading up, they at least knew there were stairs in front of them. Then, suddenly, there was a landing, where they all stumbled into one another.

"I'm going to open the light on my torch," Jasper said. "I'll shine it around so we can see where we are and where to go. Then I'll turn it off to save the bulb."

He turned it on. They could see other stairs leading down from the landing—stairs to another passageway. They could see how several stairways led up to this same landing. Shining the torch up and around, Jasper found the stairway up.

Jasper pointed. "We have to keep going up. We started a long way down." The stairway beyond the landing was very long and seemed to have no end. That's where they went. Despite the darkness, Jasper turned off the light once they were all on the stairs.

They ran up as fast as they could, but the stairs kept going. They turned once, and Jasper flicked on the light to be sure everyone caught the steps. They ran, then ran slower, then, finally, walked. Jasper flicked the switch on his torch to see if he could see an exit.

Pop. His bulb went out.

No one said a word.

They kept going.

"Will the stairs ever end, Miss Brett?" asked Lucy. "I counted two hundred steps last time. Do you think there will be more now?"

Strange as it seemed, Miss Brett had to wonder the same.

At last, they could see a thin light from above.

"I can see my feet!" Lucy cried with pleasure.

As they got closer, they could see that the light came from beneath the door at the next landing. But it was a very small landing and they had to press together to fit.

"It's locked," Jasper said.

"Wallace, try the sphere," Noah said, standing right behind Jasper.

Jasper helped Wallace, and they felt along the door. But there was no lock, no astragal, no groove along the edge—nothing. "Where? How?" he asked.

"Let it free, Wallace!" called Lucy from behind Jasper. "Let it go under the door and find the lock on the other side."

Of course, thought Wallace, as he removed the magnetic sphere and laid it gently on the floor.

It rolled across the doorjamb and bumped against the bottom of the door.

"It's too big to fit under." Wallace's voice cracked. "It's not going to—"

Miss Brett flicked on her torch and looked around the doorway. Wallace fumbled in his pocket. "Maybe my coin—"

Suddenly, the door opened. But it was not Wallace's coin that had opened it.

"Lock this door," Bo Peep said to Miss Brett. She looked around and saw that, somehow, they were back on the second floor of the manor house. Robin Hood stood on the other side of the door. Bo Peep did not ask how they came to be there, though he had asked them to stay in the castle. But they were shocked to see him standing there.

"How?" she asked.

"You have key," he said.

Miss Brett shook her head. "No, we left it in the—"

"Iron key," said Robin Hood.

Miss Brett remembered the big iron key that hung in her room. *Very well*, she thought. She ran to get the key—the iron key hanging in her room.

Robin Hood turned and shouted something. Seven mysterious men in black came running down the hall. A man in a tall, pointed hat led the way, followed by a man in a black fez, the feather man, the man in the big beret, a man who looked suspiciously like a large black carrot, a man in a tall black wig, and, bringing up the rear, Bo Peep. Without so much as a greeting, tall wig, fez, and beret ran down the stairs from which the children and Miss Brett had just come. Pointy hat, feather man, and big black carrot ran down the front stairs and, from the sound of the door below, into the garden.

"You are hurt?" Bo Peep asked. "Not hurt?" Miss Brett was sure she heard kindness in his gruff words.

"Not hurt, thank you. We are not hurt." She put a hand on his arm. "But what are we to do now?"

"Must go." Bo Peep nodded to Robin Hood, who picked up his skirt and led the way down the hall.

It was then that they felt the earth shake. This time, they could see the light and smoke from the explosion through the window at the other end of the hall. It came from the far side of the garden. Was it in the orchard? Or in the beast garden? There was no way to tell from where they were.

"What is happening?!" Miss Brett cried.

"We're under attack!" said Wallace.

"Komar Romak come," Bo Peep said with a growl. "Must go down. *Now!*"

CHAPTER FORTY-TWO

TWISTS AND TURNS

OR

WHAT THEY FOUND IN THE DARK

"Down?!" said Miss Brett. "There's someone trying to break into the castle! We can't go down!"

Suddenly the room shook. They almost fell off the landing.

"Take stairs now," Bo Peep demanded. "There are. Wall. But not. No wall."

"What?!" Faye shouted, but there wasn't time.

"I don't want to go down!" cried Lucy, clinging to Miss Brett and reaching for her brother at the same time.

"We don't have a choice." Faye tried to sound strong, but her teeth were chattering.

"Sweet angel . . ." Miss Brett said to Lucy, but hoping to soothe them all with her voice. "We are all together, and we will do what we need to do to stay out of harm's way."

"Wait!" shouted Wallace, running toward his room. Bo Peep tried to grab him, but Wallace managed to slip around Bo Peep's skirt.

"Wallace!" cried Miss Brett.

Within seconds he was back, running toward the others. "I've got them," he panted, opening his fist. He held a handful of small light bulbs. There was one for each torch.

Miss Brett smiled. "Good thinking, Wallace."

"Now!" bellowed Bo Peep.

"Hey, just one second." Noah tried to keep from stepping on his own feet.

"No!" Bo Peep said, pushing them into the dark passage.

Miss Brett led the children back through the door. She held an electric torch in front and looked at what lay ahead down the long, long flight of stairs. Then the door closed with a slam. The torch light popped and went out.

"Please, let me change the bulbs," Wallace said anxiously.

"Yes, heading down with no light sounds like a dangerous proposition," said Noah, leaning over and bumping into Faye. She pushed back.

"Rather snug, isn't it?" said Noah, righting, then over-righting himself and tipping again.

"Don't push me!" said Faye as Noah bumped into her for the third time.

"I'm sorry. I can't see."

Jasper whispered to Wallace, "Faye has her torch. We can change the other bulbs by the light of hers."

Faye flicked her torch. No light came.

"There's no room here, anyway." Wallace couldn't even move his elbows.

"I'll move down the stairs to make room," said Jasper, handing his torch to Wallace. "I'll meet you at the bigger landing."

"I'll come with you," said Faye, handing Miss Brett her spent light. "Take Jasper's torch so Wallace can use its light to change the others." She started down the stairs after Jasper.

Going down in the dark was much more dangerous than going up in the dark. Falling up steps was nothing compared to falling down them. And as soon as Jasper and Faye took the first turn from the manor door, the darkness overwhelmed them. Jasper felt Faye's fingers digging into his shoulders. Her breaths became short and fast. He knew she was feeling the darkness closing in on her.

"Let's take it slow," said Jasper, gently. "This place might be dark, but right here, the walls are wide, aren't they? It makes me think of being out in a wide open space at night. A big wide black sky can sometimes feel close."

He could feel her fingers loosen somewhat and her breathing become steadier. After a few seconds, she took a deep breath. "Thank you, Jasper. That helps."

When they got to the landing, Faye insisted that they stay close to the wall. "We cannot see where the railings are," she said. Jasper didn't mind.

As they waited, they heard banging noises.

"Is that coming from ahead or behind?" asked Faye.

But Jasper did not know. Could it be the others coming down? Or something they did not want to think about? Either way, they had to wait.

And then there was light. Coming down the long stairs, they could see a bright torch guiding the others down.

"They're coming," said Faye, relieved.

"Wallace is a genius," said Noah. "Oh yes, that's right, we already knew that."

Gazing down the long stairs, they could see what they could not see going up—that there were several stairways, crossing and interlocking. It was like an underground maze. It must have been two hundred feet from the stairs to the house to the depths of the tunnels. The walls were all stone, except where the stairs veered into the middle, which had wooden railings on both sides.

For Jasper, this was dizzying. He leaned back and saw Wallace standing with his eyes shut tight. Jasper took Wallace's hand. "It might be easier if we walk together," Jasper said quietly, and Wallace looked grateful.

But when he turned to go down the next flight, Jasper found that, from this landing, there were no stairs. He shined the torch in front of him. There were no stairs anywhere.

"That's impossible," Noah said. "We came up these stairs."

Jasper felt along the walls. Stone everywhere. Then Faye saw a glimpse of it.

"Wait!" she called, taking the torch from Jasper, "Look."

There, carved in the stone wall, was the symbol of Wallace's coin. But this was not the same one they'd first found in the tunnel.

"Why here?" asked Noah, "What is it here for?"

Wallace went over and placed the coin in the wall. It fit, like it did in the tunnel carvings. But nothing happened. Wallace tried to pry the coin out. It was stuck. He turned it slightly, and then it came out in his hand.

The floor began to shiver and the walls began to shake—or at least that wall began to shake. As if from nowhere, a door opened in the stone.

"The stairs!" Lucy said, pointing into the darkness.

But when he shined the torch down there, he couldn't see stairs. Instead, it looked like a chute.

Without warning, the door in the wall slid shut.

"Jasper, we missed it!" cried Lucy.

Wallace quickly put his coin back into the slot. He turned it and, again, they felt the floor shiver and saw the wall open up.

This time, however, when they shined the light down the opening, there *were* stairs.

"That's impossible," said Noah

"Stop saying that," said Faye.

"Should we take these stairs?" asked Wallace.

Jasper leaned over. Something burned the inside of his nose.

"No," he said pulling back. "I smell smoke."

"Is it coming from down there?" Faye came over just as the door closed.

Jasper looked at her. "I'm not sure. I can still smell it."

Wallace quickly put his coin back in the slot.

"Is this whole crazy castle built on a rotating device?" Noah asked as the floor shook again.

"I wouldn't be surprised if it was," said Jasper as the door opened again.

From above, they could hear what might very well have been gunfire.

"We have to take this stairway," said Jasper as the door opened again, revealing yet another passage. "Follow me." And he went first down the stairs.

Miss Brett was about to shout to let her lead, but Lucy clung close to her, and Miss Brett knew it was too late to even try.

Jasper shined the torch down what was a much narrower passageway. The stairs were steep and uneven.

"I can feel air coming up, can't you?" he said to Faye, who was breathing heavily.

It was a long while—perhaps several minutes—before they reached another small landing.

Miss Brett looked around. "How do we know those were the other stairs that the gentleman mentioned?"

"*Gentleman?*" Noah laughed. "I'll have to remember that you consider men wearing bonnets and bloomers gentlemen."

"We have to hope those were the ones he meant," said Jasper.

"You don't think we missed them?" Wallace squeaked, still clinging tightly to Jasper's hand.

"No, of course we didn't," Jasper said firmly, though he worried they may very well have.

The next landing was larger. They stopped again. There were stairs. But unfortunately, the stairs did not go down. They went up.

"Now what do we do?" Wallace adjusted his glasses.

"There has to be a wall," Jasper began to feel around the new stairwell. "If there are stairs, there's a—"

And he found it. Wallace quickly retrieved his coin and found the keyhole in the wall. He turned the coin, the walls moved, and a doorway opened where there had been only wall.

"Follow the door!" called Lucy.

They all ran through the opening—all except Wallace.

"Wait!" cried Wallace, fumbling with something. Jasper grabbed his hand and pulled the boy through, just as the door closed. There was a tinkling of glass.

"What was that?" asked Noah.

"The last light bulb," Wallace said.

"No worries," said Noah. "We still have—"

But he was cut short by the flicker of a dying bulb.

"Stupid thing!" cried Faye, shaking her torch. The light flickered again and went out. Faye threw it in frustration. It flew over the rail and down beneath the stairs. From where it landed below them, they could see the flickering, and still functional, light.

"Why did you do that?" asked Jasper.

"It was useless!" said Faye. "I—I shouldn't have. I…I'm sorry."

Jasper reached and squeezed her hand. It was too late. The torch was gone.

Miss Brett flicked her torch. Nothing. No one said a word. They were now in total darkness. Miss Brett shoved the now useless torch back into her bag. Jasper flicked on his torch. They had only two left and no extra bulbs.

The new passage had an arched ceiling and led to a winding stairwell. These stairs, carved of wood, were more elaborate than the others, and certainly as old as any they had climbed. The steps creaked slightly as they all descended. The wood was smooth, though, and Jasper thought these stairs could have been found inside a house instead of an underground cavern, except that they seemed to go on forever.

"This is a blasted labyrinth," groaned Faye.

"I'm getting dizzy," said Lucy as the stairs went round and round. "I've counted 225 steps."

Finally, they reached the stone floor. Jasper shined his torch around. They were definitely back in the tunnels. But where?

"A chute!" cried Faye, pointing to an opening that led down from where they stood. "Is it the one from the beast garden? Or is it the one we saw at Christmas?"

"Perhaps it's the one we saw from the landing above," said Wallace.

"Or is it a totally different one?" said Noah, reasonably.

No one could be sure.

"Let's take it," said Faye.

Jasper felt Wallace's hand tighten.

"Maybe we should—" Noah stopped. "I smell smoke again."

"It'll be fine," Jasper said softly to Wallace. "We can go down it together."

"I love slides," said Noah, rubbing his hands together.

"Oh, I love slides, too!" cried Lucy.

Miss Brett bit her tongue. She had never loved slides. Never. But whatever their feelings were about sliding down the chute, they all set to it and slid.

Jasper held Wallace and Miss Brett held Lucy, or perhaps it was Lucy who held Miss Brett. They all slid down the chute and found it was longer to the bottom than they had thought. It felt like ages, but it was only a few very long minutes.

"Do you smell that?" Jasper asked. This was not good. As they arrived at the bottom of the chute, there was definitely a stronger smell—a chemical smell—and it made them cough.

"What is that odor?" asked Lucy, holding her nose as she stood. "It makes my eyes sting."

"Something's burning," Miss Brett said, trying to remain calm. If there was a fire in the tunnel, they were trapped.

"Yes. Where is it coming from?" Faye said, taking Jasper's torch and looking around. They were instead in a tunnel.

"We've passed this chute lots," said Lucy. "We're back in the tunnel where we were."

"Where is that, Lucy?" asked Noah.

"Here," said Lucy, rolling her eyes.

"And where is here exactly?" he asked.

"Silly," said Lucy, pulling Miss Brett along down the passage to the right. "Oh, goodness!"

"No, Lucy," Noah said, coughing. "This is not goodness."

By the light of Jasper's torch, the others could see they were facing the massive doors to the castle. Now they could see what they had only smelled—smoke so thick they could not see beyond it. But there was far too much smoke for a fire they could not see, feel, or hear.

Soon they were completely surrounded by smoke.

"We need to get out of here," Faye said, feeling panic as the smoke filled her lungs. She coughed. "This smoke isn't just smoke. It's a chemical fire somewhere in here. We've got to go in the opposite direction!"

But now she wasn't sure which way that was. She couldn't even see anyone else around her.

Suddenly, Noah felt someone grab for him in the dark. "Get off!" he cried. But he couldn't see who was where. No one could. He could only see that the hand wore a steel-studded, black leather glove, and he knew that none of them was wearing gloves.

"Everyone behind me!" cried Miss Brett. She reached out, feeling for the heads of each of her children. Then, from the darkness, a hand grabbed at her, too. It missed. A growl emerged from the darkness. And then they could see what it was.

A huge, hulking form emerged. With the shadows against the smoke, he seemed bigger than a man. In his arm, he carried a gun or a machine, or something that was a bit of both.

"It's Mr. Tesla's death ray!" cried Noah.

"You horrid little beasts," came a menacing growl from the man as he stomped his foot. "I want it. And I want it now."

Desperate to get away, the children and Miss Brett backed up toward the doors. Lucy began to cry.

"What do you want from us?" demanded Miss Brett, backing away.

"Give it to me!" the man growled, shaking his fist in the air.

"It's them," Lucy whimpered. She pointed at the huge man. "Komar Romak."

Jasper could see the man's face as a swirl of smoke wafted away from his raised fist. There was a scar from his forehead down to his cheek, his nose was bent and misshapen, and he clearly had only half of a thick black moustache. It *was* Komar Romak.

Miss Brett pulled the children behind her. "This?" she pointed to her bag—the bag that held the electric torch. "Is this what you want?"

With a swift swing of his arm, the giant grabbed the bag and tore it from her arm.

"Run!" cried Jasper as the man swung the gun into position. They ran back into the darkness, Jasper fumbling to turn off the torch as he ran.

"Let's go back up the chute!" cried a running Lucy, but even had they been able to climb a chute, there was no chute—only a stone wall.

"This way!" cried Noah, running down the left side of the fork in the tunnel.

Behind them, they could hear a blast from the death ray. The giant was shouting at them, firing the death ray against the walls of the tunnel. But up ahead of them, there was yet another noise. This time, it was a grunting, snuffling sound.

"What is that?!" said Faye.

"It's the other half!" cried Lucy.

"That didn't sound human," Wallace said, whimpering.

Again came the snorting, grunting sound.

"Whatever this is," said Miss Brett, "that Komar Romak is human." Her arm still ached where he'd grabbed the bag.

There came another loud snorting grunt, this time sounding closer.

"I think there's a wild boar in here!" cried Noah, clinging to Faye.

Jasper flicked on his torch. They were headed toward another fork in the tunnel. He shined down one that turned sharply to the left. The other path looked straight, but the torchlight reflected a pair of eyes. Grunts and snorting came from that side. And then, a *pop*, and darkness.

"Come with me down the other side, children!" cried Miss Brett as she gathered them all as close as she could. They ran, feeling along the walls as they did. Wallace flicked on his torch—the only one left. Soon, they found they could see a bit better, though the smoke was still filling the air. There was no sign of either man or beast.

"Against the walls, children," Miss Brett said in as loud a whisper as she could manage. "Wallace, shut off the torch." That way, she reasoned, no one could see them in the darkness with their backs against the wall. That, and they could save their last light bulb. Komar Romak had seen where they were going. It was only a matter of time before he caught up to them, for he knew by now that nothing important had been in her bag—not Antonio's orb, and certainly not anything else he might have wanted.

"Let's keep moving, children." Miss Brett tried to keep her voice calm.

The sound of the growling giant was faint, but it seemed to be getting louder.

"Listen, Wallace," Jasper whispered, "get the last electric torch ready. If anyone jumps out, we can shine the light in his face."

"Do you think that would stop him?" asked Faye. "That was Komar Romak. An enormous Komar Romak, armed with a death ray!"

"We have to make him go away!" cried Lucy, her face in Miss Brett's skirt.

"Once we blind the fellow, then what do we do?" asked Noah. "We can't very well pelt him with light."

"I know what to do!" said Faye. She had nearly forgotten the bag she still had over her shoulder. She grabbed it, pulling free of Noah. Swiftly, she pulled out the pieces of her snowball-throwing machine. She attached the disassembled weapon.

"He's coming!" cried Lucy. The floors shook as a flash of light appeared far down the tunnel.

Wallace gulped. Keeping his back touching the wall at all times, Wallace handed Jasper his torch, then reached into his pockets. He retrieved the bismuth pellets. He removed from his other pocket the magnets, which were in a clump, clinging tightly to each other. When he held his hands near each other, the magnets and the bismuth felt as if they were alive, wiggling and fighting.

Suddenly, the smell of smoke filled their noses.

"Hand me some of those small rocks!" said Faye, noticing many on the floor of the tunnel. "Hurry! Just pile them here." Jasper bent down and swept over some of the rocks.

Faye knew that the machine would scoop up the rocks as it did the snowballs.

She set her machine to aim directly into the cloud of smoke. She was going to start with the rocks first.

Faye looked up at Jasper, who was holding the last torch. She wound up the machine.

"Torch ready, Jasper?" she asked. Jasper nodded.

Something moved in the darkness.

With a flick of the wrist, small rocks were suddenly flying into the smoke. Jasper switched on the torch.

Cries of anger emerged from the smoke-filled tunnel.

"More rocks!" cried Faye.

But the growls of man or beast or both were now closing in on them through the smoke. Suddenly, there was a blast and a high-pitched squeal. Komar Romak had hit the boar.

They could hear the lumbering steps on the gravely stone. And then, Komar Romak was standing before them. He raised the death ray and aimed. Miss Brett jumped in front of the children.

"No!" she cried. "You cannot kill them."

Wallace's mind raced at lightning speed. The death ray. The iron and mercury alloy. The bismuth. Together, the bismuth pellets were strong. They could reverse a magnetic field.

With strength he did not know he had, Wallace hurled the handful of magnets at the death ray. Several hit their mark, and others hit the giant in the face, clinging to the steel studs on his upraised hand that flew up in defense. Distracted, the giant aimed high, and in a flash, a stream of mercury shot from the gun. At that exact moment, Wallace threw the bismuth. As if in slow motion, they all watched as the mercury turned from its path, moving away from the bismuth and finding the magnets on Komar Romak's hand. The mercury flew back. With a sickening scream, Komar Romak dropped the gun and writhed in agony on the cold stone floor.

Faye's face was streaked with soot, cold sweat, and hot tears. Jasper grabbed her arm as she took a step toward the flailing Komar Romak. With a stifled groan, she tried to pull away from Jasper, who knew what she was thinking. Faye wanted to go after Komar Romak, for all the sorrow and hurt. For the death of Signora Fornaio. But Jasper knew they had to go, and go now. They didn't know how hurt Komar Romak was, or even if he was alone.

Finally, Jasper felt the tug of Faye's arm ease. She turned back toward them.

"If we run down that way ..." Jasper started, but suddenly, with a *pop*, they were in total darkness again. So they just ran.

They ran through the serpentine tunnels, scraping their fingers along the walls. They ran until they hit a wall.

"No, it can't be!" cried Faye.

"No, it can't," said Jasper, desperately feeling along the wall. There had to be a round carving. There had to be a keyhole. Sure enough, he felt one, just the size of Wallace's coin.

"Your coin!" he called to Wallace. Wallace's hand shook as he tried to get the coin into the groove. A sharp cry from the tunnel made him jump and he dropped the coin.

"Wallace!" shouted Faye, who heard the coin hit the stone floor.

But Jasper was already on the ground, feeling for the coin.

"I've got it," said Lucy, who had clearly been doing the same.

"That's my girl," Jasper said, feeling in the dark for his sister's hand.

"Here," said Noah, feeling for Jasper. He had the coin from Lucy, and he was not going to let it go until Wallace had it in the keyhole. His hand searched until it found Wallace's hand, and together they put the key into the slot.

With a turn of his wrist, Wallace pulled the coin back out. With a grinding of stone, the cave door opened. Though the light was very dim, there was light. They ran toward it. After turning twice to the left, they found the light to be closer and the air clearer. Another turn to the left, and there it was: Faye's torch, lying on the ground.

"I guess it was a very good thing you threw it, Faye," said Jasper, picking it up. "And the throw seems to have wedged the loose wires back into place."

They could see the tunnel ahead and kept running, putting as much distance between them and that man. But as they ran and ran, they still could find no way out—only many ways within. They found locked passages and blocked passages, and some tunnels they were sure had been a way out only hours before. They felt as if they were going in circles, and circles that constantly changed.

When they smelled smoke again, they realized that they really were going around in circles.

"Go back!" cried Jasper. "We must have missed a passage. I'll shine the torch along the walls."

Sure enough, they came to a dark passage that had been hiding in the shadows before. Once inside the passage, they slowed down.

"I know this place," Jasper said, running his hand along the wall. "Or, at least I know we've been in this part of the tunnel."

"Look, there's the first carving that fit Wallace's coin," said Lucy.

"Yes, it is," said Wallace, running his hands over the ancient carvings on the wall. There was the etching of the bird. He remembered it from that first time. "And there." He pointed ahead.

The pile of rubble was in front of them. However these tunnels worked, they were now in a familiar place.

"Even if we could dig our way through the rocks again, we'll never get through the beast garden door," said Faye, disheartened. She had not wanted to even consider digging through the pile of rubble that collapsed moments after she had brought Miss Brett, Lucy, and Wallace back from their fall.

"But we can get out the passage from the chapel," said Jasper. "It might be a far walk, but—"

"This way," Lucy said, pointing to the right.

"Where are you going?" asked Noah. "How can you know?"

"Because it's the right way," insisted Lucy. "Even if the castle moves, the tunnels connect themselves."

"What?" Noah shook his head.

"Just follow her!" said Faye.

"I know where I'm going," said Lucy.

"To the chapel?" said Noah.

"No," said Lucy, pointing now to the left and picking up speed. Everyone followed quickly. Within a minute, they could see moon-light up ahead. "That's one of the tunnels to the garden."

THE ARCHER'S FOLLY

OR

THE FALL OF FRIEND OR FOE

They could hear the raven before they saw the full moon up in the sky. There was a light dusting of snow, and the scene, coming through the vines, felt almost like a fairytale. From the dark stifling tunnels into the icy freshness of the winter air was like stepping from one strange world into another. The chill of the night made Lucy's teeth chatter. She pulled Miss Brett's cloak and found a warm embrace.

"You did it, Lucy!" said Miss Brett, kissing Lucy's cold, rosy cheeks. "You did it!"

They found themselves in the olive orchard garden of the *palazzo*. They looked up at the house. Jasper and Faye took a few steps toward it. But then they stopped dead in their tracks.

Another explosion lit the sky. This time, it sounded as if it came from the manor house itself, but they could not see for sure through the trees that hid the entrance. What if it had been the house? Wallace looked up and adjusted his glasses, now fogging from the cold air blowing into the mouth of the tunnel. Miss Brett stopped, too. Did that explosion mean the ancient manor house of Solemano was being destroyed? All the history? The art and the books? And what about the mysterious men in black?

Wherever it had come from, someone had set it off. Someone was there—someone who meant them harm.

"We can't go up there," said Miss Brett, her face aglow in the moonlight.

"But we can't stay here," said Wallace, suddenly feeling quite exposed.

"And we can't walk down the street," Jasper said. "The moonlight is so bright. We'd easily be seen."

"I know!" said Lucy. "We can take the short tunnel to the chapel."

Noah was about to ask what she meant, but everyone had already started off after Lucy. They ran through the gardens, with nothing but moonlight to keep them from falling into ponds or off bridges. When they came to the hidden archway under the bridge connecting the olive orchard with the beast garden, Lucy pushed aside the hanging vines. "This is the tunnel I found when we first met the garden."

"You knew this was here?" asked Jasper, following his sister into the night.

"I didn't go in here because I don't like the dark," said Lucy, fumbling in the pocket of her pinafore.

"So you don't know where it goes." Faye stated this as a fact, not a question.

"This leads to the chapel," said Lucy, looking at the compass she now had in her hand.

"How do you know for sure?" asked Faye.

"I traced it with my fingers," said Lucy. "I imagined where they went after we walked through them."

"Did anyone understand that?" asked Noah.

"I think you mean you mapped out the tunnels once you had

been in them, right?" asked Jasper. "I mean, you mapped them in your mind."

"So we should go?" asked Wallace timidly. He, too, was not fond of the dark.

Another explosion lit the sky. And then a blast came from the orchard.

"We have to get out of here!" said Noah.

"I'd say we don't have much choice." Jasper gestured for them to enter, and no one argued. They followed as Lucy read Noah's compass.

This time, the tunnel went almost straight. There were no stairs, but the floor descended at a rather sharp angle. They came to a cavern. While the passage was new to the others, Lucy was sure the cavern was connected to the same tunnel they had taken at Christmas. The tunnel began to even out, and then it inclined upwards. They climbed up with some difficulty, especially for those in skirts and dresses. Again, the ravens, with their unmistakable chatter, signaled they had arrived at ground level. With the light of the moon, they could see an outline of light around the door in the chapel alcove. Jasper felt the door and, yes, he found a doorknob.

The doorknob was icy cold against his bare hand. This had to lead to the outside. Jasper pushed hard against the mossy door. It did not move. He and the others searched for a round keyhole that would fit Wallace's coin. Jasper could not see well enough, and no one was able to find a keyhole. They all pushed and pulled at it, but the door didn't move. Was there some crazy lock from the inside? Or outside?

Jasper took a step back and pushed as hard as he could. In one try, he broke through with a force that sent him stumbling out onto the ground. They were not inside the chapel. This was not the entrance they had used before. This time, they found themselves in what had once been the chapel's small herb garden. The remains of flowerbeds, now containing wildflowers and weeds, lined the outside walls. It was yet another entrance to, or exit from, the ancient chapel. Jasper crawled into what he thought was a bundle of rags. Only it was not a bundle of rags.

"The shepherd!" Jasper cried, scrambling to get away from the man. But when the shepherd leaned over, Jasper could see that he had a handkerchief tied around his mouth. Ropes tied his feet together, with a pile of ropes around him, one hand still tied, the other partially freed. It was clear he had been trying to untie himself but did not have the strength.

"He's been tied up," Noah said. "And look." Noah pointed to a bench. Leaning on the bench was a shepherd's crook—a wooden staff. It was not the one they had found, the one with the deadly knife. If he had another, that one couldn't be his.

Faye was hit with a sickening sense of guilt. The poor man, she thought. They had thought him a monster, but he was a victim, just like Signora Fornaio.

"Is he not a bad man?" Lucy asked Miss Brett. Wallace hid behind his teacher, but Noah shook his head.

"I . . . I don't know," Miss Brett said, still unsure and cautious. Clearly, this was not the monster in the tunnel, but were there not always two?

"He's not moving," said Noah.

"Is he . . ." But Wallace didn't want to say the word "dead."

Full of remorse for thinking the sweet little man was Komar Romak, Faye stepped forward.

Just then, the little man groaned, as if he were in pain. Then he let out a little whimper. Faye pulled off the gag so he could breathe. She quickly untied his hands.

"Signora Fornaio." He could barely speak. "*Dove* . . . where she is?"

Faye's hand flew to her mouth to cover the sob she could not stop. Lucy burst into tears.

"No, no . . . non è possible!" he cried in a painful groan that seemed to cost him his strength. Faye untied his hands. Then the little man tried to rise, but fell back down. One hand clutched his stomach. With his other hand, he reached up.

"He can't stand alone," Wallace said, gulping. Was he ill? Was he hurt? Was he going to die? Wallace turned that lucky coin in his pocket.

Jasper reached to help, offering his hand. When the tiny old man's shaking hand came up, Jasper felt his surprisingly strong grip. It was a grip so strong, in fact, that Jasper's hand began to hurt. Unable to pull the shepherd up, he found himself being dragged down.

Suddenly, something whizzed past Jasper's ear. The old man fell back to the ground.

"No!" screamed Faye in horror.

Jasper turned around and saw a mysterious man in black standing on the chapel's ruined wall—it was Robin Hood. In his arms he held a bow and arrow. He loaded again and aimed the arrow at Jasper.

"No, Robin Hood, no!" cried Lucy, who ran to her brother. Jasper tried to push Lucy out of the way, but she refused to let go of him and he could not shake her loose.

"You shot the shepherd!" Jasper screamed. "He was bound and gagged! We were wrong! And now you've killed him!"

Bo Peep came running up through the herb garden passageway. He must not have been far behind them. He said something to the archer, who still had his bow trained on the still figure of the shepherd.

"Are you going to kill him again?!" cried Noah, ready to step between the archer and the shepherd.

Bo Peep stepped over to Jasper, who could still feel the shepherd's grip on his hand.

Bo Peep pulled his skirts back and bent at the knees next to the fallen shepherd. With a push, he turned the old man over. The shepherd's other hand was still tight against his stomach, where they all thought he had been hurt. Bo Peep pulled the hand from the folds of rags.

In it, the old shepherd clutched a knife. It was a long, sharp knife made for one purpose—to kill.

Faye let out a loud, groaning cry. Miss Brett gasped. Lucy had been hiding in Jasper's legs, and he held her tight so she would not look.

"He...he...he was going to kill you," said Noah to Jasper.

"Was...is it him?" Miss Brett's voice was shaky. She swallowed hard, but still could not clear her throat.

"Not him," Robin Hood growled. "Never him."

Bo Peep took the knife from the shepherd's hand and placed it in his apron. He reached up to the face and pulled at the beard. It did not move, but half of the moustache fell to the ground.

Shaken, the children slowly followed Bo Peep from the chapel. The cold was not the only thing sending shivers through their bones. Each of them found the weight of the world noticeably upon them. Faye's tears stung. Jasper put his arm around her.

As always, Miss Brett tried hard to be a calming force. But there was little she could say, even if she had been capable of speaking. So overwhelmed with the tragedies they had just witnessed, she did not know if she would say something foolish that might hurt more than it helped. She simply kept near, placing a hand on a shoulder or an arm, embracing anyone who reached out to her. Wallace and Lucy both stuck close to her, and she walked slowly to stay as close as possible to the children. Noah walked ahead, his head hanging down.

"Gajnuna!" came a cry from behind them.

Bo Peep stopped in his tracks, hiked up his skirt, and ran back to the chapel. The children and Miss Brett followed.

They found Robin Hood on the ground, blood coming from his cheek—but he was not dead.

And apparently, neither was Komar Romak. The shepherd, Mezzobaffi, or whatever he should be called, had disappeared.

CHAPTER FORTY-FOUR

THE PATH AHEAD

OR

CALLING CARDS FROM ARIANA

"It's not like we shouldn't have expected it," said Faye, handing her last bag to the wide-beret man with the triangular dark glasses and the enormous, pointy beard. He was loading their bags onto the carriages.

"Expected him to vanish?" Wallace said, adjusting his glasses.

"No, Faye's right," said Noah. "We should have known. Someone should have stayed with him to make sure he didn't pull another disappearing act."

"Maybe the giant came and got him," Wallace suggested, adjusting his glasses.

"Or maybe he did just disappear," said Faye, rather mysteriously.

"Maybe. After all," said Wallace, "he's done it before."

"Not he," Noah said, wagging his finger.

"Never he. They," said Faye, rolling her eyes. "Yes, yes, we all know." She looked in the carriage as Jasper placed Lucy onto the seat and covered her with a warm blanket.

Miss Brett came from the kitchen with a large basket of treats. This morning after their long night, she felt more numb than tired.

She had been baking since before the break of dawn. The manor house kitchen was intact. The back of the house and much of the gardens were not. One wall in the library had caved in from a blast. The upper floors were in shambles, so Miss Brett and the children had slept around the fire in the salon. After making sure the children were warm, Miss Brett had found herself wandering the halls. She had been unable to sleep, her head heavy with thoughts of what had happened and why. It was like a flood breaking through a dam, and she could not stop thinking.

She thought about the artist and wondered who had mourned him. She thought about the parents of the children and their own childhood as young inventors. She thought of the sweet Miss Bird and whether her own fate was bound to that woman's. And she thought of the kind Signora Fornaio, who would never again appear with bundles of delights for the children.

She needed that time alone in the kitchen. She was preparing. Was she certain they would be leaving? No, but she suspected. They could no longer be here and be safe. She baked and cooked and prepared for their long journey. If it came, it would be soon.

After the children had gone to sleep, she had sat alone, watching the snow fall upon Solemano. She sat by the big bay window, by the fire, and cried for a long time. She cried for the sadness that came with the life she and the children were living. She cried for the kind and gentle woman who was only trying to help her own son. She cried for the still mysterious men in black who she saw being carried by the others—men who surely had laid down their lives for the children and for her. She cried for her failure to see a villain in shepherd's clothing. She cried for her own sorrows. She cried for the losses she had endured in her own life. Astraea Brett had not cried for her parents in many years. But she did then.

As she packed her copy of her mother's *Alice's Adventures in Wonderland* and her old *Strand Magazine*, mementos of her own childhood, she had thought of her mother bringing books to America when she'd come from England as a young woman. Miss Brett touched the pages of the book, remembering her mother's voice. It brought the pain of her loss flooding back into her heart. And it made all other losses all the heavier to bear.

Her heart felt so weighty over the loss of Signora Fornaio. It was a loss for the whole of Solemano—for the mysterious men in black. The town would surely be in mourning for some time to come. The echo of the wailing ravens, perched on the baker's window, could be heard into the night. Even now, the birds' lament lingered in the air.

Odd, she thought, wiping her eyes. Everyone was dressed in black now—even the children, even herself. They were dressed for mourning. The villagers, always. And the men. How does one become like that, like these people, like those men? Her thoughts went to the mysterious men in black and their sorrowful darkness. It was as if they were in perpetual mourning. She had never considered this before. Behind the strangeness of the men, was there sorrow? Had they suffered some loss? Were they showing reverence for someone or something they would forever mourn?

Wiping her eyes in the night, she'd thought of the cheer and warmth of the baker. Signora Fornaio's heart had seemed to open to people who made a home in Solemano. Miss Brett had taken a deep breath then, looking out the window into the darkness. She had come to love this village. It had been their home.

She touched her own cheek. She felt that she had aged a hundred years and wondered if it showed on her face. Would she ever know the answers to the mysteries around her?

She had fallen into a light sleep in that chair by the fire. She woke to the chill of the first dawn and the fireless hearth.

"We go," came a voice familiar to her ears. Bo Peep spoke softly, but Miss Brett understood.

She went to her room and packed her bags until light from the rising sun came streaming through her window. It was then she washed her face and went to the kitchen to collect the baked goods for the journey.

"All is ready," Bo Peep said to Miss Brett, taking the hamper of biscuits from her hands.

She touched his arm. "Will you be taking us?" she asked.

Bo Peep stopped and looked back at her, their eyes meeting. He nodded, then picked up the last of the bags.

———————

"Where is Mummy?" mumbled Lucy, groggily. She had been sleeping for an hour as the carriage wended its way through the mountains.

"Don't worry, sweet angel. Just rest," Miss Brett said, gently.

Lucy wiggled the sleep from her body, her eyes seeming to focus.

"Are we going to meet them?" Lucy seemed to realize where she was.

"We go to Castle of Suleyman," Bo Peep said.

"Where is that?" asked Faye, rubbing her eyes. She must have fallen asleep as well. Jasper still had his head on her shoulder. He, too, had found some peace.

"Boy will know," Bo Peep said in what was, for a mysterious

man in black, a kind voice.

"Boy?" Faye asked.

"Ginger boy," Bo Peep said, again in a gentle voice.

Faye turned to Noah.

"Him?" she asked.

"Me?" Noah asked. He seemed startled from his daydreaming.

"He," Bo Peep agreed.

"I'll know what?" Noah asked, rubbing his eyes.

"Where we're going," said Faye.

"How would I know?" said Noah.

"Letters," Bo Peep said. "Post."

Noah, in fact, did have a package of letters clutched in his hand. They were bound with a ribbon. Each and every one of them was from his mother.

"Your mother's postcards!" cried Lucy. "They've come back!"

"I did wonder if they had gotten lost," Noah said. "This set came by post carriage today, or at least I received them today. Why these blighters decide to hold some of them until the last minute is a mystery to me. But maybe it isn't their fault. This whole lot may have just arrived. You know what the post is like."

"Well, let's have a look, then. Have you read them?" Faye remembered each time Noah received a batch of cards from his mother. They were full of colorful stories from all over the planet. This time, they apparently contained something more.

"Not all of them. Not yet," Noah said, though Faye raised an eyebrow, finding that hard to believe. She would have read them all the moment they arrived.

Noah pulled them from his overcoat pocket. He had savored the pleasure of just holding them in his hand. He often waited to read her letters, because finally reading them would somehow feel like a closure. Holding them unread felt like a promise.

"Well, we're waiting," Faye said.

Both reluctantly and with anticipation, Noah pulled the ribbon from the bundle. Lucy held out her hand, and Noah deposited the ribbon into it.

Noah looked at a couple, then cleared his throat and selected a postcard from the stack.

> *London, 29 November, 1903*
>
> *Dearest Noah—*
>
> *Off to Stockholm. My friend, Marie, and her husband will be presented the Nobel Prize, and I will sing at the reception. King Oscar has asked for a palace event. I shall stop in Paris for a new gown . . .*
>
> *With fondest embraces, Mama*

"I wonder what color gown she'll be getting," Lucy said, beaming. "And if it will have ribbons—lots and lots of ribbons."

"Perhaps it will have flern," said Noah.

"A gown doesn't have flern, silly." Then she looked thoughtful. "Does it?" Lucy looked to Jasper for an answer. Jasper, waking to the sound of Noah's voice, shrugged.

"Why not?" Noah said. "Why can't something learn from what it knows?"

"You mean a thing might learn from what happens to it?" asked Lucy.

Jasper considered this. It was interesting, the idea that a thing, not a person, could learn in some way. Does a lock, for example, learn to know its own key?

"There is no such thing as flern, Lucy." Faye rolled her eyes. "And the postcard was written in November. The gown has been bought and worn by now. The Nobels are always presented the tenth of December. Go on, for goodness sake."

Noah cleared his throat again. "Dearest darling, wonderful amazing son who is more fabulous than Faye could ever—"

"Oh, I seriously doubt that," said Faye. "Honestly, clever lad, you really are an inventor. Read the actual letter, will you?"

Noah cleared his throat again. "Very well."

> *Milan, 15 December, 1903*
>
> *Darling Noah—*
>
> *Back to London for an extravaganza with Bertie and Lexi. Haven't seen the Windsors since the launching of the HMS* Edward VII *last July. Expecting a fabulous New Year's bash, since Bertie is the leading figure of style in the world today.*
>
> *Love always from your mother*

"Oh! That's my birthday!" exclaimed Lucy, who had been sitting on the edge of her seat, curling and uncurling the ribbon. "She wrote that on my exact birthday."

"Imagine that," Noah said, taking another card from the pile.

> *New York, 15 January, 1904*
>
> *Darling Boy—*
>
> *I have a box of rainbow for you! The Binneys, whom I met at one of my performances at the Met, gave me*

a box of their newest product—coloured wax drawing sticks called crayons! The company, Crayola, is sure to get a gold medal for these unique and wonderful inventions. I will be attending the Louisiana Purchase Exposition in April (people are calling it the Saint Louis World's Fair!), for Mannie Masqueray has insisted I be present. He has designed the most fabulous architectural structures for the extravaganza. Alice says she and Eddie have a whole collection of crayons for you that you can share with Miss Brett and the others.

Kisses and embraces,
Your Mother (still west of you, sweet boy)

"Oh, how exciting!" Lucy waved the ribbon. "I'd love colored crayons for drawing!"

"What a brilliant invention," Miss Brett said, considering how lovely it would be for children and adults to have such a thing.

"I do hope they've registered a patent," Wallace said.

"Of course you do," Noah said.

"Read another!" cried Lucy, now fully awake and thrilled.

The next one he selected was not a postcard, but an envelope. It was addressed, by hand, to "Noah and his Friends," but inside was a card printed in beautiful scarlet ink. Inside the card was a folded, rose-colored paper. "It's an invitation," Noah said with some surprise. "My mother is performing at the Royal Opera House in Cairo."

"Cairo?" Faye was surprised. "Cairo, Egypt?"

"Is there another?" asked Noah. "Of course, Cairo, Egypt. If there is another Cairo, my mother would not be there, for it would only prove to be an imitation—a lesser representation of Cairo in its purest form."

"Oh, give it to me if you're not going to read it," demanded Faye, reaching for the invitation. "It's for all of us."

Noah held the invitation out of reach.

"Children, please," Miss Brett scolded. But she, too, was eager to learn what it said.

"Sorry," Faye said. "Dearest Noah, would you be so kind as to read the invitation?"

Noah tilted his head slightly toward Faye, then shook out the rose paper first and held the invitation in his hand. They all sat quietly as Noah read aloud:

4 February, 1904

Dearest Noah, Jasper, Faye, Wallace, Lucy, and Miss Brett:

You are most emphatically invited to the fabulous Royal Opera House in the magical city of Cairo, Egypt. In the spirit of global embrace from the April signing of the Entente Cordiale, the performance will be in celebration of the international spirit of Verdi's fabulous operatic creation, Aida. The incomparable Ariana Canto-Sagas will perform in Cairo. The celebration will culminate in a performance this November by Emma Eames and Enrico Caruso at the Metropolitan Opera in New York City.

We shall all celebrate the newly established Maadi neighbourhood and repair to the villa of the French ambassador.

The printed invitation gave the details of the event.

"Are we going to see the pyramids?" Lucy clapped her hands and wiggled her toes.

And suddenly, they were all talking at once. Was it true? Would they be going to Egypt? Miss Brett looked over the invitation. It looked like it. Cairo, Egypt. Land of the pharaohs. Land of the great pyramids. Land of wonder.

"I'm excited to see your mother perform," Faye said. She smiled one of her heart-stopping smiles that Jasper could feel, even though it was not directed toward him.

Yes, thought Miss Brett, they'd finally get to see the wonderful Ariana Canto-Sagas performing, and at the famous Royal Opera House. What an adventure that would be.

"So the castle is in Cairo?" asked Lucy, leaning toward the front to ask Bo Peep.

"One in Cairo," said Bo Peep.

"One?" Noah looked at the others. "How many castles and manors do you have?"

There was no answer.

It was only as the light began to fade and a bit of a chill entered through the thin glass windows that Miss Brett lit the fires in the small braziers built into the carriage doors. The children huddled close.

Faye stretched as Lucy reached for Jasper. At the same time, Wallace took his coin out of his pocket to look at it. He took out his remaining magnetic sphere as well. Jasper reached up for a stretch, and when his hand came to rest on Faye's shoulder, Faye suddenly jumped in her seat.

"That hurt!" she cried.

"Sorry," said Jasper, remembering that this had happened before. He realized, just then, that this is what had concerned Wallace on Christmas Eve.

"Wallace," he said, his eyebrows raised, "what do you know about these bracelets?"

All eyes were on Wallace.

"Wallace knows something?" asked Faye. "I mean, about your bracelets?"

"Well." Wallace adjusted his glasses. "It's not the bracelets. Or rather, not just the bracelets. I noticed that my coin was creating a strange, well, static electricity, or some other kind of reaction when it came near Faye's necklace."

"And now you tell me?" Faye said, rubbing her neck. "Maybe you created some kind of magnetic infusion, messing with all those rare earth alloys. Or somehow altered your coin."

"I wondered about that," said Wallace. "But with the carvings on the wall and the way my coin acted as a key, I felt there must be something more. And something changing."

"Faye, don't move," said Jasper. "I want to just see…" Faye jumped as Jasper took Lucy's hand and slowly moved their hands toward Faye's necklace. They felt an electric shock, like the one at Christmas, but this time, the bracelets gave a tug and clicked onto Faye's necklace. When Jasper tried to pull his hand away, it dragged her necklace with it, cutting off her hair.

"Get that off me!" she cried.

Jasper managed, but with difficulty.

"There's some kind of magnetic force!" Noah said as he reached over to Lucy's bracelet. Just then, Wallace's coin slammed his fingers into a sandwich between bracelet and coin. Then the coin and bracelets began to move menacingly toward Faye's neck. With Miss Brett's help, they pulled and pulled at arms and hands, trying to prevent what might be a painful shock for Faye.

Finally getting them apart, each of the token-holders felt their tokens quivering.

"It's like they're coming to life," said Lucy.

"Whatever it is, it's getting stronger," said Jasper. Even being next to Faye made his wrist ache.

"I think you made it happen with those magnetic spheres. Did you ever think you could be turning everything into magnets?" asked Faye.

"I don't think I did," said Wallace. "But they got a lot stronger after we had Antonio's orb. It was almost as if his sphere was a catalyst. A trigger."

An element? thought Jasper.

"Okay, this is really too strange," Noah said, moving closer to the window and farther from Wallace.

"It is." Wallace again wondered about his coin.

"I'd say it might be best to put everything in a box," Noah said, "if only we could get these bracelets off your—"

"No!" shouted Bo Peep, pulling the reins of the horses and turning to his passengers. "Must never be as one."

With no further explanation, Bo Peep gathered the reins and turned back to driving. In response to his reaction, the children moved their tokens farther apart.

"Could they have come into contact with some other kind of element—another catalyst of some kind?" Faye asked, rubbing her neck.

"Perhaps," Wallace said, though he suspected it was more than that.

"It's one thing or another," Noah said. "It's always one thing or another."

"Or both," Faye said.

"It's 'The Strange Round Bird,'" said Lucy.

"What is?" asked Wallace.

"Only that's just the story about it," Lucy said. "The pieces of our things."

They were without a clue as to what she meant—except Jasper.

Lucy shook her bracelet in frustration. "They are pieces of a thing, aren't they?" Lucy asked Bo Peep, leaning forward.

"They are one," he said, "but never to be touched."

"Never to be touched," Lucy repeated.

Bo Peep said nothing else, and no one dared ask. Miss Brett tidied up and unfolded a blanket to cover the soon-to-be very sleepy children.

"What did he mean, Miss Brett?" asked Wallace, his eyelids growing heavy.

"Well, I have a feeling we will find out soon," said Miss Brett.

Lucy smiled, yawned, and blinked her eyes rather slowly. "Never to be touched even if you are bold," she said. "Turns the world to dust and lead into gold."

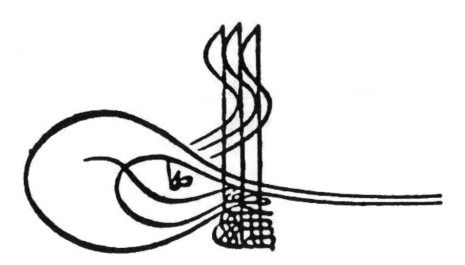

ACKNOWLEDGEMENTS

So many people have inspired these pages, from the inventors and authors who still teach us from centuries long ago, to travelers and friends.

My amazing husband, Nate, is my sword and shield whenever I head into the unknown territory of the unwritten story.

My children, Julius, Lyric, and Cyrus motivated my heart and hand.

Both Harrison and Bruce at Bancroft are beacons of light in the journey through the forest of words.

And I want to thank those who spent time visiting these pages in earlier formulations and made them the better for it.

Finally, a bow and a tip of the hat to a very special man of words, Dr. Abe Bortz.

ABOUT THE AUTHOR

Eden Unger Bowditch has been writing since she was very small. She has been writing since she could use her brain to think of something to say. She wrote at the University of California, Berkeley, and she wrote songs as a member of the band enormous.

She has written stories and plays and shopping lists and screenplays and dreams and poems—and also books about her longtime Baltimore home. She has lived in Chicago and France and other places on the planet, and has been a journalist, as well as a welder, and an editor, and other things, too.

The Ravens of Solemano, which is the second installment of The Young Inventors Guild trilogy (the first was *The Atomic Weight of Secrets*), is her second middle-grade/young adult novel, and she has been as excited writing it as she hopes you are reading it.

Presently, Eden lives with her family (husband and three children) in Cairo, Egypt. But that's another story entirely…